Marquesses at the Masquerade

A Regency
Novella
Anthology

SUSANNA IVES
EMILY GREENWOOD
GRACE BURROWES

Published as a three-novella compilation, Dukes In Disguise, by Grace Burrowes Publishing, 21 Summit Avenue, Hagerstown, MD 21740.

Cover design by Wax Creative, Inc.

ISBN-13: 978-1987665949

TABLE OF CONTENTS

NOTE FROM THE AUTHORS

What's next? Vanishing Viscounts? Barons Behaving Badly? We're not sure!

For these novella anthologies, we kick around a premise until something pops up that feels interesting, but flexible enough to take off in a lot of directions. For *Marquesses at the Masquerade*, that's pretty much all we had: Three marquesses, one masquerade where each man crosses paths with his true love. Go!

Off we went to our separate writing caves, to emerge weeks later, happily-ever-afters in hand. Some interesting similarities emerged: All three heroines have suffered loss of a loved one, though one lady still has plenty of family. Two heroes are widowers, only one recalls his wife with uncomplicated loving fondness. Two heroes have to deal with an old flame complicating matters, two have to deal with helpful/meddling family. All three novellas drew upon myth or fairytale, but our choices were Norse gods, Cinderella, and Greek legends.

Despite some similarities, we were struck by how unique each story is to the author who wrote it. Susan's hero has the intensity she conjures for all of her protagonists. Emily's is a perfect gentleman, and yes, that would be Grace's hero confiding in his horse. (One of these days, Grace is going to write a hero with a ferret. Don't laugh. It worked for Judith Ivory.) Our heroines went in similarly distinctive directions, as did the supporting casts, the settings, the authorial voices.

We hope you enjoy our ***Marquesses at the Masquerade***. We had great fun writing them, and comparing our results from a simple shared premise. We do believe the Vanishing Viscounts have some potential, but aren't so sure about Barons Behaving Badly. Let us know what you think!

Happy reading!
Grace, Emily, Susan (and Lord Tyne's horse)

MASQUERADE BALL

THE PLEASURE OF YOUR COMPANY
IS REQUESTED AT A BALL
HOSTED BY
THE MARQUESS OF BOXHAVEN

SATURDAY NIGHT
NINE O'CLOCK

Once Upon A Ball

Emily Greenwood

CHAPTER ONE

"Mundie, you're taking too long," came an irritated female voice from the doorway of Rosamund's room. "How am I supposed to make the final adjustments to my attire for the Boxhaven masquerade ball when you are taking so long to complete my gown?"

Rosamund, who hardly remembered the last time she'd used her surname and at age twenty-two was years beyond the sensation of cringing at the detested nickname, merely said, "I'm just finishing the final stitches, Aunt."

She would not, of course, mention that it had taken her longer to finish the adjustments to the gown because the alterations required her to do far more than "just sew on a few ribbons to refresh the look," as Melinda had ordered when she'd handed the gown to her. Melinda had put on a significant amount of weight, which no one was meant to mention, but it was a fact of which Rosamund, effectively Melinda's personal seamstress, was well aware.

Melinda's eyes traveled over Rosamund's small room, which was on the top floor of the Monroes' London town house, as far away from the main family quarters as possible, and came to rest on Rosamund's untouched lunch tray, which contained a piece of toasted cheese and an apple.

"You'd have more time to do what little is asked of you if you weren't always eating."

Rosamund managed, from long practice, not to laugh. Since Rosamund was kept constantly busy sewing for the household—and with Melinda and her daughters, Vanessa and Calliope, there was always mending, and her two cousins being out, new dresses to sew—Rosamund undoubtedly made up for her keep in what they would have spent hiring a seamstress. And as she was rarely invited to join the family for meals, she was not costing them a great deal in food. She knew from the housekeeper, Mrs. Barton, that the kitchen staff had been instructed "not to be lavish" with Rosamund's trays.

"Of course, Aunt." Rosamund might have pointed out that if she was not allowed to consume food, she would eventually run out of energy and be of no use, but she'd learned, from the moment she'd come to the house at age fifteen, that it was best to agree with Melinda and say as little as possible.

"I don't know why I should have to remind you of your responsibilities, Mundie. One would think you'd be grateful for being taken in and cared for as you have been."

This was a familiar refrain.

"I am very grateful, Aunt." And she truly was. She had a roof over her head, and meals, such as they were. More important, she had the company of Melinda's uncle Piggott, who lived in a room down the hall from Rosamund's little cell, and of the housekeeper, Mrs. Barton. Sometimes of an evening, the three would take a mug of tea together in Uncle Piggott's room. Rosamund called him Uncle Piggott even though he wasn't actually her uncle, but Melinda's uncle by marriage. From the first, he'd insisted that Rosamund was the sort of person anyone would be proud to have as a niece and that he'd be delighted if she wished to call him uncle, as his real, "less pleasing" nieces did. Uncle Piggott, despite having been a vicar or, he would say, because of it, preferred blunt speaking.

Melinda peered closely at Rosamund's work and offered a brief snort in judgment, then leaned into the hallway and called for Mary, one of the maids. Mary arrived in the doorway with an armful of fabric, and Rosamund's heart sank. The Boxhaven ball was only two days away, and she'd foolishly hoped both her cousins would wear the gowns they'd worn to their last ball. But Mary was holding Calliope's favorite gown from the previous season, which would never fit her without letting out the bust.

Melinda plucked the gown from the maid's arms and dropped it on the small table next to Rosamund. "You know what to do, Mundie, and she wants crystals sewn along the neckline as well. You'll need to finish it tonight, because you'll be working on Vanessa's gown tomorrow."

Which meant more rushing to finish in time for any last-minute nips and tucks before the ball. Rosamund had often suspected that Melinda took special pleasure in seeing how fast she could make her sew.

"I'll make certain the gowns are ready in time."

"See that you do." Melinda gestured to Mary. "Take this tray away. We don't want Rosamund to be distracted while she works."

With an apologetic look that Rosamund returned with a quick, understanding smile, Mary removed the tray.

The hour was late when Rosamund finally finished the last stitches on Calliope's gown, but she knew Mrs. Barton had brought up Uncle Piggott's evening tea and was lingering in his room to chat. Rosamund hung Calliope's gown neatly on the hook in her room that had been installed for just that purpose and crept down the dark corridor toward the light of Uncle Piggott's room.

Uncle Piggott's living had been a poor one. Now nearly eighty, his financial circumstances necessitated accepting the charity of his niece Melinda, who'd offered him a room and meals in exchange for the right to let all her acquaintances know how charitable she was.

"I'm her ticket into heaven," Uncle Piggott liked to tell Rosamund with a wink. As the stairs were now too much for him, he passed all of his time in his room, contentedly. The tall stack of books that stood on his night table and was frequently refreshed by Rosamund accounted for a large part of his contentment, along with his beloved pipe. If his body had betrayed him in age, though, his mind remained sharp.

"So, Melinda has you working your fingers to the bone so those awful daughters of hers can be paraded before the *ton* in the hopes of catching husbands," Uncle Piggott said when Rosamund joined him and Mrs. Barton in his room.

"This will be the first time madam and the young ladies have been invited to Boxhaven House," Mrs. Barton pointed out.

"Not surprising, as the Marquess of Boxhaven is surely too sensible a man to want anything to do with either Melinda or those chits," Uncle Piggott said cheerfully. "It's actually quite remarkable how rotten they are, considering how nice they look. I have often observed to our Lord that if He only made everyone look on the outside as they are on the inside, so many of our human problems would resolve themselves." He shook his head. "Lemon-suckers, the pair of them."

"Shh," Rosamund said, giggling. "They might hear you."

"What, all the way up here in the Outer Reaches?" Uncle Piggott liked to refer to the fourth floor as the Outer Reaches. His room was comfortable but modest, a chamber obviously meant for guests of little importance. At the far end of the corridor, in a dark, perpetually chilly spot, was Rosamund's own tiny chamber.

"Melinda would have to be a witch to hear that well," Uncle Piggott said, filling his pipe. "Though I have not discounted the idea that she might be some sort of devil's imp."

"I despair of your sense of decorum," Rosamund said, "though I like it more than I ought to when you speak badly of Melinda. My own relations, and they're providing my meals and shelter." She shook her head. "I am shocking."

"They're the shocking ones," Uncle Piggott said around his pipe stem. "For your mother's own sister to treat her niece so shabbily is appalling."

But they all knew that it was the very fact that Rosamund was her mother's daughter that had doomed her to the position she now had in the Monroe household. Melinda had never forgiven Rosamund's mother for marrying "a penniless sailor." Her sister marrying beneath her, Melinda believed, had dragged down her own consequence, resulting in Melinda's marriage to the "worthless" (and now dead) Mr. Monroe, instead of the viscount who had once pursued her.

Melinda had clearly felt vindicated when Rosamund's father, a captain in the Royal Navy, had been involved in a public scandal related to some men who had deserted their posts. Rosamund had never wavered in her faith that her father had done the right thing throughout the affair, but he had been court-marshaled, and their distinctive family name had been dragged through mud that stuck to it forever after.

"If your mother hadn't married a man with such an unforgettable name," Melinda said on the day seven years before when Rosamund arrived to stay, "perhaps you could recover *somewhat* from the scandal. But no one will forget it, or his infamy, and I won't have my generosity to you repaid by subjecting my family to derision. You will keep to yourself and not draw attention in any way. And you will never, under any circumstances, give anyone your last name."

Uncle Piggott poked the air with his pipe. "You ought to be attending the Boxhaven ball. As a member of the family, you were invited."

Rosamund had privately felt more than a few stings of disappointment while laboring over gowns for a ball she could not attend—because she couldn't attend, she knew that. Melinda had never once included her in a social event in all the years she'd lived with the Monroes.

"Why would I want to go to the ball when, with my aunt

and cousins gone for the evening, the three of us can have a whole lovely evening together?" Rosamund said. "Perhaps we might even purloin some wine."

"Your ideas of a wonderful evening are truly pathetic," Uncle Piggott said in a peppery voice, but Rosamund thought, for the briefest moment, that she saw a hint of moisture in his sharp old eyes.

* * *

"It's the very thing for you, Marcus. I knew the instant I laid eyes on it. Him."

"Er, you did?" Marcus Hallaway, the Marquess of Boxhaven, said to his mother, Lady Boxhaven, trying to keep any note of dismay out of his voice. But she had just presented him with a small spaniel. A lapdog! She'd brought the dog, concealed in a basket, into the sitting room in Boxhaven House, his London home, when she'd come for tea that afternoon. She'd lifted the top of the basket with the flourish of one offering a wonderful treat.

The dog, released from his confinement, now placed his two front paws on the top edge of the basket and yipped excitedly. With his chestnut and white coloring and enormous brown eyes, he would have looked at home in the arms of a well-dressed lady.

The dog also looked barely past the puppy stage, and Marcus had visions of him tearing through the corridors of his house with servants trailing after him. He wondered dismally whether the creature was housebroken, though he supposed his mother would not give him a gift that would create disgusting messes in Boxhaven House.

Still, he had plenty of dogs at his country houses, not that he was closely acquainted with any of them. Why had she brought him a *lapdog*, and with all this ceremony?

His mother gave him a shrewd look. Lady Boxhaven was the mother of four grown children, and she was no stranger to parsing the nuances of her offspring's demeanors. "I know you have dogs at Weldwood and the other estates. But you aren't often in the country these days, and I hate to think of you... without a companion."

"A companion," he repeated. Was the dog meant to be a new salvo in his mother's longtime campaign to get him to find a wife? If so, he couldn't comprehend her reasoning, because theoretically, if he now had a "companion," then might not further companionship become a less pressing issue? As this line of thought in regard to a dog standing in for a wife quickly turned ridiculous, he abandoned it and mentally threw up his hands as to his mother's motivation. His mother was not averse to eccentricity, but she was infinitely dear to him, and if she wanted him to have this small dog, he would accept her gift graciously, even if it meant the possibility of tooth marks in his best boots.

"Exactly," she said with a grand smile.

He nodded slowly. "Well, thank you very much, Mother. Extremely thoughtful of you."

She beamed, and the dog took this opportunity to launch himself out of the basket. Marcus braced himself to save any number of breakable and bite-able objects the animal might make for, but it was not to the divan legs or the rug tassels that the dog made his way.

"Oh!" cried his mother gleefully, "he likes you! I knew the two of you would suit."

The dog, ignoring even the plate of biscuits perched on a low table a few feet from his basket, had raced over to Marcus and was now at his feet, wagging his tail excitedly.

"See, he's already realized you're to be his master."

"A veritable example of the forces of fate in action," Marcus muttered.

"Isn't it?" she crowed.

The drawing room door opened at that moment to admit Marcus's younger brother, Jack, and their sister Alice.

"Oh!" squealed Alice, who at sixteen frequently found occasion to squeal. She rushed over and dropped to her knees before what Marcus was privately already calling The Creature.

"He's darling! Or is it a she? Is this your dog, Marcus? It must be, why else would it be here? But why did you get a dog?"

"A wonder she ever manages to draw a breath, isn't it?" Jack observed, apparently not equally overcome at the sight of the dog. But then, Jack was a gentleman of twenty-seven, with interests that inclined toward horseracing and the sort of discreet carousing favored by young men who were beloved by their families and friends as good fellows but nonetheless not immune to the pleasures of, well, carousing.

"It's a wonder you're even upright this morning," Alice said, directing a withering look over her shoulder at Jack as she proceeded after the dog on her hands and knees, "considering—"

"Thank you, Alice," their mother said firmly. "I don't think any of us need to entertain such considerations."

Jack shot Marcus a look that spoke volumes. He had been looking for his own town house to buy and was staying with their mother and sisters in the meantime.

"*Is* this your dog?" Jack asked as the dog returned to his apparently preferred spot at Marcus's feet.

"Yes," Marcus said, restraining a sigh. "Mother has just this morning presented him to me."

Their mother, standing behind Jack, could not see the way her younger son's eyes danced at these words. Marcus treated him to the sort of glare that an older brother who was a marquess learned to cultivate at an early age by practicing on his siblings. Jack only grinned.

"The little fellow certainly seems to like you," Jack said.

"It is rather unfair," Alice said, sitting back on her heels. "Here I am, prepared to dote on the little thing, and he only has eyes for Marcus, who's not even paying attention to him."

"Dogs, much like young ladies, can easily become spoiled by too much attention," Marcus observed meaningfully.

"Don't listen to him," Alice said to the dog, having coaxed him to a sitting posture at his master's feet, from which position he gazed upward adoringly. "Just because someone is a marquess doesn't mean he knows much of anything."

Marcus did not dignify this with a response.

"Have you decided on a name yet?" his mother asked.

"I think you should call him Rex," Alice said.

"Brute," Jack suggested.

"*No*," their mother and sister said as one.

Marcus looked down, thereby receiving the full effect of the devoted canine gaze directed up at him. "Socrates," he pronounced. "Let us hope he grows in wisdom."

"Perfect!" Alice said. "You ought to bring him to the ball, dressed in a little toga. It would be the very thing."

"Yes, wouldn't it?" Jack said gleefully. "And Marcus could go as Caesar. I should pay handsomely to see him sporting this fellow about the ballroom in matching togas."

Marcus reflected that, though he was on the whole glad he was no longer fourteen, there were times when he wished it would not be considered unseemly for him to pummel his brother.

"About the ball," their mother said. "I am a wee bit concerned, because we've had quite a response to the invitations. Of course I'm delighted that so many are eager to attend our ball, but I do hope it won't become a terrible crush."

The siblings all shared glances of affectionate exasperation. Overcrowding at *ton* events was a perennial concern of Lady Boxhaven, who felt that a hostess ought to be occupied with her guests' ability to circulate freely and drink a cup of lemonade without being jostled.

"It will be fine, Mother," Marcus said kindly. "Boxhaven House is quite up to the task of hosting everyone we know all at once."

"I do hope so," she said, not sounding convinced. "I would hate for anyone to feel hesitant to attend because it would be an uncivilized crush."

"Some of the people you invited are people I would not mind in the least being discouraged by the idea of a crush," Alice said, abandoning her efforts to secure Socrates's attention and standing up. "Tell me again why we had to invite Lord and Lady Winstonhurst and the Monroes."

"The Winstonhursts are friends of friends. And we can hardly avoid asking the Monroes, as we've asked everyone else in the neighborhood."

"But they're so incredibly tedious," Alice said.

Marcus, who had been cornered by Mrs. Monroe at a concert a few weeks before and subjected to a disquisition on the magnificence of her two daughters, whom he had not seen for some time, was inclined to agree.

"If the ball is as much of a crush as Mother fears it may be, perhaps they'll find the event inhospitable and leave early," Jack observed. "Perhaps we should invite more people to ensure that that happens."

"You just don't want to dance with Florence Drummond," Alice said.

"Does anyone?" Jack asked.

"Don't be a beast," their mother said. "Florence Drummond is a sweet young lady."

Jack sighed. "I know she is, as sweet as treacle. But she talks constantly. It's like a river of words rushing over a person, drowning you before you can either respond or escape."

"She only does that when she's nervous," Alice said. "Kate says Florence is actually a very interesting person. I believe those were her very words."

"Where is Kate, anyway?" Marcus asked, surreptitiously trying to nudge the dog away from his boots, which were in grave danger of being besmeared with drool. Kate, the elder of the two sisters, was twenty-three.

"Shopping," their mother said. "She said she needed some ribbons for the ball."

"More likely she just wanted to sit in Gunter's watching people," Jack said. "Ever since she attended that lecture on poetry, she's been 'making sketches of ideas.'"

"Well, I hope she buys some ribbon as well, because the gown she means to wear is decidedly prim," Lady Boxhaven said. "Despite its reputation, I don't think poetry has brought as many people together as a pretty gown. Not, of course, that I am suggesting that a pretty gown is of ultimate importance."

"Of course not," Marcus agreed reasonably.

"But primness is rather discouraging to suitors. Now," she said, looking around the room speculatively, "I'll just go have a word with Hendricks about chair placement for the ball. That is, if you don't mind, Marcus."

Lady Boxhaven had been the mistress of Boxhaven House until she moved, with Marcus's younger siblings, to a town house two blocks away the year Marcus turned twenty-eight. Though he'd told her it wasn't necessary, she'd insisted that a man of twenty-eight deserved his own lodgings. Marcus suspected her design had also been to leave him to his own devices so he might be more motivated to find a bride.

"By all means," he said. "Perhaps you'd like to take Socrates with you, to show him about the house?"

His mother merely laughed as she swept out the door.

It had not escaped Marcus's notice that his family had been hosting more balls than usual this year, increasingly on very thin pretexts. He was not unaware of the reason for this, which was that his mother wanted to see all her children married and married well, and not one of them had yet obliged her.

Being the oldest and the one most expected to fill a nursery, Marcus knew that nothing would give his mother more pleasure than for him to marry. While he liked to oblige his mother whenever possible, he did not feel a pressing need to hasten to the altar. One thing was in his favor: His mother's marriage to Marcus's father, who had died in a carriage accident five years before, had been blissful, and she wanted nothing less than bliss for her children.

"Life is unpredictable," his mother would say with a sad sigh now and again. "Think of your poor father, cut down in his prime. None of us has any guarantees. Which is why I so want for each of my children to know the happiness of a marriage founded on love."

None of her children, who all adored her, ever replied to these thoughts with anything but a kind smile or a gentle patting of her arm. They all agreed with her that marriage to a person one loved was a very good idea, but finding such a person was not as easy as their mother seemed to think. She had met their father at a ball, where, as the night wore on, she would recount, they both just *knew*. Having found her perfect match so effortlessly, Lady Boxhaven was not considered by any of her children to be quite reasonable on the subject of finding a mate.

"How do you compete with love at first ball?" Kate had muttered to Jack the night before, after their mother had been reminiscing about the fabled "night of romance" she'd shared with their father.

"It's not supposed to be a competition," Alice said. "She only wants us all to know the happiness that she and Papa did."

"It's easy for you to be relaxed about the whole thing," Kate had moaned. "You're not twenty-three and attending your five hundredth ball."

"Some people would be happy to attend five hundred balls," said Alice, who, having only come out that Season, had begun attending balls only the month before.

"Just you wait," Kate said.

These words were not delivered in a tone of menace, but rather, one of realism. They all knew that their parent believed that each of her children, like her, would find love at a ball. Their mother was not otherwise superstitious or prone to flights of fancy, but from this belief she could not be dissuaded. Consequently, she encouraged her children to attend as many balls as possible, and she looked for any excuse to hold a ball.

In addition to balls celebrating Jack's return from his European tour and Marcus's thirtieth birthday, both unobjectionable reasons for celebration, there had been balls to celebrate the redecoration of the ballroom and the successful cultivation of a new rose variety at Weldwood, the family seat. Marcus would not have been surprised had his mother announced the following week that she wanted to hold a ball in honor of the arrival of Socrates in Marcus's household, though he dearly hoped she would not.

Tonight's ball was in honor of Kate's ankle, which she had sprained a few weeks before and which had only recently been pronounced safe for dancing by their family physician.

"I wish she wouldn't refer to the ball where she met Father as a 'night of romance,'" Jack said. "And when she goes into that part about how he got that dreamy look in his eyes..." He shuddered. "It doesn't bear thinking about, one's parents at balls."

"Well, I think it's wonderfully romantic," Alice said. "And I hope I do meet my husband at a ball, whoever he'll be. I think nothing would be nicer."

CHAPTER TWO

As soon as Melinda and her children had left for the Boxhaven masquerade, Rosamund made her way to Uncle Piggott's room, very much hoping Mrs. Barton would bring wine.

"Rosamund," he greeted her. "Where is your ballgown?"

"Er..." Uncle Piggott liked to joke, but a ball Rosamund could not attend seemed like a poor topic for teasing.

"My dear," he said with unaccustomed gentleness, "it was a rhetorical question. Of course I know Melinda didn't suddenly become a decent person and decide to bring you to the ball. Which is why I have taken matters into my own hands." He raised his voice and called out, "Mrs. Barton, if you please."

Rosamund hadn't seen the housekeeper in the shadows, but now she stepped forward. She had a pile of fabric draped over one arm and a basket on the other, and she gave Rosamund a smile tinged with conspiracy.

Rosamund drew in a quick breath, already concerned about

what was brewing. "What—" she began, but Uncle Piggott cut her off.

"But me no buts, young lady. I know you are conscientious and moral and grateful to be given shelter and food, no matter that you have to work for it, and that you do not wish to cross your aunt. You are a member of this family, and thus you were invited to the Boxhaven masquerade ball. And you are going."

Rosamund opened her mouth, but she couldn't seem to form words.

"Now then, Mrs. Barton," Uncle Piggott said.

Mrs. Barton set the basket and gown on the bed. "Let's have that old thing off of you, Miss Rosamund," she said and began undoing the row of buttons on the back of Rosamund's frock as Uncle Piggott covered his eyes.

Rosamund found her voice. "You've both gone mad."

"I hope so," said Uncle Piggott, "if going mad means doing something for once. Melinda treats you in an appalling and completely un-Christian way, and tonight, it's time for revenge."

Mrs. Barton tugged off a sleeve. "I don't think revenge is a good reason to go to a ball. Or," Rosamund cleared her throat meaningfully, "a very Christian one."

"As the authority on matters Christian in the Outer Reaches," Uncle Piggott said, reaching blindly for the pipe on his bedside table as he kept his other hand over his eyes, "I deem revenge to be an excellent reason to go to a ball, particularly in this case. But it's not the main reason you're going. Mrs. Barton has it on good authority that there will be not one but *three* marquesses at the ball." He knocked a book on the floor but finally lighted on his pipe. "Not that the Marquess of Boxhaven would not be enough to entice a young woman to a ball. I was at a dinner at which he was present ten years ago, and none of the rest of the gentlemen in the room could gain the attention of a single woman."

"Uncle!" Rosamund said. "You once had dinner with the Marquess of Boxhaven? Why didn't you ever tell me?"

He chuckled and wedged his unlit pipe in the corner of his mouth. "Piqued your interest, didn't I? He has a younger brother as well, who will likely be at the ball. You could do worse than attract the attention of the younger brother of a marquess."

Rosamund could only blink, feeling lightheaded. "I should count myself lucky even to glimpse the younger son of a marquess."

Mrs. Barton held up the dress.

A little gasp escaped Rosamund. Uncle Piggott chuckled. "Our Mrs. Barton did well, didn't she? Hurry up and put the thing on so I can see."

If the sea under moonlight could be captured, this was what it would look like. Blue satin cascaded in soft ripples and glimmered with silver lace and scatterings of embroidered flowers done in silver thread. Tiny crystals here and there twinkled, completing the impression that the gown was pure enchantment.

"Where did you get this?" Rosamund breathed.

"A castoff from a previous employer," Mrs. Barton said. "It would never fit me"—this was surely true, as Mrs. Barton was tiny and the dress looked to be about the size of Rosamund's taller frame—"and I don't have a ball invitation. But you do, Miss Rosamund."

"I can't wear this," Rosamund said.

"Of course you can." Mrs. Barton smiled. "And nothing would delight me more than to send you to that ball dressed as you ought to be."

Standing there in just her chemise, Rosamund felt her eyes begin to mist. She sniffed.

"None of that, Rosamund," Uncle Piggott said with mock sternness. "You'll end up with red eyes, and take it from me: Gentlemen are leery of ladies with red eyes."

"What if someone recognizes me?"

"It's a masquerade," he reminded her. "You'll have a mask, and since Melinda has kept you hidden all these years, it's not as if anyone there will know you."

"But what if I see Melinda or my cousins?"

"They would never expect to see you there, and so they won't. Now, do you want to go to this ball or not?"

"Yes," Rosamund whispered fiercely. "Yes, I do."

"Then there's no time to waste."

They had thought of everything. In addition to the dress and a fresh petticoat, there were ribbons for Rosamund's hair and a pair of slightly worn dancing shoes with paste jewels.

"Where did you get them?" Rosamund asked in wonder.

"I had a few shillings lying about, and Mrs. Barton found them at the market." Uncle Piggott held up a hand as Rosamund looked dismayed. "And before you go into hysterics of concern about the state of my purse, consider that I am an old man, and if I want to spend a few shillings on my favorite young lady, I ought to be allowed that pleasure."

"Then I won't say anything but thank you," she said as she slipped into the shoes. Miraculously, they fit, which seemed just right, because already this night seemed like some kind of enchantment had befallen her.

She was to go in the family coach, which would take her the five blocks to Boxhaven House and bring her home at midnight, well before the time when Melinda and her daughters would wish to return. She'd been concerned about involving John Coachman in this plan, but Mrs. Barton had assured her that he, along with all the servants, was in support of the plan.

Right before Uncle Piggott sent Rosamund down to the waiting coach, he gestured to Mrs. Barton, who produced a beautiful strand of pearls.

"Are those… my mother's pearls?"

"Of course," he said. "What else would you wear to the ball?"

"But Melinda—"

"Had no right to take them from you."

It had been the hardest moment after a succession of hard

times. When she'd arrived at the Monroes' house after the wrenching months of her mother's final illness, Melinda had told her, "You shall be given a chance to make up for all the trouble your arrival is causing and all that is being provided to you."

"Of course, Aunt," she'd said. "I shall be happy to be of any help."

Melinda had held out her hand. "The pearls, if you please."

"Excuse me?"

"The pearls," Melinda had said impatiently. "They should never have been given to your mother."

Rosamund had swallowed. The pearls were the only thing she had left from her mother—in truth, the only thing at all she had left from her family. Everything else, all the bits and pieces that hadn't amounted to much, had been sold to pay the bills.

"I had always understood Grandmother gave them to Mother at her wedding."

"A misunderstanding," Melinda had said, and Rosamund's heart had sunk at the insincerity stamped on her aunt's features. "I will keep them, as a sort of down payment for your care."

Rosamund had surrendered the pearls.

Now, she stared at them lying across Mrs. Barton's palm, the jewels lustrous in the firelight. Her heart squeezed. Her mother had hardly ever had occasion to wear them, but sometimes she had put them on for one of their meager family dinners, and their glamour had brought a wisp of cheerful elegance to their homey surroundings.

"Well, don't stand there gawping, girl," Uncle Piggott said. "Put them on."

Melinda would be livid if she ever found out Rosamund had worn them, but then, that response would likely pale in comparison to what her aunt would do if she found out that Rosamund had gone to the ball.

She put on the pearls, then performed a pirouette. "What do you think?"

"You'll do, my dear," Uncle Piggott said, his gravelly voice suddenly thicker. "Oh, yes, you'll do."

"You look wonderful, Miss Rosamund," Mrs. Barton said, dabbing at the corner of her eye. "Now go and have a wonderful time."

And they sent her down to the coach.

CHAPTER THREE

Marcus, not normally particularly excited about masquerade balls, admitted to a deep gratitude for that evening's event because it was relieving him of the company of Socrates.

Not that he disliked the creature—Socrates was a sweet fellow, and he brought delight to any woman in the vicinity merely by his presence.

But Socrates had yet to cease behaving as though Marcus was his sole reason for existing, and it was slightly unspeakable being on the receiving end of the kind of adoring attention his dog dispensed. Since even Socrates's most ardent admirer (Alice) agreed that dogs really shouldn't be present at a ball, Socrates had been spirited away by Cook, whom the creature had shown a willingness to tolerate for a brief amount of time (due mostly to the application of kitchen scraps) before he began the mournful howling that marked his every absence from his master.

Marcus was dancing with his grandmother, Lady Tremont,

who, in accordance with the masquerade theme, was wearing an extremely tall wig he suspected had been fashionable in her debutante years, along with a club-shaped patch positioned below her left eye. Though she was well over seventy, Marcus thought she looked charmingly young, and he told her so.

"Rogue," she said tartly, but the corner of her mouth trembled with pleasure.

While many of the guests had come to the ball dressed as kings or dairy maids or mythological characters—he suspected the Thor who'd just moved past him was the Marquess of Tyne—Marcus's only concession to the masquerade was a black satin demi-mask. Scores of other gentlemen were also dressed like him, in black evening coats and pantaloons with matching demi-masks, which effectively deepened his concealment, because it would be hard to tell one gentleman from another.

"You are deliberately using up one of the waltzes you might be sharing with a young lady by dancing with your ancient grandmother," Lady Tremont informed him.

"I am waltzing with you because I adore you." His grandmother, not known for effusions of emotion, blushed. Marcus hid a smile.

"I'd forgotten how charming you can be when you wish, young man," she said. "You are becoming so serious. One might even think that you don't much care to laugh."

Marcus frowned. "Who doesn't like to laugh?"

"You, sometimes, from the looks of it. Take care that the duties of the marquessate don't weigh you down. There, see, you're frowning now."

He supposed he did sometimes feel weighed down by his responsibilities. He certainly liked to laugh and enjoy himself, but he did often have a great deal on his mind, things that had to be seen to. "That's only because you are casting aspersions."

"I think your mother is trying to get your attention." Lady Tremont squinted. "Oh, look, she's just realized you're wasting a waltz with me."

"Would you cease this talk of wasted waltzes? I have not

waltzed with a more pleasing companion in quite some time."

"Which only speaks volumes about the young ladies with whom you've been dancing."

Marcus sighed. "There's a list this time."

"A list, you say?" Lady Tremont chortled. "Debutantes ranked by beauty, age, size, and goodness?"

"I'm sure nothing like that," Marcus said, which was true. His mother was far too kind to treat anyone, least of all harmless young ladies, as cattle. Well, mostly harmless—Miss Clarinda Faraday kept sending him bold, meaningful glances over the shoulder of her dance partner. Having observed her eyeing a fellow he suspected was the Marquess of Exmore, Marcus was fairly certain that Miss Faraday's goal was to snare a marquess, any marquess.

"The perils of being so very eligible," Lady Tremont said with mock pity. "At least there are two other marquesses present tonight to attract the attention of the matchmaking mamas."

It was at that moment that Marcus's eyes, carelessly passing over his grandmother's left shoulder, fell on a woman dressed in blue. She was striking, even with part of her face hidden by her silver demi-mask. A delicate wash of pink warmed the fair skin of her cheeks, her glossy dark brown hair looked as rich as sable, and she had a shapely figure that showed to advantage in her gown. But her beauty wasn't what riveted him—there were scores of beautiful women present. Partly, he was drawn to her mouth, which was curled in an expression of benevolent amusement. But mostly, he was drawn to her eyes.

He couldn't see their color—he was a good dozen feet away—but they had light in them. And he suddenly knew that he had to know more about that light.

But who was she? Even though she was wearing a mask, he was certain that if he'd ever seen those eyes before, he would remember.

"See something interesting, do you, Marcus?" his grandmother asked. As the movements of the dance brought them in clear sight of the woman in blue, he inclined his head in her direction.

"Do you know who that lady is, the one in that silvery blue gown?"

Lady Tremont squinted, and he was reminded that she was not wearing her spectacles. "Is that Francesca Gaitskill? I believe she's recently arrived in town, and she has dark hair."

"It's not Francesca Gaitskill," he said as the music came to an end.

Marcus took his grandmother's elbow to lead her off the dance floor, all the while keeping the mystery woman in sight, which wasn't easy in the crowded room. He suspected, from the heads turned in her direction, that several other gentlemen had their eyes on her as well.

"Go," Lady Tremont said.

"Eh?"

She patted his hand where it touched her elbow. "Never mind about me, I'm not so nearsighted that I can't find my way to the lemonade table. Go speak with this blue-clad lady. If she's some new mystery beauty, every unmarried man in the room will already be scheming to make her acquaintance, and a disgraceful number of married ones as well."

Marcus didn't need to be told twice. He dropped a kiss on his grandmother's forehead and muttered his thanks.

* * *

Rosamund, twirling around the ballroom in the arms of a gentleman wearing a wine-colored demi-mask, already knew that she would remember this night for the rest of her life.

She was at the Marquess of Boxhaven's masquerade ball, in his grand town house, surrounded by happy, lovely people dancing to beautiful music. From the tips of her jeweled dancing shoes to the topmost swirl of her hair, she felt grateful to be alive and young. Across the ballroom, she had spied her aunt and cousins standing amid a group of ladies watching the dancers, and nothing had happened. The ballroom was so crowded, in fact, that Rosamund doubted her relatives would even see her. Even if they did, she felt *fairly* safe behind her mask, and she knew that she looked nothing like the shabbily dressed person on whom they regularly dumped their piles of holey stockings.

She had been prepared to simply watch the dancers. She had not danced since she was fourteen, and she had thought that simply being at the ball was already so wonderful that it would have been enough. But hardly had she entered the ballroom when a gentleman had approached and asked for a dance, and she hadn't lacked for partners since.

When *it* happened, her gallant partner in the wine-colored mask was playfully, though with increasing focus, trying to guess her name. Rosamund's eyes, passing over the shoulder of her partner, met those of a tall gentleman, and something electric passed between them.

Her dance partner was still talking, but it was as though everything and everyone in the ballroom were falling away, and the only other person now there with her was the tall gentleman whose gaze held hers.

He was dressed in black with a beautifully crisp white cravat and a black satin demi-mask. His hair was golden brown, and she thought—or maybe she felt, or just knew—that his eyes were blue. He smiled at her, collapsing the space between them as the dance came to an end.

"Won't you please tell me your name, oh mystery lady?" her partner asked, breaking the spell.

Before she could reply—not that she intended to give her name—the tall gentleman was at her side.

"I believe the next dance is mine," he said, his eyes glittering at her conspiratorially.

She smiled. She'd never tasted champagne, but she'd seen it freshly poured in a glass, and she felt as though champagne bubbles were rising inside her. "Is it?"

He cast a look at her dance partner that was equal parts haughty and warm, and she wondered who this tall gentleman was. He might be some lord, perhaps a friend of the Marquess of Boxhaven. He might even *be* the marquess, she thought giddily, before discarding the idea. The Marquess of Boxhaven would be far too busy at his own ball to be taking note of someone like her. He was probably dancing with at least a viscountess.

"You'll excuse us, won't you?" the tall gentleman said to her partner.

Her partner inclined his head—she had the sense the two men knew each other, though the conventions of the masquerade encouraged anonymity. With a last glance at Rosamund, her dancing partner walked away.

"I'm not certain that was polite," she said to the tall gentleman, but she was smiling.

"He'll live." The music was starting. "Do you really want to dance?" he asked.

The next dance was a quadrille, whose steps she remembered finding confounding as a girl. The waltz was, in fact, the only dance she really knew how to do, probably because she could practice it alone in her room, humming as she twirled around with a broom handle.

"Actually, a lemonade sounds more the thing," she said.

"Lemonade it is." He placed a gloved hand lightly at her elbow and guided her through a throng of people toward the table. The room had been crowded when she'd arrived and since then had become only more so, and now it was rather difficult moving about.

"How thirsty are you?" he asked as their progress was arrested by a seemingly impenetrable mass of people.

"Not terribly," she said. "I suppose it's more that I've become warm."

"Oh, there you are," an older woman in a cream mask said to Rosamund's partner, squeezing past a man dressed as a bishop. "It's just as I feared."

The tall gentleman laughed. "A success, you mean? Yes, I fear the ball is quite horribly successful."

"Cheeky fellow. You know what I mean. People will be

feeling terribly crowded. I really don't know what to do."

"I don't think there is anything *to* do," he said. "And I don't think anyone else particularly minds that it's a squeeze. What do you think?" he asked, turning to Rosamund, who was watching him and the woman in the cream mask with dawning comprehension.

The woman who was expressing such hostly concern—and who had, now that Rosamund was noticing, hair nearly the same color of golden brown as the tall gentleman—could only be Lady Boxhaven. Which would mean that the tall gentleman was a member of her family, and Rosamund would lay odds he was her son. That meant either her younger son, or the marquess.

From the way he'd sent her dancing partner scurrying, she had a pretty good idea which son he was, and her heart skipped in her chest.

They were looking at her, waiting for a reply.

"I don't mind being a little crowded when a ball is so wonderful," she said.

His eyes twinkled at her before he turned to the other woman, surely Lady Boxhaven. "There, you see? An impartial observer. The ball's a success and not at all horrible."

Lady Boxhaven's attention finally came fully upon Rosamund. She had very kind, soft eyes, and she seemed to pause as she regarded Rosamund. "Well, an impartial observer is a very good thing," she said with a smile. "Do excuse me, please, I think I am wanted," and she disappeared back into the crowd.

"I suppose that little conversation has given you clues about my identity," the tall gentleman said.

"I suppose it has," Rosamund agreed, liking the way his eyes teased hers. A lady passing next to Rosamund jostled her, and the marquess—for she was now certain her companion must be him—steadied her with a hand on her elbow.

"Shall we go out to the terrace?" he asked. "It will be cooler outside, and I should think less crowded."

"Yes, please. This truly is a wonderful and successful ball, but too much successfulness at one time could make a person's head spin."

"Successfulness." He chuckled. "A very nice way of putting not being able to move."

With a stride that clearly expected to encounter no opposition—and, to Rosamund's delighted amusement, didn't—he led her to the open doors leading to the terrace. Outside, the air was cool and fresh, and only a few couples stood about here and there. He guided her to a spot away from the others, near where the balustrade led down a short set of steps to a garden.

"Now then," he said, leaning a bit closer and offering the kind of beguiling grin that had probably stolen more than a few feminine hearts, "since you've had clues to my identity, don't you think it a good idea to offer me some clues to yours?"

She laughed. "No. This is supposed to be a night of mystery."

"A night of mystery," he repeated. "But my identity isn't a mystery to you anymore, is it?"

"Not unless you aren't the Marquess of Boxhaven and that wasn't your mother speaking with us just a minute ago."

He inclined his head with playful dismay. "Will you at least tell me if we have ever met before? Though I feel certain I would know if we had."

She felt certain she would know if they had even passed each other on the street, because there was something about him, something that made her heart race and her skin feel warm, and she knew she hadn't stopped smiling since their eyes had met on the dance floor. He was special, but not because he was wealthy and titled. He was handsome and commanding and, for whatever reason she could not have named, completely interesting to her, and she wanted to know everything about him. She *liked* him.

"We've never met before," she said.

He nodded, as if he too would have known her. "Did you

come tonight with your family?"

She smiled, feeling that nothing in her life had ever been more fun than teasing this man. "That would be a helpful clue, wouldn't it?"

CHAPTER FOUR

This, *this* was what he'd been waiting for his entire life, without even knowing that he'd been waiting. This feeling of being so incredibly alive, like every inch of his skin was awake, all because of the lady in blue.

He was about to ask her if she had been in London long—he was already forming a list of innocuous questions that nonetheless ought to narrow down something about her identity—when, with no warning, he felt something thump against his legs.

"What—" he started to say, even as he realized that somehow his dog had escaped the footman tasked with his care. Socrates gave a happy yip and immediately laid his body across Marcus's feet. Marcus had so far succeeded in discouraging the jumping up and the licking of his boots and shoes, but Socrates continued to seek whatever contact he could manage.

"Oh," the lady in blue gasped, "what a sweet little dog!" The next moment, she had crouched down and pulled off her gloves, and then she was petting the creature as he reclined on Marcus's dancing shoes, and Marcus stared in fascination. Socrates, interestingly, began emitting whimpers of canine delight. "How adorable."

"Yes," Marcus agreed, gazing at the top of her head.

She looked up at him, the torchlight glowing on her lovely features and dancing in those eyes whose lights were spinning an ever more powerful spell over him. "He seems quite attached to you. Is he yours?"

"Yes. My mother presented him to me as a gift, though I am still not certain why she thinks I need a lapdog. I'm afraid Socrates is somewhat ridiculous—since the moment he arrived at Boxhaven House, he's behaved as though destiny brought us together."

She stood up, her eyes laughing through the holes in her mask, and he tried not to think about kissing her even as he laughed with her. He must have laughed more this night than he had in ages. Perhaps his grandmother was right, and he was becoming too serious, or, at least, he was allowing fun to fall by the wayside.

Or maybe it was simply that he'd been waiting for this woman. And now she was here, like a long-awaited arrival, and he thought that he would never want to stop smiling. He was giddy, and everything was wonderful, and he didn't want the feeling to end. He had no intention of *letting* it end. He was confident he would persuade her to reveal who she was, because he knew, he *knew*, that this night was the beginning of something important.

"How lucky you are to have such a thoughtful mother, and of course, such a devoted dog."

"Your being charmed by Socrates's less-than-civilized behavior suggests to me that your household must be deficient in dogs."

"Sadly, it is," she said.

"Perhaps you reside in Town, then, and there's not much need in your household for a dog?"

"Perhaps," she said lightly, evading his attempt to discern her address. Was she perhaps a relation of someone they knew? He racked his brain for the kind of family news his mother so frequently shared with him, and to which, somewhat shamefully, he did not pay a great deal of attention. Had she told him of some friend's lovely cousin coming to Town, or something similar? Nothing came to mind.

"Oh!" she said as the warm weight on his feet disappeared. "Your dog has just installed himself on my feet."

Incredulous, Marcus looked down. Socrates, who had taken little more than passing interest in anyone but him since arriving at Boxhaven House, let alone actually seeking the attention of anyone else, was now lying across the lady in blue's feet. As Marcus had already moved some way toward laying his heart at this woman's feet, the sight of his dog there was a little galling.

"Goodness, I feel quite chosen," she said with not a hint of sarcasm. She sounded, in fact, delighted.

"Socrates!" Marcus said. "Get up this instant." Socrates ignored him.

"Oh, do let him stay where he is," she said and caught his arm as he was about to crouch down to address the matter. "I don't mind a bit, really. He is so sweet and very, very soft."

"You really must be deficient in dog exposure." How different she was... open, as if she was ready to be delighted by whatever happened.

"Oh, there you are," came a breathless voice as a footman appeared on the steps coming up from the garden. "I'm terribly sorry, miss, that this dog is bothering you."

It was Johnston, the footman who'd been tasked with assisting Cook with Socrates, and he stopped abruptly as he took in the full situation. "My lord," he said, bowing to Marcus. "I regret most seriously that Socrates escaped from me. I had brought the dog into the garden because—"

"I can imagine why, Johnston, thank you," Marcus said.

"Yes, my lord. I thought I had hold of him, but he ran off

suddenly. He must have known you were here."

"Indeed," Marcus said dryly. "Thank you, Johnston, that will do. If you will remove Socrates from our guest's feet?"

* * *

Rosamund knew she would pay for this night. With luck, not because her aunt or cousins discovered her presence, which, now that she and the marquess had moved to the terrace, seemed not as likely since few other people seemed inclined to venture out there.

No, she'd pay for this night because being with the Marquess of Boxhaven was so wonderful that everything else in her life would pale in comparison. She would be thinking about him every night before she fell asleep, probably until she departed this mortal coil, and all day long too, as she worked her way through the piles of sewing and mending Melinda found for her.

But she already knew that she would never regret what would surely become bittersweet memories in the months and years to come, because she would always know that she had met him and that he had looked at her as he was doing right then. She might have gone her whole life without looking into his eyes and feeling as though they were touching each other's souls.

But the future was for later. She didn't care about the future right now, because she meant to savor every moment of this wonder-filled night.

"Now that you are no longer being pinned in place by a dog, we might go inside, if you like," he said. "Everyone else out here has done, probably because they're playing a waltz, and those are popular."

She glanced around the terrace, surprised to see that he was right. They were alone.

"I can hear the music," she said. "It's so beautiful. Everything here is beautiful. It must be wonderful to live here."

"I can't complain, though I sometimes do," he said cheerfully. "For one thing, all sorts of people are terribly interested in what a marquess does, so one feels *watched* all the time, never mind that my family treats my home as if it is theirs."

"Is your family all as nice as your mother?"

"Nice is not exactly the word. My brother, Jack, is generally wanting to hide from the consequences of something he shouldn't have done, my sister Kate is generally wanting to hide from my mother's matchmaking efforts, and my sister Alice, who is sixteen, ought to want to hide but never does."

"They sound lovely," she said wistfully. She hadn't realized until that moment how very much she missed having her very own family. Not Melinda—she and her daughters might be relatives, but they weren't *family*. Uncle Piggott was like family, of course, and so were the other servants in the household. Still, there was nothing better, was there, than a whole family of related people who all truly loved each other? It was what she'd known for the first fifteen years of her life, and what she'd learned to do without since coming to Melinda's house.

He chuckled. "If you insist that I turn sentimental, I will go so far as to admit that they each have a number of redeeming qualities."

"And I imagine that they each feel very lucky to have you as their brother."

He inclined his head in answer. "Have you any brothers or sisters?"

"I was an only child."

"And?"

"There's not much more to say."

"Don't think I didn't notice that you are evading my attempts to learn more about you," he teased, "while, quite unfairly, you know exactly who I am."

"There isn't that much to know about the mundane details of my living situation. I'm afraid it would destroy all the mystery of this lovely night if I revealed them." And because she could see that he wanted to ask why, she said, "Though I think it quite fun to know who you are."

"Because I am the Marquess of Boxhaven?" he asked with a trace of disappointment.

"Because you are you," she said. "And because I can see you are the very best sort of man, the kind of man who clearly doesn't need a lapdog, but accepted one cheerfully because his mother wants him to have one."

"Will you call me Marcus?" he asked.

"Marcus," she repeated. "It suits you."

"You might tell me your name at this point," he said lightly, but his eyes looked serious. "It is a customary exchange."

"Not when one is at a masquerade." But then she said softly, "You may call me Poppy." It had been her mother's nickname for her. No one had called her that for years, but tonight, it suddenly felt right that this special man might know this private name.

"Poppy," he repeated, and she heard the pleasure in his voice that she had trusted him. He took a step closer, and her heart thumped in response. "Will you dance with me, Poppy?"

He smelled extremely good, like some sort of expensive soap. He probably had drawers full of expensive soaps, and other drawers full of crisp, pressed linens, and closets full of boots, and rooms full of furniture. These were all things, and she understood that while he might not even particularly care about any of these things, they were part of why his life was completely different from hers.

Things made a difference. If she owned things like houses and carriages and fine jewels, she would have choices in life that she did not. She'd understood about such things from early in childhood, when choices had to be made about how to live within what her father's erratic captain's salary could provide. But her family's decisions had always been made out of love, out of the knowledge that they each wanted the others' happiness, and that if there was to be any hardship—skimpy meals, clothes worn past respectable use—they would bear it cheerfully, because they were sharing it. Money gave a person a great many options, and because she had no money of her own, she had but two choices: live in her aunt's house, or starve.

Only now, just for tonight, she, as Poppy at the ball, had other choices, ones that would never be offered to her again. Did she want to dance? She could almost laugh that he would even ask, that he couldn't perceive that every part of her was whispering assent.

"Yes," she breathed.

She had removed her gloves to pet his dog, and as he was about to take her hands, he paused to take off his own. Then he enclosed her hand in one of his, and she nearly sighed with the pleasure of his warm skin and the strength of him. His other hand came to her waist, and he drew her closer. They began to move slowly around the terrace in a sort of half time that was entirely their own.

And then gradually they moved more and more slowly, until they finally came to a stop as the music played on and a few night noises from insects reminded them that the terrace was otherwise deserted. His eyes shone in the torchlight, and his expression was serious.

"I know that we have only just met tonight, but I feel as though I've known you much, much longer."

"I feel that too," she said, hardly daring to believe that he'd spoken of exactly what was in her heart.

"I want to know everything about you. I want to *know* you."

For the briefest of moments, she entertained the idea that they might have infinite time to get to know each other. She almost wished he hadn't said anything, though, because his words could only remind her that this night, while magical, was only one night, and that was all they would ever have.

But she was also glad, heart-brimmingly glad, that he had spoken, because his voice and his words told her that being with her meant something to him, and that was what she would treasure most.

"That would be wonderful," she agreed.

"Do you know what else I feel?"

"What?"

"That I want to kiss you."

Excitement fluttered in her like a thousand butterflies, and she gave a small nod. His head slowly dipped, and then his lips touched hers. She had thought that the night was already almost too perfect, but this... his kiss was beyond perfect. Tender at first, as though he was leaving her room to accept him, but then when she circled her arms around the breadth of his chest, he deepened the kiss, and she felt the whisperings of hunger, his and hers. Her heart hammered with a wild joy that she never wanted to end.

Time and place ceased to have any meaning, and all she knew was that this night and this man would be imprinted on her heart forever.

But finally, something did penetrate her cloud of happiness, and she became aware of a sound that was the knell of doom.

The distant sound of a clock chiming midnight.

Dear God, midnight! Panic rose in her instantly. She had to leave.

She broke the kiss and stepped back.

"What is it, Poppy?" he said.

"I—I have to go."

"What, now?" His lips curled in a smile that expressed confidence that he would convince her she didn't want to spend a minute apart from him. She wished more than anything that she could answer with one of her own.

"Yes, now, actually," she said, her mind racing. They'd been on the terrace for a while, and she knew Melinda had ordered the carriage to collect the Monroes at one o'clock, but she had no way of knowing where Melinda or her cousins might be in the ballroom. They might very well be between her and the path to the door. They shouldn't recognize her, since they wouldn't be expecting her—but they might.

"You can't go now," he said, his brow touched with a crease as he understood that she wasn't being playful. "You haven't yet told me nearly enough about yourself. How will I be able to call—"

Oh God, she couldn't bear it. And she couldn't waste another moment either, because she had to get to the coach so the driver would have time to take her home and return for her aunt and cousins.

A clean break was the only thing to do, and without another word, Rosamund turned away from Marcus, meaning to run down the steps behind her. But she tripped a little in turning, and he reached out to steady her, and his hand brushed her shoulder and caught the strand of pearls. She barely registered a tugging sensation, but she didn't dare stop. And in that moment, she had a piece of luck.

"Oh, there you are, Marcus," came a feminine voice. "Mama says dinner is about to be served, and you are wanted to lead Lady Catterton in."

Rosamund raced down the steps and into the dark garden.

"Wait!" she heard him call, but she only ran faster, making for the glow of the torch by the mews with everything she had and hoping that the Marquess of Boxhaven would be above sprinting after her. She thought she heard the sound of feet pounding the ground, but she had the element of surprise on her side, and she gained the mews, and in another few moments, she had run out to the street and reached the waiting coach.

"Waste not a moment," she cried to the coachman as she climbed in. He didn't need to be told twice, and they were off.

It wasn't until they were almost home that she realized the pearls must have come off when Marcus tried to steady her, and they were gone.

CHAPTER FIVE

The loss of the pearl necklace was a disaster.

Uncle Piggott and Mrs. Barton were waiting when Rosamund got home from the ball, eager to hear all about it. She told them right off about losing the necklace, though without mentioning how or who was involved. No one needed to be told that there would be repercussions, and that if they did not fall on Rosamund, they would necessarily fall on the servants, especially the maids.

"And I won't let that happen," Rosamund said firmly. "I shall go to Melinda as soon as she returns and tell her I took them."

"You'll do nothing of the sort," Uncle Piggott said. "We'll figure something out, won't we, Mrs. Barton?"

Mrs. Barton, who looked less convinced of the possibility of solving the problem of the missing necklace and therefore somewhat stricken, nonetheless said, "Perhaps we should send a footman to inquire about a necklace that was lost. Surely the marquess would wish to return such a thing to a guest."

But Rosamund could easily imagine that the marquess would not surrender the necklace without first discovering from whose house the footman had come. Or, even if the Marquess of Boxhaven did give it back immediately, the footman would still be a clue, a very large clue, to her identity, and she knew the marquess was far too smart and persistent not to make use of it.

"No," Uncle Piggott said, "it would be too great a risk."

"Agreed," Rosamund said. "Maybe I could sneak into Boxhaven House in a few hours, when the ball is over and everyone has finally gone to bed."

"No," Mrs. Barton and Uncle Piggott said in unison. Rosamund knew it was a preposterous idea, but what else could she do?

"I'll speak to Bronwen," Mrs. Barton said. Bronwen was Melinda's personal maid. "When she undresses Melinda tonight and puts her jewels in the box, Bronwen will say nothing about the missing necklace. And she can do whatever is needed to make sure Melinda doesn't notice."

Uncle Piggott nodded. "And in the meantime, we'll think about how to get that necklace back."

Rosamund knew this was not a very good plan in terms of its likelihood for ultimate success, but it was the only sensible course any of them were likely to come up with.

She took their hands. "I haven't yet had a chance to say that, aside from the loss of the necklace, I had a truly splendid time. I never dared dream that I might go to a ball—and such a fabulous ball—and I can't thank you both enough."

Uncle Piggott grinned. "You met a handsome fellow and danced with him, didn't you?"

"I did," Rosamund said, and her heart squeezed. Marcus was so much more than a handsome man, and all she now wanted in life was the chance to get to know him more. Which would never happen.

"But that's wonderful!" said Mrs. Barton. "Surely you

could ask the gentleman to help you. Perhaps you could send him a note, and he could procure the necklace on your behalf."

"It's impossible," Rosamund said.

"But if you had a wonderful time together, which I can see from your face that you did, he'll be wanting to see you again, Miss Rosamund."

Uncle Piggott had been watching this exchange. "Unless he's the sort of gentleman whose station in life would require him to be very… discerning."

Rosamund nodded, forcing down a lump that wanted to form in her throat. "He doesn't know who I am, but I figured out who he is. He's someone who could never know me outside of a masquerade."

"One of the high-and-mighty lords, is he?" Uncle Piggott asked.

"Yes," whispered Rosamund.

"Oh, my dear," Mrs. Barton said. "There must be some way."

"There's no way," Rosamund said. "But nothing can ever take away my memories of the ball, and for that, I'm very, very grateful. Now," she said briskly, needing to stop talking about the ball whose like she'd never see again and the marquess she'd never get to know, "Mrs. Barton had better speak to Bronwen before the others come back."

Bronwen did as she was asked and breathed not a word of the affair. The next day, everything in the Monroe household proceeded as usual. Rosamund was left to fix the tears that had been made in the ladies' gowns from the evening before (Calliope in particular was a great one for stepping on the hems of her gowns), and no one made any accusations or suggested the ridiculous notion that Rosamund herself had gone to the ball.

But it couldn't last, and Rosamund was torn between delirious memories of the ball and awareness that she had done something that could not go unnoticed forever. As she sewed, she tested scenarios in her mind of what she might do if, or rather, when Melinda found out about the pearls. But none of the scenarios was of any help, because if she had had anywhere else to go, she would long ago have gone there.

* * *

How hard could it be for a powerful marquess, with all the avenues that riches and connections could offer, to find one woman in London who did not wish to be found?

Very hard, apparently. This was what Marcus discovered in the days after the ball.

His masquerade lady had fled into the garden for whatever urgent reason had possessed her, taking a little piece of his heart with her and, he imagined, though he could not know, without a backward glance. This last part was somewhat pathetic on his part—for all he knew, she'd raced across the garden gazing regretfully over her shoulder the whole time, but he was in all honesty a little hurt.

How could she run off like that, after everything that had passed between them? What could possibly have been so pressing that she'd had to leave so suddenly? And who the devil was she?

He began trying to find out who she was as soon as possible on the day following the ball. He had one additional clue beyond the name Poppy, the few details she'd revealed, and the unremarkable gloves she'd left behind: the pearl necklace that had come loose as he'd tried to catch her. It wasn't much to go on. Pearls being fairly indistinguishable, all the necklace had to offer was the clasp, which was engraved with *SDW to HPW*. He brought the necklace to his mother, who knew the most of any of the family about the members of the *ton*.

"SDW to HPW," she mused. "I'm flattered that you think me so knowledgeable, but this is really very little to go on. And you say she gave her name as Poppy?"

"Yes."

She nodded, thinking. "Very likely a nickname."

"Right." He'd already thought of that, and it wasn't a comforting thought.

"And a last name that might begin with W, and we don't know if the initials refer to the present generation, or an earlier one, though it's probably safe to assume the pearls were a gift from either a husband to a wife, or a parent to a daughter. Ward, Wilcox, Warner, Wallingford," she listed, squinting. "Wilson. I can think of dozens of people, and that's not including Williams. So many people named Williams." She paused. "And then there's the fact that these initials could refer to people from a hundred years ago. A strand of pearls is the kind of thing that gets handed down in families for generations."

"I get your point, Mother," Marcus said tightly.

"I'm sorry, dearest." She touched his cheek. "I'd love more than anything to help you. Your Poppy seemed like a very nice young lady."

"She is."

His mother tapped her chin. "I suppose the best thing would be to create a chart for different generations and match up names. We ought to be able to narrow the possibilities down that way."

Having no other sensible course of action, Marcus sat with his mother, and together, they filled several pieces of paper with names. In the end, all they determined was that HPW must be the initials of a woman, since a man would not receive a gift of pearls, though Marcus had assumed that to begin with. Beyond that, he now had a lengthy list of people with initials that matched at least one set of the initials on the clasp, and a much smaller group of those who could be reliably matched in the sort of relationship that would occasion the gift of a costly necklace.

"And this is all supposing the two people were not unrelated people with last names that started with the same initial," his mother pointed out. "Or someone whose family is not well known to us."

"I know," Marcus said, trying to keep his frustration in check.

But he did at least now have a place to start, so he compared their list with the ball's guest list and arrived at eight families with possible family members that might have, or might at one time have had, at least one of the sets of initials.

Marcus made eight calls, one to each family, and drank many more than eight cups of tea while he tried obliquely to tease out whether any of the families might have a young lady previously unknown to him who'd attended the ball and lost a necklace. This was a tricky undertaking—he didn't want to give too much away, because the consequences of the Marquess of Boxhaven going house to house looking for a woman whose last name started with W, but about whom he knew little else, did not bear thinking about. If nothing else, he would be besieged by everyone within a fifty-mile radius who had a marriageable daughter, cousin, or friend who had a last name starting with W.

None of the calls yielded anything helpful.

Meanwhile, every night, he dreamed of her.

In his dreams, they danced and laughed and kissed, and then she told him her *full* name. But in that maddening way of dreams, he could never quite hear it.

By the end of the week, his frustration was mounting. Surely it couldn't be that he'd found the woman for whom he'd been waiting all his life, only to never see her again. Surely fate wouldn't be that cruel.

But as the days continued to pass with no sign of her, he began to think that fate might be exactly that cruel.

* * *

The axe fell six days after the ball, when Melinda was picking through her jewelry box to make a selection for a dinner party that evening. Her scream of outrage could be heard all the way in the Outer Reaches, and Rosamund, putting the finishing touches on the new gown Vanessa was to wear that night, immediately knew that the jig was up.

Bronwen had been instructed that if Melinda discovered the pearls were missing, she must tell Melinda that Rosamund might know where they were. Rosamund was thus summoned immediately, and a livid Melinda demanded an explanation.

As there was nothing for it, Rosamund simply said, "They were mine and I took them."

"Shocking creature!" Melinda cried. "Where are they? Bring them to me at once!"

"They're gone."

Melinda's features hardened. "You sold them, didn't you? You little thief! But what should I have expected, inviting someone like you into our home? I have been a fool, a fool who was far too generous for her own good."

Melinda then demanded the money from the supposed sale, which Rosamund of course didn't have. Amid Melinda's resultant pronouncements that Rosamund was a thief and no longer welcome in her house and shouts for a Bow Street runner to be called, Rosamund threw her few belongings in a bag and said a hasty goodbye to Uncle Piggott.

"She's the thief!" Uncle Piggott nearly spat. "The necklace was yours."

"It doesn't matter."

His fury melted away as his dear old features sagged with concern. "But where will you go, Rosamund?"

"I have some money saved." Only a very little bit, but Uncle Piggott, who had so little himself, didn't need to know that. "And I'm sure I'll find work somewhere."

"This is an outrage! She has treated you abominably."

"Shh," Rosamund said gently. Uncle Piggott would never be thrown out on the street, but he needed to preserve the goodwill of Melinda lest he find himself neglected and mistreated. "It will be all right."

She hugged him, blinking back tears, and asked him to relay her goodbyes to Mrs. Barton and the servants. And then, in case a Bow Street runner might really be coming for her, she left in haste.

Rosamund found a cheap room in a boarding house and began visiting employment agencies and shops, seeking work anywhere that looked likely. But work was not easy to find for a woman with no references, and as the days wore on and her meager funds dwindled, she had to ration what she spent on food. When she was finally offered work as a seamstress, at wages that would barely allow her to feed herself, she ignored the irony and accepted the position with alacrity.

As the weeks ground on, hunger settled in as a permanent guest and her own clothes grew threadbare while she sewed new gowns for fashionable ladies. She'd been right about one thing, though: the memories of Marcus and her night at the ball became the one bright spot in her days, bittersweet though the memories were because of the knowledge that she would never see him again.

CHAPTER SIX

Marcus, who about to set out on a journey north to visit his grandmother, had just stepped into his coach and was closing the door when Socrates unaccountably jumped out of the coach. Before Marcus had even dismounted, his dog, who had previously never run anywhere if it was not toward Marcus, had raced a good way down the street.

Marcus took off after him, calling fruitlessly, trailed by a footman doing likewise. He was still some distance from the dog when a carriage turned the corner ahead at a smart clip. Socrates was but a few feet from its wheels, and Marcus barely had time to conceive of imminent and appalling disaster, when a woman stepped into the road and snatched his dog out of harm's way with moments to spare.

The coach rolled on obliviously as Marcus reached the woman, who was still holding his wayward dog. She was young, though he couldn't see her face because she was wearing a bonnet and her gaze was directed at Socrates. Her worn and faded frock and the dated look of her bonnet suggested slender means, and he took her for a servant of some kind.

"Excuse me, miss," he said, approaching. "That's my dog you just rescued from certain disaster. I can't thank you enough."

She looked up, and as his eyes met hers, he was struck by the entirely unexpected, and strangely intense, sensation that he'd met her before. And was that an answering light of recognition in her own eyes?

He hardly had time to formulate these thoughts, though, because she immediately directed her eyes woodenly to his chest. As this was a not uncommon reaction among the servant classes when encountering someone like Marcus, he took little note.

He tried for a moment to place her. Had he perhaps passed her on the street before, or glimpsed her working in the home of an acquaintance? He must have encountered hundreds of servants over the years. Or perhaps she simply looked like someone he knew.

However, he really had no time for such inconsequential considerations. He was about to leave for a journey to the home of his grandmother, who'd retired to her country home as the Season was coming to an end. It had been almost three months since the masquerade ball, and despite his continuing lack of success in discovering anything about Poppy, he couldn't forget her. She popped into his head at all sorts of odd times— when he was eating breakfast, while riding in Hyde Park, at dinner with friends. Never mind how often she appeared in his dreams. He was hoping that his grandmother would be able to provide some thoughts as to the possible identity of the owner of the pearl necklace, and thus of his mystery lady from the ball.

"He was almost hit by that carriage," the young woman scolded him. Marcus couldn't remember the last time he'd been scolded by anyone, being that he was thirty years of age and a marquess. Her bonnet must have come loose while she was running after Socrates, because it now began slipping toward the back of her head. As she pushed it impatiently off, he saw her face better.

She was pretty, a slim slip of a thing with thick dark brown hair escaping here and there from a careworn knot and those eyes that interested him more than they should. They were brown with flecks of gold.

She rubbed her cheek consolingly across the top of his dog's head, though Socrates seemed unbothered by the notion that he'd just escaped death. That his dog was not merely tolerating the attentions of a stranger but making no attempt to reattach himself to Marcus was astonishing, because the only other person Socrates had shown any real interest in since Marcus had acquired him had been Poppy of the Ball.

It seemed his dog had a fondness for females or, apparently, certain females, since Socrates had not taken a particular liking to Marcus's housekeeper, nor any of the maids, his mother, or even, inconveniently, his sister Alice, who'd volunteered to take care of him while Marcus was away. Much as he would have liked to accept her offer, he could not in good conscience have done so, since experience had taught him that as soon as Socrates perceived that his master had left the house, he began howling and didn't stop until Marcus returned.

So far, all of Marcus's efforts to train Socrates into better behavior had been completely ineffective. But apparently, and inexplicably, Socrates liked this young woman. Perhaps this was because she'd rescued him, but Marcus had no time to puzzle over the issue, because he needed to be on his way. He had, though, just had an idea.

"I am keenly aware that he was in great peril and that you saved his life," he said. "For which I am extremely grateful. He's a good-hearted fellow"—considering what he was about to propose, Marcus thought it best not to mention the diabolical howling yet—"but, I'm afraid, young and untrained. He was in my carriage, and I was closing the door when he bolted out. I can't think why."

"Dogs will do things like that," she said reasonably. "Perhaps he saw a cat, or smelled something appealing to him, like a cheesemonger's cart."

Her speech was educated, her manner pleasant. He suspected she might be one of the numbers of women of good families who had fallen on hard times. And then her eyes met his again, and he was struck anew with the thought that he knew her.

"I say, is it possible that we've met before?"

"How—" the word came out as a croak, and she cleared her throat. "That seems highly unlikely."

He grinned. "It does, doesn't it? But I have the strangest sense that I've seen you before."

"Oh, well, I've walked through Mayfair many times. Perhaps we've passed each other on the street."

He nodded slowly, though he felt that this wasn't quite right, that it was too thin an explanation for the jolt of connection he felt when looking in her eyes. But what difference did it make if he had once passed her on the street? He didn't know her.

"Shall I relieve you of my dog?" Socrates had laid his head shamelessly on her shoulder and appeared supremely content.

"Could I hold him for a moment longer? He's so dear."

"Certainly." Marcus would have gleefully agreed that she might hold Socrates for the rest of the day, since such an occurrence would allow him to do any number of things he had put off while he'd been busy keeping Socrates out of trouble. As Marcus watched, his dog licked the area of his rescuer's neck right below her ear.

"Socrates," he said sternly, "behave yourself."

She laughed. "I don't mind. He's just a puppy."

Something about her laughter made him want to laugh as well, even though there wasn't anything especially amusing about their conversation. Or maybe it wasn't only the sound of her laughter, but the way her eyes twinkled that made him feel as though they were sharing something fun.

"Well, I can't thank you enough for saving him. It was

fortunate that you were here."

This was the moment when she might say why she had happened to be on the street, whether she perhaps worked in one of the neighborhood households.

"Yes, it was," she agreed, not offering so much as a hint as to why she was there.

"Are you perhaps employed in the neighborhood?" he prompted.

"I am a seamstress."

This made sense. Not a few seamstresses were gentlewomen fallen on hard times, and the more he talked with her, the more certain he was that she had had a good upbringing.

"Ah. Well, I hope that I might perhaps tempt you to make a change in position. I have a proposition of employment for you: I would like to retain you as a minder for my dog. As evidenced by recent events, Socrates is in need of someone to keep him out of trouble."

"I'm sorry, did you say you wish to retain a companion for your *dog*?" she said, clearly puzzled.

He couldn't blame her, as he would never have expected to find himself attempting to hire a woman he'd just met to be a companion for a dog, but he knew that he would not be able to bear the disappointment in his mother's eyes if something happened to Socrates. Not that *he* wanted anything to happen to Socrates either, at least, not most of the time. Also, this woman presented the possibility that Marcus might have time unencumbered by his dog, which, after months of nearly constant canine companionship, sounded incredibly appealing.

"Yes. Suffice it to say that he was a gift and that, excepting yourself, it seems, he will not tolerate the company of anyone but myself. As you might imagine, this can create problems. Namely, if I can't be with him, he howls constantly."

"Ah," she said.

"I'm journeying north today, as soon as possible, in fact, and I should be obliged if you would consent to accompany me—or, more specifically, my dog—on the journey."

Not surprisingly, she looked taken aback by this abrupt proposal.

He smiled encouragingly. "I would pay you handsomely, of course."

His words did not appear to put her at ease, and he thought she hugged his dog a little more tightly to her chest, as if Socrates might protect her from him. He was slightly offended, until he remembered that he hadn't introduced himself and that a pretty young woman had good reason to be nervous about the idea of a strange man offering employment suddenly, particularly employment that would require a journey alone in his company.

"Please excuse me," he inclined his head politely. "I have not introduced myself. I am the Marquess of Boxhaven."

* * *

He didn't recognize her.

She'd known it was him the minute their eyes met and she heard his voice, even as the carriage behind him with its gilded crest silently mocked her. But he didn't know who she was.

True, he'd clearly felt some recognition—she'd seen it in his eyes and the wrinkling of his brow. The jolt when their eyes first met had been a shared jolt. But that had meant nothing. He didn't know she was Poppy, and he apparently wasn't under any kind of lingering enchantment from the ball that might have swept across the chasm between them and made everything into a happily ever after.

Rosamund knew she should be glad. None of the circumstances that had allowed them to meet at the ball was in force anymore, and she now was of an even lower status than when they'd first met.

Still, it stung that he didn't know her, after they'd shared what had felt like the most special hours of her life. Over the past months, just thinking of him, of the fact that he was somewhere in London while she was there as well, had filled her with secret joy. Forbidden joy, but joy nonetheless. Now she was being shown how meaningless all that had been.

She briefly considered simply telling him they'd met before. *Oh, this is funny*, she might say, *we met at your ball.* But then she would eventually have to tell him her real name, and he would know her as the daughter of a man who was, however undeservedly, a national disgrace. And if Melinda then also discovered her whereabouts and made an issue of the "stolen" necklace, Rosamund might be in a great deal of trouble. Considering her father's sad infamy, she could not, as his daughter, expect leniency.

She wished that none of those details about her mattered and that she could once again look in Marcus's eyes and see that he thought she was special. But wishing was for people who were not in the kind of desperate straits she was in.

Marcus was offering her what would likely be a better wage than she was making as a seamstress, and for much easier work. Though she knew it was foolish to consider accepting his offer, not just because of the potential harm of her aunt's accusations, but because she couldn't bear for Marcus to find out that his mystery lady from the ball was really a poor, shabby seamstress, her future looked bleak, and his offer was tempting. The seamstress work paid barely enough to keep herself, and she had no hope of securing anything better. Was there really any choice?

"My name is Rosamund, my lord." Socrates started to shift in her arms, and she held him out to Marcus, who accepted him.

"Well, Rosamund, what do you think? Will you agree to be Socrates's companion, at least for the next month, or until he grows in wisdom and acquires civilized behavior, which might be rather further in the future? I would, of course, make it worth your while to set aside your current employment, and I would provide you with a character reference, should your work prove satisfactory."

He then named a wage that would solve a great deal of her troubles, the kind of money that might allow her to leave

London and establish herself somewhere else, perhaps as a dressmaker. Such a vision of the future was so vastly better than what she was now facing that she could hardly believe it possible.

"Your offer is unexpected," she said, stalling for time as she considered whether it was the height of idiocy to be a companion to Marcus's dog and thus inevitably put herself in Marcus's charming company when he could never be for her. Now that he was not wearing a mask obscuring half his face, she could appreciate fully how handsome he was. His eyes were a gorgeous shade of dark blue, and he was just as tall and broad-shouldered as she remembered. Simply standing there talking to him was making her heart beat faster. "I would imagine there are not many dog companions employed these days."

He gave her an amused look. "I would imagine so as well. Just think, it might be the start of a new sort of occupation, and you can be proud to say that you were the very first."

She couldn't resist smiling back—really, the man was too charming for his own good, never mind everyone else's—and gave an inward sigh. Charming people, and likely charming women, probably came as easily to him as breathing. She would doubtless regret this, but she had little choice.

"Very well, I accept," she said, hiding a smile as Socrates attempted to lick his master's ear. "When should I start?"

"Well..." He grinned sheepishly, deftly evading Socrates's little pink tongue. "Now, actually. I really was just about to depart on my journey."

"Now? As in, this very moment?"

"Well, as soon as possible. I did want to get an early start so as to make the trip in one day."

"But I would need to give notice and let my landlady know I won't need a room now and pack my things." Only a very few, since she didn't have much.

He waved a hand, dismissing her concerns. "A footman can be dispatched to your employer to give notice for you and sort things out with your landlady, and someone at Boxhaven House can pack a valise for you. I'm certain there are any number of my sisters' castoff clothes lying about."

"Oh. Well, I suppose that would all be agreeable." Since he was neatly doing away with all these details for her, *agreeable* was an understatement, but he didn't need to know that.

"Excellent. You can have a cup of tea and a sandwich, if that would suit, while the valise is packed."

"That would be welcome," she said, trying not to sound absurdly eager about his offer of food. Since her dwindling store of coins had necessitated measures such as simply telling herself she wasn't hungry when she was, the possibility of eating an entire sandwich in one sitting sounded like heaven.

"If you will come this way, Rosamund, I will take you to Boxhaven House, where I can finally put down this squirming bundle of fur-coated insanity."

CHAPTER SEVEN

Rosamund had not quite believed that tea could be served and a bag packed for her with such speed that in little more than half an hour, she and Marcus would be ready to leave, but that was what happened. The benefits of being a marquess were clearly many.

She took a seat in the coach opposite Marcus, a servant handed Socrates to her, and they were off.

"I appreciate your willingness to travel on the spur of the moment," Marcus said. Considering that he was a marquess and she was a lowly dog companion/former seamstress, he was being remarkably gracious toward her, but what else would she have expected? He was the same considerate man she'd met at the ball.

"There really isn't any comparison between the work I was doing and what you were offering," she said. He nodded in acknowledgment, his gaze lingering on her for a moment, and her heart thumped in anticipation of she didn't even know what, but all that happened was that his brow wrinkled a little.

While she was in his house, she had begun to worry that, in the close confines of the carriage, he might remember her, but that didn't seem to be the case. *Good*, she told herself unconvincingly. All for the best.

Socrates, meanwhile, grew unsettled as the carriage rolled through the streets of London and into the countryside, alternately standing up and sitting down in Rosamund's lap and on the seat next to her. After yet another trip across Rosamund's lap, he whimpered and looked at Marcus.

"Here, hand him over," Marcus said. "I suppose he's not used to coach travel."

With an apologetic look, Rosamund passed the little dog to Marcus, and there was quiet in the coach for about three minutes, at which point Socrates began pacing back and forth across Marcus's lap.

"Must you?" Marcus asked his dog.

"Perhaps he would like to be on the floor," Rosamund said. So Socrates was gently deposited on the floor, where he curled into a ball for some time before standing up again and looking imploringly at Rosamund. She leaned down and scooped him up.

"At this rate, you will be ready to give notice by the time we arrive at my grandmother's house," Marcus observed.

"Nonsense, he is the dearest thing," she said, petting the dog's soft head. This seemed to calm Socrates a bit.

"You have not yet heard him howling. Have you always had a particular way with dogs?"

"I've always loved dogs. We had one when I was little, though it's been a long time since I've been in a household with a dog." Rosamund couldn't imagine Melinda even petting a dog, let alone welcoming one into her household. Though it was just as well for the world of dogs that none of them had to be part of Melinda's household, however much Rosamund would have loved a dog like Socrates to curl up with her in her cold little room.

He nodded, a man with impeccable manners marooned in a coach with a woman so far down the social scale from him— or at least, to his knowledge—that normally he would not be expected even to acknowledge her existence.

"I have a number of dogs at my country estates, but they are bigger, naturally, and housed in kennels. Socrates was a gift from my mother, and thus of special concern to me." He chuckled. "It was the oddest thing. He took to me from the first moment. I can't say the sentiment was shared initially, but he has grown on me. Slightly."

She'd seen Marcus at the ball with his mother, seen the easy affection between them, and she nearly chuckled at the idea of his mother presenting him with a lapdog. Her father had given her a puppy for her third birthday, and Tatter had been her constant companion.

She smiled at Marcus, and he smiled back, though with a wrinkled brow again. His smile gave her a little spark of happiness before she reminded herself that she was the only one in the carriage dreaming dreams. She simply needed to not care, for the next few weeks, that he didn't know who she was, and then she would be free to begin a new life.

* * *

Rosamund was quite pretty. When he'd first encountered her on the street, Marcus had merely noticed this fact in the reflexive way that a man notices an attractive woman.

That he was noticing her prettiness now, again, as they sat across from each other in his coach was because of that same reflex, and not because he was on the alert for pretty women. Far from it, since there was only one pretty woman he wished to know better: Poppy. She was the reason for this journey to the country, where his grandmother had repaired, because he hoped she might be able to shed some light on the initials on the necklace clasp and thus Poppy's identity. Still, he was a man, and he'd long ago learned that some things about being a man were fixed, and noticing pretty women, whether he wished to or not, was one of them.

When he'd proposed the plan to visit Lady Tremont, his mother had pointed out that he could easily send her a letter. It wasn't as if seeing the pearls themselves would help his grandmother solve the mystery of Poppy, since pearls were pearls. But it had been almost three months since the ball, and despite the fruitlessness of Marcus's efforts to find out who his mystery lady was among their acquaintances, he couldn't forget Poppy, and he needed to do something.

Besides, his grandmother had also seen the mystery lady at that ball, if briefly, and maybe in talking about her, one of them would remember something more, some detail that might help identify Poppy.

My Poppy, as he had taken to thinking of her. Ever since the ball, he'd actually had trouble focusing on much besides her and the hope that he would either discover her identity, or she would somehow contact him. He hadn't forgotten for a moment how it had felt to be with her, and he'd spun more than a few fantasies about what it might be like if she were part of his future.

Still, anyone, male or female, would have said that Rosamund was pretty, and he would have to be made of stone not to be a little charmed by the way her eyes danced when she was talking to his dog.

"I really think you might prefer choosing one place and staying there for a bit," she counseled Socrates, who had adopted a vexing pattern of pacing in circles on the floor, followed by looking imploringly at his two companions in turn, apparently seeking to be picked up again since he was too small to jump onto the seats.

Socrates whimpered.

"You were just in my lap a moment ago," she pointed out to him patiently.

"I suspect Socrates's concept of time is not the same as ours. But then, his command of the English language is perhaps not very deep either."

"I'm sure you're right. I was mostly thinking of trying to

distract him, because he doesn't seem quite content."

"Mostly?" He chuckled. Really, there was something so refreshingly amusing about Rosamund. Refreshing... That was a funny way to describe a person, but *fresh* actually seemed to work because she was different. She had an open quality, as though ready to be delighted by life, which was surprising in a woman who'd surely been spending most of her waking hours in drudgery, sewing for little pay.

Or maybe it was the way she made him feel—wait, *no*. He frowned. She didn't make him feel *any* way. She was only a nice young woman who was good with dogs and happened to be pretty and have a sense of humor.

"Does that mean that in some respects you think he understands you when you address him comments about his behavior?" he couldn't resist asking.

"I suppose it does," she said. "Something about his eyes— don't you find that when you look into his eyes, you sense understanding?"

He snorted and found himself thinking that his sister Kate, who had a sense of humor that was attuned to life's absurdities, would like Rosamund. Not because Rosamund was absurd, but because—blast, there he went again. He tamped his wandering mind down firmly.

"His eyes? I don't think I've spent even a second gazing into Socrates's eyes."

"That's a shame," she said with a perfectly straight expression, though mirth tweaked the corners of her mouth. "You can tell a lot about someone by looking into their eyes."

He believed this, though he'd never thought of extending the idea to include dogs. But he could remember how it had felt to look into Poppy's eyes, how from the first moments, he'd felt that something special was meant to be between them.

He was vexed that he couldn't entirely recall the color of her eyes, but it had been night, and most of the time they'd spent together had been on the terrace, which had been fairly shadowy. He remembered only that her eyes were brown. At least, he was nearly certain they were brown.

Rosamund had brown eyes with gold flecks. They were lovely eyes, and though he'd put aside that sense of familiarity he'd experienced when he first encountered her, he did wonder about her and how it seemed likely that she had been gently bred. Was it possible she was from some family perhaps distantly known to his family? The idea was not comfortable.

"I was thinking again about that sense that I've met you before," he said. "Even your voice, now that I think of it, seems familiar. Do I look at all familiar to you?"

She coughed. "You? Familiar?"

"Yes. This feeling that I know you—it's like a puzzle I can't solve."

"You must have me confused with someone else."

"I agree that's likely, but still, there's this sense of familiarity." He cocked his head. "Do you ever go to Gunter's?"

"I have never been there."

He nodded. Gunter's was probably too costly for a seamstress. And yet... "But you haven't always been a seamstress, have you? I mean, you have clearly been educated."

"I was fortunate as a girl. Our vicar allowed me to sit in on lessons with his daughter."

He nodded. "And your father?"

"He was a working man," she said.

"And your last name? You didn't give it earlier."

At that moment, she leaned down and plucked Socrates from the floor and simply handed him to Marcus. "I'm certain you did not know my family, my lord, unless you've spent a great deal of time in Liverpool."

"No, I can't say that I have," he said, distracted by the way Socrates was fidgeting in his lap.

"There, you see?" she said. "Nothing to puzzle about."

Why was he pressing her anyway? Did he think she had met him before and was *hiding* that information for some mysterious reason? But he couldn't seem to let this go.

He gave up on trying to get Socrates to sit still and put him back on the floor. "Why did you come to London to work?"

"Because there is work in London."

"But might you not have done something else with your education, been a governess perhaps?"

"So many questions, my lord. But I'm afraid my history is quite dull and that all I have to say for myself is that I've done a great deal of sewing."

He had the sense that Rosamund's history was far from dull. A person so engaging as she was bound at least to have an amusing perspective on her experiences. But it would be ridiculous to press her further.

"Oh dear," she said to Socrates, who had begun pacing in a slightly panicked way. "I do wonder if you're feeling quite well. Perhaps we'd better—"

But Marcus had also noticed Socrates's increased agitation, and he was already getting the driver's attention. They just managed to stop and get the dog outside the coach in time for him to cast up his accounts in the grass.

"Carriage travel doesn't seem to agree with him," Rosamund observed as Socrates retched again.

"Indeed."

Marcus could not have imagined watching a small dog be sick in the grass with any other woman of his acquaintance, but standing there with Rosamund was oddly companionable, as though they were parents patiently attending a sick child.

Socrates, apparently instantly recovered, moved several paces from the scene of his handiwork and began nibbling grass. Rosamund crouched down next to the dog. "Are you feeling better now?" she inquired of him.

The spectacle of Rosamund addressing his dog made Marcus want to laugh, but then Socrates began to wander away, and she dropped onto all fours and crawled after him, and the laughter died in his throat as he watched her from behind.

He wanted her. He liked her and he wanted her.

He tore his gaze away. What the devil was wrong with him?

He was besotted with Poppy! He was! He was not making this trip to seek his grandmother's help on a whim, but because he'd truly felt something important, perhaps even eternal, when he'd been with Poppy. She was very possibly the woman for whom he'd been waiting his entire life, and he wanted more than anything to see her again, to talk to her, to know her.

So why was he noticing and thinking about and wanting Rosamund?

He'd never been so disgusted with himself, and he clenched his teeth and vowed he would master this. Clearly, he needed to stop being so friendly to his dog's companion, and he needed to remember that that was all Rosamund was. And that he had urgent business to attend to.

"If you and Socrates are quite finished, Rosamund," he said abruptly, "we will get back on the road."

"I think perhaps another minute or two, my lord," she called over her shoulder, still crawling after his dog, her rump swaying erotically, though he was certain she was oblivious to the effect she was creating.

"You don't need to crawl around after him," he said sharply. "Just pick him up and let's go."

She sat back on her heels and looked up at him, and he saw that she had perceived that his manner had changed. "Of course, my lord."

She picked Socrates up gently, but all traces of her previous playfulness were gone, which only made Marcus testier.

"Have you considered, my lord," she said with only the barest hint of injured dignity, which he knew he would not have noticed had he not shared all those other, nicer moments with her, "that since coach travel does not agree with Socrates, this episode may repeat itself?"

"We'll stop again if that becomes necessary," he said, holding out his hands for Socrates so she could mount into the coach. He was determined not to engage with her beyond what was required.

She was right, of course. They were obliged to stop nearly

every twenty minutes for the duration of the ride. After the first episode, Marcus simply allowed Rosamund to get down from the coach alone to see to Socrates, which, as he reminded himself when he felt a twinge of something he didn't want to examine, was what he was paying her to do.

The result of having to cater to Socrates's delicate stomach was that they arrived at Lady Tremont's home far later than Marcus had planned, in the middle of the night to be precise. His grandmother had long since retired, and Marcus was left to make arrangements with the housekeeper, Mrs. Clark.

"Please give Rosamund a guest room," he said. However determined he was to keep her at arm's length, being Socrates's companion meant that she would likely sometimes be in Marcus's company and that of his grandmother. A companion was a companion, and such women were not treated as servants.

"That's not necessary," Rosamund said quickly. He could see Mrs. Clark was confused.

"You are Socrates's companion," he said, "and you also need to be available should he require you, not far off in some distant part of the manor."

"I'm sure we can find a suitable guest room for Rosamund," Mrs. Clark said.

"Thank you," Marcus said, eager to seek his own chamber, where he could fall into bed and finally have some undistracted moments to think properly about Poppy and his plan to find her. Tired as he was, a practical detail occurred to him. "And Rosamund?"

"Yes, my lord?" Despite his less-friendly behavior toward her, her manner betrayed no trace of dismay or insolence, and somehow he would have expected no less of her.

"Socrates will need to go out early in the morning. You may knock on my door and collect him after dawn."

He thought he saw her swallow—the hour was late, and she was bound to be as tired as he was—but no trace of anything except cooperation colored her reply. "Of course, my lord."

This was a little wicked of him, but after all, she was being paid quite handsomely to see to his dog. And he needed to not look on her as anything but a person in his employ.

Marcus, accompanied by Socrates, repaired to the handsome guest room where he always stayed when he visited his grandmother's house and fell into bed gratefully. He did dream of Poppy, but this time Socrates was in the dream, and Rosamund as well, both of them quite maddeningly distracting Poppy from paying any attention whatsoever to Marcus's dream self.

CHAPTER EIGHT

Rosamund arose early the next morning and put on one of the gowns that had been packed for her by the Boxhaven House maids. The cream muslin was miles prettier than anything she'd worn since she was a child, and it fit surprisingly well. She felt a spring in her step as she left her bedchamber, but she reminded herself not to get used to such luxuries.

As instructed, she knocked lightly on Marcus's door. There was no response, so she opened it a few feet, her eyes sweeping quickly past the form that lay unmoving on the bed under a coverlet. Socrates was lying on several folded blankets on the floor next to his master's bed, an adorable scene that made her smile partly because of how much Marcus clearly disliked being associated with adorableness. Socrates opened his eyes, and she gestured for him to come out. He yawned but made no move.

She must have leaned against the door then, because it inched inward and creaked lightly. Marcus groaned a little and shifted, turning on his side to face her, and the coverlet slipped low on his body. She froze as she realized he was naked, or at least the part of him she could see was naked.

And, she saw as her heart pounded wildly, he was still asleep.

Having been kept a virtual prisoner in Melinda's house since the age of fifteen, Rosamund had had no occasion even to glimpse a man's naked torso, never mind the naked torso of a man she'd been dreaming about for months. Though she ought to have looked away or simply closed the door, she couldn't make herself do it. Nor was Socrates cooperating, because his eyes had drifted shut again.

She tossed propriety to the wind and looked her fill.

She had danced closed to Marcus, on the terrace at Boxhaven House, and felt his athletic grace as he'd deftly guided her, but nothing could have prepared her for the sight of the dark ruffle of hair across an endless expanse of muscled chest, or the way the flat plane of his stomach arrowed downward and disappeared under the edge of the coverlet draping low on his hips. The arm falling carelessly across his chest was long and lean, the chiseled curve of his biceps evident even in his relaxed state.

He was beautiful and strong, and she felt an almost irresistible pull toward him across the space of the room. She swallowed, as if seeking relief for a thirst that could never be quenched.

He opened his eyes.

It took only a moment for him to take in the fact that she was standing in his doorway looking at him. He sat up abruptly, the coverlet falling even lower, which apparently didn't bother him at all, because he made no move to adjust it.

"Rosamund? What are you doing?"

"I—" Her voice sounded throaty and hesitant, and she tried again, more forcefully. "I came for Socrates. Socrates, come."

Socrates jumped up as though he'd only been waiting for her command.

"Socrates, stay," Marcus said, crossing his arms, which made them look more muscled. Socrates paused on his pile of blankets, ears pricked to his master's voice. She swallowed, half giddy with a sort of fearful excitement. She wasn't afraid of Marcus, but she *was* afraid of what the increasing slant of his dark brows might mean.

"He needs to go—" she began, but Marcus cut her off.

"You were lingering, weren't you?"

"Lingering?" she repeated, the astute look in his eyes making the hairs along her neck prickle.

"I felt someone, a presence in my dream, just before I awoke. It was you, looking at me."

"No, I—"

"Rosamund," he said, and the husky, questioning note in his voice whispered volumes to her. He was not immune to her. Even from across the room, she felt the intensity in his gaze, and her skin warmed. To feel Marcus want her again, as he had that night, chased every other thought from her head.

"Rosamund," he said again, "come here."

Come here. The sensual fog that had been gathering in her brain immediately cleared, however much she didn't want it to.

No gentleman lying in his bed would have asked a lady to come closer to him. But he didn't think she was a lady, and thus his interest in her, *his dog's companion*, could only be the interest of a man looking for a dalliance.

She gathered all her self-control and said, "Socrates, come," with as much authority as she could muster. Like a long-overdue rescuer, the dog raced gleefully across the room, and she quickly closed the door behind him.

Fortunately, Socrates's excitement to go outside gave her an excuse to rush along the corridor after him, away from Marcus's room and wild thoughts of rumpled sheets and warm skin. They reached the garden without meeting anyone, for which she was deeply grateful, since she didn't feel capable of composing a sensible thought. All her mental energy was going toward banishing tempting thoughts of Marcus.

He was not an easy man to ignore, as she'd discovered during the coach ride after he'd made it plain that he saw her as nothing more than the companion of his dog. She couldn't fault him for that, since being hired as Socrates's companion was the only reason she was even in Marcus's presence.

But she knew how it felt to be the focus of all his attention, and just now she'd felt it again, that consuming, wonderful feeling that Marcus wanted her.

Which he couldn't, not in the way she wanted him to want her. He was a marquess, and she was a nobody. He might be attracted to her—she knew now that he was—but the only way he could possibly see her would be as the kind of woman who might be a mistress, and she could never bear that.

Did he ever think about Poppy? Had that night at the ball meant even a little bit as much to him as it had to her? She would never know, of course, since as the companion of Marcus's dog, she would not be having any kind of conversation with him that would hint at such matters.

She and Socrates reached the garden, where he happily set about sniffing pretty much every blade of grass while Rosamund tried, with limited success, to replace thoughts of Marcus with thoughts of sensible things, such as names for the dress shop she might establish, or patterns for gowns she could make. When Socrates had finished in the garden, she took him to the kitchen to see if there might be some scraps for his breakfast.

Two young scullery maids were at work in the kitchen when Rosamund and Socrates entered, and they squealed when they saw him. One of them covered him with kisses, while the other patted his head, leaving a puff of soap that made both the women giggle. Even Cook, a woman with quite a bit more gravitas than the maids, was charmed by him, and she gave him a scandalously large portion of a beef pie that was on the table.

"The marquess's dog must eat well," Cook explained when

Rosamund raised an eyebrow.

"Perhaps not too many rich scraps would be best," Rosamund said, thinking of his digestive troubles of the day before.

Some plain chicken was found, and some peas, which he liked remarkably well.

"Like a little lord," the maid with the soapy hands cooed as she set down a bowl of water. "And such a handsome fellow." She giggled. "Just like his master."

"That will do, Bessie," Cook said, but with the kind of smile that suggested she did not disagree.

Rosamund had been considering what she and Socrates might do next. It wasn't as though he was a child, who might be entertained with a book or paper and pencil, but as his hired companion, she intended for him to be happily occupied and not, in the unfortunate way of young dogs, causing trouble and making messes. Also, there was the matter of grooming, since the fur on his ears was long and looked prone to tangles. Perhaps he would sit by the fire while she brushed him, she mused as they went up the stairs to the main floor.

But Socrates had ideas of his own, and he abruptly took off at speed through the corridor and across the foyer. Rosamund was forced to run after him, passing a maid polishing a table and giving her a smile that she hoped looked as though she knew what she was doing. Rosamund was, it turned out, not as fast as an energetic lapdog, and before she could catch him, he disappeared through the open door of the drawing room.

As soon as she came into the room, Rosamund realized why Socrates was so excited. Marcus was there, with a remarkably handsome older lady who must be his grandmother, Lady Tremont.

"Excuse me," Rosamund said from the doorway as Socrates ran to his master and dropped adoringly before him into a sitting position. "I'm terribly sorry. He got away from me."

Lady Tremont, whose gray hair was pulled into a smooth, elegant coil and whose tall, still trim figure gave hints as to the origins of her grandson's lean physique, subjected Rosamund to a thorough scrutiny. "Who are you, young lady? And why have you brought a dog into my drawing room?"

Lady Tremont's voice was pleasant, her demeanor graceful, her gown subtly flattering, and nothing about her beyond her hair and a few wrinkles that had dared to form around her eyes and mouth suggested a person who'd lived quite a few decades. Rosamund supposed she must have always been vigilant about wearing a hat.

"Rosamund came with me, to help with Socrates, my dog," Marcus said. "I did tell you I had brought him."

"When you said you'd brought a dog, I thought you meant a hunting dog, but this"—Lady Tremont indicated Socrates with the swirl of a slender digit—"is a lapdog. I never figured you for a fellow who'd want a lapdog."

Rosamund almost laughed at the pained expression that flitted over Marcus's face. "He was a present from Mother, and he has an inordinate attachment to me. And by that I mean he howls incessantly if he feels I've abandoned him. Rosamund has accompanied me here so that she can be a sort of companion to him."

"But this is absurd, Marcus! You are indulging this dog, and he will become spoiled and end up ruling your household."

"I think I will manage to keep him from dominating my household," Marcus said dryly. "But he is still young and in need of training."

Socrates, perhaps sensing that it would behoove him to cultivate the goodwill of his hostess, condescended to sniff Lady Tremont's shoe, causing the older lady's eyebrows to drift slowly upward.

"Already he has made some improvement," Marcus continued, "because he now tolerates Rosamund."

"I see," Lady Tremont said, still looking at Socrates. Finally, she turned sharp blue eyes on Rosamund, which, while there was no reason for the older lady to guess there was anything amiss with her nephew's dog-minder, was still not a comfortable experience. "Interesting."

Rosamund was eager to leave. "If I may, I'll collect Socrates and take him somewhere else."

"Certainly," Marcus said.

"Oh," said Lady Tremont, looking at Socrates, who had curled his little body into a tidy circle on the blue rug with his head resting on his paws, "you may as well let the creature stay. He doesn't look as though he'll cause any trouble. And he is rather adorable."

"Ma'am?" Marcus sounded truly puzzled, and Rosamund couldn't blame him. Lady Tremont looked as though she'd be more comfortable arranging a bunch of flowers into artful perfection, or judging the subtle variations among different-quality silks, than enduring the close company of an animal.

Lady Tremont lifted her chin airily. "He's of a suitable size to be inside the house, and he might as well get used to the drawing room, since if he can't bear to be parted from his master for long, that is where he will often be. Now, where were we, Marcus?"

And with that, Rosamund was released to attend to Socrates, who was nosing around the feet of a divan she dearly hoped he was not planning to nibble.

"As I was saying, what is it about this young lady?" Lady Tremont said to Marcus. "Is it just that she's a mystery to you? In truth, you hardly know her."

"She's different," Marcus said. "Special."

Rosamund could not help but wonder about this conversation, which sounded like he might be speaking of Poppy, though it seemed odd that he should wish to discuss her with his grandmother. She sneaked a look at them as she knelt to direct Socrates's little teeth away from a decorative tassel.

"And I venture to guess you found your mystery lady quite pretty as well?" Lady Tremont said.

"She is utterly memorable."

Rosamund started, knocking a book off a nearby end table,

and Marcus and Lady Tremont stopped talking and looked at her.

"Excuse me," she muttered, replacing the book and hoping her blush wasn't noticeable. But they *were* discussing her!

Her first reaction was excitement that Marcus hadn't forgotten her, that he had found the time they'd spent together as memorable as she had.

This was followed by something more than disappointment. If he'd really found her so special and memorable, why didn't he know her now?

She acknowledged this was an irrational complaint, since only disaster could be in store for her if he discovered that the servant he'd hired to watch his dog was his enchanting lady from the ball. But still.

She was blocking Socrates from chewing the tassel for the sixth time and wondering if she could make a discreet exit by encouraging him to dash out of the room, when she glanced toward Marcus and saw him showing something to his grandmother. Rosamund barely stifled a gasp as she saw her pearls.

He held the necklace out for Lady Tremont's inspection, apparently unaware that across the room from him, a woman was nearly expiring. "Right here on the clasp, you can see the initials."

Rosamund had forgotten about the initials. The pearls had belonged to her mother's mother. But surely it would be extremely difficult for anyone to discern to whom they belonged, never mind connecting them to Rosamund herself. Or, for that matter, for anyone to deduce that the granddaughter of the couple represented by those initials was currently on all fours on a rug a dozen feet away.

"And you say she gave her name as Poppy?" Lady Tremont mused.

"Yes, though that could be short for Persephone, Penelope, or any of a number of other names."

It was short for Penelope, her middle name, and Rosamund's

stomach fluttered crazily.

"It could," Lady Tremont agreed, peering at the clasp as though it might be induced to yield its secrets through sheer intimidation. "Woodward, Wentworth," she mused. "Wilkes."

As the W in the initials referred to Rosamund's mother's maiden name, she felt a moment anxiety that Lady Tremont might stumble on that name and begin to make connections. But then she realized that, for once, her father's unusual surname might be to her advantage, since they were unlikely to consider her mother *because* of Rosamund's father's infamy.

Marcus and Lady Tremont then proceeded to have a long conversation about who Poppy's relatives might be, and Marcus revealed that he had taken tea with no less than eight families of the *ton* trying to find out. Rosamund might have felt thrilled that she'd made such an impression on him—and, of course, she didn't want Poppy to be forgotten—but what she was starting to feel was annoyed.

How easy it was to become smitten with someone at a ball, when you were both at your best. But her "best" hadn't been who she was at all. Her clothes had been borrowed, her persona a sham.

Marcus had been real, of course. He really was a marquess, and he really was handsome and wealthy and a good man. But now, as she listened to him sing the praises of the wondrous Poppy, he was also a little insufferable. She'd spent far longer sitting with him in the coach yesterday, alone, than she'd spent with him at the ball, and he certainly hadn't been swooning over her then. In fact, he'd become downright unpleasant in the coach, and since they'd arrived at Lady Tremont's, he'd behaved as though he hardly noticed her.

Well, except for the moment in his bedchamber, when she'd felt his desire like a live thing across the space of his room, desire that answered her own.

But she was not so naïve that she didn't know that men might desire women with whom they had no other interest. It happened all the time. But she couldn't bear the idea that

Marcus would see her that way.

Of course, she couldn't expect a marquess to become enchanted with a servant, or even to really see such a person. But the fact that he didn't seem to feel anything beyond lust for her now meant that the timeless connection she'd thought they shared the night of the ball wasn't something that would endure once all the sparkle of the night was brushed away. Marcus, still caught up in the dream of his mystery lady, simply hadn't realized this yet.

Preoccupied as she was, she hadn't noticed that Socrates had disappeared under the divan. He emerged now, with what proved to be a dancing slipper in his mouth, and Rosamund shook off her thoughts.

"Dearest, you know that's not yours," she told him, attempting to take it away from him. This, of course, was the game, and after a few feints as she tried to snatch it, Socrates took off across the room toward Marcus, who stood by the hearth.

CHAPTER NINE

Marcus was only peripherally aware of Socrates and his minder—or at least, he'd made certain not to glance toward the other side of the room, where Rosamund was on all fours. Again. He ought to have considered, before hiring such a pretty woman to be his dog's companion, that minding a young, energetic dog would involve her in activities such as crawling around on the floor. Or perhaps another person hired for the job wouldn't have found it necessary to do so. But Rosamund wasn't someone to do things by half, he had observed, and while that was in many ways an admirable quality, at that moment he could not appreciate it.

He realized that he didn't even know her last name, and he'd been dreaming about her, dreams that were far from chaste. But why *should* he know her last name? She wasn't supposed to be someone to whom he gave any thought at all.

Yet, he had still not recovered from the sight of her standing in his bedchamber, returning his avid gaze with what he knew—*he knew*—was desire. It had thrummed between them like an insistent pulse.

He tried telling himself now that the moment had only been a temporary madness, some remnant of erotic dreams on his part, some shock on hers, but he knew this wasn't true. All the more reason to make certain he did not allow his attention to wander to her.

Being intentionally unaware of what was going on across the room, though, meant that he wasn't prepared for Socrates to come speeding toward him like a cannon blast. Marcus reacted to the sudden approach of his dog by stepping backward. His arm hit the mantel, knocking into a small, ornate clock, which tipped over the edge.

He reached for the clock, but he had to step to the side at the last minute to avoid crushing Socrates, who was dancing at Marcus's feet. He was startled when his arm knocked into Rosamund, sending her backward. He hadn't realized that she'd raced across the room and was also reaching for the clock.

Marcus jerked around, the clock in his hand, and there was Rosamund, sprawled on the floor. "Rosamund, Good God! I'm sorry. Are you hurt?"

Socrates rushed over and began to lick her face. Marcus picked the dog up and handed him to his grandmother.

"I don't think so," Rosamund said, but then she put her hand to the floor as she tried to stand, and he saw her wince.

"Yes, you are."

"It's nothing. I only bumped my hand."

But he ignored her and dropped to his haunches. "May I?" he asked, gesturing to her hand.

"If you insist, but it's nothing."

He took hold of her hand, which was small and capable looking. A red mark was spreading in the area around her wrist.

"You must have hit your hand against the table leg. You'll surely have a substantial bruise. The doctor should look at it to make sure that you haven't done any further damage."

"That's really not necessary," she insisted.

"Humor me," he said, ringing for a servant. "I can't undo being the cause of you falling and injuring yourself. At least allow me to arrange proper care."

"You really didn't—"

But a maid appeared at that moment. She was given instructions to send for the doctor and given Socrates to bear away. Fortunately, Dr. Cranwell was already on the estate, seeing to a footman, and it seemed likely he would be along shortly.

"That was quite clumsy of you, Marcus," Lady Tremont pointed out as the maid left the room amid the plaintive whining of the disgruntled Socrates. "You quite knocked Rosamund over."

"I'm well aware of that," he said grimly. "And I am abjectly sorry, Rosamund."

"It was an accident, my lord," she said. "You couldn't have known I was there."

"But I *should* have known you were there."

She laughed. "Why, are marquesses omniscient?"

Lady Tremont sniffed. "They like to think so."

"I just should have known," he said.

"I merely took a tumble, and I'm sure the doctor will agree it's nothing."

But Dr. Cranwell, when he arrived, did not say her injuries were nothing.

Marcus and Lady Tremont left the room while she was examined. The doctor was as courtly and gentle with her as he might have been with a delicate flower, which Rosamund suspected had a great deal to do with him believing she was a guest of the marquess. In her borrowed dress, she didn't look much like a servant, and no one had explained to him who she was.

"I'm afraid your shoulder will be sore for a day or two, miss," he said, "and your hand in particular should not be used. Rest will be the best thing."

"Thank you, but—"

A knock sounded at the door, followed by Marcus's voice asking if he might come in. Dr. Cranwell opened the door and proceeded to alert the marquess that the young lady had indeed sustained injuries from the fall, injuries that, while not serious, required rest. Rosamund opened her mouth to protest being discussed like she was an invalid, but Dr. Cranwell kept talking.

"The young lady ought to rest for at least three days, and she must not use her right hand at all during that time."

This was getting to be ridiculous. Her hand might be a little sore, along with her shoulder, but her hurts were mild and hardly limiting. She didn't want to be ungracious, but she had a purpose here and a real need for the wage she was to earn. "But Socrates—" she began.

"Will be fine," Marcus said.

"Socrates?" repeated a puzzled Dr. Cranwell.

"My dog," said Marcus, as if that explained anything. As though on cue, the sound of a dog howling somewhere in the house could be heard. Rosamund hid a smile at the doctor's look of befuddlement.

Marcus saw Dr. Cranwell out, then turned to her.

"Well, then, Rosamund, where would you like to rest? In here? The library perhaps? Or if you prefer, I can assist you to your chamber."

"You've been very kind, my lord. But as I've told you, I really don't feel much injured at all. Dr. Cranwell was being unnecessarily cautious, as I'm sure you know."

"I know nothing of the sort. You had a fall, and you need time to heal."

"My lord," she said, trying to keep the impatience out of her voice, since he was being thoughtful, even if he was also being ridiculous, "I'm only a little bruised, and I certainly don't need to sit around resting." She stood up. "See? I am perfectly fine."

"Rosamund," Marcus said sternly, "you are to follow Dr. Cranwell's orders. Please sit."

She didn't need to sit, but his commanding tone did not invite argument. She sat—for the moment. "But they are entirely unnecessary! I am not hurt."

"Your hand is bruised."

"I have done far worse to myself walking clumsily through a doorway, and I have certainly never required rest for such a thing."

"Nonetheless, I insist that you follow Dr. Cranwell's instructions."

"My lord"—she was beginning to feel exasperated—"I am here to be a companion to Socrates, and I intend to do so."

"Rosamund, please. Even if putting your feet up for a few days won't make you feel better, your doing so will make *me* feel better."

"Oh," she said, startled by the kindness in his tone. "Well, that is extremely—really, excessively—considerate."

"Think nothing of it. Socrates can wait a few days for you to recover."

She laughed. "How can you say that when, at this very moment, he is howling like a banshee?"

One corner of Marcus's mouth curved up, and her stomach fluttered at the boyish amusement in his eyes. "He is making an unholy racket, isn't he? One almost has to admire it, considering he's such a small fellow."

"Yes, but he's also a dear little fellow."

"Not so dear when he's getting underfoot."

"I'm sure it's hard *not* to be underfoot when one is a small dog."

"Are you always so unfailingly patient?"

As they talked, Marcus was having the worst time not looking at Rosamund's mouth, which was the color of a ripe berry. He forced his eyes to move to a neutral place on her face, but her chin was charmingly pert and her forehead interesting in a way that he would not have expected of a forehead.

He was vastly relieved that she was not much hurt, but wasn't it just as well for him if she was consigned to a room where he was not? Because, far from putting her out of his mind, he kept getting ideas about her, ideas he should not be getting when he wanted more than anything to see Poppy again. Already, his grandmother had suggested several families with members who might fit the initials on the necklace clasp, and Marcus had begun mentally drafting letters delicately inquiring whether these families had any members named Poppy. He would mention having found something engraved belonging to her that he wished to return.

There was the possibility of success, and nothing could have pleased him more.

But even simply standing near Rosamund was making him itch to close the gap between them and touch her.

He cleared his throat. "Well, I shall make certain you're settled for the afternoon, then I'll go see to Socrates, lest my grandmother's servants all give notice en masse."

Her brows drew together in vexation, which only made her more adorable. "I really don't wish to collect money I have not earned."

"None of us can have everything we want," he said, cheerfully cutting her off. "Now, resting place?" He grinned. "Not the final one, of course."

Her lips quirked a little at his joke. "If you insist—"

"I absolutely do."

"Then I should be quite happy to spend some time in the library." She actually *looked* happy at the thought of spending time in the library.

"Do you like to read?"

"Reading," she said with a giddy sigh, "is just about the best thing there is."

Marcus liked to read also, but on the issue of it being just about the best thing there was, he felt that Rosamund was sorely misguided. Being an innocent, she was surely unaware of other choices that could easily best books.

What if you showed her about those choices? It wasn't as if he was engaged to Poppy, or courting her. For all he knew, she had forgotten him. As a single young woman, Poppy could not simply write to him or visit. But there were a hundred little ways she could have arranged to contact him—by showing up at events where he would be, contacting his sister Kate, asking someone to introduce them. She might even have sent an anonymous note. Marcus knew *he* would have been creative if he'd been in her shoes.

And, what argued in particular for her contacting him again, *he had her pearls.* She had to know where she lost them, since she would have felt the tug when he accidentally grabbed them as she was dashing off wherever it was that it had been so urgent for her to go.

For the first time, he felt the tiniest bit annoyed with Poppy. Why did she have to be so mysterious? Why couldn't she make some effort to contact him, even if it was only a note to his mother to ask about the return of her pearls? He felt certain that she'd been as enchanted as he had been that night.

He had not, until now, considered the possibility that he might never find her, but now he did. Only for a moment, because he did have hope. He was going to write those letters that afternoon, and there was every chance something might come of them.

Socrates gave a particularly pathetic howl as Marcus helped Rosamund to stand. She thought of protesting that obviously she didn't need assistance standing, since she'd done it unassisted a minute ago, but clearly Marcus would not be gainsaid, so she accepted his hand up.

The minute their hands touched, a warmth that had nothing to do with the temperature of his skin stole up her arm, and she had the sense, from his quick intake of breath, that he'd felt something too.

He gently tugged her upright and placed her hand on his arm, then led her out of the room and along the corridor. Socrates was still howling piteously, but all she could think about, shamefully, was the springy feel of Marcus's muscles under her hand. His shoulders had felt like that too, on the night of the ball, resilient with firm muscle and leashed strength, and she wanted more than anything to touch them again. As they walked through the corridor, she felt his eyes on the side of her face several times, and a blush warmed her cheeks, but she kept her eyes facing forward.

"I was hoping he would tire himself out and fall asleep," Marcus said after one particularly plaintive wail, "but his volume doesn't seem to have diminished at all."

She was grateful for an innocuous topic of conversation, anything to keep her from thinking about Marcus's arm and how it had been bare that morning when she'd seen him in bed. "He is a dog who feels things keenly."

"He is currently the bane of my existence."

She glanced at him. "Oh, come now, you know you adore him."

"I'm certain I've never said such a thing."

"But that doesn't mean you don't feel it," she teased, even as she told herself it was foolish to be playful with him. What could possibly be the point of such banter when what she needed was for him to treat her like any other person in his employ? But she couldn't resist the pleasure of talking with him. "I imagine, if nothing else, his presence makes you think of your mother."

He sighed. "She is a remarkable woman, but I still don't understand why she thought I needed a lapdog. However, I have in general learned it is best not to inquire too deeply into the motives of the women in my family, because they're frequently diabolical, even if they are well-intentioned."

"Diabolical seems a little strong."

"You haven't met my sister Alice. She's never encountered a piece of what she likes to call social news that she doesn't believe it's her mission to verify. She's sixteen, but she knows as much about the affairs of the *ton* as the oldest dowager."

"She sounds fun."

"She is a terror, but she's our terror."

Rosamund could easily imagine him as a wonderful older

brother. In truth, despite the alternately friendly and chilly ways he'd treated her since hiring her and the fact that he was annoyingly besotted with a memory of her, she liked pretty much everything about Marcus. Which really was terrible.

CHAPTER TEN

They reached the library, and Marcus led Rosamund to a divan by the hearth, where a modest fire was chasing away the last of the morning chill.

"Now then," he said, rubbing his hands together, "what would you like? How about some cakes?"

"It's eleven o'clock in the morning," she pointed out.

"Right." His eyes roamed around the room. "Is there anything you wish from your chamber that might be brought to you? Some embroidery?" He frowned. "Or not embroidery, since that would require the use of your hands."

"I'm not much for embroidery anyway."

"Right," he said vaguely, at a loss, and he thought he saw the edges of her mouth quiver with amusement at his discomfort. But hell, what did one suggest to entertain a woman who was not exactly a servant, but not a woman of his class either? He had no idea, but he wanted to be certain she was comfortable.

He also wanted to sit down next to her and take her in his

lap, but that was out of the question.

"Perhaps Socrates would like to sit with me?" she suggested.

He gave her a look. "Don't let him manipulate you with his howling. That dog lives like a prince."

"But I really would enjoy his company."

"Perhaps later," he said, knowing that if he brought Socrates into the library, Rosamund would ignore her sore hand and play with him, because that was the kind of person she was.

"Then if I might I avail myself of the books?"

"The books?" he said distractedly. He was having trouble not focusing on her lips again.

She gestured to the tall bookcases that filled the room. "There are a few books in here."

"Well, of course! If you tell me what you'd like, I'll get it for you."

She smiled, and he nearly groaned. She was so pretty—no, she was lovely, that was the word for her. Her eyes had such warmth in them. *She* was warm.

From the hallway came a familiar sound, the excited yapping of his dog. It quickly grew closer, and Socrates must have reached the door, because the yapping turned into a plaintive yowl.

Marcus sighed. "He must have escaped from whichever servant was tasked with seeing to him. That's not very restful, having him outside one's door, is it?" he said.

"Not very," she said, her eyes twinkling. "He must miss you."

"Or you," he said. "I begin to wonder which of us he prefers."

With a few suggestions from Rosamund, Marcus selected some books and piled them close to her. Then, to save his grandmother's servants from losing their minds—and really, to save himself from turning into a pile of smoldering embers—Marcus left Rosamund to see to his dog. He and Socrates repaired to his chamber, where he began drafting the letters to the families his grandmother had suggested might be related to

Poppy. Socrates slept on his feet.

A man with a young dog for a companion couldn't spend the whole day in the house, though, and the afternoon found him taking Socrates to romp in the garden.

* * *

After several hours lying on a divan with a pile of books, Rosamund was beginning to think that falling had been the best thing to happen to her in ages. Oh, her hand hurt a little, though certainly not so much that she needed to sit around. But since Marcus felt so terrible that he couldn't bear the idea of her moving about with a bruise, she was apparently to be a lady of leisure. Lying about with nothing to do was, not surprisingly, utter heaven.

She couldn't remember the last time she'd sat around reading during the middle of the day. Reading at Melinda's house had been done in stolen moments very early in the morning, or late in the evening if she had not used up her monthly allotment of one candle.

At lunchtime, a maid brought a tray overflowing with delicious treats, which Rosamund nibbled while reading a novel. She felt lavishly indulged, and she refused to think about how mundane such an afternoon would have been for any other lady of Marcus's acquaintance.

Around teatime, Lady Tremont arrived in the library, apparently to visit with her, which Rosamund found unexpected, considering she was a lowly companion for a dog.

"This is an absurd sort of job that Marcus has hired you for, isn't it?" Lady Tremont asked once she'd settled into the armchair opposite Rosamund. She still looked as fresh and impeccable as she had early that morning and not the least fatigued, despite the fact that she must surely have been near seventy. She might have been older, or she might have been younger. What she seemed was ageless, in an effortless way, though Rosamund, accustomed to making just the right adjustments to gowns so they would flatter, knew that *ageless* was another word for *well-maintained*.

"I thought so too, when the marquess proposed it," Rosamund replied. While she couldn't afford to give Lady Tremont any details that might cause her to guess anything about Rosamund herself, there didn't seem to be any harm in discussing how she'd come to be in Marcus's employ. "I'm not sure if he explained how it transpired?"

"You saved Socrates from certain death, apparently, and the creature took to you immediately."

"Something like that," Rosamund said.

"You look familiar," Lady Tremont said without further preamble.

Caught off guard, all Rosamund could say was, "I do?" She racked her brain for reasons why Lady Tremont might think this. Might she know Melinda or one of Rosamund's cousins? Rosamund didn't think she looked much like any of her relatives, but most people weren't very good at seeing their own family resemblances.

"Something about the color of your hair."

"My hair?" Rosamund knew she sounded like an idiot, but Lady Tremont had been at the ball, and she had seen Poppy. Rosamund wanted to squirm, but she kept herself still.

"My grandson said you were previously employed as a seamstress. Is it possible we met at a dressmaker's?"

Rosamund nearly collapsed with relief. "Yes, that's probably what happened."

"Hmm," Lady Tremont said speculatively. She had left the door ajar when she entered, and now they heard the marquess's voice in the corridor.

"Socrates, you are forbidden." The sound of tiny claws clicking on polished marble could be heard.

"Extremely forbidden," Marcus continued, his voice growing louder as though he was coming nearer.

Apparently, Socrates had not yet learned the meaning of *forbidden*, because as Rosamund and Lady Tremont watched, he nosed the door open farther and trotted in. He gave a happy yip when he saw Rosamund and made for where she was sitting.

"Socrates," Marcus said in tones of deep exasperation, entering the room briskly, "you are the most infuriating dog."

With three strides, he had reached Socrates, whom he plucked from the carpet just as he was almost to Rosamund's feet.

"All my other dogs understand what's what," Marcus said with a frown, "but I begin to despair of him."

"I'm sure your other dogs have spent some amount of time being trained," Lady Tremont said. "Surely it is a bit soon for Socrates to have learned all the necessary commands."

"He knows how to sit," Rosamund pointed out. "And he's learning to stay. We were practicing earlier."

"There, Marcus, do you hear that?" Lady Tremont said, standing. "A veritable little gentleman in the making. Now, if you'll excuse me, I need to speak to Mrs. Clark."

As soon as his grandmother was gone, Marcus asked Rosamund how she was feeling.

"Completely fine," she said.

"That's because you've been resting." His eyes lingered on her, and she had the sense he wanted to say something more. But all he said, after a moment, was, "I suppose I ought to take Socrates off somewhere that he can't get into trouble."

"Oh, let him stay here," Rosamund said.

"He might jump on you."

"I think I can manage not to be overpowered by him," she said. "Besides, I've had quite a few quiet hours today."

Marcus gave a long-suffering sigh. "If you insist, I suppose he might have a supervised visit with you." He put Socrates on the floor and admonished him to behave. "That means no jumping on Rosamund."

Socrates immediately trotted over to sniff her foot, and she leaned down to pet him.

"Is that a good idea with your injuries?" Marcus asked.

She gave him a speaking glance and petted some more. Socrates licked her hand in apparent gratitude, then trotted over to Marcus. He sat down at the tips of his master's shining black boots and gazed up at him adoringly.

Marcus returned his gaze impassively.

"He wants you to play with him," Rosamund pointed out.

"I had gathered that," he said dryly, though he made no move to do so.

"How can you resist him? Look at those big brown eyes. Look at the devotion and the hope."

Marcus gave her a ridiculously haughty look, which made the edges of her mouth quiver. "He's a pampered and indulged lapdog with his very own personal companion, not a destitute orphan."

"Is it that you don't know how to play with him?" she asked sweetly, tempted by she knew not what devil to tease him. "I could show you some of his favorite games."

"You're supposed to be reading."

"I finished my book. Why don't I show you the way he likes to play with a ball?"

He arched a single, lordly brow at her. "Sit, Rosamund. Stay."

She gave him *her* best haughty look back, though it did not have the effect, apparently, of making him quake in his boots.

"I believe I am meant to be regretting the error of my ways, or rather, my speech," Marcus told Socrates, "but I am unable to do so."

"That's because he's a marquess and used to doing only as he likes," she observed to his dog, though she knew it wasn't true. Marcus hadn't wanted a lapdog, for instance, but despite his feigned disregard for Socrates, she knew he cherished the dog for the sake of his mother. She was fairly certain that as the honorable brother, son, and man he was, he did a great deal of things he didn't care to do. But she couldn't resist the urge to tweak him.

Though she really, really didn't want to admit it, no matter how much she'd told herself that she must simply deny her attraction to this man, she couldn't. He'd slipped under her skin.

He grunted in reply and disappeared behind one of the shelves, Socrates trotting after him.

After a few moments, she called out, "What are you doing?" She felt silly just sitting there, and so she stood up. Goodness, it felt wonderful to stretch her legs.

With an eye toward the bookshelf shielding her from Marcus's view, she leaned over and touched her toes, then dropped to a crouch and held it before standing up again, movements she'd accustomed herself to performing to loosen muscles that were cramping after too many hours sitting and sewing. Her shoulder felt almost entirely better, which was not surprising, since it hadn't been much injured to begin with.

"I'm looking for another book for you to read," he called out.

"Very kind of you." She tiptoed to a row of books on a different shelf than the one Marcus had gone behind. Occupied with a series of titles about the flora and fauna of the Lake District, she didn't notice when Marcus stepped out from behind the bookcase a few minutes later.

"What are you doing, Rosamund?" he growled.

Her heart fluttered in giddy response. "Looking at books."

"You're supposed to be sitting." He stalked toward her, his brow lowering a bit more with each step, Socrates at his heels spoiling the effect somewhat. Still, he did look menacing— something about the hardening of his jaw—and his eyes had gone squinty in a way that was clearly meant to intimidate lesser mortals. In that moment, Rosamund did not feel like a lesser mortal.

"While I certainly enjoyed reading for hours," she informed him, "and I am grateful for the luxury of such leisure time, the only result of that little fall I took earlier was a bruise."

"Dr. Cranwell prescribed rest," he rasped, sending a shiver down her spine.

"And I have thoroughly benefited from it. But I am starting to feel like a captive."

Marcus stopped right in front of her, emanating the outrage of a thwarted marquess and also looking very, very handsome.

"Help me, Socrates. Your master looks scary."

But Socrates for once was not interested in either of them. Instead, he wandered off to nose around a particular patch of carpet a few feet away. Marcus dropped his chin, giving Rosamund the full benefit of blue eyes glinting with something much different than exasperation. He moved closer, backing her up against the bookcase behind her.

"Rosamund, what are you doing to me?"

"I… don't know," she said, feeling her legs turning to jelly. "I'm not trying to do anything."

"I know," he said, a note of what almost sounded like anguish coloring his voice. His dark blue eyes held hers. "I know. But just you being you is enough."

"Oh," she breathed.

His eyes dropped to her mouth, and she knew that he wanted to kiss her. The knowledge spread a ripple of warmth through her. He had kissed her when she was Poppy, a seemingly suitable woman, and now he wanted to kiss her as Rosamund, the dog's companion. Knowing he was still searching for Poppy, she didn't know how she felt about this shift in his affections. On the one hand, she was real and here now, and she was already a little in love with him, so of course she wanted him to notice her and want to kiss her.

But she didn't know what it meant that he did.

Mostly, though, she wanted him to kiss her again, and she held his gaze as the air between them simmered and his head dipped lower. His lips touched hers, gently at first, a kiss that expressed attraction and sought permission, his lips on hers both familiar and achingly different. *She* was different. She knew him more now.

She responded, and he put his hands on her shoulders and deepened the kiss, nuzzling her lips, seeking entry, and she opened to him. His tongue stroked hers, and a little moan escaped her at how good it felt. In response, he gathered her in his arms, crushing her to him as he plundered her mouth.

Every thought left Rosamund's head, save the knowledge that being in his arms was the most wonderful thing she'd ever felt and she never wanted it to end.

But it did end, far too soon. With a groan, he tore himself away and stepped back.

"I'm sorry," he said thickly.

"I'm not," she said, allowing herself a completely honest response.

His eyebrows slammed together. "Rosamund," he began, but at that moment, Socrates gave a little woof, and the door to the library opened.

CHAPTER ELEVEN

"Oh, you're still here, Marcus," Lady Tremont said, unaware that in at least one breast in the room, a heart was racing. Or perhaps she was not unaware, Rosamund thought, as the older woman's eyes lingered on the two of them for several seconds.

"Rosamund and I were looking for a book," Marcus said, apparently feeling a need to explain why they were standing so close to each other.

"Ah. I gather you are feeling better, then, Rosamund, as you are standing," Lady Tremont said.

"Yes, ma'am, I feel quite recovered," she managed to say, despite the way her head was swirling. Marcus had kissed her! Every second of it had been glorious, and all she could think was that she hoped he wasn't really sorry he had kissed her. She forced herself to focus on Lady Tremont. "I was just telling his lordship that I won't need to rest any longer."

"That is certainly good news," Lady Tremont said.

"Were you looking for me?" Marcus asked.

"Yes. I wanted to ask if you'd sent those letters about your, er, acquaintance yet. I thought of one more likely family that matches the initials."

Rosamund's breath caught. Marcus was sending letters to people he thought might be related to Poppy, she guessed. These would have to be families whose surname started with W, and since the only family Rosamund had left were the Monroes, the risk of his letters eliciting any information was perhaps not high. But not impossible. Those initials belonged to her mother and grandmother, and someone *might* recognize that.

But beyond the fear of being found out, Rosamund wanted to know how he felt about Poppy now, after their kiss.

"Not yet. I mean to do it today."

"Sarah Westover's middle name is Diana, and she has a daughter who should be about the right age. I'd forgotten about the Westovers because they were out of the country for quite some time, but I heard they've recently returned."

"That sounds promising," Marcus said. Rosamund, urgently wanting to know just how promising Marcus actually thought this news was, could not determine how he felt about this additional possibility of finding Poppy. She thought he seemed distracted, and some part of her hoped that he *was* distracted, very distracted, after their kiss.

But this was the height of foolishness, she told herself sternly as she glanced around for Socrates, who seemed all of a sudden to be more capable of looking after himself, or at least of not causing a commotion. Marcus had kissed her, and it had been wonderful, but she reminded herself that even if he wasn't looking for a mystery woman who'd enraptured him, Rosamund, with the scandal clinging to her and Melinda's threats of Bow Street runners, could never be anything to him.

And she didn't need to stand around and listen while he made plans to find the woman he *really* cared about.

Having spied Socrates partially, and shamelessly, hidden behind a throw pillow on a divan, she said, "If you'll excuse me, I think Socrates is in need of his afternoon walk."

Lady Tremont looked past Rosamund's shoulder. "He looks quite comfortable to me."

If she hadn't been so intent on leaving the room so that she didn't have to listen to Marcus yearning for a woman who didn't exist, Rosamund might have savored some amusement at the fact that Lady Tremont seemed to have been won over to the idea of dogs in the house, or at least one particular, spoiled but dear dog.

"It won't last," Rosamund said, going to the sofa and picking up Socrates, who thought this was a lovely idea and promptly put his little head on her shoulder. She gave an inward sigh. Even Marcus's dog had won her heart.

As she passed by Marcus on the way out of the room, his eyes lingered on her significantly with some meaning she couldn't read. Though why he should be looking at her meaningfully— let alone kissing her—when he was so besotted with Poppy, she didn't know. Trying to sort out any of her thoughts about Marcus only made her feel utterly confused, and she resolved then and there not to think about him anymore.

She also resolved not to think about whether she even *could* stop thinking about him.

* * *

Marcus finished the letters to the families who might be Poppy's family the following morning. The notes urged the families to write him back if there was any information to be offered, and it was entirely possible that within a week, he would have an answer about Poppy.

As he sealed the last letter in the stack, he wasn't certain how he now felt about finding his mystery lady. Ever since meeting Poppy, he'd been so convinced that she was the woman he'd been waiting his whole life to meet. He'd dreamed of her night after night, and he'd imagined countless times what it would be like if he ever saw her again.

But now he was attracted to Rosamund. More than attracted. In the library, overcome by the spell of her presence, he'd told himself that if he once kissed her, he would know she wasn't for him the way that Poppy was, and he would be able to forget about her.

That wasn't what happened. The minute his lips touched hers, he'd only wanted more of her, and he'd had to force himself to stop.

What the hell kind of man was he?

He'd always believed that when he loved a woman, he would love only her. His mother's hope for him and each of her children, that they marry for love, had been his own hope and desire as well. It was why he'd waited so long, waited for the woman who would be his perfect match. And he'd thought that he'd finally found her, and that her name was Poppy.

But now he couldn't stop thinking about Rosamund and how special she was. Because she *was* special, and if she'd been a young lady of a good family, his choices would have been different. What was he supposed to do with her? He couldn't *marry* her, even if he did want to abandon his hopes of Poppy. Her family had apparently been rough and poor, and she'd been a seamstress before she'd been a dog's companion. Her education and gracious manner might allow her a certain acceptance into polite company, but the only position a woman like Rosamund could have in relation to a marquess was as a mistress.

Was he considering asking her to be his mistress? *Was he?* After all, he hadn't found Poppy, and he might never.

And Rosamund was special.

He pointed out to himself that being his mistress would offer Rosamund many advantages, not the least of them his protection. She was seemingly without any family or friends to help her. She had no position now, having left her seamstress job, and from what he could tell, no plans for the time after which her help would not be needed with Socrates.

The idea of Rosamund simply disappearing back onto the streets of London was abhorrent. She was too good and too lovely and—he thought of how readily she'd agreed to accompany a man she didn't know on a carriage trip—far too trusting. Really, he didn't know how she had survived as long as she had, considering the way she conducted her life.

He could change all that for her. He wanted to protect her. He liked her a great deal, and he wanted her so much he could hardly think of anything but her.

All he needed to do was convince her of the wisdom of his plan. She was an innocent, of that he was certain, but considering she apparently wasn't sorry that he'd kissed her and that she surely had a grimly narrow future awaiting her, surely she wouldn't need too much convincing.

He found her in the garden, sitting under a tree and brushing Socrates.

"Good afternoon, my lord," she said when she saw him. He didn't miss the glimmer in her eyes at the sight of him, and he thought, *Good.*

He stood over her, aware that Rosamund was not a woman to do the predictable thing. He crossed his arms, drawing his mien of authority over him, and got right to the point. "Rosamund, as you are aware, I engaged you to be Socrates's companion for a period of about a month."

Wariness crept into her eyes. "Yes, I understood that."

"Have you thought about what you might do when your time with Socrates is done? What your plans are for the future?"

"My plans for the future?" Her brow wrinkled. "Do you mean that you wish to end my employment?"

"No, I mean that as your employer and thus the person concerned with your welfare, I wish to know what plans you have for when Socrates no longer needs a companion."

She pressed her lips together and returned her attention to the long fur on Socrates's ears. "My plans are not your concern."

"Of course they are," he insisted. "I'm the only man responsible for your safety, as far as I can tell."

"I don't need a man or anyone else to be responsible for my safety."

"Yes, you do," he said impatiently. Since she wouldn't look up at him, he dropped to a crouch right in front of her. That, she could not ignore, and her head came up. "You're being obtuse, Rosamund. Do you want to go back to being a seamstress, so that you can work from dawn to dusk and earn barely enough to keep yourself alive?"

"You don't need to worry about me. I will be fine."

"But I will worry. Do you think I want to think of you alone and vulnerable out in the world?"

She made a dismissive sound. "Disaster is hardly waiting behind every corner."

He reached for patience, realizing with a hitch of anxiety that Rosamund was too spirited to be simply bullied into doing what he wanted. "It is when you don't have money. Which you don't, or you wouldn't have been working as a seamstress and looking so hungry."

"Looking hungry?" She had the nerve to roll her eyes, and he wanted to grab her and shake her—and kiss her—until she understood what good sense he was making. "Now you are being presumptuous. My lord—"

"Marcus."

"Excuse me?"

"My name is Marcus, Marcus Hallaway."

"Fifth Marquess of Boxhaven," she supplied.

"But Marcus to you."

Color flared in her cheeks. "I'm a dog's companion! A dog's companion doesn't call a marquess by his Christian name."

"Since a dog's companion is untested ground," he said, "I think we can establish our own rules. Call me Marcus."

"Fine, *Marcus.*"

He drew in a breath, tamping down his frustration. He had to make her see that what he was offering was her best possible choice. Life presented so few options to a woman like her, but she did have choices, and he meant for her to have the best. "Think about it, Rosamund. I could set you up in a lovely little cottage somewhere. You wouldn't even have to go back to

London if you didn't want to."

"And then you would come and visit me, I suppose?"

"Yes, as often as I could. Rosamund, I quite like you."

Rosamund, her heart sinking into her well-worn half boots, looked at Marcus crouched before her and forced herself to see not merely the man who had kissed her so passionately and just admitted he quite liked her. Because she loved that man. There was no use in avoiding the truth. Marcus was kind and good and smart and achingly handsome and desirable, and she loved him.

But he was also a wealthy aristocrat, the pinnacle of everything their society valued, and thus not for her. How could he ask her to surrender herself to him, to give up all hope of respectability? And, most painful of all, to become to him an amusement for which he made time?

"And when you marry?" she made herself ask.

He had the grace to look uncomfortable. "I don't know. I am not in a rush to get married."

"But there is someone special, isn't there? Wasn't there a mystery lady you and your grandmother were discussing?" She ought not to hope that he would abandon Poppy, since *she* was Poppy, and she treasured that he had been so smitten, even as she felt impatient that the thin veil of illusion was of so much more value than a flesh and blood woman.

He frowned. "There was someone who I thought was special, but I don't know—" He cut himself off abruptly, as if he could not say anything further on the topic. "Rosamund, you and I might have a great deal of time together. I would make sure you were always well taken care of." He cleared his throat. "And I would of course see to any children who resulted."

She felt sick at the thought of children. Not of having children—nothing would have made her happier than to share children with a man she loved who loved her too. But that was the problem: She loved a man, but he didn't love her.

Marcus liked her a great deal, she knew that. And he

wanted her, quite a lot, considering the offer he was making. But his sights were rightly set on marrying a woman from the realm of lords and ladies. This was how life functioned, and one young woman from a scandal-plagued family who was facing an accusation of theft wouldn't change that.

She stood up, needing to put distance between them, but he followed suit. "I can't."

"You can."

"Very well, I won't."

Anger flickered in his eyes, though he kept his tone reasonable. "It's the only good choice before you, Rosamund."

Realistically, it probably was. Her wages for the time with Socrates would take her far, but they wouldn't provide security. Marcus was offering her security, because she knew that once he assumed responsibility for her, he would never shirk it, no matter if he married or simply lost interest in her. He was that good of a man. A man who was entirely worthy of her love, but who could never be hers.

"I have to go inside."

"We're not done talking," he said tightly.

"There's nothing more to say. Socrates, come," and he did, saving her from having to say anything more, and she left Marcus standing under the tree.

CHAPTER TWELVE

Rosamund followed Socrates into the manor, resolutely not looking back at Marcus. Socrates, meanwhile, predictably took off at a trot. It was as though everything in his life was so exciting that he needed to run everywhere, Rosamund thought as she hurried into the library after him. She didn't think he'd chew any of the books—so far, he'd shown an interest only in putting shoes in his mouth—but she couldn't be certain.

Worrying about the safety of Marcus's books after the conversation they'd just had felt strange, but she needed to remember that Socrates was the reason she was there, not Marcus. However much she might be tempted by him, Marcus represented nothing but danger to her heart. What she needed was to focus on her work, finish her time with Socrates, collect her wages, and make a new life for herself.

She'd survived scandal, the loss of her parents, and seven years spent sewing in an attic, and she'd survive a little heartbreak as well.

Much, much more than a little, an insistent voice whispered, but she ignored it.

She was surprised by the scene that greeted her when she entered the library. Lady Tremont was sitting on a divan, and curled up next to her, his head on her lap, was Socrates. She was petting him.

"Ah, Rosamund," Lady Tremont said as she entered the room. "I suppose you are looking for Socrates."

"He seems to be more comfortable running through the house than I am."

Lady Tremont chuckled. "He is a scamp, isn't he?"

"If you'll forgive me for making a personal observation, ma'am, you seem to have taken to him."

But Lady Tremont didn't look offended. She just nodded slowly and continued to pet Socrates. She looked surprisingly... relaxed.

"At my age," Lady Tremont said, "I've learned that if something makes you happy, then you must seize the day and allow it to make you happy."

She paused after these surprising words. "Of course, I'm not speaking of the kind of false happiness people sometimes ascribe to such things as gambling or shopping or drink, but something—or someone—that makes your heart feel bigger." She smiled at Socrates and gently stroked his floppy ears, which Rosamund happened to know felt like silk. "In those cases, one ought to take note."

Rosamund felt her so recently buttressed defenses crumbling as she watched Lady Tremont pet Socrates. *Someone who makes your heart feel bigger*, that little voice she'd been ignoring repeated triumphantly. And there was the full truth: She needed to be practical, but she also needed Marcus. Of course she could live without him, she could *survive*. But life wasn't only about survival.

Marcus made her heart feel bigger. When she was with him, she felt as though everything in her life was ever-expanding.

Love made you stronger, love made you grow. Love opened

you up to receive what life had to offer you. Wasn't that what her parents had taught her? Without the foundation of their love, the deep knowledge that she was loved and accepted, and that love never died, how could she have borne the narrowing of her circumstances after her parents were gone, the days and years of hardships that living in Melinda's house had meant?

Love changed everything.

She loved Marcus. And she felt changed.

* * *

Rosamund was avoiding him. Ever since the day before, when Marcus had asked her to be his mistress, she'd made herself scarce. He wasn't exactly surprised—the openness and sense of wonder she seemed to have for the world spoke of someone to whom many of life's experiences were an untried realm. He wanted to be the one to show her those experiences.

She'd rejected his offer, but he couldn't stand the idea of her alone in the world, trying to make her way. Where would she live on the kind of money she could earn, some kind of flea-ridden rooming house? And how would she have enough to eat?

Of course, he could simply give her a substantial sum of money to ensure her security. But money could do nothing to ensure that Rosamund had *people* in her life, good people who cared about her. Rosamund was made to laugh and share affection, and how was she supposed to do that if she was alone? Even if nothing bad happened to her—a big if—the most likely path facing her, since she'd refused his offer, was that of a lonely spinster. And that would be a tragedy.

He was aware of his own ulterior motives, of how much he wanted her. But that didn't cancel out the fact that she needed someone to care for and protect her. And Marcus meant to be that person.

It was midafternoon, and he knew, because he had passed by the open door of the drawing room a quarter of an hour before, that Rosamund was sitting on the rug by a window, petting Socrates while she read a book. He rang for a servant and ordered a tea tray to be delivered there, meaning to join her. Perhaps he could appeal to her reason…

When he arrived in the drawing room, though, Rosamund was looking intently out the window.

"Rosamund?"

"Marcus!" She spun around. "Oh, Marcus, Socrates is gone!" Her words came out in a rush, but he quickly gathered what had happened as she explained about being distracted when a maid arrived with a tea tray.

"And when I turned around, he was gone. I've looked everywhere in here, but he's nowhere to be found. And now I've realized," she said, distress tightening her voice, "that he must have hopped onto that footstool, which gave him access to the chair and the window. I'm so sorry! If only I hadn't looked away."

"Rosamund, he's an imp, and no one could watch him every minute."

He could see she was distracted by her worry and not really hearing him. "I'm going out to the garden to look for him."

"We'll go together," Marcus said firmly. "He's got short legs, and he shouldn't be that hard to find."

But Socrates was not in the garden, nor anywhere close to the house.

"You don't think an animal might have found him," Rosamund said bleakly as they stood at the back of the garden, where a small meadow gave way to a wood.

"Unlikely." Though not impossible, but he wasn't going to admit that to her. "I have an idea where he may have gone. I took him for a walk the other day, so perhaps he followed that path again."

He led them along the somewhat overgrown path that passed through the wood. They looked to the left and right as they went, calling out encouragingly.

"He's so small," Rosamund fretted.

"He'll be fine."

"But what if he's been snatched by a hawk, or fallen in a

lake?" she said morosely. "The possibilities are endless."

"Endless, really?"

"You know what I mean, and don't be unfeeling!"

Marcus hid a smile. Rosamund was completely endearing when she was outraged. "I suspect that Socrates is perfectly fine. I haven't seen any hawks around here lately, and most dogs can swim."

And, in fact, when they found him, Socrates did not look as though he'd had any dire adventures. As they stepped out of the wood and into a clearing, there he was, curled up in the shade of a rosebush that stood in front of the miniature house Marcus's grandmother had had built for her grandchildren when they were young. Socrates did actually look adorable sleeping in front of the small house, though Marcus would have preferred to have been drawn and quartered than admit it.

* * *

"Well," Rosamund said quietly, so as not to wake Socrates, "this is unexpected. He seems to have found a Socrates-sized house. Thank heaven he's safe."

"And apparently very sleepy. You'd think he'd have heard us calling him, but I suppose he must be exhausted after coming all this way on such short legs."

"What is this place?"

"A playhouse, built for us grandchildren when we were young. It has a working fireplace, where my brother Jack and I loved to burn things—sometimes even wood. We pretended it was our hunting lodge. My sisters always wanted it to be what they called a Ladies Holiday House, which apparently meant a place to arrange elaborate social events for their dolls."

"I'd love to look inside," she said, moving closer. "Though I suppose it must be disgustingly dusty after all these years."

"Actually, it might not be," he said, following her. "My cousins were visiting with their children last month, and I imagine it would have been cleaned for their use."

Socrates stirred as they approached. He yawned, stood, and

stretched, waiting while Rosamund opened the door.

"Goodness," she said, entering. "I love this place." The main room was small but cozy, with a table by the fire and four chairs, all just the right size for a couple of children to sit down to a meal. In the corner, under a window with real glass panes, stood a bed made of what looked like branches, giving it an appealingly rustic look. A colorful quilt beckoned with the promise of the perfect place to curl up with a book.

"It has its charms," Marcus said, standing behind her.

Socrates followed them inside and promptly curled up in front of the empty hearth.

"Oh, Socrates," she said, "we can't stay."

"Why not?" Marcus said behind her, and a deep note in his voice made her turn. "You just said you loved this place. Why rush off?"

He grinned boyishly, and Rosamund's heart turned over. "I…" She didn't really know what to say. The truth was, she did want to stay there with him. She wanted it more than she'd ever wanted anything.

He took a step closer, close enough that every part of her was aware of his body so near to hers. "Stay," he said. One little word. An invitation, not a command.

"I wish I could."

"Don't just wish, do."

How she wanted to. Beyond wanted.

When she didn't say anything, he kissed her.

They had kissed before, but the experience had lost none of its newness and enchantment. In the tender brush of his lips and the way his tongue explored her mouth, she felt his desire to please her and bring her pleasure. How—*why?*—would she say no to this? She loved this man. There was no one else like him, and she knew with certainty that there never would be.

She wrapped her arms around his neck and pulled him closer, whispering his name as her cheek brushed his earlobe. She couldn't think of any future beyond the next moment. She wouldn't.

With a growl, he broke away to kiss her neck, his mouth traveling over her skin hungrily, dragging along her neck, and pushing against the neckline of her gown, as if he couldn't get enough of her. He traced her shape through her bodice, and her breath caught as his hand cupped the swell of her breast. He thumbed the tip, and she moaned.

She pushed her hands through the thick waves of his hair and slid them over the light bristles on his cheeks. Her blood rushed deliriously through her body, chasing every sensible thought from her head. All she knew was that she needed Marcus with everything she was.

"Rosamund," Marcus rasped. His hands shaped her bottom and pressed her against his hips, letting her feel what she had done to him. With deft fingers, he unbuttoned her gown and loosened her chemise, baring breasts that were so lovely he ached at the sight of them.

"Rosamund, Rosamund," he whispered, drunk on her name, on her.

He kissed her satin skin and captured her nipple in his mouth, blood roaring in his ears. Guiding her backward, he helped her to the bed, and they collapsed onto it, laughing.

"So beautiful," he said, positioning himself at her feet. Pushing her skirts up as he went, he kissed along the inside of her leg.

"You." Kiss.

"Are." Kiss.

"So." Kiss.

"Beautiful."

Every inch of her intoxicated him, and he drank her in like a man dying of thirst.

By the time he reached the tops of her thighs, they were both trembling, and he dragged himself up her body to taste her mouth again. For a moment, the thought penetrated that if Poppy was the woman for whom he'd waited his whole life, who was Rosamund? Because he couldn't imagine any woman being more to him than Rosamund was right then.

Aching for her, his breath coming in pants, he nudged her legs apart and slipped his hand through her intimate curls.

"Marcus?" Her voice was a shaky whisper, and he smiled crookedly and rubbed one little spot in delicate circles. "Oh, Marcus," she whimpered.

"Yes, love, I know."

She was ready for him, and thank God, because he didn't think he could wait another minute.

He'd never been with a virgin before, but he knew how this might be for her. "I'm sorry, sweet, this will probably hurt a little," he said as he eased himself to her entrance, dearly hoping it wouldn't hurt very much.

"I don't care," she whispered urgently, wiggling against him.

And then all words were beyond him, because she was so tight and slick, and it took every ounce of control to go slowly.

As he inched more deeply into her, she stilled. "Marcus, wait, this is too much. *You're* too much."

"I am?" He paused, though his blood was screaming.

"Maybe," she whispered, "you're too big."

A pained chuckle escaped him. Chest heaving, he rasped, "I'll fit, trust me. Just another"—he pushed a bit farther and reached her resistance—"moment." And then he was through.

"Oh," she gasped. She began squirming again, making his eyes roll back in his head. "Oh, I don't think—"

"Shh," he said, beginning to stroke slowly, resisting every urge driving within him. "I want this to be good for you. It gets better." At least, he desperately hoped it would. It was taking everything he had to go slowly when she felt so incredible.

When her breath caught a few moments later, he felt her desire shift. She clutched his back. "Marcus, I—I want—"

"I know," he grunted. "I know what you want." With sweat-inducing patience, he worked her slowly and was rewarded with her cry of pleasure. And not a moment too soon, as his own climax raced through him, filling his veins with the sweetest sensation he'd ever known. Wanting nothing more than to stay buried deep within her, he forced himself to pull out and spent himself on her stomach.

He collapsed against the mattress, not quite certain what had just happened to him. Making love with Rosamund had made him feel completely overtaken. He was hardly a novice in the bedroom, but he felt as though he'd been only practicing before, and now he had finally arrived at the real thing. As if everything in his life had prepared him for this woman. As if he'd been waiting for Rosamund all this time.

His brows drew together slightly as he recalled that he'd had a similar thought the night he'd met Poppy.

Rosamund lay quietly beside him. After a few moments, he reached for his coat and pulled a handkerchief from the pocket and gave it to her with a rueful look.

"It seemed unwise to risk pregnancy."

"I appreciate that you were thinking more clearly than I was," she said, accepting the cloth.

"I'm not sure I can take credit for much clear thinking just then." He shifted onto his side toward her. Her hair had come loose and fell across her chest in long, straight sections of brown satin.

"I didn't know how it would be," she said, "but that was…"

"Amazing?"

"Yes," she admitted, sounding dazed. He grinned, ridiculously pleased that he'd put that note in her voice.

"You know"—he leaned forward to kiss the back of her hand—"you never told me your last name." He chuckled. "I really think I should know it, considering."

She stiffened in his arms, and the next thing he knew, she was sitting up and pulling the coverlet around her. "I don't."

He laughed, puzzled by her reply. "Why not? You're being oddly mysterious." He traced his finger along the back of her arm, stopping to circle the pointed place where it bent. Even her elbow fascinated him. "Unless there's something you're hiding?"

She moved to the edge of the bed and cast a glance over her shoulder. "You don't need to know my last name, Marcus. I'm the companion of your *dog*."

He sat up as well, annoyed. Why was she being so difficult?

"Rosamund, I *obviously* look on you as more than the companion of my dog. I want you to be a great deal more. I want to take care of you."

"You can't."

"Don't be silly. Of course I can. I *want* to take care of you."

"Well, I don't want to be taken care of."

"Why?" he demanded.

Her only response was to button up her gown.

He growled and got out of bed, jerking on his breeches. "What are you doing? Why are you in such a rush to go? I thought you enjoyed what we did."

She finally turned and drew in a breath, as if gathering herself. "I did, Marcus. It was wonderful and magical, and I've never experienced anything like it. I'll always treasure this time we've had together, but I can't do that again."

He crossed his arms, treating her to his most commanding glare. "You can't tell me that you don't like being with me."

"No, I can't tell you that. But it doesn't also follow that I want to be your mistress. You know that I'm not the kind of woman you're destined to marry."

He absorbed her words. "Well, no," he agreed, because it was only the truth. Rosamund was delightful, she delighted *him*, but the idea of a seamstress becoming a marchioness seemed like something from a fairy tale.

A rebellious voice whispered that Rosamund had grace and sensitivity and charm, surely essential qualities in a marchioness.

"But…" he began, not knowing what he would say.

She shook her head. "You know what is expected of you, and you're too good a man not to do the right thing. And what about that mystery woman you're looking for, the one your grandmother is helping you try to find?"

He pressed his lips together. "There was a woman I met who I thought was special. But it seems she was not so taken with me, at least not enough to further our acquaintance, or even allow herself to be found."

She swallowed and looked away from him. "What if she did seek you out, this mystery woman?"

That was the devil of it. He thought he'd given a piece of his heart to Poppy, but he could no longer deny that Rosamund had claimed more than a little of his heart as well. Poppy was from his world, and therefore, a choice for her would be easier. But Rosamund was so special, the idea of ever letting her go seemed impossible.

When Marcus hesitated, she said, "You don't have to answer that," and he was surprised by the kindness in her voice, because she had every right to be bitter or angry. But hadn't Rosamund been a surprise from the first?

"I don't know what I would do," he said honestly, because the choice for Poppy was no longer clear at all.

She nodded once and told him she would return to the house alone so as not to attract attention. Socrates, the traitor, followed her.

CHAPTER THIRTEEN

Marcus was in the drawing room the following morning, making plans while his aunt sat doing embroidery on the sofa. Despite an overwhelming desire to try to *make* Rosamund understand that she was being utterly foolish, he'd acknowledged this wasn't possible and forced himself to allow her some time to think. At least, he hoped she was thinking. If she wasn't seriously considering his proposition, he didn't know what his next step would be, because all he knew was that he couldn't let her go.

Rosamund and Socrates were somewhere in the garden, he knew—he'd asked her to bring the dog to the drawing room when they were done. He meant for them all to have tea. Well, not Socrates, obviously, but he and his grandmother and Rosamund. Marcus reflected that it was a shame he couldn't tell his grandmother about his attachment to Rosamund, even though he suspected Lady Tremont had grown fond of Rosamund too.

She'd become so incredibly important to him. And he still didn't know her last name, he thought, vowing to remedy that once and for all when she came in to tea. She was the one he wanted to talk to, the one he wanted to be with. She made him laugh. She made him want to spend the entire day in bed. And he didn't think he'd ever tire of her.

Which was problematic, if he considered Poppy.

He didn't want to consider Poppy, actually. She'd been so special, and he didn't doubt that the night of the ball had been dazzling because of her and that she was a truly delightful woman. But he didn't know her. He *knew* Rosamund, and while being with Rosamund felt wonderful, what they shared wasn't a dream—it was real.

A knock at the door brought a servant to announce visitors: Mrs. Monroe and her daughters, Calliope and Vanessa.

"Mrs. Monroe?" Marcus repeated. The Monroes were London neighbors with whom he had a passing acquaintance, but hardly people he expected to see at his grandmother's house. They had been invited to the masquerade, he remembered now. Alice had moaned about them coming, because she thought them rather awful.

"Interesting," Lady Tremont said. "Show them in."

Marcus just had time to lift a questioning eyebrow in his grandmother's direction when the door opened and their guests filed in.

All three performed very deep curtseys. Marcus hadn't seen either of the daughters in some time.

"How nice to see you, Mrs. Monroe," his grandmother said. "And your daughters."

Mrs. Monroe blushed with pleasure at the greeting. "Thank you, Lady Tremont. Please forgive us for arriving at your home in this somewhat abrupt manner, but I think when I have explained the reason for our visit, you will be glad indeed."

"Please," his grandmother urged. Marcus waited with only vague interest.

"As you know," Mrs. Monroe said, "we were invited to

the masquerade ball held at Boxhaven House held earlier in the Season, and we gladly accepted that invitation. At that magnificent event, as I have come to understand, the marquess met a remarkable young lady." She smiled. "A young lady whose identity he does not yet know because of the masquerade, and of whom all he has is a necklace she lost at the ball. A necklace, I suspect, that bears the initials HPW and SDW."

Mrs. Monroe paused, and Marcus, who had been toying with a button on the front of his coat, stopped as her words penetrated. He had not divulged the fact of the engraving to the families with whom he'd taken tea months ago. He nodded once.

Mrs. Monroe's hand went to her heart. "My family lost a pearl necklace that night," she said, "bearing the initials of my grandmother, Sarah Warwick and my mother, Helen Warwick."

"Ah," said Lady Tremont after a long moment.

"How did you know I was looking for the owner of the necklace, ma'am?" Marcus asked. He'd only just sent the letters, and he hadn't sent one to her anyway. He glanced back and forth between the daughters, trying to compel his brain to ascertain if one of these young women was Poppy. He felt that he ought to feel something if he was in her presence, but nothing indicated to him that either of these young women was any more special than any other woman of the *ton*.

Mrs. Monroe cleared her throat delicately. "I was speaking with a lady recently who knew a family whom you visited after the ball, and she told me of the necklace that was found at the ball. I realized that this must surely be our family heirloom, which was lost that night."

"It seems Marcus and his visits to certain families have been much discussed," Lady Tremont observed.

Mrs. Monroe nodded, apparently unconcerned about this breach of etiquette. "And it was fortunate they were, too, since if we did not know about the necklace being found and the marquess's interest in its owner, we would not have known to bring ourselves forward. Because our family, my lord"— she smiled grandly at Marcus—"is the one you've been searching for. One of my daughters –we can't remember which—was wearing the necklace that night, and she is your mystery lady from the ball."

She presented her daughters to him—he'd met them once or twice before—and he exchanged greetings with them. They were both pretty, but within a minute of speaking to them and perceiving not one bit of vividness or joy bubbling over in either of them, he knew that neither was the woman with whom he'd once danced. And he also knew that it no longer mattered to him who Poppy was.

* * *

Rosamund had not been alerted that visitors had arrived, so when Socrates trotted ahead of her and disappeared into the drawing room, she merely followed him, knowing that Marcus wished them all to have tea together. Which she thought was a foolish idea for a number of reasons, not least that a dog's companion should not take tea with a marquess and his grandmother. But he'd insisted that his grandmother wanted Socrates to come to tea, and therefore, Rosamund must come as well.

As she reached the doorway, she saw that three ladies were inside, facing away from her, and she hesitated. But Socrates had gone ahead of her, and now he went over to sniff the feet of the arrivals. Rosamund's first thought was that she ought to collect him before leaving Marcus and Lady Tremont to their visitors, who would surely be more appropriate entertainment for teatime. Then she realized who the visitors were.

She nearly gasped.

Melinda, Vanessa, and Calliope were here, in Lady Tremont's drawing room. Rosamund didn't know why or how, but it couldn't be anything that would be good for her. In fact, it was very possibly to do with the pearls, and it occurred to Rosamund that gossip might have carried news of the necklace being in his possession to her aunt.

So while Rosamund might not need to worry about Bow Street runners—Marcus himself knew how the pearls had come into his possession— Melinda could now do her harm in another way.

Fortunately, Socrates had come to Rosamund when she entered, and intending to quit the room before anyone saw her, she quickly picked him up and turned to go.

"Rosamund," Lady Tremont said, "do stay. I'm sure our guests would like to meet Socrates."

She froze. All eyes turned toward her. Her cousins gasped, and Melinda made a sound that was closer to a growl.

"Mundie!" she cried. "What are you doing here?"

Marcus was looking back and forth between Rosamund and the guests with an expression of puzzlement. "Ma'am? Are you acquainted with Rosamund?"

Melinda drew herself up with all the gravitas of a grievously injured party. "Yes, my lord, unfortunately, I am. She was until recently living under my roof."

"I had understood Rosamund was working as a seamstress."

"That might be the way she passed herself off to you, my lord. But you should know that she is not respectable."

Marcus's eyebrows slammed together at these words. "I would ask you, ma'am, what reason you have to suggest that about someone in my employ."

"Rosamund is in your employ?"

"She is the companion to my dog."

"To your dog?" Melinda repeated quizzically. She absorbed this information with a furrowing of her brow, and Rosamund knew she was thinking about how best to arrange things to her advantage in light of what she knew about her niece. But that information was Rosamund's to share, and she would not let her aunt speak for her.

"Mrs. Monroe is my aunt," Rosamund said.

Melinda reddened with fury. "The connection is not a happy one. In fact, my niece's father was an infamous enemy of the state. We did her a kindness by taking her in and allowing her to live quietly among us when she would otherwise have been shunned by all respectable people."

"I see," Marcus said. His eyes were hooded, making it impossible for Rosamund to read his expression. But it was too late now to keep secrets, and she was almost glad Marcus would now know who she was.

"My father was a good man who was made a scapegoat for those who should have acted more nobly," Rosamund said, her voice gaining strength. All those years ago, while everyone had vilified and mocked her father and called him a traitor, Rosamund and her mother knew that he had only done what was right and that he had paid the price for what others refused to see. Now was her chance to speak the truth that no one would listen to before. Perhaps no one would want to hear it now, though she believed Marcus would at least listen. His eyes had not left her, and she kept her gaze on him.

"My name is Rosamund Shufflebottom, and my father was Captain Frederick Shufflebottom of His Majesty's Navy."

"Silence, Rosamund!" her aunt said. "How dare you speak of our family's disgrace?"

"No, Aunt, I won't be silent. I have been silent for too long," Rosamund said, steeling her voice when it would quiver. "You have perhaps heard of the Shufflebottom Affair, which took place half a dozen years ago, my lord? With our family name being so memorable, I believe the news of my father's disgrace spread even farther than it would have otherwise."

"Yes," he said, "I remember the Shufflebottom Affair."

She nodded, swallowing down the lump of emotion pressing in her throat. "He was a captain in the Royal Navy, and he gave comfort to deserters from another Navy ship by taking them onboard when they were trying to escape pursuit. I'm sure you saw the mocking cartoons and the cries of traitor, the calls for him to be hanged."

He nodded slowly, his eyes on her. She couldn't know what he was thinking, but at least he would hear the truth.

"He was vilified, and my family was assumed to be of the

lowest character. My father maintained that he'd helped the men because their captain was a cruel madman who'd had many sailors beaten horribly for minor offenses, three of them beaten to death. But no one would listen. He'd acted against his country, and that was all that mattered. He died of an apoplexy during the court martial proceedings. My mother died soon after of a broken heart."

"No one wanted to listen to him because he was wrong and a scoundrel," Melinda said sharply. "He was an embarrassment to our family, as are you."

Marcus's jaw seemed to turn to stone in that moment, and his eyes glittered with ice as they shifted to Melinda. Rosamund realized she was seeing the steely core at the heart of the man she loved, and she shivered.

"Rosamund could never be an embarrassment to any family," Marcus said in the kind of commanding tone a general might use in battle. His words had only begun to penetrate when he continued, "I see now how it was, Mrs. Monroe. Rosamund was orphaned, and you took her in because you felt bound by duty to do so. But you made her pay for it, didn't you?"

Melinda blinked rapidly several times. "I don't know what you're trying to imply."

"Quite simply that you must have treated her abominably. I knew of your daughters, but I never once heard of a cousin living with them. And that was because Rosamund was to remain hidden, wasn't she?"

Rosamund could only stare, comprehension beginning to dawn. He believed her, and he understood. Relief and happiness nibbled at the edges of her anxiety and made the corners of her mouth tremble. For Marcus to know and understand was everything she had so dearly wanted—or nearly everything. It would be enough.

"Her family brought nothing but scandal to the rest of us," Melinda said, her chin held high. "Her duty has been to lead a quiet, useful life."

"I'll wager it was useful to you," Lady Tremont said darkly. "And I'm in no doubt there's more to the story of those pearls than you've described."

"Those pearls belonged to my mother and should be returned to me," Melinda screeched. "Rosamund took them—"

"Only because you forced me to surrender them when I came to your house as a girl," Rosamund said, amazed her voice sounded as even as it did, but Marcus had given her strength. "They were given to my mother and were meant for the oldest girl in every generation. Which is, in fact, me."

Melinda wisely said nothing to this.

"Nothing else to say?" Marcus said in that hard, marquess's voice. "Never mind, I've heard enough. My housekeeper will see you out. Good day to you, Mrs. Monroe."

"But," Melinda began, "your lordship, you're not thinking to keep *Rosamund Shufflebottom* here as a servant. Mundie, come along!"

"No, I'm not thinking to keep her as a servant. But she's not going with you either," Marcus said, and if Rosamund had been on the receiving end of that icy glare, she felt certain her knees would have been knocking together. Melinda seemed to shrink as the marquess's dark blue eyes bore down on her. "*Good day*, ma'am."

Lady Tremont stepped into the hallway and could be heard calling for Mrs. Clark, but Melinda and her daughters were already leaving. As they passed through the doorway, Vanessa turned and gave Rosamund a hard look of the kind she'd dispensed many times, but this time Rosamund only smiled back. What did it matter what any of them thought? With any luck, she'd never see her aunt or cousins again.

And then Marcus was at her side.

"Why didn't you tell me?" he demanded, all traces of the imperious marquess gone.

"What could I say?" She realized, as he took her hands in his own large, warm ones, how much she was shaking. "The daughter of Frederick Shufflebottom is not a woman whom the Marquess of Boxhaven could possibly want to employ, never mind..." She blushed as he gently placed a fingertip over her lips.

"The daughter of Frederick Shufflebottom is a firebrand for justice and the finest woman I know."

He waited, as if to see whether she had truly heard what he'd said. "Marcus," she said, her heart in her throat, "your words mean so much to me. But—"

"I don't want to hear anything that starts with 'but,' Rosamund. I love you, and I don't care if your name is Shufflebottom, Fingerpuller, or Jellyleg."

He loved her? Could it really be? Her lips started to tremble, but she managed to say, "Do you know a lot of people named Jellyleg?"

"What I know is that you haven't yet said whether you love me." He kissed her, and her heart swelled with such happiness that she thought she might burst.

"And I *think*," he continued, "that you very likely have a ridiculous idea that I need protecting from the likes of scandalous you."

"You're a marquess," she said seriously. "You can't consort with a scandalous woman."

"On the contrary. I'm a marquess, so I shall do exactly as I like. And one of the things I should very much like is for everyone to know that your father was the sort of patriot of whom this country ought to be very proud."

"Oh, Marcus." Tears of joy filled her eyes. "This all feels too good to be true."

"And yet it is true." He kissed the tip of her nose. "But I can't tolerate another moment of suspense. *Do* you love me, Rosamund?"

"Yes, Marcus, yes!" She wrapped her arms around his neck and kissed his cheek. "With all my heart."

They held each other for long moments, and then he leaned away so he could look into her eyes. "Then say you'll be mine.

Will you marry me, Rosamund Shufflebottom?"

"Yes! Oh, yes, I will, Marcus!"

After quite a lot of kissing, they found themselves on the divan with Rosamund curled up in Marcus's arms. She realized that someone, likely Lady Tremont, had discreetly closed the door to the drawing room at some point.

He dropped a kiss on the top of her head. "Shufflebottom certainly is a memorable name."

"It is, and yes, I was teased about it as a child."

"Poor you. So... Poppy."

She smiled. "Yes, Poppy. My middle name is Penelope, and my parents called me Poppy as a nickname."

He nodded. "When you first walked into the room and saw your aunt, I began to put it together. But I think in some way, I always knew. From the minute I met you on the street, after you rescued Socrates, I felt something every time I looked into your eyes. I hope you know that you put me through an appalling time, thinking I was enchanted with one woman while I was falling in love with another one."

"I'm sorry about that," she said, kissing him a number of times and reveling in the fact that now she could kiss him all she wanted, whenever she wanted. She cupped his cheek, her expression turning serious. "Though I had my own appalling time, knowing who you were and believing you could never be mine. Never mind knowing that you loved the memory of me pretending to be someone I wasn't more than you liked the real me."

Marcus gave her a mock stern look before his expression turned serious. "But Poppy *was* you. Her clothes weren't what dazzled me: It was simply her. Which is you, simply you, Rosamund Penelope Shufflebottom, soon-to-be Hallaway. I've been waiting for you all my life, and now you are truly mine."

"Oh, Marcus, I do love you," she sighed.

A muffled snort drew their attention to Socrates, whose presence had been forgotten, but who was now standing a few feet away, looking up at them.

"He was being so uncharacteristically tranquil, I'd forgotten he was in here," Marcus said.

Rosamund cocked her head. "It almost looks like he's grinning."

Marcus nodded. "Like he's pleased with himself."

A moment passed, then Rosamund said, "He was a sort of matchmaker, when you think about how he brought us together."

Socrates yipped insistently, and his master gave him a haughty look, though the effect was somewhat spoiled by the grin teasing his lips. "I don't think I can tolerate too much smugness in a dog, but I suppose this is where I'm meant to admit I'm grateful that my mother gave me this creature."

"I think it is," Rosamund said, laughter filling her eyes. And he kissed her again, laughing.

"I am," he said. "Oh, I am."

THE END

Dear Reader,

I hope you've enjoyed ONCE UPON A BALL, my own spin on the Cinderella tale and the first story in the Hallaway Family series.

I've had such fun working with Grace Burrowes and Susanna Ives on this anthology collection! In addition to being wonderful writers, they're both lovely people, and I feel pretty lucky to get to write Regency stories with them.

My next release, now available for preorder, is A ROGUE WALKS INTO A BALL, which is the story of the Marquess of Boxhaven's younger brother, Jack, whom readers meet in ONCE UPON A BALL. Visit my **Books** page at emilygreenwood.net/my-books/ for more information and ordering links. You can also subscribe to my mailing list while you're there if you want to be alerted to my new releases (the only time I send emails).

From one book lover to another, happy reading!
Emily

A ROGUE WALKS INTO A BALL
BY EMILY GREENWOOD

Sarah Porter knew that life was not fair. No sensible woman could reach the age of twenty-five and not know this in her bones, though Sarah had had particular and personal proof of this truth from a young age, in the shape of a nose that could not be ignored.

She'd first begun to experience the effects of her singular nose when she was thirteen and it became apparent that her nose was growing far faster than the rest of her face. Her mother began to wring her hands when Sarah appeared at the breakfast table each morning, as though startled anew at the sight.

"Oh, my dear, it's your father's nose," Mrs. Porter would wail, her own button nose sitting unremarkably amid her fine features. "Why should you have been so cursed? If only there were something that could be done."

"Don't pay it any mind," Sarah's father would sometimes be moved to counsel from behind his newspaper. "Having a prominent nose has never bothered me."

But as Sarah was to learn, large noses on men were not the same thing as large noses on women. And her nose was growing into the same shape and, she was dismayed to find as the years passed, nearly the same size as her father's nose. What fate had given her was a hawk's assertive beak, and the only question was how large it would ultimately be.

Quite large, it turned out. Large enough that it was the first thing anyone noticed about her, and people were never shy about remarking on it.

If people knew her family, the remarks were commonly

expressed variations of "Oh, you have your father's nose," uttered in the tones one might use for a person who'd suffered a great calamity.

Then there were the ladies who condoled with her: "I know just how you feel— my feet are far too big." Since feet could be hidden, Sarah could rarely take comfort in such expressions.

By far the worst were people who thought they were funny, and of these, the most disastrous was the shopkeeper who'd handed over Sarah's purchase with a wink and said, "I nose you will like it!"

Gideon Grant, the most handsome and popular boy in the village of Scarborough, had heard the comment, and he'd laughed uproariously. He'd followed her out of the store, chanting "I nose you will like it" after her as she hurried away, willing herself not to cry. For years after that, whenever he saw Sarah, Gideon found a way to use the hated "I nose" construction, saying things like "I nose you don't want to get wet" if he saw her with an umbrella, or "I nose you live nearby" if he passed her on the street.

By the time Sarah was sixteen, she'd decided that Gideon had done her two favors. The first was that his relentless teasing taught her to rely on herself. Sarah had always been clever, and she loved to read. She liked novels and poetry, but what she loved best were travel stories and maps. The allure of foreign lands, and the idea of an escape from the narrow world of Scarborough, helped her not to care about the likes of Gideon Grant.

The other thing that Gideon's teasing did was to demonstrate, in a way Sarah learned to accept deeply, that people who were attractive were generally shallow. He was helped in imparting this lesson by other mocking boys, and several of the lovely young ladies of Scarborough, who tittered appreciatively at the witticisms he uttered at Sarah's expense.

These lessons insulated Sarah from the, to her, entirely foreseeable disappointments once she was old enough to go to social events such as parties and balls, where she was an instant wallflower. And while she stood at the edges of dance floors and watched as the gentlemen's eyes moved past her to rest on prettier women, she consoled herself with thoughts of Constantinople and Paris, of the olive trees of Italy and the fishing villages of Greece. She conjured daring schemes of how she might one day reach these places, and she *mostly* didn't care that her nose made her a nobody.

Visit my Books page at emilygreenwood.net/my-books/
to preorder A ROGUE WALKS INTO A BALL

Only Unto Him

Susanna Ives

CHAPTER ONE

Lord Exmore decided Miss Annalise Van Der Keer was beyond any hope. He, like the rest of Society, already knew her to be headstrong, ignorant, and silly. After all, he had warned his cousin Patrick away from the socially disgraced lady only days before. He and Patrick's father agreed to send the impressionable young man packing to India, putting almost two continents between Patrick and Miss Van Der Keer. But now, as the woman in question stood in Exmore's parlor in the late evening, having arrived with no hat, no gloves, and no chaperone, he realized that he had woefully overestimated what little sense the wild chit possessed.

"What kind of hideous, unfeeling monster are you?" she blasted him when he strolled in to meet her.

She brandished a crumpled letter in her hand. Her dark curls, wet from the rain, had escaped the mooring of her hairpins and were plastered about her cheekbones. Her enormous brown eyes were luminous with tears and hurt.

"What the devil?" He had neither the time nor desire to be hospitable to the girl, who had been plucked far too soon from the schoolroom. "Where is your uncle? Does he even know you are gone?"

Miss Van Der Keer had come to London for the Season and had stayed in the home of her uncle, Mr. Harry Sommerville. His was a well-respected family that was a hairbreadth above middling. Annalise's aunt was as silly as the young lady, but Mr. Sommerville was a serious, ambitious man, who brooked no nonsense. Annalise must have slipped from under her keepers' noses.

"You sent Patrick away." Her girlish soprano voice cracked with emotion.

He crossed to the side table, where a tray holding a decanter and several tumblers waited. He poured a glass of brandy and took a sip, letting his anger simmer down before he spoke. "If you are referring to Mr. Hume, he left England of his own free will."

Exmore did not lie to Miss Van Der Keer on this count. Patrick's father had sent an urgent letter upon learning that his son had been caught in the snares of Miss Van Der Keer, who had made quite a name for herself in Society. The small age difference between Exmore and Patrick was such that Patrick regarded his cousin as a wiser older brother, rather than a disapproving father. Patrick had been easily swayed by his cousin's arguments against a match with Miss Van Der Keer. Exmore, who had fallen in love and married young, had impressed upon Patrick the importance of choosing the proper wife for his station. Exmore had used his own wife's superior characteristics as an example of an ideal wife for a gentleman: gentle, well-mannered, yielding, responsible, charming, and beautiful—all the attributes lacking in Miss Van Der Keer.

Exmore had then stroked his cousin's ego by saying Patrick had the makings of a great man. Patrick would prove himself in India, making a name and a fortune. Upon his return to England, Patrick would secure a better wife than Miss Van Der Keer could ever make him.

Patrick had put up a weak defense of Miss Van Der Keer,

claiming she was "rather pretty." Exmore had waited for a more ardent defense of the lady in question, but when none came forth, he had explained to Patrick that a marriageable lady for his station needed more to recommend her than being merely pretty.

Now, as Exmore studied the miss in the intimate setting of his parlor, he realized that Patrick was right. She was pretty, but she didn't possess the type of beauty that would have tempted him. Her pale, heart-shaped face, with her small, rather pointed chin, accented her overly large lips and luminous eyes. Her nose was slightly turned up at the end. Her brown hair parted in the center and fell about her cheeks and neck in thick, heavy waves. Her face hadn't the elegance of his wife's classical symmetry, but fit her giggling, girlish personality.

Nor did her prettiness make up for her atrocious behavior in any small measure.

"But you are a marquess and his cousin," she retorted, her hands balled. "He had little choice but to do as you directed."

"Mr. Hume decided on his own."

"Impossible!" Tears dripped down her cheeks. "He loves me! He would never leave me on his own accord. We are to be married."

Exmore's fingers tightened on the glass he held. "Did he propose?" Patrick had said nothing of an engagement. They would have to pay a tidy sum to Miss Van Der Keer's father to keep the matter quiet. The imprudent alliance must be avoided at all costs. Miss Van Der Keer could not be let near his family tree.

"It—it was understood," she stammered.

Exmore released a relieved breath. Clearly, the engagement was a construct of her overactive imagination.

"We knew each other that way. We knew there could be no one else for either of us." She raised her eyes to his. Hers were a deep brown, almost black. The candlelight reflected in them like moonlight on water. They were potent, somehow capable of transmuting her emotion into him. He could feel the wild sorrow that drove her tonight.

"I'm sorry." He drew out a handkerchief.

"No, you're not," she spat, staring at the offered cloth. "This is what you wanted. You never liked me. I can tell. You are so humorless and deadly proper. You've never thought me good enough."

He measured his words. His father had died a few months before, and he watched now, powerless, as his wife struggled with her first pregnancy. He had real concerns that truly mattered, concerns that this silly girl with her lovesick tantrums would know nothing about. He returned the handkerchief to his pocket and took another sip of brandy. "I never thought your manners and conduct were good enough for him… or any gentleman in proper society, for that matter."

"You are wrong. My father may not be titled, but he is a gentleman."

"It is immaterial if your father is a gentleman. You decided not to behave as a gentlewoman. You thought it clever to steal a gardener's wheelbarrow and have your friends push it about the park at the fashionable hour. You think it's proper to play scandalous parlor games in respectable homes."

One of her favorite tricks was to ask a gentleman for a handkerchief at a ball and then hide it from him, making him search the vases and furniture drawers while she giggled at his discomfort. Once, at a dinner party, she proposed that the young people sneak away to another room and play a game she devised where one person was blindfolded and had to guess who kissed them on the cheek or hand or such. However, Miss Van Der Keer kissed Patrick on the lips, scandalizing the other poor guests she had dragged into the game.

"You make your affections for Patrick wildly known by chasing him about with singular determination, following him about, making a spectacle of yourself to receive his attention, including lifting your skirts in public to repeatedly tie your slippers and pretending a column at the Royal Theatre was Patrick and suggestively kissing it."

"It was a dare."

"One you foolishly took. Have you not seen the crude cartoons of yourself in the papers this week? Have you not read your name disparaged in the Society columns? Do you not see the people avoiding you in the streets?"

She turned silent.

"My sentiments of you echo those of the Duchess of Brysessy when she warned her granddaughters away from you. You are an ignorant girl with no idea of proper behavior or gentle manners." He was almost yelling. All the worry about his wife's condition and father's death funneled into his annoyance at Miss Van Der Keer. He took another sip of brandy to calm himself.

"I don't care," she declared. "The Duchess of Brysessy is a gossipy old harpy who finds pleasure in creating drama wherever she goes."

"I know you feel this way about your better, as does the rest of Society, for you made your sentiments about the duchess known aloud on Rotten Row. Tell me, Miss Van Der Keer, do you give no thought to the consequences of your actions?"

She didn't reply.

"If I did influence Patrick, it was to show him the facts of the matter. Your wild behavior would have dire repercussions on his station and future. I'm sorry your feelings have been hurt. But you're young, and I'm sure in a month's time, your heart will have sufficiently repaired to fall violently in love again with some other poor fellow."

"Don't patronize me! What—what do you know of love? You're a marquess. You marry according to a Debrett's entry—a heartless, cynical affair."

The wrath he had tried to hold back surged forth. *Had this girl no restraint on her tongue?* It was a joke among his old friends that he was overly protective of his wife. But in her weakened condition due to carrying his child, that primitive urge to protect compounded. "Don't you dare make assumptions about me and my affections for my cherished wife," he barked.

"I love her with a depth that you will never understand."

She winced as though his words inflicted a wasp-like sting. "Forgive me," she whispered. "I didn't mean to say those words. I didn't mean…" She pressed her hands to her face, and her body trembled with her sobs.

Again, he felt that annoying prick of compassion for her. What quality about this addled, reckless girl cut close to his bones? It wasn't attraction—how could he be attracted to another woman when he was married to the most beautiful, most gentle creature in all of England? What about Miss Van Der Keer seemed to amplify whatever feeling passed through him? A mystery he didn't care to explore. She had taken up too much of his valuable time.

He gestured to the door. "I shall have a footman accompany you to make sure you get home safely. I shan't breathe a word of this to your uncle, although I should. Coming here was as reckless as it was improper. Should you be found out, your already severely impaired reputation would be beyond redemption, if it isn't already so."

"It doesn't matter." She shook her head. "My uncle is sending me away. He says I have shamed him because you have cut his family."

"I have in no way cut his family because I don't approve of a match between you and Patrick. It is no reflection upon your uncle that you require another year or two, or a dozen, in the schoolroom to mature. Good night, Miss Van Der Keer."

"But I love Patrick." She didn't budge, but gripped her gown in her balled hands. "He has to come back. You can't do this."

"What you are feeling is adolescent infatuation. Nothing more. It's not real love."

"I love him with every fiber of my being. You say that I couldn't understand the profound love that you have for your wife. But I do. I love Patrick that way. I will always love him. I am steadfast in my affections." Her eyes pleaded, as if he possessed some kind of magic to undo her hurt and have Patrick return. Telling her how easily her lover had been persuaded to leave her would only hurt her more. And he doubted she would believe him. Best to let time or another man quell her obsession for Patrick. He drew in a breath. "One day, you will come to love another man more wisely and with more maturity than this frenzied infatuation for Patrick. You will look back upon this moment and thank me."

"You are wrong!" the impertinent girl persisted. "I will love only him forever. You must believe me. You must repair what you have done."

"I have done nothing but talk sense to a young man, and therefore, I wouldn't repair it if I could."

"I love him." Her voice was a trembling, broken whisper. "Don't you understand?"

He rested his hand on her elbow, attempting to escort her out. Yes, he knew what it was like to be deeply in love. And each day, as his wife struggled with her pregnancy, he prayed that sickness or death wouldn't part them so soon.

"I'm sorry," he said softly.

In an abrupt motion, she pressed her cheek against his chest, clearly desperate for comfort—even if it came from her perceived villain. Without thinking, he wrapped his arms around her, taking in her warmth. He closed his eyes. In her quaking sobs, all the worry for his wife and their unborn child, all the anxious thoughts he tried to keep hidden, rushed to the surface. Even in her manic sorrow she must have perceived his fears. She drew back, her lips parted in surprise. Then he saw something in her eyes—a wisdom he didn't know she possessed. He began backing away, his heart racing, ashamed to be vulnerable before her.

"No," she whispered, reaching out to him.

"Go—go home, you silly girl," he growled. He turned from her and fled the room.

"I hate you," she called to Exmore, her voice echoing in the corridor. "You have destroyed my life."

"So be it!" He broke into a jog toward his wife's chamber as if the devil were on his heels.

* * *

Cassandra lay in bed, curled on her side, as Exmore had left her to receive the hysterical Miss Van Der Keer. Candlelight flickered on the shape of Cassandra's body shrouded in quilts and on her glossy dark curls that spilled onto the pillow. He studied her in the firelight, not wanting to disturb her. His heart began to calm in her presence. She had always had the power to soothe him. She didn't have to say any words. Being near her healed him.

"Exmore," she murmured, sensing his presence. He loved the sound of his name on her tongue. Her soft voice seemed to caress the syllables.

He rested a hand lightly on her shoulder. "Are you feeling better, my love?"

They had been so joyous when the physician determined she was finally increasing after years of trying to conceive. But he and Cassandra hadn't expected how exceptionally ill the infant would make her. She could hardly move from her bed, and she vomited what little she could eat. The physician said it wasn't uncommon for a woman to do poorly in the first weeks of pregnancy, but the sickness would pass in the later stages. Exmore wasn't reassured. His wife was losing weight, not gaining. At times, she could hardly sit up for dizziness and nausea.

"Yes, the broth Cook's sister recommended is working a little."

He smiled. "Thank heavens for wise grandmotherly types. They seem to possess more common sense knowledge than all members of the Royal Society combined."

He sat carefully on the mattress beside her. She turned and studied him.

"What is wrong?" How she could read him. He could keep nothing from her. His every aspect was open to her.

"Do you remember the ridiculous girl chasing after Patrick?"

"Oh, *her*. What outrageous thing has she done now?"

"She paid me a call this evening. Unaccompanied and in a wild state. It seems I'm a heinous villain because, in her addled mind, I forced Patrick to leave her."

"How shocking," she said, but her voice lacked any outrage. "What—what did she say?"

"That she will love Patrick forever. That I don't understand true love. The stuff of Drury Lane melodramatic rubbish."

Her brows creased.

Exmore continued, "I played the wise father—heaven forbid, we should raise such a rag-mannered hoyden—and told her that she would fall in love again with equally wild fervor and other such nonsense."

"Maybe she will," Cassandra whispered.

Exmore lifted her hand and kissed the gold band he had slipped on her fingers years ago. "I'm sure of it. Most likely next week."

"No, I mean perhaps she will love Patrick forever. After all, I was hardly out of the schoolroom when we married."

"But you were far more wise and mature than this foolish child."

"Yes, such a foolish, foolish child," she murmured, her gaze softening, focusing inward.

Exmore wished he could pry into her mind and study its workings. She had an ethereal quality, as if another part of her dwelled somewhere else. Her mysterious inner life drove him wild, making him insatiably hungry for her.

He leaned down and snuggled next to her, keeping his feet off the bed. He only wanted to be close to her. When he carefully rested a hand protectively on her belly, she stiffened.

"My dear, I'm—I'm not feeling well," she said.

"I thought the tea helped."

"It did, but..."

"My love, I'm content merely holding you." They hadn't been intimate since she'd become ill.

"I just... I would prefer, that is, I should like to be alone."

There was an inflection of a question in her voice. He knew if he asked again to hold her, she would acquiesce. She always did as he asked. But he couldn't be a selfish, clinging husband. He understood her desire for solitude. Whenever he came down with a chill, he wanted only to lie in bed, alone in his misery.

"I love you," he whispered and kissed her ear.

She made a sweet, soft humming sound.

"Rest, my love."

He strolled to the door and then turned. She had shifted onto her side again. The gold firelight danced on her curls. He watched her for a long moment and said a small prayer for her and their child's safety, and then he slipped into the dark corridor.

CHAPTER TWO

Three years later

Annalise clutched the leather portfolio containing her late father's naturalist work as the carriage rolled past the Hyde Park gates. Here, Patrick had whispered, "I love you." Gazing deeper into the park, she spied the spreading oak where they had first kissed—a quick, nervous brush of the lips. Later, in a darkened, empty room beside a ballroom, they'd enjoyed a more indulging kiss. How these memories had comforted her at night as she'd kept vigil beside her sick parents' beds as the lonely country wind keened in the grate.

"You are smiling, miss," Mrs. Bailey, Annalise's family servant, remarked from across the hired coach. "I haven't seen you smile since your papa was alive."

"I'm so happy to be back," Annalise cried, gazing out at the streets that she and Patrick had once walked. "So happy."

She had chosen to come back to London after living under

a cloud of dread for more than three years, nursing her dying parents in the quiet, lonely countryside. And now, although she still walked the earth, it felt as though huge parts of her were buried in the churchyard along with her parents.

"I don't understand how this city—Satan's broadside—can make you so happy," Mrs. Bailey said.

Annalise couldn't explain to poor Mrs. Bailey, who was country-bred and, until now, had never ventured beyond the county of her birth, how London shined as bright as the crown jewels in Annalise's mind. Although her one Season had ended in shameful ruin, for a small time in London, when Patrick had loved her as much she loved him, she'd felt more alive than she ever had in her life. She wanted to live that way again—filled with hope, laughter, and love.

The coach skirted Mayfair's perimeter before finally reaching its destination, a stately town house on Wigmore Street.

"This is it?" Mrs. Bailey hmphed. "This is your uncle's fine London home? I was expecting one of those fancy houses by the park. This is a teensy thing. How do they get everyone in there?"

"It's larger than it appears from the outside," Annalise said diplomatically. Uncle Harry's family, like their home, hung at the outer edges of fashionable Society.

The front door flew open. A young lady in vivid blue cotton rushed out. Her spiraling honey-colored curls bounced around her as she cried, "She's here! She's here!"

Good heavens, was that little Phoebe all grown up now and rolling her hair? Aunt Sally had written that Phoebe was enjoying her first Season, but in Annalise's mind Phoebe remained the adolescent who fawned over Annalise's gowns and stayed up until the early hours for her return to listen, wide-eyed, to tales of the balls that she had attended that evening.

Behind Phoebe, two more girls followed—Shelley and Caroline, who had been a toddler when Annalise had been sent away. The three hopped about the walk excitedly, soon to be joined in their makeshift dance by their mother, Sally Sommerville. The daughters and mother all shared the same physical characteristics—creamy skin flecked with freckles, golden hair, long noses, and bow-like lips. Annalise took after her Dutch father in looks, but it was always said that her personality matched that of her maternal aunt and cousins. It was a long-standing family joke about the excitable nature of the female members. "Silly and high-strung the lot of them," her uncle often quipped.

Annalise reached for the door handle and hopped down before the carriage driver could let down the steps. Her aunt and cousins crowded her, enclosing her in a large, boisterous hug.

"There's to be a masquerade!" Phoebe announced before even inquiring about Annalise's well-being or if her trip had been pleasant. "I wanted to go as Anne Boleyn—with my head off. It would have been delightful. But Papa says I must go as a boring shepherdess. What will you be?"

"So many parties this Season," Aunt Sally cried, repeatedly kissing Annalise on her cheeks. "You shan't have a single dull moment. Not a one. Oh, but you are so pale. My poor, poor dear, what you must have suffered. I'm sorry I couldn't visit after the funerals. The children, you know. But I have the perfect potion from my apothecary that will put blooms on your cheeks again. Oh, and the draper received a darling new shipment of fabric from India. We must go tomorrow. We must! There is the most delightful gown featured in *The Ladies Mirror*."

"It's beautiful!" Phoebe agreed. "Mama said that I may have one made up. And you too! Everyone will find it so darling."

"I thought Papa said that we must be careful taking Annalise to parties because of her reputation," Shelley said innocently.

"Hush, Shelley!" Phoebe admonished her sister. "You weren't supposed to say anything. And everyone would have forgotten by now."

"She's here. She's here," said a male voice in mocking falsetto tones. Annalise glanced up. Her uncle, Harry Sommerville, leaned against the threshold, arms crossed. He was a slender man with slightly receding hair that he brushed forward. He possessed a strong nose and heavy eyelids, which made him appear perpetually bored. "Why don't you girls let your cousin inside and stop dancing about and clucking like excited, mindless hens on the walk for our neighbors' entertainment?"

Her aunt laughed. "Ha! Mr. Sommerville is so witty."

Annalise didn't see the joke but laughed along to be polite.

"You may as well bring her trunks inside," he commanded his manservant. "Sally, see to dinner. You girls can catch up on your inane gossip later."

"Of course, my dearest," his wife said obediently.

"You there," Mr. Sommerville addressed Mrs. Bailey, "see to putting away Miss Van Der Keer's things. Annalise, come to my library after you have freshened up and no longer smell like every coaching inn between here and Exeter."

* * *

"Sit down, Annalise." Her uncle pointed to the winged chair in his library. He took his usual chair beside his writing bureau and crossed his legs. He adopted the mocking falsetto tone again. "Oh, Annalise is coming, how she will love to shop. Oh, Annalise is coming, whatever parties shall we attend?" His voice lowered to its normal range as he studied Annalise. "I had no choice but to allow you to return to my home. I would have no peace otherwise. I entrusted you to my wife during your last visit, not realizing the full extent of her irresponsibility to her matronly duties. I did not see the damage of your silly, thoughtless behavior until it was far too late. Hear me, my child, you will not be ill-supervised again. I shan't have you ruining Phoebe's chances. Dear God, may I rid myself of one troublesome female." He paused. "What do you say to me?"

Annalise blinked. "Pardon?"

"You should thank me for kindly giving you a second chance."

A second chance? She had often contemplated her disastrous Season, which had been fueled by an obsessive love that overwhelmed any reason. Everything had been about Patrick. Nothing else had mattered to her. Back at home in the quiet country, as she'd had hours and hours to think as she replaced her father's sheets, softened his food, and made up the medicines the physician recommended, she'd wondered if her problem was that she felt more than other people. Maybe her idea of love—all-consuming, frantic with desire, and unending—wasn't everyone else's conception. But she still loved Patrick that way, and she couldn't imagine feeling any less.

"Thank you," she said quietly. "I am very happy to be in London again, to be near my cousins."

"How poorly you deceive, Annalise. You came only to attend balls and shows and to sink your pretty lacy hooks into some poor gentleman, who, up until that point, had been contently swimming about in the sea. What else would you have to talk about? Astronomy? Mathematics?" He chuckled, tickled at his witticism.

Annalise couldn't explain why, but the image of her father in his invalid chair, sitting in the sunlit garden, filled her mind. In the last years of his life, father and daughter had grown close and spent hours together, talking about botany and his scientific papers—things she'd once found so boring.

She hadn't realized that she'd sunk so deeply into this gentle memory until she heard her uncle loudly clear his throat. "You, ramshackle girl, have you not heard a word I've uttered?"

Annalise glanced up. No, she couldn't remember a word of her uncle's lecture, but it didn't take a far leap of the imagination to speculate. "You needn't worry, Uncle. I shall not attend balls or parties, and shall make myself content instead with walking in Hyde Park or attending lectures." In truth, she would be content merely revisiting the places associated with Patrick.

He studied her, as if not expecting the reasoned answer. "Not attend balls? Why must you always upset my household?

No, you will attend those balls, so that I may have some small peace in my life. Have mercy, silly girl."

Annalise stared. Others considered her uncle droll. He prided himself on making the wry observation upon the follies of others, including his own family. She had always laughed along. Now she felt a stab of annoyance at his put-upon cynicism. What had he to be cynical about, after all? She had watched her mother writhe in pain in the last days, begging for relief. She had listened to the minutes tick, tick, tick by for weeks at her father's deathbed as cancer ravaged him.

She burst out, "Did you know that in Sweden, coveys of partridges will crowd together beneath the snow to keep warm?"

He jerked his head back. "Excuse me?"

"Certain species of cuckoos lay an egg in the nest of other birds, and then the young cuckoo chick hatches first and tosses out the other eggs."

He stared, one brow raised. "Well," he said after a moment. "That must have occupied most of your brain." He made a shooing motion. "There, there, go. I'm assuming from the ear-piercing shrilling when the post arrived that a new *La Belle Assemblée* or other such rubbish has come. I'm sure it will entertain you and your cousins' simple minds until dinner."

Annalise stifled the desire to mention something derogatory concerning her uncle's mind and the copy of *The Rambler* on his desk. She quietly rose, crossed to the door, and rested her hand on the door handle. She couldn't leave yet. She had to know. "Have—have you heard if Mr. Hume is still in India?" She tried to sound casual.

Her uncle hiked a brow, "Still angling for him, old girl?"

"No, I'm—I'm merely curious."

"Lying ladies are so transparent. No, child, he's in India, and for my sake, I desire that he will remain there for the duration of your stay, which I hope shall be brief. Perhaps you will find a gentleman who hasn't the sense to run away from you like the last one." He chuckled, amused at himself.

She didn't humor him with a response but turned and walked away. She found Phoebe waiting in the corridor, waving a magazine. "We have received a new *La Belle Assemblée*. You must see this most darling gown."

* * *

Dinner at the Sommerville house was a boisterous, giggling affair. The females chatted over each other, holding multiple simultaneous conversations about gowns, bonnet decorations, parties, who had come to call that morning, and who had danced twice at a ball. Their father quietly stabbed his food, his expression pained.

Annalise didn't recall having so much difficulty swimming in the swirling conversational current three years ago. Now, she struggled to keep one strain of thought in her mind. Had she grown more like her father, turning over one thought like a rock in his hand, quietly examining each facet and fissure, before setting it down and picking up another?

"Annalise, darling, I went through your gowns," her aunt said. "Why, they are the ones you brought last time."

"I'm afraid I've been in mourning clothes for so long that I hadn't noticed," Annalise confessed. She had lost her sense of time. Her parents' deaths still seemed very recent, but all her mourning clothes felt new, even though they were more than two years old.

"It can never do." Her aunt dabbed currant jelly on her slice of pork. "We must have new gowns made in haste. I dare not let you out in those clothes. What if someone recognizes them?"

"What if someone recognizes her poor behavior?" her uncle said in a low voice, sliding his insult into the conversation.

Her aunt laughed as if it were a joke, but Annalise felt the prick of the words.

Phoebe continued her recital of upcoming engagements. "We have the masquerade on Thursday. I must spend the entire day working on my costume. And then there's the Danvers' ball on Friday."

"Mr. Sommerville," his wife said in an imploring tone, "may we use the carriage to go shopping tomorrow?"

"If you promise to stay out of the house for several hours."

His wife chuckled. "You are so witty, Mr. Sommerville."

"May I come?" Shelley begged. "I should like new gloves."

"Of course, my love," her mother said.

"And we are going to the theater on Saturday," Phoebe continued.

"Oh, I haven't been to the theater in ages," Annalise said. She remembered how she and Patrick had playfully sneaked glances at each other with their opera glasses.

"It's *Love's Joy and Misery*!" Her aunt clapped her hands. "All my friends are talking about it. We simply have to go!"

"Phoebe wants to go because Edgar Williams plays the lead." Shelley rolled her eyes. "She thinks he is handsome."

"I do not!" Phoebe cried.

"Well, he is handsome!" her aunt agreed, causing her daughters to giggle behind their hands that her mother would acknowledge another man as handsome. Aunt Sally blushed at her daring. "Of course, he is not as handsome as your papa."

Uncle Harry glanced heavenward as if to say, *Why, Lord, have you saddled me with this lot?* and then cut into a parsnip.

"Tell me who are the handsome gentlemen this season," Annalise said to Phoebe to make conversation. "Whom are all the ladies wild for? Whom shall I set my caps for?"

Phoebe began naming names. Mr. That, Sir This, Lord Who. Her mother inserted annual incomes and estates with each. Naturally, some of the titled gentlemen were above the Sommervilles' touch, but Phoebe said their names with the wistful look of a young girl who dreamed of capturing the heart of a handsome fairy-tale prince. Phoebe finished her list with, "And the Marquess of Exmore, of course."

Annalise blinked. Exmore?

Oh, yes, his wife died, she remembered. The marchioness had passed away about the same time as her mother fell ill. He had been so devoted to his wife that, in Annalise's mind, he remained eternally married. She couldn't imagine him with a different wife.

Her aunt shrieked, "That... that man!"

Uncle Harry set his fork down. "Phoebe, do not use that man's name in our decent home."

"But why?" Phoebe asked.

"I've told you before," Uncle Harry said. "He is not respectable."

"Pardon?" Annalise burst out with a bark of laughter. Was this a joke? The Marquess of Exmore not respectable? Had the earth changed its rotation? Was winter now summer?

"But... but... he is at all the balls," Phoebe said.

"Surely, you are in jest," Annalise said. "Uncle, I cannot believe Lord Exmore to be anything other than a model of propriety."

Her uncle pointed his fork at her. "Do not question me, foolish girl. I said you may not mention his name at my table. His deeds are not fit for innocent ears."

Annalise still couldn't believe they were speaking of the same Exmore she knew. The man who had admonished her for reckless behavior. Who had counseled that one day she would love more wisely and maturely. "That cannot be."

"He changed after his wife died," her aunt quietly explained.

"Not another word!" her uncle boomed. "Or you will have to leave the table."

Silence ensued for several seconds.

Aunt Sally squirmed uncomfortably in her seat. She couldn't abide silence for very long. "Then... there is the Cornish gentleman who owns a coal mine."

"I should like a coal mine," Shelley said and licked the pudding off her spoon.

"I should like to put you in a coal mine," Phoebe responded.

* * *

The ladies gathered in the drawing room after dinner, where Phoebe regaled Annalise with the plot of every London play for the last three months and descriptions of what the leading ladies wore. Annalise said, "How fascinating," or, "What a wonderful plot," or, "What a lovely gown," at appropriate times, but her mind continued to drift to Exmore.

He had remained a villain in her mind. As if he had been cast a part in a play like the ones Phoebe described, and Annalise had never recast him. She still blamed him for sending Patrick away. Often, in the evenings, when she was exhausted from taking care of her mother or father, she would stare out at the night beyond her window. She could still make out the unextinguished lights from the neighboring village, twinkling over the fields. She would imagine that Patrick never left. That he was beside her, whispering comforting words.

Now she gazed out the window onto Wigmore Street, the sound of Phoebe's voice muting in her mind. The London fog had settled in that evening. Horses and carriages seemed to emerge from it like ghosts and then disappear again. She remembered how dearly Exmore had professed to love his wife. How worried he had been about the late marchioness that evening. She had felt his deep anxiety and concern, breaking through her own pain, when she had embraced him.

The death of his wife must have destroyed him. What else would cause him to act against his nature?

"And have you decided on your costume, Annalise?"

Annalise glanced up. "Pardon?" She shook her head. "What play are we discussing?"

"Not a play, goose," Phoebe said. "For the masquerade tomorrow night."

"I think I shall go as a country girl who forgot her costume. Or perhaps as a young lady whose clothes were in fashion three years ago."

"No, no, we must come up with something jollier. It's my very first masquerade. I can barely contain myself, I'm so excited. I do hope something almost wicked happens to me." Phoebe ran through a list of costume ideas. Annalise didn't care for any of them. She wanted to ask about Exmore. How did he fall from respectability? What had he done?

* * *

A little after eleven, Annalise retreated to her chamber, a cozy room near the servants' quarters on the upper floor. There would be no escaping from this room and sneaking away on a rainy night to Exmore's home. The chamber was small, but she had it to herself. A lush carpet covered the floor, and heavy blue brocade drapes kept out the cold and outside sounds. On one side of the four poster bed was a toilette table and on the other a writing desk. The fire in the grate lit the entire tiny room.

Mrs. Bailey helped her out of her clothes and into her nightgown, all while complaining about the other servants. "Their fancy manners and ways, as if I wasn't good enough for their filthy city with its black-soot sky. This city is fit for sinners. It's not for us, miss. And look at this clothespress, miss. A wee church mouse would be hard-pressed to fit his clothes in it. No, we should go to your relatives in Holland like your father wanted, though it would break my English heart."

"If I go to Holland, you should return home. In fact, if London is not to your pleasing, why not go home?"

"What? I'm not leaving my little girl alone in the world," Mrs. Bailey said, outraged. "Good night, miss. You are holding up well, you are. I'm proud of you."

But when the door closed behind her and Annalise was all alone, she felt her strength falter. Mrs. Bailey had put away her clothes and toilet bottles, but she had set the two leather portfolios on the writing desk.

She opened the top one, drew out father's delicate drawing of *Digitalis purpurea*, and studied it as the shadows from the fire danced over its surface. Her papa had been a quiet man. He had once told her that some people you knew by their conversation and others by their silence. She hadn't known what he meant until the last year of his life—that some kinds of silence held much more meaning than words could express.

She carefully let her fingers touch the edges of the image as tears sprang to her eyes. Futile homesickness filled her. When she had given her keys to the new tenants of her childhood home, she had known she would never pass its threshold again. Even if she could, it wouldn't be her home without her parents. She wished she had tried to know her parents better when they were healthy, rather than waiting until the last months of their lives.

"Annalise." Phoebe's head popped around the door. "I had another idea about what you can dress up as for the masquerade. A siren! That would be wonderful."

Annalise discreetly blinked away her tears before they could fall.

"Yes, then I could go naked and not worry about a costume."

"Oh, you are very naughty, Cousin," Phoebe said admiringly.

Annalise studied her cousin. "May I ask you a question, and you needn't answer it if you feel that I shouldn't ask it... but I have to know. What has happened to Lord Exmore? I cannot believe he is disrespectable."

Phoebe's eyes lit with mischief. She closed herself into the room. "He is the most wicked rake in all of London," she said in an excited whisper. "The most handsome and the wildest. All the ladies want to tame him. It's better than anything at the Royal Theatre or Covent Garden. He keeps company with actresses, and there are rumors of fights and deep gambling. Wicked, delicious stuff."

"You shouldn't know such things," Annalise said, but not in an admonishing way.

"No, goose, I'm to pretend that I don't know such things. Such as a wealthy marquess will always be respectable no matter what Papa says. Every lady speaks of him behind her fan, except in our home because of Papa."

"But he loved his wife so dearly."

Phoebe pretended to dramatically faint upon the bed. "Perhaps sorrow has driven him mad." Then she burst into giggles. "I should hope that a man would love me so much that he would be driven mad with passion for me... You know, like in *The Fatal Love of a Maiden*?"

"You do realize that Lord Exmore is a real man? He is not an actor."

"Of course, I do, dear cousin. I've seen him at balls. Well, from across the dance floor. I've never really talked to him or danced with him. But he is ever so wickedly handsome."

"I meant he's made of flesh and bone and warts and has to make water like everyone else. I have never cared for him, but I know that he sincerely loved his wife in a deep way. And his hurt must be true."

"I should like it very much if he would fall in love with me in a deep way." Phoebe sighed.

Annalise opened her mouth to try again to get her point across to Phoebe but stopped. Maybe the problem was with Annalise. Perhaps she needed to relax and giggle again and care only about gowns and plays.

Phoebe must have got an inkling of her cousin's thoughts. "My dear cousin, you are far too serious. You must be happy again. Go to the masquerade as a siren but in a gown. That will be great fun." She bounced off the bed. "I know you are worried that people may cut you. But that was a long time ago. Don't listen to Papa. Everything will be jolly. You will see." She hugged Annalise. "I'm so happy you are here. We shall have a lovely time shopping tomorrow." Phoebe made a silly little dance out of exiting the room.

Annalise crawled into bed. She was exhausted but couldn't drift off. She waited until the entire house was silent with sleep, and then she slid out of her bed, opened the other portfolio, and drew out the contents: letters and letters to Patrick that she had never sent. She flipped through the pages, glancing at the words she had written through the years.

Today my mother stared up from her pillow. "I'm going to die," she told me sadly. We have known this, but now she is resigned. My heart is broken.

Spring is here. The wildflowers are in bloom, so I took my paints to the field. As I painted, I wondered what landscape you saw. I wondered about everything you had ever done since leaving England and if I were so far in your mind as to be forgotten.

I sat Papa up in bed and read to him from Mr. Visser's new volume, which arrived from Holland today. Papa complimented my Dutch, which had vastly improved. Remember how you teased me that Dutch was the most unromantic-sounding language?

Papa has passed from this world, and although I am alive, I feel great swaths of my heart have died too. Did you feel so lost and alien when you arrived in India?

And the last she had written:

I am coming back to London. The last place I remember being wildly happy. I know you are still in India, but somehow, I feel closer to you in London. Isn't that silly? I wonder what I will say or do should I see you again?

She turned the last letter and dipped her pen in the ink.

I was mistaken. London is not the same. The memories remain, yet I am different. Can you ever return to the person you were before? I must find a way to make her come back. Can I find a way to make you come back?

CHAPTER THREE

Exmore's head pounded with a dull throb, his mouth was dry, and his stomach clenched at the thought of eating the toast and butter that the servants at Brooks's had placed before him. The last twelve hours were snatches of images in his mind: a lovely actress at curtain call, the firelight on his glass of brandy, the dice rolling down a table, a paste diamond ring glinting on the actress's finger, and the rain trickling down the filthy gutter as he held his stomach.

The owner of the ring had whispered into his ear, "Let me comfort you. Let me help you forget."

But nothing could help him. She had kissed him against the door to her flat and fondled his privates, but he hadn't reacted. She wasn't *her*, and he was too drunk to pretend. He weaved home, his vision blurry, his steps unsteady, to where *her* portrait rose high in the entrance hall. The one he'd commissioned on their honeymoon. She stared shyly over her creamy shoulder at visitors. The artist had painted the lovely sunlight upon her pink gown and dark hair, capturing that radiance about her. The light had seemingly followed her, keeping her bathed in its glow. No woman could be more beautiful to him than she was.

He had drunk some more spirits, despite his butler's warning. Then he had fallen into bed, letting his valet pull his clothes off him. Then he had drifted in and out of nightmares.

This morning, he had awakened reeking of the actress's perfume. His face was bloated, his chin rough with stubble, but in the hall, *she* remained radiant in her silken gown, gazing upon him, her sweet expression unchanged.

Damn her.

He couldn't stay in his home. It was the least emotionally comforting place he knew. So, he'd scooped up his correspondences and taken them to the club. He'd found a table in the back corner. He wanted to be left alone, but he didn't want to be alone. He guzzled black tea and rested his clammy head on his hand as he read over missives concerning a vote that would take place in Parliament that afternoon.

"You look dreadful," a familiar voice said.

He glanced up to find Wallis Hume standing before him in a somber gray coat with a matching cravat. His eyes had that watery quality that came with age, and the hand that held his cane shook.

"I had a trying night."

"Every night is trying for you, I hear." Wallis sat and then eyed Exmore in that assessing manner of a physician. "You need to leave London, my good man. Take in the fresh air instead of the brandy. Find a gentle wife and leave the actresses alone."

"I'm needed here." Exmore tapped his letters concerning the vote.

The man waved his trembling hand. "Britain will roll along quite well without you for a few months. Why not go to your estate in the lake country?"

She was there too. He couldn't escape her.

Wallis leaned in. "You know, I was married before Beatrice.

A lovely lady. Died of a chill after our first year of marriage. I took her to Spain, but nothing could help her poor lungs. I tried to save her, but the Lord wanted her more." He turned silent and peered off with those filmy eyes. His gnarled gripped tightened on his cane.

"I'm sorry," Exmore said after a long pause.

"Listen to me. You will find another wife. You will feel affection for her. You will care for her differently than the first. But she will bring you consolation."

"Thank you," Exmore muttered and then took a sip of tea to keep back the words, *You know nothing.* And it was clear that the man had never got over the death of his first wife, who was clearly loved more than his next one. Exmore changed the subject to direct it away from himself and any more unwanted counsel. "How is Patrick?"

"Ah. Glad you should ask. I have a little healthy pursuit for you should you be inclined." Wallis held up his hand. "Now don't protest until you hear me out. My son is coming home, and he needs to be set up properly. I thought perhaps that you knew a place befitting a wealthy, distinguished gentleman to let. It is time he established himself and started his own family. Patrick has always looked up to you. You could advise him. Reacquaint him to London Society and find him a proper wife, so that we may avoid the last unfortunate episode. Whatever became of that wild girl?"

"I'm sure she saddled herself to some unassuming country gentleman by now and has more children than she can handle…" Exmore trailed off. A trim young man possessing arresting pale silvery blue eyes entered the room. The rest of his him was dark: his hair that spiked at the edges and his sun-tanned skin. He wore a fashionable blue coat and carried a rolled newspaper under his arm. His eyes hardened with animosity when he spotted Exmore. He started to turn away when Wallis hailed him.

"Good morning to you, Colonel Lewiston."

A polite smile stretched on Lewiston's tight lips. He made

a small bow. "Lord Exmore. Mr. Hume. I hope you are well."

Exmore's fingers tightened on his teacup. Luckily, Wallis answered the man's greetings, saving Exmore the trouble.

"Well?" Wallis made a humphing sound and continued talking, oblivious to the tension between the other two men. "My son—my only son—is coming home."

"Ah, I have heard much of the fine young man. I hope you will acquaint us when he returns." Lewiston was always congenial and polished, and that aggravated Exmore's hatred of the gentleman.

"Very kind of you, sir. Very kind. Aye, he has been gone for so long, I fear his old set have all scattered. Won't you join us?"

The younger men's gazes met. Lewiston glanced away first. "I beg you would forgive me," he mumbled. "I have previously arranged to meet a friend."

He bowed again. Exmore watched Lewiston stride toward the front tables.

Lewiston's presence in the same room set Exmore on edge. Exmore had come here to get some peace, and now what little he had garnered was destroyed. He couldn't concentrate on Wallis's recitation of humdrum daily news when he could hear Lewiston greet other members or his affable chuckle rise above the rumble of conversation.

"Pardon me." Exmore abruptly cut off Wallis's listing of whom he had seen at Tattersalls. "I remembered that I have an appointment with my man of business."

Wallis's mouth dropped at Exmore's rudeness. "I'm sorry. I didn't mean to keep you, forcing you to listen to the droning of an old man."

"Not at all. I'm afraid I had almost forgotten the appointment. Do send Patrick directly to me when he arrives. I shall introduce him in Society." A contented look of accomplishment passed over Wallis's features. Wallis had got what he wanted, for he surely didn't seek out Exmore unless he wanted something. That was really the only reason people reached out to Exmore—for what he could give them.

Exmore hurried away. He could feel Lewiston watching him. Exmore shoved on his gloves and hat as he exited the club. Wind whistled down the street, blowing up loose papers and the rotting scents from the gutter. He hadn't any appointment, of course. He had lied to Wallis, and he didn't feel a tinge of guilt about it. Living as he did now required many lies. Lies to conceal, omit, deceive, and to mercifully spare the feelings of others. The first lies were the hardest to tell. Now, they flowed easily from his tongue.

He glanced up and down the street. He didn't want to go home. Parliament didn't start for several hours. He thought about a drink. No, he wouldn't. Even he was beginning to worry about his deteriorating health. But that left him with nothing to numb his mind for the next few empty hours of the day.

He wandered down the street with no destination in mind. He greeted passing people he knew, pretending to be like everyone else with destinations, appointments, and reasons to be out in the world. He continued in this fashion until he came to a print shop. He stopped and took in the illustrations in frames that were propped by the window. They were botany images of flowers and insects he couldn't name, but they alleviated his mind for a few minutes, so he entered the shop.

The bell tinkling on the door announced his presence, and a clerk shifting through prints at a table glanced up. Exmore waved him off and ambled to a bin of images behind a marble vase on a pedestal. He and the clerk were the only souls in the shop. He flipped through prints of political caricatures, turning his head to read the small text. He didn't chuckle at any of the grossly drawn images, except the one of him in Parliament, throwing dice with one hand and holding playing cards in the other.

The caption read, *Lord Exmore wagers on the fate of the country.*

The bell rang again. He looked up as a young woman entered, her body silhouetted against the bright light flooding from the glass door.

* * *

Annalise survived the glove maker, milliner, hosier, and the first draper perfectly well. She joined in with her cousins' and aunt's squeals of delight over kid gloves or a darling straw bonnet. But after the next shop and the next, she found her smile waning, her nails digging into her palms, and her head aching. At every stop, three women were simultaneously asking for her opinion of a slipper or shade of green against her skin or a lace design. She remembered she once could shop all day, delighting in loading boxes into the carriage. She had never worried about the money. All items had been put on an invisible bill that was sent home to her father. Now, the money was hers, and whenever she demurred on an item, her aunt would flick her wrist and say, "My love, you can't go about in those old unfashionable threads."

It was to be a shopping expedition to replenish Annalise's wardrobe, but her aunt bought far more for herself. For everything she picked for Annalise, she had to have one for herself or her daughters. By mid-morning, they had sent the loaded carriage home with boxes and were walking to the Burlington Arcade, where the carriage would return to retrieve them.

Annalise stopped on the walk, arrested by the images in the print-shop window. A dozen prints by Dutch naturalist Christiaan Visser, whom her father had esteemed, were neatly set about in carved frames. She had seen tiny, etched reproductions in Visser's books that she had read to her father in their garden, but here were the same images in detailed precision and vivid color.

"Please," Annalise implored. "May I visit this shop?"

"Why ever would you want to do that?" Phoebe asked. "It's pictures of bugs and such."

"No, it's just that, my father… his work…" She stumbled over her words in the face of their confused stares. She couldn't make them understand that these images stirred cherished memories. "He was a naturalist too. It would mean a great deal to me."

"My poor darling." Her aunt embraced her. "We shall be at the draper's two doors down selecting fabric for you. Come, girls."

Annalise watched them leave, releasing a long breath. She opened the door and stepped inside the gloriously quiet shop. It was empty except for a clerk and a gentleman in the back. More of Mr. Visser's work was exhibited on tables or hanging on walls. She gazed around herself, feeling as if days and days of tension were draining away.

The clerk approached. "May I help you, miss?"

She smiled. "I want to stand here and quietly study the glorious illustrations of Mr. Visser."

* * *

It couldn't be, Exmore thought.

The serene woman clad in the soft lavender of half mourning resembled Annalise Van Der Keer in all aspects of outward appearance. Same large eyes, heart-shaped face, and turned-up nose. Yet, it couldn't be her. There was something very different about this woman. Something he couldn't articulate.

He edged behind a statue of Athena so that he might safely study the mysterious woman. There was nothing particularly fashionable about her gown. It had none of the numerous bows and lace that had characterized Annalise's country-aping-city dress. The sunlight that fell at an angle from the window gave her a Madonna-like quality as it rested on her cheekbones and strands of hair falling from her bonnet. She gazed at the illustrations with a gentle smile that curved her lips and lit in her eyes.

But this serene vision couldn't be Annalise Van Der Keer, the love-sickened, hysterical girl who'd arrived at his home during a rainstorm to blame him for destroying her life. The wild, frenetic energy of that girl wasn't present. It seemed as if someone had taken the shell of Annalise Van Der Keer and poured another woman into it. He continued to watch her, unable to take his eyes from her. Her radiance infused the space around her.

The young clerk was not immune to her power either. He nervously rubbed his hands as he approached her.

"You—you admire the work of Mr. Visser?" he stammered.

She spun around as if surprised. She must have been wholly mesmerized by the images. Her smile widened as her dreamy eyes focused on the clerk. His mouth dropped open, and his ears reddened.

"Yes, I do." Her voice was silken and light. "So does my father. I mean, so *did* my father. He *was* a naturalist." There was an inflection in her last words, as if she wanted the man to ask about her father.

"I think they are quite nice prints," the man said instead. "But sadly, none are selling."

Exmore watched her face fall a fraction. *No, you ignorant, young clerk. She wants to talk about her father. You make her feel insignificant when you say no one wants what she and her father found valuable.*

"I suppose they aren't very exciting to someone who doesn't study botany or zoology," she conceded. Exmore could hear the tinge of hurt in her voice. "But to me, there are so many tiny miracles in these prints. For instance, have you noticed something particular about this print you have among the Australian floral illustrations? The *Phyllopteryx taeniolatus*? It's not a plant at all, but a sea horse. Or sea dragon, to be more precise." Excitement sped her words and brightened her face.

My God, it could really be her.

She turned and walked in Exmore's direction, but her gaze was fixed on the wall above him. He slipped farther behind his statue, concealing his face.

"And don't let this sweet-looking flower fool you," she continued. "It's a sinister Australian pitcher plant, or *Cephalotus follicularis*. These dainty petal-looking things actually trap flies and digest them."

She stood at least fifteen feet away—too far to pick up her

scent or reach out to touch her. Yet, some odd energy shot through his veins, speeding the beat of his heart and bathing him in heat.

And he knew it was truly Annalise Van Der Keer. He remembered the same wild energy that emitted from her body into his that night she embraced him. The sensation had scared him and sent him rushing to his wife.

What had happened to Annalise that so radically changed her?

He remembered the morning his wife died. In a matter of hours, he had gone from knowing who he was and what he wanted, to being a stranger in his own home. The servants had been the same, all the furnishings had remained in place, he had met the same people along the walk by his home, yet he had had the disorienting sensation of being lost. Of not knowing what he had thought he knew. His world had completely turned upside down, yet everyone else had carried on in the normal cycles of their everyday lives. But maybe Annalise's world had changed too.

"Would you like a print?" the clerk asked Annalise. He was painfully smitten now.

"Why, yes, all of them."

"Shall I—"

She tossed back her head with a musical chuckle. "I'm sorry. I was jesting. I'm supposed to be buying fabrics and bonnets and such annoying little things." She sighed with a drop of her shoulders. "But this duck-billed platypus wants to live on my wall and so does this koala bear. Oh, I can't decide. There's nothing for me but to go to Australia and collect them all."

The clerk's mouth dropped open again. She gave that laugh that seemed to resonate in Exmore's chest. "I'm still jesting. I guess I shall take the platypus—my father adored it. My other monies I shall waste on silly ball slippers and such."

Exmore suppressed an appreciative smile. The poor young clerk's hands were positively shaking when he lifted the desired illustration from the table and began to wrap it in paper.

Meanwhile, Annalise returned to studying the pictures. She turned toward Exmore again, and her gaze was about to take him in. He couldn't hide. Instead, he rose taller, bracing for the impact of eye contact. His heart hammered as if it were located behind his eardrums. What would she say? Would she still hate him? Did she love someone else? Did she know his wife had died? Did she know how low he had sunk?

Then the door flew open, the bell ringing violently. Annalise spun around as Sally Sommerville rushed in. Two young ladies were in her wake, one he had seen dangling about the woman at balls. He made himself as invisible as possible behind the statue and lowered his head. He could not see the ladies, but he listened to their conversation.

"Annalise, it was all for naught. The shipment from India is late," one of the girls said.

"How thoughtless of the Indian and Atlantic oceans to delay us," Annalise quipped. Again, his lips curled into a smile.

"Thank you, miss," the clerk said.

"Did you buy an illustration?" Mrs. Sommerville asked.

"Oh yes." Annalise's voice was breathy with joy. Paper crinkled as she must have opened the package for the others to see.

"What is that?" one of the girls asked.

"It's a duck-billed platypus." Annalise enunciated each syllable. "Isn't it delightful?"

"It's rather homely."

"I'm sure to other platypuses it's quite ravishing," Annalise declared. Exmore smirked.

"I'm thinking of dressing as one for the masquerade," Annalise continued. "Then, should I see another duck-billed platypus, I shall know that we are destined to be together. Perhaps you should like to be a sea dragon, Phoebe? Imagine the costume."

"I should love to be anything other than a boring shepherdess."

"But then you may use your crook to herd your dance

partner," Annalise pointed out.

They must be referring to the Boxhaven masquerade tomorrow night.

"Oh, I'm vexed that the shipment hasn't arrived," Mrs. Sommerville complained, putting an end to the banter Exmore had enjoyed. "Now we must try that other shop in the arcade. Hardly my favorite. Come along, girls."

The bell jingled as the door closed. He raised his head, assuming the ladies had left. But Annalise had remained behind, her hand resting on the door handle. She took one last sad glance around. Exmore could see her eyes fill with tears. He heard his uneven exhale and stepped forward… to do what? Comfort her? But she blinked away the tears, turned, and left. Never realizing he was there.

He continued to stare at the empty space she had occupied. Although the light continued to shine through the window, the room felt darker, as if someone had extinguished a glowing lamp.

"Did you find an illustration, sir?"

Exmore looked at the inquiring clerk, not seeing him for a moment.

"Yes," Exmore said, making a reckless decision to try to chase away the oncoming despondency. "I would like that one." He pointed to the illustration of Australian bears that Annalise had rejected for the platypus.

Minutes later, he held the paper-wrapped print under his arm as he navigated the crowded streets. A cynical thought bubbled up. How convenient that Annalise should return at the same time that Patrick was returning to England. As if planned. Had the two corresponded all these years? Patrick had made no mention of her in his letters to Exmore. In fact, after six months in India, Patrick had written of his appreciation to Exmore for helping extract him from Annalise's influence. Away from London, Patrick had come to realize the folly of his affections and now could see the numerous faults of Miss Van Der Keer that everyone else had realized but him.

Patrick had described her as an *ambitious, witless, unmanageable piece of fluff* and had promised that he would choose more wisely in the future, citing Exmore's late wife as a model of how a gentle, graceful wife should behave. Had he lied to Exmore? Exmore wouldn't be surprised. He harbored little faith in humanity these days.

Once he was away from her arresting image, his senses returned. How could he assume from one chance meeting that she had changed? Maybe her wild character waited below the surface.

He left the print, still wrapped, on his desk and chided himself for the foolish purchase. Being at home did little to raise his spirits, so he headed out again, finding a welcoming tavern where a fire roared and actresses mingled about.

He never made it to Parliament that night, but stumbled home in the early hours, his world rocking like a boat on a sea—a sea of brandy. He studied himself in the mirror, as his valet undressed him, and loathed what he saw. What had he become? His eyes were reddened from drink, dark crescents carved beneath, an unhealthy pallor to his skin. His valet tried to extinguish his lamp, but Exmore waved him off. He resented that when he overindulged in spirits, his staff treated him like a child who might burn down the house. Left alone, Exmore unwrapped the illustration of the Australian bear and studied it. He had been thinking about Annalise since that encounter. She had called the bear a koala.

He stroked the edge of the image like it was that mythical jar that contained a genie. Maybe some mythical version of Annalise would emerge and calm his pain with the peace that had enveloped her in the gallery when the beautiful light fell on her smiling face.

CHAPTER FOUR

Annalise did not go to the masquerade as a platypus, but neither did Phoebe go as a shepherdess. Annalise had an inspired idea that Phoebe should be Titania from *A Midsummer Night's Dream.* Annalise spent the day putting together Phoebe's costume and helping her aunt transform into Queen Elizabeth. It seemed that her aunt knew only that Queen Elizabeth wore a large dress.

Annalise, Phoebe, and Mrs. Bailey spent the morning running about finding ingredients to redden her aunt's hair and whiten her face, as well as locating sheer muslin for Phoebe's wings. Annalise appreciated keeping busy, because it fended off her homesickness. Yet, she found that sometimes, out of nowhere, she would pass a certain tree or home, and a memory of Patrick would rush over her like a blast of wind, bombarding her afresh with recollections of textures, scents, and magic from another time.

Annalise waited for last-minute inspiration for her own

costume as she dressed her cousin and aunt. To create Queen Elizabeth's costume took two of Annalise's old dresses and some stained brocade drapes that were stored in the attics. For Titania, Queen of the Fairies, Annalise cut leaves from green cotton and created vines from long lengths of brown cloth. She and Mrs. Bailey stiffened the wing fabric with the starch they used to create Aunt Sally's ruff.

Phoebe danced with excitement when Annalise finally let her turn and look at herself in the parlor mirror. Her cousin gasped at the wings, headpiece, and mask that Annalise and Mrs. Bailey had fashioned.

"I could be on the stage!" she squealed. "You are simply brilliant, Cousin."

Not a moment later, the house filled with her uncle's booming steps. The door to the ladies' parlor flew open.

"Annalise, you will not make a mockery of this family," he said when he saw Phoebe.

Annalise looked up innocently at him. "It's Shakespeare, you know," she said in the tone that indicated he was an idiot if he did not know.

Annalise had only half an hour to dress for the masquerade after completing the others' elaborate costumes. She thought about saying she wouldn't go, but then she would spend the evening thinking of her old home, or Patrick, with only her uncle to keep her company. Then, gazing down at the discarded string and thread from Phoebe's wings, that annoyingly elusive inspiration finally struck.

"Perfect," Annalise muttered to herself.

However, when she came downstairs all dressed up, her Aunt Sally said, "Good heavens, would you care for Phoebe's unused shepherdess costume?"

"But I'm Ariadne," Annalise said.

Her aunt and Phoebe stared at her.

Annalise tried to elaborate. "From the Greek myth, you know."

More vacuous stares. Alas, it was too late to change, and the carriage had pulled up.

* * *

Annalise didn't want to admit that London had lost its charm. She wished she could be as joyous as Phoebe, who flitted about, all smiles and laughter. To Annalise, the costumes had a scary grotesqueness about them. The perfumes hurt her nose, and the air felt like breathing in the famed thick London fog. Amid the loud laughter and music, she felt painfully alone. She loitered about the walls for the first hour. The only attention she received was curious glances at her costume, which was hemorrhaging string. Finally, a young gentleman dressed as an Arthurian knight approached.

"My friends and I are quite puzzled." He gestured to a group of more knights clad in various forms of armor and crowded in the corner. "May I ask, what is your costume exactly?"

"I'm Ariadne."

"Who?"

She stifled a groan. What had she been thinking when she made this costume? "The character from the Greek myth."

"Sorry." He shook his head. "Would you care to dance?"

She hesitated, but his smile was a pleasant one beneath his half-mask, so she consented.

The dance floor was a crush of people poking each other with protruding costume parts. Annalise sometimes danced alone in her room, but she hadn't danced with a partner in a long while. As the music began and people started to turn, she realized she had forgotten the steps. She panicked and slid her mask up to glance at her feet.

Her partner stiffened. "Are you… are you Miss Annalise Van Der Heer?"

"Keer," she corrected, pretending not to hear the alarm in his voice. "Van Der Keer."

His eyes began to dart about behind his mask. "I didn't realize—that is, I didn't know you were in town."

"I only just arrived."

"Oh."

Still holding her hand, her gallant knight took a step back from her, as if she were contagious. He didn't say another word to her for the entire dance, even though she tromped on his toes and bumped into him several times. When the torture was mercifully over, he bowed and scurried back to his friends. She watched him animatedly speak to them as they took discreet glances in her direction.

It seemed London hadn't forgotten her. Or forgiven her.

The clock on the chimney-piece chimed the eleventh hour. These parties lasted well past midnight. She just wanted to go home. Not her aunt's house, but her true home, miles and miles away, where someone else now lived.

Through the windows, she spied the large, fat moon shining in the heavens. It was the same moon she'd watched shine through the trees by her window at her old home. Tonight, the cold, distant heavenly body felt like the last thing tying her to the past. She followed it, going through double doors that led to a terrace, where she came across lovers escaping the din. She passed them, heading to a spot of solitude at the back.

There, she rested her hands on the railing and drew in a deep breath of the cool night air. The moon was luminous in the silent sky. She studied its contours, remembering her father's sketch explaining the different phases in relation to the sun. It had made sense when she'd stilled herself and finally listened to him.

"You have lost a part of your costume," a man said.

A cold tickle raced down her spine at having her quiet refuge invaded. The voice was rich and slightly blurred, as if he were drunk. She turned to find a heavily bearded and masked musketeer peering out from the shadows. He sat on a stone bench under the eaves. Had he been there before? Perhaps she was the invader of his peaceful space and not the other way around.

"I fear this costume was not the best choice." She picked up a length of string that had fallen from her gown. "It's been shedding all evening."

"May I hazard a guess at who you are?"

She chuckled at his phrasing. She almost wanted to say, *Yes, do tell me who I am, for I don't know anymore, and I'm feeling particularly lost tonight.* Instead, she said, "No one else has been able to guess."

"Ah, a challenge. I shall succeed where others have failed you." He made a dramatic show of rubbing his faux beard as he thought. "Ah!" He raised a finger. "I have it. You are a shedding Egyptian mummy."

She feigned disappointment. "Oh, had I only thought of that."

"I see that you are cleverer than I thought upon first impression. But I will discover your mystery." He leaned forward. The light from the burning sconces reflected in his dark eyes. "Yes, of course, I have it now. You are a very confused writing spider."

She laughed. A deep, true laugh that reached to her belly, breaking up some of the tension she held. "Again, another brilliant costume I didn't think of. Perhaps I should have consulted you before the ball."

He tossed up his hands. "You defeat me, kind lady. Give me the answer."

She shook her head, chuckling. "Yet, I adore your guesses."

"I endeavor to always please the ladies, of course." He rubbed his beard again. She could see an amused smile peeking below its whiskers. "But of course. You are a butterfly trying to break from a poorly constructed cocoon."

"An awkward metamorphosis of sorts? Sadly, not in this case. Here, I shall relieve your misery. I'm Ariadne."

"From the Greek myth, of course."

"You know it!"

He stared at her for a moment and then blinked. "Of course. Doesn't everyone?"

She smiled, warmth flooding her body. "That's what I thought. Yet, everyone else has looked at me when I told them as if… well, as if I should have dressed as an inmate of Bedlam."

He tilted his head. "I quite enjoy the charming inhabitants of Bedlam. One of the very few places you can hold an intelligent conversation in London. Do you ever feel the sane are locked up and the insane are roaming the streets and known as the general population of London?"

What an odd thing for a stranger to say. But she laughed. She hadn't truly laughed, it seemed, in months, maybe years.

"Very clever, indeed, Ariadne." He reached out and touched a string on her skirt. The touch wasn't intimidating, but friendly. Another string fell away at his light touch.

"Sadly, I don't think I'll be rescuing Theseus with my poor thread. The Minotaur will surely eat him."

The man dismissively waved his hand. "He deserved it for how he treated you, leaving you heartbroken after you saved his sad hide."

"Ah, but I get Dionysus in the end."

"And Dionysus is Bacchus to the Romans. I think all stories that end with Bacchus are good endings."

"I agree." She felt herself smile and then became self-conscious. While she was wildly delighted to discuss something other than balls and gowns, she shouldn't have been alone on a terrace with a male stranger. She glanced toward the door, where light and noise from the party spilled out. She couldn't help but think that this party was a modern version of the Minotaur's maze.

"Aren't you going to venture a guess at who I am?" the man asked. He affected a hurt tone. "How rude not to ask."

"I'm so sorry," she said dramatically. "I didn't mean to offend. Hmmm, let me see…" She narrowed her eyes, pretending to concentrate. He was costumed from head to toe, his intense eyes the only part of him unconcealed.

"I'll give you some hints. I'm exotic, loyal, and very dangerous." He raised his sword. "And I possess most excellent props." He set his sword between his teeth.

She made a clucking sound. "A poor adventure-seeking musketeer such as yourself must find English ballrooms a bore."

He removed the sword from his mouth. "I admit there isn't enough intrigue, mystery, threats of revenge, hidden treasure, or swordplay to pique my interest, so I had to come out in the moonlight to pine for my Spanish home."

"I find this ball full of intrigue and mystery. For instance, it's been so long since I've attended a ball that every dance has become a mystery, and as for intrigue, I feel like I'm in some miniature version of the court of Louis XIV."

"Tell me, where have you been? Say it was Spain."

"You make me laugh," she said. "I love to laugh." Then she shook her head and turned serious. "I've been at home in the country caring for my parents. They recently passed."

She could feel his penetrating gaze on her face, as if he knew her throat was burning and that her heart hurt.

"I'm truly sorry," he whispered, all hints of drunkenness gone from his voice.

"Thank you." It was the first true acknowledgment of her parents' deaths since she'd come to London. Her aunt and her family had flitted briefly on the matter and then changed the subject as if death were some vile, embarrassing secret, and by speaking of it, they hastened their own demises.

"I've recently had a death in my family," he said quietly. "Well, it's been a few years now. But it never leaves my mind for long. Memories lie in wait for me at almost every turn."

"It's very disorienting," she admitted, feeling her emotions gushing as if a lock on a canal had been opened, letting the waters rise. "I've lost my parents and my home. It was all in the natural course of things, yet now... now..." She paused. She shouldn't admit such emotional things to a stranger, but she felt as though she had been secreting away words for years, with no one to share them with, except in letters she never sent to Patrick. "I spent years caring for my parents. It consumed all my hours and thoughts. And now that I'm back in London, I feel like I'm on a beach, trying to find the seashell that I once fit in. But it's gone. Washed away. I'm different, but I don't know how." She brushed her hand on her gown. "I'm a costume of broken threads. I'm sorry, I should say—"

"Were they sick for very long?"

Only after she had sat on the bench beside the man, did she think that perhaps she shouldn't have. But why did it matter now? She didn't know how much longer she would remain in London anyway, stewing in memories of Patrick, who wasn't coming back... at least, not for her. Maybe her future rested across the ocean in Holland with her father's family. She had never been there, but her faithful moon companion would follow her.

"My mother passed quickly, painfully," she said.

"That must have been hard to watch."

"Yes. She was so vivacious… like me. Or so they tell me. In the end, I was overwhelmed with sadness, of course, but she wasn't hurting anymore. My father's death was much slower. Cancer. I only truly got to know him in his last months." She paused, remembering reading to him as he rested on a sofa in his study, while brown, twittering finches hopped about the vine growing along the sill. "He was very quiet. My mother's world was among other people." She gestured to the guests lingering about the door. "But my father lived in nature and his books. Funny the worlds we inhabit. Am I boring you?" She knew if she'd uttered such things to her aunt or cousins, she would receive only useless blank looks.

"While most dry English sorts bore me to flinders," he said, "you are an exception and do not. Please continue. Tell me more about your father. He sounds fascinating."

"He was a naturalist. He was captivated by the smallest detail, the kind most people would rush over." She turned and looked at the man, whose eyes now glowed with sympathy. She wondered if her musketeer was perhaps a kind, old man, wizened by age. Perhaps that was why she felt so comfortable with him. "Did you know the true miracles are in the smallest of things?"

"Yes," he whispered.

"He saw all the miracles. I'm still learning, but I fear I haven't my father's talents for observation."

"But he showed you where to look."

Her lips spread into an appreciative smile. "You put it so neatly. I have kept his drawings to remind me. When I finally find a new home, I shall put them on the wall so that I will see them every day, like my mother's necklace." She touched the small ruby at her neck. "I want to keep them near me."

"You have no home?"

"I'm currently staying with my aunt, but…" She shrugged. "I don't know where I'm going. I live day to day now."

"I understand."

Silence crept over the conversation. It was that kind of silence she'd learned from her father. When no words were exchanged, yet meaning filled the void. She instinctively knew this stranger lived day to day as well. She knew he hurt in a way he wasn't conveying. She couldn't articulate how she comprehended him. She just *felt* him.

A cluster of people on the side of the terrace broke into loud laughter, destroying the quiet.

"Might I recommend Madrid as a home?" the musketeer said. "Excellent climate and charming people."

She shrugged. "Madrid, Timbuktu, Saint Petersburg, Dover."

"Dover is far too remote. It's a treacherous half-day trip from London by coach and sled dog."

"And I understand the roads are strewn with highwaymen, Mongol hordes, and, of course, the famed blood-thirsty pirates."

"Have you no protector, fair maiden? No hopeless romance? You see, to a musketeer, all romances are conveniently doomed things, because, well, a musketeer must dash off to the next adventure. He can't be tied down when a quest calls."

"Once," she admitted, hearing the brittleness in her own voice. "Long ago."

"It—it sounds as though you still have emotions for him."

The amusement had left his voice. The question was a serious one.

She studied him. Who was he? His gaze was as mesmerizing as the moon above them. She knew it was reckless to admit her secrets to a stranger. But were they truly secrets if they burned to be known?

"I fear my Theseus has abandoned me," she confessed. "He has sailed away. My heart hurts, and no Dionysus awaits on the horizon to comfort me. Perhaps I should—"

"My wife died." His words spilled out, broken and raw.

She seized his hands. "I'm so sorry."

He didn't draw away but tightened his hold on her fingers. His palm was both soft and rough—not what she'd expected from an older man. The warmth of his clasp radiated through her. She hadn't touched many men, only Patrick and her father. The musketeer's touch reminded her of neither. It was kinder, lighter—the touch of a sympathetic friend.

A woman's voice broke the silence. "Lord Exmore, there you—oh my, am I interrupting something? I do hope so." She gave a light, tinkling laugh.

Annalise gasped. Exmore! The man holding her hand was Exmore!

The musketeer—Exmore—bolted up from the bench, concealing Annalise behind him. "What do you want?" he rudely responded to the woman. A hardness had entered his voice. It was the voice she remembered from years ago. Annalise began to shiver. What had she done?

"Oh, I shan't get in the way of your seduction du jour." The woman disappeared in waves of blue silk, her laughter trailing behind her.

Exmore slowly turned. Dizzying heat rushed to Annalise's head.

"I'm sorry, Miss Van Der Keer. I—"

"Wait!" The realization burst in her mind. "You knew it was me! You knew! H-how long have you known?"

He released a breath and raked his hands through his hair.

"Since you entered the ballroom with your aunt."

She glanced down. Her hands were shaking. She felt violated. He had been playing with her. He'd pretended to be so sympathetic, but a true sympathetic, kind person wouldn't carry out such mean trickery. She was humiliated thinking about all she had confided to him… about her father, about Patrick…

"Forgive me," he whispered.

"Get—get away from me." She bolted for the door.

Forgive? As if he had accidentally stepped on her toe or bumped into her, instead of ripping her beating heart from her chest. She didn't give her forgiveness so lightly. To Hades with London and Exmore. She just wanted to get away from London and all its heartbreak as fast as she could. There was nothing for her here… not anymore. She had been stupid to come back.

All the inhabitants of the refreshment room looked up when she entered. Their gazes felt like a splash of cold water on her face. News of her presence had pervaded the party. Everyone knew that beneath the stupid costume was Annalise Van Der Keer, the silly girl who'd disgraced herself chasing after Patrick Hume. She could see the malicious laughter trembling on the guests' lips. She glanced back at the terrace, where Satan waited. She was cornered. She swallowed, raised her head, and walked across the room, ignoring the whispers.

The ball continued until two. Annalise thankfully didn't spy Exmore again. She spent the rest of the masquerade wandering from room to room, pretending to look busy. All the while, she planned. It would take several weeks to arrange for a stay at a relative's home in Holland. Tomorrow, she would write the letters. Upon receiving a positive response, she would buy a ticket on a boat and tell Mrs. Bailey that she didn't require her employment. Dear, loyal Mrs. Bailey would be miserable away from her motherland. It was time Annalise truly grew up and left her memories of Patrick behind. He wasn't coming back. He was gone forever. Her love for him was like having an amputated limb—she had to go on living despite the pain, scars, and missing part.

After Mrs. Bailey removed Annalise's hideous costume and left her alone to sleep, Annalise opened her portfolio and drew out her last letter to Patrick. She turned the letter, writing across it.

Dear Patrick,

Sadly, our correspondence must end. I will always love you. But you do not love me, and I need to let go of the fantasy that someday you will again. Good-bye.

She read over her words as the ink dried. No! She wadded up the letter and then stopped and pressed it out. Why couldn't she let go of him? Why had she chased his memory to London when he clearly didn't love her? What was wrong with her?

* * *

Nothing could blot out what happened. The smoke and noise in the gaming hell hurt Exmore's head. He couldn't seem to add up his cards or remember what card led. Alcohol didn't bring the sweet numbing sensation he craved for his self-loathing. Having lost ten pounds, he gave up and ambled home, hoping the cold air would clear his mind. He carried on a logical argument in his head as he wove through the streets

He had tricked Annalise. Why did he follow her to the terrace? Because he had to solve the mystery: Had she truly changed?

Yet, why did he keep talking once he had determined that her temperament had indeed calmed? Why did he ask her intimate questions when he had known he was violating her trust?

He looked up. The swollen moon was directly above him.

Because she made him happy. For the moments that he was with her, he felt lifted above the despondency that followed him. He hadn't thought the conversation would go very far. He hadn't thought he would have to admit who he was. He had wanted only to keep her near him. He could tell she hadn't known happiness in a long while. She hadn't appeared to know that Patrick was returning. She was simply lost, as he had been after Cassandra died—unsure of who he was and the world he inhabited. She had wanted to talk, and he had been the wrong gentleman at the right place and time. Like him, she was surrounded by people, yet she was painfully alone. He wanted to make her happy too.

Of course, he had ended up making her feel worse. *Damn him.*

He was sober by the time he entered his home. He kept his eyes averted from his wife's portrait as he climbed the staircase to his chamber. He lit the candle on his writing desk and sank into the chair. He drew out a clean sheet of stationery from the drawer, dipped his pen, and wrote.

Miss Van Der Keer…

CHAPTER FIVE

Annalise had written and dispatched three letters to Dutch relatives by luncheon. She kept her plans to herself for now because Phoebe and her mother were bubbling with excitement from the masquerade. They subjected Mr. Sommerville to a detailed recounting of every costume and every dance partner.

"Enough, good wife!" he bellowed. "What have I done to deserve this torment?" He glanced down the table. "You are mercifully quiet, Annalise. Are you not in boughs over the masquerade too?"

Annalise jumped at the sound of her name. She had been staring out the window, wondering about the flora and fauna of Holland. They had tulips, of course, but she wondered what she might find that wasn't in England.

"Ah, she's daydreaming," her uncle said. "One night in London, and she's already ridiculously in love. Maybe this one will stay around, and I can pop her off. I need to start ridding myself of my female problem. It's an infestation I have on my hands."

His wife laughed.

"I was thinking about botany," Annalise said flatly.

"Turning into a bluestocking, are you?" he quipped. "I suppose the ball must have bored you."

"I had a wonderful time," she lied. Aunt Sally and Phoebe had been too caught up in their excitement to have noticed the ripple Annalise's presence had caused at the masquerade. Annalise decided it was best to remain silent about the problem since she would be leaving soon enough.

"Sadly, Annalise's new gown won't be ready in time for tonight's ball at the Danvers'. She'll have to wear an old one," Aunt Sally said.

Lud, another ball? It didn't matter what she wore there. She was only going to linger in the corner, trying to be as invisible as possible. This would be her battle plan until she could retreat to the Continent.

"Oh dear, whatever shall we do?" Mr. Sommerville adopted his falsetto tone again. He dabbed his face with his linen. "Annalise must wear rags. I feel a faint coming on." His family laughed merrily. Annalise managed only a stiff smile. Thankfully, her uncle's tirade was cut short when the manservant entered, holding a package and several letters.

"Pardon, sir." He bowed. "A letter has arrived in the post from your solicitor. You had asked that I inform you as soon as it arrived, sir."

"Yes, yes." Mr. Sommerville rose, signaling the end of luncheon, and took the letters from the servant. "I shall be in the library seeing to important business," he said. "Should you require my audience for some trifling matter, my door will be locked." He walked out.

"Come, Annalise, you must help me with a darling new hairdressing for tonight," Phoebe said, coming to her feet.

Before Annalise could answer, the servant thrust the package before her. "For you, miss."

Annalise slowly took it, noticing the frank. Her belly

tightened.

"Ooh, what could it be?" Phoebe asked.

Annalise quickly turned the package, hiding the frank.

"Is it from a dance partner?" Phoebe continued. "I wondered that we should receive no flowers this morning. But maybe because it was a masquerade, our partners won't send any because they aren't to know it was you."

"I suppose," Annalise said casually, hoping to conceal her racing heart.

"Come then, open it!" Phoebe said.

"It's from a friend from home." Annalise changed the subject. "Flowers in your hair would be lovely. Don't you think, Shelley?"

"Yes!" Shelley grinned to be included with the older girls.

"Then I shall dress both my cousins' hair?" This was met with great approval, and the mystery of the package was quickly forgotten.

Minutes later, Annalise tossed the package onto her bed in her chamber. "There is nothing I want to hear from you," she told the package as though it were Exmore himself. She turned to leave and help her cousins but stopped and groaned. "Very well."

It was best to get these vile things over with. She recklessly tore the paper away and then gasped. Below was an illustration by Visser—the koala she had not chosen that day in the shop. How had he known? Had he been there? But she didn't remember anyone being in the shop but herself and the clerk before her cousins arrived.

She removed the illustration from the trappings of paper, and a folded letter fell onto her lap. She set the illustration carefully on the mattress and then opened the letter to reveal neat, unadorned script.

Miss Van Der Keer:

Please accept my apologies. I betrayed your kind trust, and for that I am deeply sorry. I must own that I knew you had returned to London after I spied you in the print shop. You did not see me in the back behind a statue because you were enraptured by the illustrations of Visser. I hope you will accept the gift of the illustration you left behind that day in order to purchase "silly slippers."

I should have made my identity known to you at the ball, and pardon if I am presumptuous, but it seemed as if you wanted to talk, that you hadn't had someone to speak to for a long while. Had you known my identity, I fear you would have remained silent. I found our conversation delightful and regret its abrupt ending. Please know that all your words I keep in confidence, as I have your call to my home years ago. How our lives have changed since that time. I have nothing but the kindest wishes for you. I apologize if I upset you, and I give you my word that I will kindly stay away from you for the remainder of your time in London. God bless you.
Exmore.

She drew in her breath and reread the letter. She was struck by Exmore's kindness, as she had been when she had known him only as a musketeer. He had been a villain for so long in her mind, it was hard to think of him in any other role. Had what she thought was betrayal of her trust merely been confused compassion? Should she write him back of her forgiveness?

Did she forgive him?

"I don't know," she whispered.

And hadn't she not been entirely without fault the night she called, unchaperoned and unkempt, to his home? Theirs was a tangled mess of emotions and history, and she would rather avoid him and the memories he kicked up.

She studied the koala, and suddenly, an image of her father cradled in her arms, laboring for breath as he died, filled her mind. She had squandered most of their lives together, assuming he was dull and boring. It hadn't been until the end that she truly knew him. Exmore had lost someone too. She remembered the pain in his voice. *My wife died.* Who was she to judge? She was foolishly holding on to Patrick, a man who didn't love her. Exmore had told her as much that evening long ago, but she had refused to believe him because the truth hurt too much. No, she had never learned to love more wisely, as he had said she would. Her heart was as stupid as ever.

Yes, perhaps she could forgive.

She crossed to her desk, drew out a piece of paper, and dipped her pen. What to say? A large blob of ink dripped onto the page. Again, that old anger she had nursed for Exmore returned afresh. She hastily scribbled.

What do you want from me? Why couldn't you leave me alone?

Her door opened, and Phoebe popped her head in. "Are you coming to help us with my hair for the ball or not?"

"Yes, yes, of course." Annalise turned the page over and rose from the chair. She needed a little more time to think about forgiveness before she wrote any more.

* * *

Exmore cursed himself for sending the letter and illustration as he ambled toward his club. He might as well have tossed them into a void.

Although he had written that he would kindly avoid her, he desired to see her eyes and hear what she had said when she read the letter. Their conversation had been left dangling. Its incompleteness bothered him, because he had so much he wanted to say to her. He couldn't explain it, but the only person in London he really wanted to talk to was her. He wanted to speak about more than Patrick. He wanted to tell her about Cassandra and how disoriented he had felt after she died.

But the kindest thing he could do was keep silent and walk away from Miss Van Der Keer. Too much bad history rested between them for any kind of friendly acquaintance. But during that time with her, as the fat moon had looked on, she had raised him above the gloom that weighed daily in his chest. He had a glimmer of hope that he could be attracted again to a proper lady and not sink to emotionless, soulless trysts.

He found himself standing before the print shop window where he had spied Annalise a few days ago. The small optimism in his heart faltered. All the illustrations of Visser had been taken down, replaced with political cartoons about the Prince Regent. He didn't know why, but it felt like an omen as he gazed at the grotesque, exaggerated images of the corpulent prince instead of the beautiful drawings that had captivated Miss Van Der Keer.

He stepped inside. A different clerk, older than the one Annalise had enthralled, was setting out more ugly caricatures.

"Where are the Visser images?" Exmore demanded, a strange note of panic in his voice.

"Couldn't sell them," the man replied with a shrug. "We sold the lot of them to a shop on the Continent." The clerk then nodded to a newspaper folded on the table beside Exmore. "Aye, but if you're interested, Mr. Visser is in London lecturing. Perhaps he will have some prints with him."

"May I?" Exmore lifted the paper and flipped through the pages until he found:

Mr. Christiaan Visser, renowned Dutch naturalist, will speak at the Royal Institution. Interested ladies and gentlemen are invited to attend.

The article went on to give the specifics of the time and room. Annalise needed to know about this lecture!

Yet, he had written that he would keep his distance from her. *Hang it all.*

"You may take the paper, sir, if it pleases," the clerk said.

Exmore shook his head and replaced the paper on the table. "No, thank you." If Annalise were meant to attend that lecture, she would have to learn about it through another means. He had given her his word.

He left, feeling that old edgy restlessness set in. For the rest of the afternoon, he could settle nowhere for very long, moving from club to club until the day's session of Parliament began. He wanted to disappear into a gaming hell, letting brandy and the thrill of the turn of cards crowd out his gloominess. But dammit, he had to get better. He couldn't live his life this way. He had to find a way out.

Back at home after Parliament, he shuffled through his invitations. He received six or so invitations for balls or recitals for any given night during the Season. He rarely received invitations to dine anymore, having left too many embarrassed matrons with an empty seat at their tables. As he glanced at the names, he wondered where Annalise might be.

Why can't you stop thinking about her? Let her go, good man.

He tossed the invitations face down on the table and blindly picked one—a ball given by Lord Carruthers.

He had his valet adonize him and the carriage sent around.

For all his trouble, he danced three sets with pretty young things who possessed sweet smiles and insipid conversation. He could see the large moon looming through the windows—the same full moon that had shone the night of the masquerade, yet this night had none of the previous night's magic. He caught himself scanning the crowd, looking for Annalise. But she wasn't there. Frivolity surrounded him, yet he felt miserably alone and despondent. The sirens sang in his ear, *Come away to a gaming hell. Stop trying, it's no use.*

By ten o'clock, he had succumbed. He slumped in a chair around a card table, drinking his second brandy and pondering whether to hold or ask for another card in a game of vingt-et-un. He held a ten of spades and an eight of diamonds. Good, but perhaps not quite good enough to win. But as he considered the probabilities of his cards, he realized he didn't care about winning or losing. They felt the same—empty and dull.

Behind him, two young bucks were drinking at a small round table. They had been there for almost half an hour, but now their conversation drifted to his ear.

"Miss Littleton. I'll wager she will be engaged in two weeks," he heard one say. "Many fellows are vying for her."

He glanced over his shoulder. The two men had been joined by a third, a dandy wearing a padded black coat and a collar so high it brushed against his earlobes. A book was set on the table before the men, and a servant had brought over an inkwell.

"I'll put down ten pounds that she'll be engaged in six days," the dandy said in an affected bored drawl. "She has tolerable looks and possesses a very tolerable dowry."

A gentleman with reddish-gold hair and dry skin spotted with pale freckles wrote down the wager. Their friend, a slight man with dollop-like blond curls that fell over his eyes, put forth another name. "Miss Poplin. Let us discuss, gentlemen."

Exmore returned to his cards. He accepted another from the dealer. A seven. He had overplayed. He laid down his cards, took another sip of brandy, and waited for the next hand to be dealt because he couldn't think of anywhere else to go. Going to the theater or another party seemed like too much effort.

The name Miss Van Der Keer seemed to pop from the conversation behind him.

He spun around.

"You are cracked, Ronald," the curly blond said. "Don't you know who she is? Let me enlighten you." The man launched into tales of Annalise's previous Season, either embellished or plainly false. Exmore's fingers balled into a fist.

"No one will ask for her hand," the curly-haired man concluded. "I'm betting ten pounds Miss Van Der Keer won't be accepted in any homes by next week, let alone receive a proposal. Write it down, Simon. Write, man. Seven days to social disgrace." Delighted maliciousness filled his laugh.

The dandy waved his hand dismissively. "That's too easy, my boy. She's already been cut by the Danverses tonight."

"What?" Exmore exclaimed.

The men's faces brightened from Exmore's attention.

"Good evening, Lord Exmore!" said the freckled man

recording the wagers. "We were placing bets on the fates of this year's crop of ladies. Care to wager?"

Exmore bit back the retort to put him down for one hundred pounds that his fist would bloody their faces within the next five minutes. "What did you say about Miss Van Der Keer?"

"She's been cut by the Danverses." The dandy's mouth was twisted in the smug smirk of a man who knew a piece of news before anyone else. "I was there myself not fifteen minutes ago. The old girl was in tears because no gentleman of any consequence had asked her to dance. I recall you weren't very fond of her. Warned your cousin off that wild hoyden. Care to wager?"

"Go to hell." Exmore headed for the door.

CHAPTER SIX

"I'm terribly sorry your niece is suffering such a headache and must go home," Mr. Danvers told Aunt Sally. The Danverses had herded Aunt Sally, Phoebe, and Annalise into a corner. The host wore a stiff smile, trying to disguise the unpleasant conversation. Annalise didn't have a headache. It was merely a flimsy excuse cooked up by the host to politely expel her.

All of Mr. Danvers's delicate diplomatic work was undone by his wife, who wept into her lacy handkerchief. "But I planned this ball for months, my love," she wailed. "All the food, flowers, musicians. She's ruined it."

Mr. Danvers rested his hand on his wife's arm. "Dearest, please, contain yourself. Others are watching."

Annalise felt the prickling heat of the guests' curious glances like hot ants crawling along her skin. She wanted to shout at them, *You mean nothing to me.* In a few weeks' time, she hoped to board a ship to Holland and put miles of cold, turbulent ocean between herself and this snobbish city. Its shine had been tarnished. But she had to maintain her civility for Phoebe's and her aunt's sake. They had to continue to swim in these infested waters.

"Come away, Aunt Sally." Annalise beckoned her aunt quietly, hoping to escape without creating an even bigger scene.

"Mr. Danvers, she is like my own daughter," Mrs. Sommerville implored. "Let her stay." Aunt Sally's pleading tones were edged with hysteria.

"I understand that this is a delicate matter," Mr. Danvers said. "I assure you I'm only thinking of Miss Van Der Keer's well-being."

Annalise stifled a bark of bitter laughter.

"This is cruel," Phoebe cried. "I shall tell Papa."

Annalise couldn't see how that would improve matters by any measure.

"Phoebe, you can remain and enjoy yourself," Annalise said, trying to remain calm. "My feelings shan't be hurt. I assure you that a quiet evening of reading in my chamber would do wonders for my, um, headache."

"I shall speak to Mr. Sommerville tomorrow," Mr. Danvers said. "Of course, this little incident will not lessen my esteem for the gentleman. These things do happen from time to time."

Annalise bit back the desire to say, *Oh yes, it's always unfortunate when you must humiliate someone because you have no backbone and always bow to Society's whim. Well, I would rather have the approval of innocent daises in the fields than yours.* No wonder her father had preferred animals and plants to people. Of course, he had always been far wiser than she.

"Let my niece stay," Aunt Sally pleaded. "My husband will be so vexed. He has such a temper." Aunt Sally pressed her hands together as if praying. "Doesn't Annalise look lovely? I know her gown is a few years old, but she has done her hair differently for your ball. You can't turn away someone so lovely."

"I concur," a rich baritone interjected.

Mr. Danvers wheeled around. There stood Lord Exmore. Annalise sucked in her breath. This wasn't the Exmore she remembered. He had been the stiffly proper sort, perfect in manner and manicure. He had gazed at the world with reserved, disapproving eyes—or, at least, that was how he had gazed at her. This Exmore sported a reckless smile, and his hair was unkempt. Dark curls lined with prematurely silver threads fell over his forehead. Dry wrinkles crowded the corners of his eyes. His once chiseled face was slightly bloated, sagging at the corners of his mouth. This was the face of a dissipated libertine whose lifestyle was aging him before his time. Annalise struggled to reconcile this Exmore with the man she had known years ago. She couldn't. The death of his wife had altered his soul beyond recognition. This man was a stranger.

The Danverses turned, as shocked as Annalise at seeing Exmore.

"My lord." The hostess fell into a deep curtsey. "You honor us."

What was happening? Had Exmore not been invited? This party was a few social tiers beneath him, so she hadn't expected to see him here.

"And I would be exceedingly honored if Miss Van Der Keer and her cousin Miss Sommerville would save a dance for me, if their dances are not spoken for." He spoke in pleasant tones, although his chest heaved as if he had run here.

What was he doing? He had given his word that he would stay away from her.

"Yes!" Phoebe cried.

Exmore shifted his gaze to Annalise. A beckoning glow warmed his eyes, and he held out his hand for her to take. She studied his long fingers that tapered at the ends. She realized that he was offering to be her savior. He might have been a rake, but his title and wealth solidified his place on the Mount Olympus of London Society. Was he trying to save her? It was too late for her, but she knew she had to take his hand for Phoebe's and Aunt Sally's sake. Still, she remained unmoving;

everything seeming to slow down around her.

Then he whispered, "Please."

She shivered at the intimacy of the sound, as if he were aware only of her and not everyone staring at them. She reached out and clasped his hand.

His warm fingers wrapped around hers. Her lips parted. His touch felt as it had the night before—like an old, comforting friend.

* * *

Exmore continued to hold her hand, afraid that if he let go, she would be washed away by an invisible ocean. He could tell that the stares of others unnerved her. They didn't bother him, because he had grown accustomed to them. He had learned in these last years, after some of the most notorious nights of his life, to keep his head high and wear a cocky, dangerous smile, no matter what he had done.

He began, "I know I gave you my word that—"

"I meant to write you, but I couldn't find the right words," she broke in. "I thought if I waited a bit, the perfect words would magically appear. Such as when you're not even thinking about it, but simply setting about lighting candles or mending a sleeve, and suddenly, 'Oh my goodness, those are the words!' Typically, it happens after I've posted a letter." Her laugh was brittle, in the manner of one making a joke to hide nervousness.

"Ah, then you still have time. Perhaps the words will come to you as we dance." He led her onto the floor as dancers were assembling for the next dance. Her hand clenched in his.

She shook her head. "I think the only word I have is 'sorry.' I'm sorry that I reacted so strongly last night. I'm very confused now. Everything is…" She shook her head. "I can't explain it."

"Try," he encouraged.

Her brows dropped in concentration, and then she said, "This thing on your waistcoat. What is it?"

"A button."

"What?" She shot him a comical look. "No! That is not

what you call a button. That is a spinneybob. Everyone knows it's a spinneybob."

"What?" He played along with her game. "I've called it a button my entire life."

"Well, you were wrong your entire life. It's a spinneybob."

"Ah, I see what you're getting at."

"You do?"

"You've changed so drastically that you don't recognize your own world."

Her bright expression fell to a more serious one, which fit more comfortably on her nervous features. "Yes. Precisely."

"I know that feeling well."

"You see, we are supposed to be enemies. But now it seems we are not."

"We can still be enemies if that is your preference?"

"Perhaps." She smiled teasingly and then added, "No. I like you better this way."

That radiance he remembered at the print shop enshrouded her as she studied him with tender eyes. It seemed that his entire day had culminated in this moment. As if he had known at some hidden level in his mind that it would, and he had simply been killing time, hanging about clubs and hells, waiting for this dance to arrive.

"I didn't see you at the party earlier." A nervous quality entered her voice. "How did you know…well…"

"That you were in social peril?"

"I adore how you phrased that."

"I heard from somewhere that you may be in a spot of trouble. And although I left my musketeer beard and trusty sword at home, I couldn't resist the beckoning of a lady in distress."

She laughed. The sweetness had a calming effect—like hot tea on a dreary morning. "I'm not so distressed, but I thank you on behalf of my aunt and cousin."

"Not distressed? You hurt my chivalrous pride, señorita."

She glanced about the room. "The thing is, I'm leaving

London for Holland—where my father is from." There was no excitement in her voice, only resignation and sadness. "There's nothing for me here except my cousins. And it seems they would be much better off if I were gone as well."

He couldn't deny the prick of panic. *I'm here. You can't leave me alone.*

Patrick would soon be here as well.

Exmore decided it was better to keep this knowledge to himself and lure her with something more innocent and uncomplicated. "Ah, I know a secret that may change your mind. I shall tell you on the dance floor."

"Ooh, I dislike when people do that. You must tell me now. No secrets."

"You must wait for this secret that I know you will adore. It's a scintillating tale."

"You are cruel," she said and then chuckled. He remembered once comparing Annalise's beauty to Cassandra's, finding fault in Annalise's more countrified features. Cassandra belonged on carved marble. The cool, idealized beauty. But Annalise's face was meant for kindness and playfulness. You couldn't love her face without falling in love with all of her. Not that he was falling in love. He truly didn't know, because he couldn't trust his emotions anymore. He was merely happy to be with her at this very moment. That was enough.

She groaned. "Must we dance? Couldn't you have saved this damsel in distress for a card game or a glass of punch?"

"Hold on to me, and all will be well."

She shook her head. "No, it will not be well. Your toes and the toes of other dancers will suffer greatly."

"Come now, don't you want to know my delightful secret?"

She considered and then wagged her finger. "Very well, but it's your own fault if I smash up your toes."

"Smile as you do it, and I won't notice."

When he led her onto the chalked floor, numerous other couples rushed forward to claim spots. This happened whenever he attended a ball. Exmore couldn't understand his allure. In his own mind, he led a boring, embarrassing, desperate existence. He should have been banned from polite society long ago, but his deplorable behavior only seemed to fuel his popularity. Yet, the more Society desired of him, the less he desired of Society. He wished he could whisk Annalise away to a terrace, far from the curious looks. There, they could talk and laugh. He didn't want much anymore from life, only the simplest, most commonplace of things, such as good conversation.

Annalise held him tight, bit the edge of her lip, and looked down at her feet when the music started. She was stiff but responded readily to his prompting touches that sent her in the proper directions. As she moved down the column of dancers, farther from him, she would flash him a comical look each time she made a mistake. When they were rejoined, she proudly declared, "I only stepped on three toes."

"All you require is a little practice, and maybe you'll only trounce one toe next time."

"I don't think there will be a next for me. Well, at least not in England."

He didn't want her to talk this way. "Are you truly leaving?"

She glanced at her aunt. "I sent missives to my Dutch cousins this morning. I don't know when I shall receive a reply, but I shall tell my uncle tonight. I'm sure he will be relieved to see me go. This will undoubtedly be my last appearance in Society."

"After all my heroics?"

She tilted her head. "But my last cherished memory of London Society will be dancing with the handsome Marquess of Exmore." She delivered her flirtatious words with comfortable ease, making it obvious that she didn't have any designs on him. This realization shouldn't have angered him, yet it did. "It's very romantic," she continued. "Worthy of the stage, in my cousin Phoebe's opinion. Of course, to be truly stage-worthy, I would have to die a tragic and dramatic death now."

"Well, I hope you won't die this tragic and dramatic death before next Tuesday. That day is part of the secret."

"Oh yes, *the* secret. You have to tell it now, for I've done what you asked and attempted to dance and injured several men."

"I don't know," he teased. "Perhaps I was presumptuous. It's a dark, lascivious secret and may involve a ritual sacrifice. It might be too much for your delicate ears."

She raised an amused brow. "Very well, keep it to yourself. Don't think of telling me."

"But it's practically bursting to be told."

"No, I shan't hear a word of it. Not a word." She moved down the line of dancers again, flashing him an impish grin.

He felt a jolt of arousal and forced himself to focus on the dance steps and his new partner.

"I saw that mischievous smile," he accused when they came together again. "Now I must tell you my secret. It can't be contained."

"I didn't smile mischievously at you." A light rallied in her eyes.

"I'm well-versed in the language of smiles, and that one was particularly mischievous, milady."

"Oh, you mean *that* one. I was smiling at the gentleman next to you."

He repressed a chuckle and feigned an angry face. "Well, for that, I won't tell you the secret about Christiaan Visser's upcoming lecture."

"What?" She dropped her hands from his grasp. All her playfulness vanished. "No, no, you must tell me! You see, he's my father's favorite," she cried. "I read to Papa from Visser's work in our garden during his last months. I have such memories. You must tell me. No jesting now."

He gently gathered her hand in his, and they turned together. "Tuesday. At the Royal Institution at eleven in the morning."

"That's four days away! It might as well be four lifetimes."

"Patience, milady."

She flicked her wrist dismissively. "I've had enough of this patience everyone speaks so highly of. I don't find it virtuous at all, but irksome."

He wanted to dance her out of the room, onto the street, and to someplace where they could laugh and talk, away from the others. He wanted her all for himself.

"Will you attend the lecture as well?" she asked.

"Would my presence trouble you?"

She studied his face. He had to look away in the heat of her frank gaze. Were the deplorable ways he had spent his days and nights since Cassandra's death evident in his eyes?

"Yes," she whispered.

He tried to disguise his disappointment. "I understand."

Her brows drew down into confusion, and then her face lit with realization. "Oh, I meant, yes, please come. No, your presence won't trouble me. I should like to see you." He wasn't sure if she was aware that her fingers had tightened gently on his. "Do you think... Do you think that we can be friends?"

He had never been friends with a woman before. The women he knew fell into the categories of family, acquaintances, or lovers, but not friends. Yet, at this moment, he wanted to be her friend more than anything. It would be something honest and innocent. Things he hadn't encountered in a long while. "I should like that very much."

The music had ended, and they were still holding hands. "Thank you for your secret," she said quietly. "And for rescuing my family and for making me laugh."

"I believe you are guilty of causing me to chuckle once or twice."

"It feels lovely to laugh again." Her eyes were gleaming like jewels under the chandelier.

"Yes."

Another few seconds ticked by before she slowly released him. "It's Phoebe's turn," she whispered, and then that impish smile he adored returned. "This dance will be the pinnacle of her Season. Do make it worthy of her theatrical imaginings. You may want to fight a duel with another dancer or create other high drama."

* * *

Annalise marveled at Exmore's potent societal powers. After an hour spent being pointedly ignored and then asked to leave, now she had to politely turn away potential dance partners. This radical change happened merely because Exmore had asked her to dance and let her glow in his brilliant light. Society was as fickle as it was shallow. Once, she had aspired to its flimsy adoration. Now, she found it ridiculous.

Nonetheless, she smiled and conversed with her new partners and apologized for stepping upon their toes. But how could she respect them after Exmore? A true gentleman wouldn't bend to the pressures of Society. He would act according to his own mind, as gallant Exmore, the modern musketeer, had.

The dance continued until the early hours. Exmore stayed for the entire time, dancing with all the young ladies. Annalise loved watching their giddy excitement at being whirled in the arms of London's premier rake—the dashing gentleman most of them had seen only from afar and excitedly gossiped about among their friends. Annalise and he crossed paths in several dances. They would share a smile, as if they were privy to a private joke. Annalise found that dancing, conversing, and simply being with others was easier with a friend, a true kindred spirit, near her.

As she was leaving, Exmore accidentally bumped against her when he hailed a servant for a glass of punch. "Four long, miserable days," he whispered. She struggled to maintain her countenance.

* * *

Back in her chamber, Annalise was too excited to sleep. Even the most boring passages of her father's esoteric academic books could do nothing to calm her spirits. Finally, she dipped her pen.

Dear Patrick,

Tonight, I am happy. Truly happy. I have become friends with the last person you would expect of befriending me. Exmore. He wrote me the kindest letter of apology, and then he arrived like a hero to save me from disgrace. Not that I minded the disgrace. London hardly matters to me anymore. You are not here. All that remains are memories, and now I find that they are not enough to sustain me. I must go forward even as I prefer to go back. I can never be the girl I was once before. I have tried, but it is futile.

I am not the only one who has changed.

I was shocked when I first saw Exmore without his mask. His eyes appeared so painfully tired—like those old, weathered men who worked on the canal boats at home. Not the eyes one expects on a marquess. His handsome face shows the wear of the dissipated life he now leads. How his wife's death has broken him. My heart hurts for him despite all the resentment I had harbored for him for so long.

I do hope our friendship survives, but I no longer hold too tightly to hope and the future. Yet, when I'm with him, I feel as though I'm coming back to life.

CHAPTER SEVEN

Like her aunt and Cousin Phoebe, Annalise was late arriving for breakfast. Her uncle had already eaten and left for an appointment with his solicitor. Without Uncle Harry presiding over the table, the dining room took on a joyous atmosphere as Phoebe regaled her sisters with her dance with Exmore, retelling every little detail.

"And his eyes were like smoldering embers. He is far and beyond more handsome than Edgar Williams, even when he was that gladiator in *Love of a Legionary*." This was fine praise indeed. "And his fingers were long and elegant, and his coat molded to his strong shoulders." Phoebe had noticed more specific details about Exmore than Annalise had. Annalise had *felt* him and his emotions, more than she had noticed his physical details.

"Didn't you dance with him too, Cousin Annalise?" Shelley asked. "What did you talk about?"

Annalise had opened her mouth to answer when the

slamming of the front door boomed through the house.

"Annalise!" her uncle yelled. "Get into my parlor, you reckless, foolish girl."

Her aunt burst into tears. "Oh no! What have I done?"

"You have done nothing, Aunt Sally." Annalise rested her linen beside her plate and rose. "I've managed to anger him."

This must be about the ball last night and her notorious dance with Exmore. She knew gossip spread every morning in London like fire on dry straw. She wasn't angry or annoyed, merely resigned.

Her uncle had reached the parlor first. He still wore his hat, which he tore off and threw onto the sofa. "Why must you make a mockery of me again?"

"Again?"

"You can't comprehend it, can you? When Exmore sent Patrick Hume away, the marquess cut me. I wasn't good enough."

"I don't—"

"You will talk when I give you leave to do so." He paced near her. "Word is all over London about you. You seem to relish being the center of attention even if it requires making a fool of yourself."

"I do not. I care nothing for Society."

He laughed and gazed upward. "I'm not sure which is worse, having Mr.

Danvers, a prominent gentleman, almost turn away a member of my family, or I should say my *wife's* family— you couldn't possibly be my blood relation—or having you especially noticed by the Marquess of Exmore."

He edged even closer. She sensed something darkly predatory about him, as though he took pleasure in demeaning her. "What game are you playing?" he asked.

"I'm not playing any game."

"Exmore may be a deplorable rake, but you are far, far beneath him. He will not propose to you. If you aren't good enough for his untitled cousin, you surely aren't good enough for him. You must hold another attraction for him." She felt her uncle's moist, warm breath on her face. "What have you done, my girl? I will send you packing if you have behaved with any impropriety."

Annalise straightened her spine. "You are correct. The marquess's station is above mine. For the sake of your wife's and your daughter's place in Society, I danced with him. To my knowledge, I have not behaved improperly. The marquess and I are… friends."

Her uncle thought this was wildly funny. He clutched his belly, he laughed so hard. "Friends? You are *friends* with a marquess? *Friends* with a libertine?" He seized her wrist, squeezing it. "Listen to me, there can be no friendship between an eligible marquess and a young lady of your station. You have no idea of the ways of the world. You are nothing but a plaything to such a man. No better than those actresses he seeks pleasure with."

Annalise yanked her arm free. "Do not speak to me that way!"

"I am your guardian. I will speak to you as I please."

"There is no legal paper stating that you are my guardian!" Annalise fired back. "It is all in your imagination. I am an independent woman of my own means. And I very much know how the world works, and I do not approve of it."

Again, he laughed. "An independent woman? Such a mythical creature cannot exist. Women can't take care of themselves. And the world does not seek the approval of a silly girl. Exmore can only intend to get you into his bed so that Society will further mock me."

Annalise took several breaths to keep from hurling insults at her uncle. When she trusted her voice again, she spoke, low and controlled. "I have written to my cousins in Holland. As soon as I receive a positive response, I shall remove from your house."

"No one will have you, Annalise. They have more sense than to let you into their homes. You should be nicer to me.

I'm the only one who will take care of you. Everyone else sees you for the addle-brained girl that you are."

Annalise had had enough of his invective. She turned and strode out of the room.

Her uncle shouted to her retreating back, "You will not speak to the marquess again. You will not encourage him, or I shall have to do something drastic. Something you don't want to know about. Do you understand?"

* * *

Annalise rested on her bed and pondered leaving for the Continent tomorrow without waiting for replies from her Dutch cousins. She hadn't visited Holland before and knew nothing of where to live or how society worked there, but it had to be better than living under her uncle's roof and suffering his taunts. Exmore had kindly saved her from social ruin, but the idea of attending more balls and parties was enervating. Annalise almost wished he hadn't come to her rescue, then she wouldn't have to bother with Society anymore.

But if he hadn't appeared, she wouldn't have found out about the Visser lecture.

Nor would she have laughed.

How did this happen? Once, her mind had been filled with what parties she would attend and what she would wear to them. She had thought of each party as a chance to meet her potential husband. She had been consumed with falling in love then, even before she met Patrick.

Now, the only thing she truly anticipated was attending a botany lecture with Exmore. A friend.

Annalise took out a fresh sheet of stationery and dipped her pen.

Dear Patrick,

Can a man and woman simply enjoy each other's company without any further entanglement?

I know that I need to release you from my heart and marry someone else. I truly want to fall in love again, yet it frightens me.

My heart is only beginning to recover from your departure and my parents' deaths. It is tired, and I feel that I don't even know my own mind anymore.

I only want a friend who is a kindred spirit. Someone to talk to.

Annalise stopped, letting her pen hover over her words.

Alas, I shouldn't be friends with Exmore for Phoebe's and my aunt's sake. They will have to continue to live with Uncle Harry when I'm far away, across an ocean.

Again, she paused to think.

I shall meet Exmore at the lecture as I said I would and then cease any further contact.

Yet, he makes me laugh.

* * *

Exmore woke up, for once feeling something other than the heavy listlessness of another day before him. His mind was clear, free of the dullness and pain of overindulgence. In his first waking thoughts, he remembered that he would attend a botany lecture in three days' time. He chuckled aloud. Hadn't he dreaded botany at Cambridge? Hadn't he used those lectures to catch up on his sleep? Now, this lecture and seeing his new friend were the only things he truly looked forward to, and he hadn't been excited about anything in a long time.

Throughout the morning, thoughts of Annalise drifted through his mind. He didn't try to stop them, because they pushed away the gloominess. He noticed the details of people and things—the expression on the footman's face, the gleam on the iron railing outside his home, and the fresh-bread scent wafting from the baker's shop. The day felt buoyant, like it was water that sustained him, rather than letting him sink. In a bookstore, he found a journal with an article on African orchids that he thought Annalise would enjoy. He went out in

Society that evening, hoping to come across her to discuss it, but unfortunately, she didn't appear at any of the parties that he attended. He bought the journal the next day, marked the pages, and sent it to her, bundled with a pink orchid and pithy note that ended with, *Looking forward to our grand secret.*

That night, Exmore attended a painfully insipid play titled *Love's Joy and Misery*, which, of course, was all the rage in London. He hadn't realized he had enlisted for theatrical torture until after he had purchased the box and suffered through the opening scene. The second and third scenes only compounded his misery, and he was about to leave when he spied Annalise across the theater, in a box with Mr. Sommerville's family. She was close enough to the stage that he could train his opera glass on her and pretend to watch the play, all the while safely studying her in delicious detail.

Maybe it wasn't such a horrid play, after all.

While the Sommerville ladies wore tight, fashionable curls adorned with beads and other paraphernalia, Annalise's hair fell in straight strands around her cheeks. It had the appearance of being hastily pinned up, yet it suited her—unaffected and natural. She had wound her shawl around herself like a comfortable blanket. Her cousin Phoebe sat forward in her seat, practically leaning over the railing, clearly enraptured by the sentimental rubbish. From time to time, Phoebe whispered excitedly to Annalise and pointed to the stage. Annalise didn't share her cousin's enthusiasm. He watched, amused, as she tried to conceal her chuckles at the supposedly serious moments, rolled her eyes at the trite conventions, and arched a brow at the hackneyed, melodramatic plot turns. He wished she were beside him, so they could exchange sarcastic commentary.

Exmore's favorite part of the play happened when Phoebe caught Annalise yawning during a supposedly heart-wrenching love scene. A terrible sin! Although he couldn't hear what they were saying, the animated conversation between the two ladies was far more entertaining to watch than what was on the stage.

At intermission, the lobby was flooded with people. Their

chatter, echoing in the great hall, formed a roar of sound. Exmore edged through the crowd, the smell of perfumes and hair oils assaulting his nose as he searched for Annalise. He finally spotted her leaning against a marble column, just outside a circle formed by her uncle and his family. His heart quickened, and a smile spread over his mouth.

Her eyes widened with recognition as he drew nearer. He raised his fingers, a small, silent greeting. Her lips parted. She glanced at her uncle and then at Exmore again. She held his gaze for several moments, before turning and slipping into the crowd.

What?

It took a moment for him to fully comprehend the small exchange.

Annalise had cut him.

He stood there for another few seconds, staring at the column where she had stood, his anger flooding in.

How dare she treat him this way?

No woman had ever turned him away.

Did she realize how many other women vied daily for his attention?

He had an urge to chase after the ungrateful lady and tell her that he regretted saving her from social disgrace.

These were ungenerous thoughts, yet they bubbled in his mind.

He strode back to his seat. Why was he so wildly angry? Not annoyed, as he should have been, but viscerally irate. Hot, black rage coursed through him. When the next act started, he trained his glass on Annalise.

She sat, expressionless and wooden, watching the play.

Scene after scene he watched her, stewing in his anger and mentally admonishing himself. All the while, he waited for her to look his way.

What was he doing?

Then it finally happened. She glanced in his direction. Their eyes met. Then she glanced back at the stage.

Damn her.

He bolted from his seat and left the theater. He walked in the cold night, avoiding eye contact with prostitutes, peddlers, and conning thieves until he came upon a grimy tavern and entered. He edged through the eclectic, drunken crowd of dock workers, solicitors, seamstresses, and ladies of pleasure until he found a quiet corner in which to hide. He ordered a brandy, and when it arrived, he studied its warm, amber glow in the firelight and sank into his anger at Annalise.

He had saved her from social ruin, and this was how she thanked him. Did she somehow think she was his better? He was a marquess. She was a nobody. Worse than a nobody, she was almost an outcast before he had stepped in.

A drunken customer began singing at the bar. Exmore almost yelled for him to shut his hole, but the man's lush tenor was surprisingly good. Wonderful, to be more accurate. He wasn't a trained opera singer, but he had the voice of the common people. He sang of the loss of his love to another man. The tavern turned quiet and somber. The man's plaintive singing reached to the pain that had driven Exmore's fellow drinkers to this grim hellhole to drown their despair.

Exmore stared at the tenor but didn't see him. His beautiful voice summoned Annalise's face in Exmore's mind as she had been the night they danced. How her sweet smile, which lit her eyes, had made his heart light, as though he could rise above the disaster of his life.

His anger receded, leaving the seemingly bottomless despondency that had consumed his life since his wife's passing.

Why did Annalise have to turn away from him?

CHAPTER EIGHT

He told himself he wouldn't go to the lecture. The morning Visser was speaking, Exmore instead headed out in the rain to a club that was in the opposite direction of the Royal Institution. Yet, when he saw Colonel Lewiston sitting by the window, Exmore kept on walking. At another club, the conversations of others rankled Exmore's nerves, and he couldn't keep Annalise out of his thoughts. He wanted to confront her and understand why she had cut him. He composed a mental peal he desired to ring over her, which contained the words *gratitude* and *kindness*, but not the phrase, *Why did you hurt my feelings?* Maybe he had to solve the mystery of her sudden coldness, or express how he felt, even if she didn't care, or merely see her, but he was driven into the pounding rain to Visser's lecture after all.

Exmore didn't spy Annalise among the dusty men in ill-fitting clothes crowding about a man who Exmore assumed was Visser. The gentlemen appeared to know each other and were excitedly chatting about their own botanical studies.

They didn't notice Exmore slip into a chair at the back of the small room. The clock set on the mantel showed three minutes until eleven. What if she didn't come? What if he had to suffer through a lecture by Visser, who clearly struggled with English, from the snatches of conversation Exmore had overheard. At five after the hour, Visser cleared his throat, and the other gentlemen took their seats. Exmore felt deflated, frustrated, and angry after all the mental drama that had driven him here. She wasn't coming, despite having pleaded for the details of lecture, after she had said she could barely wait for days. His ire at her rose even higher for trapping him in a boring lecture.

But mostly he felt let down.

In his periphery, he saw a flutter of fabric beyond the threshold of the door and turned. She appeared, a lovely smile radiating from her face despite the wet curls plastered to her cheeks and the water that dripped from her hem. She held a leather portfolio under her arm. He couldn't deny the lightning sensation in his chest at her sight.

"Mr. Visser." She curtsied. "My father, Franz Van Der Keer, and I hold you in great esteem." She spoke quickly, her voice breathy with excitement. "I read your book on your Australian journeys to him in the last weeks of his life. I cherish your work and the memories it has given me."

"Franz Van Der Keer," Visser said and then continued in slow, laboring English. "A very good friend. Pardon me. You speak very fast."

Annalise switched to his native Dutch. Visser's stiff expression relaxed. Whatever he said to her caused Annalise to clutch her hand to her heart, tears appearing in her eyes. Although Visser gestured to a vacant chair in the front row, she strolled back to Exmore and slipped into the seat next to him and smiled as if the night at the theater hadn't happened.

"Sorry I'm rather late." She set her portfolio on a neighboring chair. "I walked here. Although, I'm sure it appears as though I swam the entire distance."

He tried to remain angry, but the emotion was cracking

about the edges. He couldn't help but quip, "Don't worry, you look quite intelligent."

"Is that a compliment or an insult of omission?" Her eyes sparkled. "I'm sorry I didn't speak to you the other night at the theater. Wasn't it a dreadful play? Phoebe thinks it's akin to Shakespeare, no doubt due to the handsomeness of the leading man. You see, my uncle… to say that he violently disapproves of our friendship is too mild a description of his feelings. So please excuse my rudeness. I only thought of you and your well-being… and, well, my well-being, to be truthful."

She smiled again and turned her attention to Visser, leaving Exmore to study her profile and to ponder how hours and hours of anguish evaporated in a matter of seconds.

The first ten minutes of the lecture were rather painful as Visser struggled with English, often looking to Annalise for help. After a point, and to the great pleasure of his audience, Visser switched to his native tongue and allowed Annalise to translate. Exmore turned his chair, putting his back to the wall beside the window, and watched Annalise's animated face as she retold Visser's stories of hacking through jungles or hiking across African plains searching for unknown species. He could contentedly have spent the entire lecture just listening to the sound of comforting rain and her gentle voice weaving through English, Dutch, and bits of Latin.

Visser spoke for little over an hour. Afterward, the other attendees clustered around his table, where various bones, furs, and dried plants were displayed. Exmore waited with Annalise outside the circle of men.

"What's in the portfolio?" Exmore asked her.

"My father's work. I wanted to show it to Mr. Visser."

"May I see?"

She opened the portfolio on a table pushed against the wall. Exmore made approving noises as she explained each one to him, although he really didn't know what he was looking at. He just enjoyed how her excitement transmuted into him and the tingle that rushed up his arm when she touched him.

Soon, Visser joined them and began asking Annalise questions in Dutch as he flipped through her images.

"Ah," he said, drawing one out.

She emitted a squeaking sound and tried to yank it from his hands. "Oh, no, that's mine!"

Both Visser and Exmore quickly reacted to keep her from hiding the illustration. Exmore held it up as Visser pointed to different aspects, speaking in admiring tones, as Annalise wildly—and beautifully—blushed.

Later, after they had helped Visser pack up his specimens, Annalise and Exmore stood in the paneled hall outside the lecture room. The rain was coming down hard, but inside the building, its sound was muffled to a lull.

"So, don't keep it a secret. What did Mr. Visser say about your brilliant illustration?" Exmore asked.

She waved her hand, flustered. "It's not brilliant."

"Don't disagree with me. I'm a marquess."

"Oh, I forgot that I must always agree with a marquess."

"It saved many a life in medieval times."

She glanced comically heavenward. "Ah, the feudal days of yore. How I don't miss them."

"Come now, what did Mr. Visser say?" he insisted.

Her lovely blush returned. He adored how it spread across cheeks and onto her upturned nose. "He liked it. He truly admired it and asked that I send him more. Can you believe that? The renowned Mr. Christiaan Visser actually approves of my work!"

"Of course, I can. You are a naturalist like your father. Even though I have no idea what I'm talking about, I can tell that you are far more talented and knowledgeable than those other fusty gentlemen here today."

She shook her head. "No, no, I'm a woman."

"A woman *and* a brilliant naturalist."

"Could you see me hacking through the jungles, escaping blood-thirsty tribes, fording rapids, and cresting summits in the quest for an exotic fern or such?" The dreamy quality of her gaze betrayed her incredulous tone.

"Absolutely. The first thing that comes to mind when I think of you. May I come along to the jungle? I'll carry your supplies and do the hacking and fording."

"How chivalrous of you. Yes, do come. Let's run away."

She was laughing, but he realized that he wouldn't have said no if she were deadly serious. *Yes. Run away from all of this.*

"Aye, miss, there you are, miss." A fortyish woman in a heavy wool coat and ruffled bonnet rounded the last set of stairs. "London was evil before, but in the rain, you would think it's Satan's own parlor. I wandered about for an hour before I found decent thread that wouldn't break off the spool. How was the lecture?"

"Wonderful," Annalise replied. "Heavenly. Mr. Visser knew Papa and truly enjoyed his work."

"But he was especially impressed with Miss Van Der Keer's illustration," Exmore interjected before a proper introduction.

"Aye, she's a special young lady who doesn't belong among the sinners," the woman said. "She needs to be back in the country with the flowers and green fields, not in this teeming rubbish heap."

"Lord Exmore, may I present my faithful servant, Mrs. Edward Bailey. She accompanied me here. We sneaked away from my uncle's house together."

"Partners in crime." He winked at Mrs. Bailey. "Pleased to make your acquaintance. Thank you for taking such good care of Miss Van Der Keer."

Mrs. Bailey made a click deep in her throat, clearly intimidated by Exmore's title, and stepped away. He wished politeness didn't demand introductions. He would have loved to continue speaking with the earthy, no-nonsense Mrs. Bailey.

"Did you really sneak away to attend?" he asked Annalise.

"Actually, I was fibbing. I simply said that I planned to attend a naturalist lecture and that Mrs. Bailey would attend me, and everyone scurried away like I had announced that I had contracted the plague."

He chuckled.

She glanced at a window in an empty lecture room, and her brows furrowed. "Alas, I fear we must brave the rain again."

"Must you?" he asked. "There is a warm tea shop tucked away around the corner, perfect for waiting out the deluge."

She paused, considering, and then shook her head. "I shouldn't…"

"I can't let you go out in the wet and cold. You will most certainly catch the dreaded plague or, at the least, a deadly chill."

"My goodness, you make hot tea sound like life or death."

"Did you ever doubt it?"

"But if my uncle finds out…"

"I'll be surprised if we aren't the only people there. And there's a table practically hidden around a chimney. No one will see you. So, you have no good reason to decline and risk your life." Exmore had spent several mornings at the tea shop, hiding and gulping down strong tea, trying to chase away all that had happened the previous night.

"But will there be good conversation?" Annalise asked.

"Only the best, of course."

She glanced again at the pounding rain on the window and then at him. "Well, if we aren't going adventuring in a jungle, we may as well have tea. Who cares what my vile uncle thinks? Let's go."

"There's the old Miss Van Der Keer. I wondered where she had gone."

"Oh, she comes out from time to time—as reckless and foolish as ever."

* * *

Annalise knew she shouldn't have followed him to the tea shop, but she positively dreaded returning to Wigmore Street. The day had been perfect, the best she had had in months, and she wasn't ready for it to end. She wanted to hang on to its shine a little longer.

Exmore was correct. The tea shop was quite cozy, and he

led her to a table that indeed was almost hidden behind the chimney and tucked in the corner, where the light was dim. The candle burning on the table gave the impression that it was nighttime.

Mrs. Bailey learned that the shop owner had been born in her home village, and the two fell into a conversation about whom they knew and whom they were related to. The rain thundered on the roof and windows, and steam rose from Exmore's tea, curling about his mesmerizing eyes and gentle smile. Annalise felt her muscles relax as a deep contentment settled over her.

Exmore poured a few drops of cream in his black tea and swirled it with a spoon. "I have to admit that I was rather upset at you before the lecture."

"Me? What am I guilty of? Do make it interesting. Larceny of crown jewels, disorderly conduct at Almack's."

"No, no, because you ignored me at the theater. But then you prettily apologized, and my grudge disappeared as if I hadn't been nursing it for days."

How odd that he should be angry at her for not speaking with him. She hadn't thought she would be significant in his vast, colorful universe. "I'm sorry. I wanted to speak to you about the fascinating article you sent me. I've been thinking about it for days. Alas, my uncle read your letter when it arrived, and well, Mount Vesuvius erupts more peacefully. Might I suggest not sending letters to me, or if you do, don't write, 'Looking forward to our grand secret.'"

"Dear Lord, I'm dreadfully sorry."

She flicked her hand dismissively. "It's ridiculous. My uncle has lascivious suspicions. He thinks that you couldn't possibly be friends with me. Only nefarious things can exist between you and a lady such as myself."

"Such as yourself? What's wrong with you?"

She studied him. He was a handsome man, but not as handsome as Patrick. Or perhaps he was a different sort of handsome. He was a little more hard-featured and intense than her former suitor. He was dark to Patrick's gingery, golden looks. In any case, it didn't seem right that he should be here, talking to her, when he could bask in the adoration of the *ton*. "You're a shining English god, living high on Mount Mayfair, and I'm a lowly, untouchable, mortal woman, baked in common mud and loitering about the edges of society."

"Do you think that? That we can't truly be friends?"

She glanced at the liquid in her cup. "I really want to be friends," she whispered. "You are the most interesting person I know, well, now that my father is dead." She lifted her cup to take a sip, but then put it back down before it reached her lips. "I know I need to marry. I know it's how I'm supposed to spend my waking hours in London, thinking about what I should wear, where I should be seen, all in the hopes of securing a husband. But…" She gazed at Exmore. "I'm tired. I'm so tired. Do you understand?"

He gave a bitter laugh. "Very much."

"I've spent all my time worrying about my parents and taking care of them and my home, and I'm not ready to be thrown into marriage just yet. I want space to breathe. I feel like I've lost myself, and I'm trying to find her. And I never really forgot…" She trailed off, too ashamed to talk about Patrick. She changed the subject. "I can't imagine that you could possibly love someone after your wife's passing. To me, you will always be married to her. I remember how much you admitted you loved her that night… well, the night of my infamous midnight visit. Her loss must be devastating."

He shifted in his chair and glanced toward the counter. "Yes," he said quietly. He ran his thumb down his cup. "The night of your so-called infamous midnight visit, you swore that you would always love Patrick. And as you look at me now, I believe you still do."

What to say? It seemed foolish to admit to all the hours she had thought about him, the stacks of letters that she had never sent. Now it was her turn to look away. "I do." She shook her head. "I know he doesn't love me. You don't have to tell me that. He never wrote to me. My love is all my own."

Exmore said nothing, but when she ventured a glance at him, she saw pity in his eyes.

"Do you ever hear from him?" She blurted the question that had been in her mind since the night they had danced together. "No." She raised her palm, catching herself. "Don't answer that." Yet, she paused, waiting for an answer. What was she doing? She already knew the answer. Hearing it wouldn't soothe her hurt but make it worse. Yet, she had to hear him say it.

"Yes," he said slowly, drawing out the one syllable. "I do."

She had gone too far already, so she kept going down this painful course. "Does he ever mention me?"

"No, he doesn't." He was holding something back. It lurked behind his words.

"I fear you are not telling the truth."

He paused for a moment. She could tell he was choosing his words to tell her gently. At last, he said in careful tones, "Your assessment that he doesn't love you is correct. Please don't ask me for more."

The rain picked up. A gust of wind splattered it on the windows. "He probably thanked you for your counsel in the matter."

Exmore remained quiet. She could see the back of his jaw work.

"You once said that one day I would love more wisely, but clearly I haven't," she quipped.

He reached across the table, touching her arm. "Please ignore what I said that night. All of it."

Her eyes burned with the beginnings of tears. "I thought of him every day. I spoke to him as if he were there. I just needed... I needed someone to talk to. I couldn't share my worries with my mother or father. They had to contend with dying. I felt…" She stopped, not wanting to admit how alone and scared she had been. "I guess that's why I came back to London. I was chasing memories of a better time."

"And now you are leaving."

She smiled. "I didn't find what I was looking for. It's gone forever." She turned, self-conscious, having admitted too many honest, vulnerable feelings. She no longer wanted to talk about herself. "Did you have someone to talk to after your wife's death?"

He thrummed the table with his thumb. She noticed his lashes. They were thick and curled, the kind women coveted. They softened his otherwise hard features.

"My wife's pregnancy was difficult." His voice was hollow. "She couldn't keep down any drink or food. Then she contracted a chill, and her body… she hadn't the strength."

Annalise took his hand that rested on the small table beside hers. "I'm sorry."

"But the answer to your question is no, I had no one with whom to confide my feelings." There was an odd quality to his voice, something she couldn't articulate. But he slid his fingers between her gloved ones and gave them a small squeeze. She waited for him to say more, but he didn't.

"I was alone because, well, I was truly alone in the country, unless you count the sheep, but they aren't very commiserating," she noted. "I've spoken to enough to say that the species, as a whole, is not a sympathetic one. Yet, you had people buzzing all about you, and you still felt alone. Feeling alone is so personal."

He tilted his head, his eyes burrowing into hers. "Do you feel alone now?"

She shook her head. "Not today. Despite the rain, today is lovely, for I have excellent company and tea. There is little else to want."

"I concur, my friend."

"Friend," she echoed. The word, the pressure of his hand on hers, and the kindness in his expression sent the smile that warmed her lips to her heart. Several seconds passed in silence. It wasn't an awkward, dangling pause of not knowing what to say, but a full and content silence. Her father's kind of soothing quiet. This silence said, *I'm here. You aren't alone. We've found each other. We are true friends.*

Moments later, they spoke again. Not returning to the subject of pain and loss but ranging across topics. He listened to her, leaning back in his chair, shaking his foot where he had braced it casually over his knee. When he spoke, he leaned forward with a smile twisting the side of his mouth, often playing devil's advocate. He declared outrageous things that he seriously couldn't believe and made her laugh. Cup after cup of tea was poured and biscuits were consumed, until Mrs. Bailey edged over, breaking into the invisible circle that seemed to have formed around Annalise and Exmore.

"Miss, I don't mean to interrupt, but it's almost three, and the rain has stopped."

"Oh heavens, I've lost all knowledge of time. I must go. My uncle!" Annalise gathered her things. "But think of the pleasure he will have in berating me."

She affected her uncle's tone as Mrs. Bailey helped her slip on her coat. "Annalise, you are late because you attended a lecture. See what happens when you attempt to think?"

Exmore seized her naked wrist. Somewhere in the conversation, she had unconsciously drawn off her gloves. A jolt of strange electricity ran over her skin. "There's a chemistry lecture next week," he said. "Please attend. You can ignore me all week, pretend I'm a homely insect that you should smash under your foot, anything to appease your vile uncle, but… but come to the chemistry lecture."

"I don't know. What if people—"

"It promises many colorful explosions."

She chuckled. "Oh, things being blown up is so very tempting. But—"

"You can sit on one side of the room and I on the other. When you see me, feign outrage and loudly announce that you would have never attended had you known I would be present. Once our fierce animosity is established, we can slip away afterwards and hide in our favorite tea shop."

She tried to object, but his imploring eyes melted her words away. "Very well. But promise to be as fascinating as you've been today."

"I wouldn't dream of disappointing your expectations of me."

She laughed as she picked up her portfolio and headed for the door. There, she stopped, turned, and walked back to him

A smile dawned on his face that caused her heart to rise.

"Did you forget something?" he asked.

She carefully cracked the portfolio and drew out her illustration. "Yes, I forgot to give you this." She set it on the table and hurried away, pretending not to hear his objections.

She met Mrs. Bailey outside the door of the tea shop.

"I don't care what your uncle and them at his home say," Mrs. Bailey said. "I know people. I can peer into their hearts. And this talk of the marquess being a cruel rake is pure rubbish. He is a good man. Good like my departed Edward, please his loving soul."

CHAPTER NINE

A game began between Exmore and Annalise: the ignore-each-other game. He left his house every night to search for her. Sometimes, he found her at the opera or theater, where their gazes might accidentally meet to share in a laugh or make an unspoken sarcastic remark. Just being in the room with her, the light in her eyes, the benign brush of their arms, gave him peace. Her presence moored him. While she orbited his world, the days no longer stretched before him like an endless ocean. The gray sameness that characterized his days lifted. He felt like he was returning to himself, the old demons fleeing.

The day before the chemistry lecture, he headed to his club with his correspondences and a journal. He had a quickness to his mind and step. His former vitality was slowly returning with more sleep, less brandy, and less time at gambling tables. Yet, his good mood dampened when he strolled into the club's morning room to find Colonel Lewiston and Wallis Hume sharing a table.

Wallis hailed him. "Ahh, the man I desired to see. Come, come sit. We have a pressing matter to discuss." He gestured to a passing servant. "More tea, please."

Exmore glanced about the crowded room. All the tables and chairs were occupied with men smoking and reading papers or discussing the day's politics. He was trapped.

"Sit, my good man," Wallis urged him, oblivious to the invisible current of animosity between Lewiston and Exmore. "You are looking quite well. You must have taken my advice."

"Err, yes," Exmore agreed, remaining standing. He didn't remember Wallis's advice. People had been trying to offer Exmore their so-called wise words since Cassandra's death. Exmore conveniently forgot all the inane counsel.

"Who is she?"

Exmore blinked. "Pardon?"

"The lady," Wallis prompted. "Remember, I told you to find a good lady. So, who is she? I'm an old man who rarely gets out to parties, and unfortunately, I hear the gossip days after everyone else. You must tell me."

Lewiston tilted his head and studied Exmore. His pale silvery eyes reminded him of cold, stark, snow-laden landscapes.

"No one," Exmore muttered. "I have found no one."

"Sit down." Wallis patted the armrest of the empty chair beside him. "We must discuss Patrick."

Exmore sank into the empty chair. Lewiston shifted in his. One of them would have to go soon.

"I have heard very troubling reports, indeed," Wallis said. "I understand that brazen girl Miss Annalise Van Der Keer has been in London for a few weeks now and is making her way into some of the finest homes. It was relayed to me only hours ago that she would be attending Lord Warrington's ball this evening. Lord Warrington! The Prince Regent shall be there. To think he would be sharing a room with that… fiendish woman. Oh, had I known sooner, this wouldn't have happened."

This was what Wallis needed to speak about? Exmore

looked down to where his hands had balled into fists. He spread his fingers as a servant arrived with more tea. He could feel Lewiston's blue-flame eyes on him. He hated being so close to the man. Although they rarely spoke, Lewiston possessed a silent smugness in his power over Exmore.

"What say you, Lord Exmore?" Wallis continued when Exmore didn't answer. "Surely you are outraged."

"I believe Lord Exmore has danced with her," Lewiston volunteered.

Exmore's restraint was cracking. How easy it would have been to strike the man's handsome face. Perhaps blacken those pretty eyes, as Exmore had wanted to for years.

"He has?" Wallis cried, outraged. "Is this true?"

"Yes," Exmore said, forcing himself to sit back in his chair. He decided that the best course to protect Annalise was to appear nonchalant, as if she meant nothing to him.

"I say, you of all men should know her true nature," Wallis said. "She's a termagant. A hellion." He waved his hand dismissively. "No doubt, you had to dance out of politeness."

Exmore didn't trust himself to answer. He drew a long sip of tea instead. Lewiston had remained silent but looked on with a small amused hike to his lips. What did he know? Lewiston always had the advantage of knowing more than Exmore did.

"Lord Exmore, I fear for Patrick," Wallis continued. "I don't want that wild gel chasing after him. He's an important man now. Five thousand a year. He doesn't need her sort dragging him to her depths, scaring away more promising prospects." Wallis looked at Exmore for agreement.

Exmore spoke in low, measured tones, aware that Lewiston was watching him closely. "I think you would find that Miss Van Der Keer has matured. I haven't witnessed any of her former misbehavior of which you speak."

"But what happens when Patrick arrives?" Wallis pressed on. "She knows he's coming. That's why she's here. She has the mind of a cunning minx."

"I feel you are mistaken." Exmore could no longer conceal

his anger. It ground in his voice.

Wallis patted his armrest. "I want you to talk to her father."

"He is dead," Exmore said bluntly.

"You appear to know a great deal about Miss Van Der Keer," Lewiston said slowly, slyly.

Exmore ground his molars. How had he fallen into this delicate game of societal chess? He had to move carefully to protect his queen.

"Then who chaperones her?" Wallis demanded. "Her uncle again? That insidiously ambitious man. You must talk to him. Remind him of his and his niece's station."

"Which is?" Exmore snapped.

"Her uncle is a hairbreadth above middling, and she herself is barely respectable." Wallis's voice was raised, thundering over the din. "You must speak to her uncle and find some means, some leverage on the man to have his niece removed from London before she can get her scheming claws into my boy. She means to make him the contempt of gentle society and ruin all he has become."

Exmore bolted to his feet, shaking the table, splashing tea.

"Come now, what is this?" Wallis demanded, lifting his tea-soaked linen from his lap.

"Very well." Exmore's voice was a low, hoarse whisper. "I shall speak to Miss Van Der Keer and warn her away from Patrick. I shall suggest that she find a gentleman who knows his own mind and doesn't require his papa to solve all his problems."

Wallis's mouth dropped. "Are you insulting my son? I say!"

Lewiston released a low chuckle. Damn the man.

"You asked me to warn away Miss Van Der Keer," Exmore said. "I'm merely thinking of a course that will work."

The old man's eyes narrowed as his mind worked. "I say," he said slowly. "Maybe that gel's sad charms have got to you in your weakened state. Listen to me, my lord, stay away from her low sort. Her kind will say and do anything to ingratiate themselves to their betters."

Exmore knew he wasn't acting wisely, but he wouldn't stand to have Annalise slandered. He leaned down, placing both hands on the table, his face inches from Wallis's.

"If you say a word against Miss Van Der Keer," he said in a low growl, "I will sink Patrick's prospects in this city forever. He may as well have stayed India." Exmore gathered his letters and journal and strolled out, stunned silence in his wake.

Outside in the vivid sunlight, his body quaked. What had he done? He was supposed to keep things under wraps with Annalise. Their friendship was the purest, most lovely thing he had in his life. Of course, he had to slip up and destroy it. Damn him.

If anything grew from this unfortunate meeting with Wallis and Lewiston, he would do everything in his power to protect Annalise. He would shoulder all the blame. Until then, he would remain silent and hope nothing came of it. But he had a clawing feeling that a powerful wave was rolling in from the sea about to crash upon him.

* * *

Annalise glanced about Lord Warrington's ballroom, searching for Exmore. Some evenings they crossed paths, other nights they didn't. She floundered the nights he wasn't around. Even though they pretended not to notice each other, when he was about she was aware of his every move. She could detect the slightest raised, amused brow or tightened lips suppressing laughter. When it was safe, their gazes would meet, and they would say without speaking, *I know you are here. All is well.* Strange how she needed only a single look from him to feel strong again.

She didn't see him among the faces, but counseled herself that she had only arrived, and the musicians were still warming up. There was still time.

She continued to furtively search for Exmore, and at the same time, she tried to assure Phoebe that her hair still appeared beautiful, even without the strand of adorning beads that had broken in the carriage on the way over.

"But I had my hair in papers all night and morning for this coiffure!" Phoebe complained.

"Don't be so crestfallen. If you were to meet a gentleman tonight, and he were to fall in love with you only for your coiffure, I don't think you should have him."

"It's still vexing."

"What if I discreetly take a leaf from this palm and place it your hair? Would that do instead?" Annalise reached for the palm, knowing well she wasn't going to snap off a branch of the hostess's magnificent plant, but she enjoyed teasing Phoebe and casting her from her frustrations.

"No!" Phoebe gasped.

"But if you don't stand beside the palm for the remainder of the evening, no one will know." She laughed. "Come now, you know I'm jesting."

"Ah, Annalise, there you are."

Annalise whirled around to find her uncle had materialized behind her. He normally didn't attend parties, but he couldn't turn down Lord Warrington's invitation. It was the greatest home he had been accepted in. His pleasant smile looked like a tight, ill-fitting garment on his face. Beside him stood a trim, handsome man possessing an intense face accented by startling pale eyes.

"Colonel Lewiston, may I present my niece Miss Van Der Keer." Her uncle had taken on the polite tone he used in public. "The colonel has expressed a desire to dance with you."

"Thank you." Annalise curtsied. "I should be very happy to dance." And she was. She had danced enough now that she no longer feared causing bodily injury to others.

"There now," her uncle said to Colonel Lewiston. "She is tame enough. Enjoy her."

Annalise took the colonel's offered arm and tried to make small conversation to conceal her embarrassment at her uncle's demeaning treatment of her. "I'm sorry, but I am at a disadvantage," she said as he led her to the dance floor. "For you seem to know me, but I do not think I've met you before." She would have certainly remembered such a striking gentleman.

"I do not attend many balls." He spoke in a blunt, clipped manner. "In truth, I knew you were coming here tonight, and I sought out your uncle to present you."

"Oh," Annalise said, because that was politer than asking, *And why were you searching me out?*

"You see, I came to warn you," he said as they took their positions for a quadrille.

"Concerning?" Annalise was becoming nervous. Who was this Colonel Lewiston?

"I'm sorry for my abruptness and harsh manner. I am a military man, and I lack the talent of delicate conversation. But it has been made apparent to me that Lord Exmore holds you in much esteem."

The dancers began to move, but Annalise remained still. "Why do you say this? It is not true."

He held out his hand. She stared at it and took it only after a neighboring dancer bumped into her.

"Please heed my advice," he said, leading her in a turn. "Take care to avoid him."

"Why do you speak this way to me?"

He edged closer to her than the dance dictated. "He cares little for your feelings," he said, only loud enough for her to hear. "He is a marquess and will have his way."

"Sir, again, do not speak to me this way. It is impolite."

"The truth is often impolite. He misused a lady. A lady I loved. He destroyed her gentle heart and her life. He... he killed her."

"What?" She yanked from his clasp. The dancing couples beside them turned, eyeing them. Annalise wanted to walk away, no, run, but knew the best tactic was to stay in the dance and then quietly slip into the crowd. Causing a scene wouldn't improve the situation.

"My apologies." He lifted her hand and drew her back into the dance formation. "You may misunderstand. He did not kill her with his hands. He tortured her heart, slowly draining away her life. She died of grief."

Sorrow imbued his dramatic proclamation, and normally Annalise would have been more sympathetic, but she felt only annoyance. "People do not die of grief, Colonel Lewiston. I should know. Please do not speak any more on this topic. We are at a ball. Tell me, have you attended Astley's Circus or Kew Gardens?" She pointedly attempted to change the subject to a more proper one.

"As a compassionate gentleman, I urge you, do not fall under Exmore's influence. Stay away from him."

The only man she wanted to stay away from was the colonel.

She knew Exmore led another life as a rake in the dark belly of London. He visited places and did things she didn't care to know about. She knew that sorrow changed a person, driving him or her to act in desperate ways. She couldn't judge him, especially when she was ignorant of the particulars concerning Colonel Lewiston or his lady friend. But she didn't want to be dragged into any sordid situation between the two men.

Then a worrisome thought struck her: If Lewiston knew about her secret friendship with Exmore, who else did? Her gaze flew to her uncle. He was drinking champagne and speaking amicably with another gentleman.

The dance began to feel like a sickening blur. She wanted to rip her hand away from Lewiston's clasp. She didn't want him touching her in any manner. Thankfully, he turned silent for the remainder of the dance, and they both moved through the figures. When the music ended, he leaned close and whispered, "I warn you. Stay away from Exmore."

She left the dance floor, shaking, and headed for the refreshment parlor. She heard the colonel say something about procuring her some punch, but she ignored him and continued on her own. How did their secret get out? She had told no one, and she trusted Exmore.

A warm hand latched on to her elbow, and Exmore whispered, "I need to speak to you."

She slowly turned. Exmore's face was politely composed but pain imbued his burning eyes. "Please." His voice had a hollowed-out quality.

She shouldn't meet him here. Not at a crowded ball with her uncle hovering about. It was too dangerous. Yet, she replied, "Yes," to his imploring gaze.

He walked to a closed parlor door, opened it, and slipped inside. She glanced again at her uncle to find he was still deep in conversation with another gentleman. She paused a moment more, having second thoughts, but then slipped into the parlor with Exmore.

* * *

Exmore seized her shoulders, holding on to her as if they were in some swift-moving current and she would be cast away from him otherwise. "What did he say to you?" he demanded.

Annalise didn't need any more explanation. She comprehended him immediately. "That man Lewiston said… that you killed some lady he loved. That she died from grief that you inflicted. He was a horrible man. I couldn't stand touching him. How dare he say these things to me? And at a ball. He is mad."

Exmore released a deep breath. He should have known Annalise would be sensible. "He is not mad, but he is a very angry and hurt man."

She held up her hand. "Please, don't put me in this situation between you two. There are aspects of your life that I don't need to know about. You are a m—"

"I'm a drunken libertine."

"No, I didn't say that."

"That's what others say. But I need to tell you something. Something I—I haven't admitted to anyone else."

The unspoken words had sat in his mind for years and affected every minute of his life, burned in his heart. His life was divided into two times periods—before Cassandra's death and then after. He had planned to bury the secret with his death and Lewiston. Until that time, he had been prepared to live with the ugly truth day to day, hour to hour. But now, as he looked at Annalise's compassionate eyes, the words were too heavy, and he couldn't carry them anymore. Something in her face—in its unique contours—made him feel safe, as though she had some power that no one else possessed to heal him.

"You can tell me anything you need to," she encouraged.

The truth he had held back so long burst out. "Lewiston loved Cassandra."

She blinked. "This—this is about Cassandra?" The machinations of her mind showed in her eyes. "Were they lovers? But—but you loved her!" she said fiercely, protectively. "You loved her so much! I remember what you told me that night. How you loved her with a depth I couldn't conceive. Oh, Exmore." She drew him into a tight embrace. "I'm sorry."

"It's not as it seems." He buried his face in her silken hair, drawing in her vanilla scent.

"Tell me now," she whispered. "The truth. All of it. You needn't worry about my feelings."

"I loved her." The words emitted from a deep, despairing place. "I loved her too much."

"You cannot love someone too much, Exmore," she said quietly.

He drew her tight... He needed her warmth, her strength, her understanding. "Unless they don't love you. Unless your love is unwanted."

She sucked in her breath. Her body stiffened for a moment, and then all the softness flooded back. "Oh, Exmore. No. I always thought… yours was the perfect marriage. I coveted it when I had been abandoned. I was jealous of it. I thought… I'm sorry. Oh God."

"I fell wildly in love with her from the start." The truth had been poisoning him. He had to get it out. "My father advised me against the match, believing I was too young. I wouldn't listen. She was all I knew, all I thought about. I didn't know that she loved another. I didn't. I thought her reserve was part of her calm countenance. Unknown to me, her father forced her to marry me because I was a future marquess, and Lewiston, then, was only the younger son of a baron."

He drew back until he could see her eyes. "I didn't know."

She caressed his shoulder. "Of course you didn't."

"I wouldn't… I wouldn't have encouraged her to marry me. I feel like a monster."

"This isn't your doing."

"I never suspected anything. She was a good wife—a model wife. Yet, I felt she always kept something from me. Her elusiveness drove me wild. I couldn't get enough of her. I spent years trying to steal into her secret world. I thought that was how love worked."

The tears he had never let himself cry filled Annalise's lovely eyes.

"The pregnancy made her ill. She couldn't hold down water or food. It was torture to watch her body writhe with retching convulsion. She… she…" He swallowed. His throat burned. "She called out Lewiston's name. Until then, I had never heard of the man. She begged her maid to come and write a letter to Lewiston. Beneath her delirium, she knew she was dying." He searched her face, soft with compassion. "I—I did something I shouldn't have," he admitted. "I betrayed her trust."

"In an emotional time, you act in ways you never thought you would. I can't judge you."

"I read the letter."

She reached up and placed her gloved hand on his cheek. "What did the letter say?"

He could tell she didn't care about the letter. She knew he needed to confess, and she was giving him permission.

"She said she was sorry that she wasn't strong enough to run away with him." His voice cracked. "That she thought of him when she touched me. She pretended the baby was theirs. That someday they—she, him, and her unborn child—would be reunited in a world without end. Just as her love for him was—without end."

Annalise slowly drew him back to her safe embrace. "I'm

sorry," she whispered.

She rested her cheek on his chest. He liked her there. Her touch penetrated all the way to his pounding heart. Damn that night years ago, and Patrick, and Wallis's vile words. Annalise was the only true thing in his life. "I couldn't keep our friendship secret," he said. "Wallis Hume was insulting you at a club, and I wouldn't have it. I couldn't have him belittling you. Lewiston was there and overheard it all."

"Shhh." She ran her fingers along his back. "Don't worry about that. It doesn't matter to me."

"The other day you reminded me that I once told you that you would love again and more wisely," he said. "Well, you don't. Love continues, even for those who don't love you. You knew that, and you fought for Patrick. I've never told you how much I came to admire you for that. You are the strong one."

"I don't feel strong at all. I'm pretending that I'm strong, because it's easier than owning how confused and sad I can be."

"Are you that way with me?"

"No. I really have nothing to hide from you. You know all my secrets."

"Thank you," he whispered. How easily she gave herself away to him, letting him know her. She didn't drive him wild like Cassandra had by hiding her true thoughts. She wasn't a beautiful enigma. She readily gave herself and that sweet, radiant calmness that he recalled from the day at the print shop. He felt safe in her arms. Wasn't it supposed to be the other way around? How could a grown man feel unsafe? Wasn't he supposed to be her hero and comfort her? He drew her tighter. "Thank you," he whispered again.

They didn't say anything more but rested in their embrace. The music and chatter from the other room could have been miles away.

Then the door swung violently open, the handle smashing against the wall. Mr. Sommerville and Colonel Lewiston stood on the threshold. Sommerville's thin neck was red and corded, and his bulging eyes burned with anger. Annalise tried to leap away, but Exmore held her close. They wouldn't get to her. They wouldn't hurt his Annalise.

"Thank you, Colonel Lewiston, for alerting me to this unfortunate situation," Sommerville said while glowering at Exmore.

Lewiston eyed Exmore. Triumph hiked the edge of his mouth. Lewiston surely thought he had done a great service to Annalise. He had saved her from Exmore's supposedly vile clutches, avenging Cassandra through her.

"What have you done, Annalise?" Sommerville demanded.

"Shut the door," Exmore said, keeping a protective hold on her. Behind them, guests were turning to see the reason for the commotion.

Lewiston shot Exmore a smug look, so proud of himself, and then walked out, shutting the door.

"You ridiculous, silly idiot," Sommerville spat at Annalise. "You insist on shaming me, and at Lord Warrington's ball. Have you any sense at all?"

"Don't speak to her that way," Exmore growled, keeping Annalise's back against his chest, his arm draped protectively across her.

"Tell me, my lord." Mr. Sommerville opened his hands. "Will you do the honorable thing by this witless girl? Will you marry her and be saddled with her for the rest of her life? She would disgrace the office held by your late beloved, perfect wife."

"No!" Annalise cried.

Exmore remained silent, assessing her uncle and the situation.

"Come away, now, you wicked child!" her uncle barked. No doubt, his voice carried to the other room. He took pleasure in his righteous anger and belittling Annalise. "You disappoint me in every measure."

Exmore made a quick calculation and reluctantly released his hold on Annalise… for now. "Go quietly with him," he whispered. "Don't worry about a thing. I'll take care of matters tonight."

CHAPTER TEN

"I'm going to Holland," Annalise whispered to herself as her uncle gripped her elbow, escorting her outside. The watch might as well have arrested her in the middle of Lord Warrington's ball for all the curious looks she garnered.

In the carriage on the way home, her uncle warned his wife and Phoebe to remain silent. Despite this instruction, her aunt begged, "What is wrong, Mr. Sommerville?"

"It's not for your innocent ears."

Phoebe cast Annalise commiserating looks but remained obediently silent.

Annalise gazed out the window, watching the blur of light outside the glass. She felt oddly numb about her disgrace and coming journey to the Continent. Shouldn't she feel more? Perhaps embarrassment, humiliation, or fear? Instead, her mind turned over Exmore's words. His personal descent now made sense: the rakishness, the self-destruction, the pain. How disorientating to learn that the person you loved most in the world never loved you, that she had been pretending all along. Exmore had unwittingly built his marriage and life on lies. Annalise and Patrick had never shared the intimacy of a marriage bed or spent years building a life together. Yet, she had been devastated at his abandonment. She couldn't imagine how Exmore must feel. Love, sadness, anger, remorse, and disillusionment. He had admitted that one never stops loving someone, and she knew that to be true, but she wished it was otherwise. She wished a powerful tide would sweep memories of old love away to a forgotten ocean, leaving a clean shore to start again, as if the past hadn't happened. She wished so for Exmore's sake.

At home, her uncle sent his wife and Phoebe to bed as though they were five years old. Annalise knew wily Phoebe waited on the stairwell, listening.

"Come to my parlor," her uncle commanded.

Annalise forced herself to take a long, slow breath. She wouldn't let him anger her. "I'm leaving for Holland tomorrow," she said calmly.

He flung out his arms. "That's it? You just leave? Do you have a ticket?"

"No."

"Do you know where you are going in Holland?"

"No."

He shook his head incredulously. "You halfwit. I don't know whether to be amused or angry with you." He stepped closer, until Annalise could smell the tinge of his sour perspiration on his coat. "Tell me, my girl, have you opened your legs to him?" There was predatory anticipation on his moist lips.

Annalise stepped back, keeping her spine erect, refusing to be dragged down to her uncle's base understanding. "Lord Exmore and I are friends. You wouldn't understand our relationship because you don't comprehend beauty or grace."

"It is you who do not comprehend these things." He pounded a side table with the padded edge of his fist. "Beauty and grace? What do you fashion yourself now? A poetess?

What you need to learn about are decency and chastity."

"I won't listen to your insults any longer. I'm leaving as soon as may be."

"You do not tell me what you are going to do." He grabbed her arm. "You will obey my wishes."

A servant cleared his throat. "Sir, the Marquess of Exmore," he announced.

Annalise turned her head as Exmore walked in. His gaze drifted from her face to where her uncle squeezed her arm. His lips made the slightest tremor, his nostrils flared, yet when he spoke, his voice was low and smooth. "Good evening."

Her uncle rushed forward, almost tripping on the foot of a chair. Barely recovering his balance, he performed a stumbling bow before Exmore. "My lord."

"I desire to speak to you in private regarding your niece," Exmore said.

"Annalise is a witless—"

"Not another word dishonoring Miss Van Der Keer," Exmore thundered. He pointed to the closed double doors at the back of the room. "Is this the study? It usually is in such drab, middling homes. How can you bear to live in this rodent's hole?"

Her uncle paled at having his home belittled by the great man. Exmore didn't wait for him to answer but strode toward the parlor. He didn't look back when he addressed the servant. "Have tea and biscuits brought to Miss Van Der Keer." He opened one of the doors. "Come, Sommerville."

As her uncle passed, he looked to Annalise for sympathy at Exmore's belittling of him. Annalise ignored her uncle. Exmore closed the study door behind the men.

What was Exmore's game? She had a nervous inkling that she knew the answer. She couldn't let him do this. He didn't love her but was acting out of honor.

She wanted to burst into the parlor and cry, *No, no, this isn't necessary*.

She had only to survive one more night under her uncle's

roof, and then she would sail away, liberating herself and Exmore.

The conversation between the men was quick, not five minutes, but it seemed like an hour to a fretting Annalise. When it was over, her uncle bounded out, his demeanor radically changed. He appeared overly pleasant, trying hard to be the congenial man he wasn't.

"Well, now, here she is. Hee hee. So beautiful. Ready to make you a very happy man."

Annalise's gaze shifted between her uncle and Exmore. "Smile, girl," her uncle commanded. "He wants to marry you."

"May I have a moment alone with my bride-to-be?" Exmore said.

"Of course, of course."

Annalise waited until her uncle retreated from the room, bowing as he went. Silence permeated the room. When she opened her mouth to speak, Exmore rested his hands on her shoulders. "No, Annalise, don't turn me away yet. Listen to my case."

"I can go to Holland. I have enough money of my own. This is all unnecessary."

His fingers slid down her arms until they interlocked with hers. "I want to marry you," he said quietly. "If you will have me?"

"But I…" She gazed up at his eyes, not expecting to see the vulnerable yearning in them. She wanted to say she loved him. She wanted to give him everything Cassandra hadn't. But she couldn't. Tears burned in her eyes. "I don't love you. I'm sorry."

"Shhh. I know you don't love me. But you are honest. You hide nothing."

"That is not enough for a marriage."

He sank to one knee. "For months, I've wandered about in a haze of despondency. Nothing could lift me from my low spirits, except brandy and gambling and…" He didn't finish, but she knew he found empty pleasure in women. "Then one day, I wandered into a print shop to waste hours, for I had so many hours in my day, and this lovely lady arrived. She had such a light around her, and she spoke of exotic creatures. Later, she met me at a masquerade and I concealed my identity to keep her near me longer, because she broke through my gloom. Then she spoke to me in a tea shop, and her presence was like sunlight in my darkness." Annalise's tears were free-flowing now. He kissed her hand, letting his lips caress her skin. "And I hope I'm not presumptuous when I say that you find happiness in me."

"I do," she choked through her tears. "Very much."

"What waits for you in Holland, Annalise? Maybe love, maybe more emptiness. I am here. I simply want your companionship. That is all. We can be a marriage of friends."

She shook her head. "No, no. Years from now, you may fall in love again. I shall hold you back."

"I've been in love before, and so have you. How did it feel?"

"Don't make me think about that!" She remembered waiting, waiting for Patrick to write, refusing to believe he had abandoned her. Days had trudged on as she had hand-fed her dying mother and learned to manage a home for her father. Her mind had known he was gone, enchanted by a new land, but her heart didn't speak the language of her mind. It had hurt and yearned. It had driven her to write letters to Patrick, to replay all their memories, trying to recapture the magic of his love while she was cleaning oozing bedsores on her father's body.

"I think friendship may be better than love," he said.

Annalise wasn't convinced. "But if we are married, you will require an heir and… and a true wife would… I don't know if…" She released a nervous breath. "I'm having a difficult time saying this. A marriage is intimate."

He rose to his feet, all the while keeping his gaze on hers. "May I kiss you?"

She studied his lips. They were soft, waiting, and she wasn't averse to knowing their touch. "Yes," she whispered.

Yet, he didn't. He gently stroked her cheek with his thumbs, taking in her face. Then he closed his eyes, slowly lowered his lips, resting them on hers. His were warm, the edges slightly roughened where he shaved. His scent—like pine trees in the winter—filled her. He began to move his lips, asking her for more. She opened her mouth, letting him inside. Their tongues tentatively touched, tasted, caressed.

Kissing Patrick had been a wild, almost desperate sensation. She hadn't been able to get close enough to Patrick, her body alive and cracking with wild energy. Kissing Exmore was a lulling, sweet sensation, like the steam off of the hot tea and the peaceful tap of the rain from that day at the tea shop. And like that day, she didn't want the kiss to end, but go on and on. He finally pulled away, but only to rest his forehead upon hers.

"Will that do?" he asked, his voice hoarse.

"Are you sure I'm who you want? Me? Odd, curious me? You don't love me either."

Again, he rubbed her cheek. "Marry me, Annalise. You once said that you felt like a stranger to yourself… I know that feeling. I will give you space to find who you are. You can study botany and naturalism, and I will tell you how brilliant you are. You can delight me with your odd, curious, and wonderful insights. We can read to each other as you did to your father in the garden. We can talk over tea and let the hours fly by. Marry me."

She couldn't go back to her old home, and she couldn't find the London she had known with Patrick. It had all passed away, like her parents. The future in Holland waited with relatives she had never met—strangers who were hundreds of miles of ocean away. She didn't love Exmore in the way she had loved Patrick. She couldn't deny the advantage of his title and that their children would always be provided for. But more than anything, she admired Exmore and trusted him. He made her laugh. And that meant so much after being lonely and sad for so long.

He kissed her forehead. "We will be content. Say yes, my Annalise."

My Annalise. No one had called her that since her father died.

"Yes," she whispered. "Yes."

CHAPTER ELEVEN

The next morning, Annalise woke to wind splattering rain against her window. Beyond the glass, the world was a blurry, watery gray with people scurrying about with umbrellas. Annalise gripped her taut belly and remembered: Today, she was getting married. Exmore wanted to remove her from her uncle's house as soon as possible. To this end, he would obtain a special license that morning, and the wedding would take place in the afternoon.

The idea of a marriage of friends was comforting. She could give up on finding love again—the passionate love she had had for Patrick and the potential happiness or pain it might cause—and just accept a situation that was good enough but not ideal. Since her parents' deaths, the world seemed much bigger and harder, and she, much smaller and fragile. But now, in the rainy, cold morning, she realized she had made a mistake. Everything was wrong. She knew Patrick was never coming back to her. He didn't love her. Yet, today would be the final end to her doomed courtship with Patrick. She hadn't realized how much she had been hanging on the thinnest thread of hope for Patrick. But now, all hope, no matter how dim, was extinguished. He was gone to her forever.

"No," she whispered. "No." It wasn't supposed to be this way.

Her aunt swept into the room, her cheeks and eyes bright with excitement. Phoebe and Mrs. Bailey were in her wake. "Oh, my darling, you must get ready for your wedding!" her aunt said in a singsong voice. "I've told everyone. And a letter from your future husband has arrived and these lovely orchids for you to carry. Mrs. Bailey, put these in a vase."

Annalise took the letter, opened it, and read.

All will be well. Come to the chapel at four, my lovely bride.

Her stomach turned. She felt she might vomit.

The only suitable wedding gown she possessed was a simple, unadorned white gown from her first Season. In her fantasies of marrying Patrick, she had envisioned having a lovely dress made that was embroidered with bluebells that matched her mother's wedding veil. Annalise didn't even know where that old veil was now. When she showed her aunt her choice of bridal attire, the woman pressed her palm to her forehead, aghast. "That old rag of a thing!"

Annalise uncharacteristically lost her humor with her aunt. "Oh, who cares what I marry in?" she said and then burst into tears.

Her aunt shooed Mrs. Bailey and Phoebe away. Then she sandwiched Annalise's face in her hands. "Come now, I know you are worried," she said with maternal knowing. "But Exmore will be gentle with his wife. It's an awkward act that a wife must tolerate. But think, my love. You shall have an infant of your own."

Annalise stared. Her aunt misunderstood entirely. How could she say, *I was supposed to marry someone else*? She knew her aunt wouldn't understand. She lived in a very small, flat, defined world, where she never looked over the edges or questioned herself because what she would discover would be too painful.

"Now, now, see yourself in the mirror," her aunt continued. "Aren't you radiant? Exmore will have a very pretty wife. You should always strive to make him happy, my dear. Your happiness will be in his happiness."

Annalise peered at her reflection. She didn't see any radiance, only dark fear dilating her eyes. This marriage would be a sham. Friends shouldn't marry.

The rain continued throughout the day. On the way to the church, Annalise clutched the flowers and watched the swollen, filthy gutters flow like rapids along the roadside. She kept telling herself that she was getting married today, yet it didn't seem like it was really happening. Wasn't her wedding day supposed to be more than this? Shouldn't bells toll and horses be adorned with white ribbon? Shouldn't she feel happy?

Her uncle's manservant held the umbrella over her as Annalise lifted the edges of her gown and dashed to the vestry. Inside, the church was gloomy, gray stone with heavy wooden beams. The chapel was empty except for Exmore conferring with the vicar by the altar. *This is wrong*, she thought. *This is not the man I'm supposed to marry.* She should turn around now.

"Ah, there she is," Vicar said.

She didn't wait for her uncle to lead her down the aisle, but walked quietly on, gripping her orchids to her chest. She needed Exmore to gaze at her with those tender, reassuring eyes to calm her fears. He needed to be her hero again, saving her from her fears. But when he turned, the lines of his face were ashen, as if he hadn't slept. His gaze was hollow and tired.

Oh God, he knows this is a huge mistake too. He acted out of honor and now he's trapped.

The next minutes were a blur in her mind. The words of the ceremony streamed through her head. "Wilt thou… thy wedded husband… forsaking all others… I will…"

Exmore held her hand, his eyes averted as he uttered the fateful, un-retractable words, "And thereto I plight thee my troth."

It was her turn to pledge her life. She gripped Exmore's hand. The vicar waited. The audience of her uncle and his family grew silent. She had imagined this scene a thousand times or more. She had planned her wedding to Patrick in minute detail. It wasn't supposed to be this way. Lovely light should shine through the stained glass like God blessing the union. Her betrothed should gaze at her with a loving glow in his eyes. Her father should be beside her as her mother looked on.

Be strong, Annalise. Stop this madness.

"Miss Van Der Keer, your vows," the vicar prompted.

Exmore lifted his gaze to hers, imploring.

Her voice cracked. "I—I t-take thee…" She didn't know how she formed the remaining words. She couldn't feel the air rising through her throat or her lips moving. The vow came out halting and brittle. "I give thee my troth."

The vicar joined their hands together. "Those whom God hath joined together let no man put asunder."

Blackness filled Annalise's vision. The flowers tumbled from her fingers, and white petals scattered on the cold stone floor by the hem of her gown. Exmore caught her in his arms before she hit the ground. He kept her nestled in his embrace as the vicar hurried through the rest of the service.

"All will be well," Exmore whispered. "All will be well."

But Annalise knew it wouldn't be so as she gazed at the gold band encircling her finger. It felt heavy and unnatural. What had she done?

* * *

The next hours were akin to watching a horse race by the fence line—the streaks of motion, the thundering of sound. She held Exmore's arm like it was a raft keeping her afloat. She was beginning to awaken to the extensive duties that accompanied her vows as the staff of Exmore's London home streamed into the rain to form a line to meet her. She mustered her courage, holding the tears at bay, and tried to be as courteous as possible. She remembered very little of his home from her one visit years ago, and she had been too distraught then to take in its enormity and ornateness. A huge portrait of Cassandra waited above the double staircases entwining up a series of balconies. Annalise was arrested by the image of the woman who had destroyed Exmore's heart. She had forgotten how beautiful Cassandra had been. She seemed to peer down at Annalise as if to say, *You don't belong here.*

Exmore must have sensed her distress, for he beckoned to a manservant and pointed to the painting. The manservant nodded.

"We must have your portrait painted and hung in its place," he told Annalise.

"No!" she cried without thinking. She was horrified at the idea of London Society entering his home and seeing her likeness towering above them. The thought reminded her that as marchioness, she would have to host balls, dinners, and musical evenings. Dear Lord! All she really wanted was to draw wildflowers. Not this!

Wasn't marrying a marquess supposed to be some kind of dream? Well, it was. A nightmare.

Again, Exmore whispered, "All will be well," in her ear, but his worried tone hardly soothed her.

She was finally shown to her chamber after an intimidating tour of her new home. And she learned there were four other grander estates that Exmore also called his residences. She was so overwhelmed she could hardly keep her thoughts straight. She remembered thinking how snobbish those old matrons had sounded at balls when they spoke of marrying near one's station. Now their advice made perfect sense: Annalise hadn't been brought up to be a marchioness. Now she even had her own lady's maid—a willowy, lovely lady named Marie. Annalise missed homey, unfashionable Mrs. Bailey. She desperately needed someone from her old life at this moment.

Marie curtsied. "My lady," she said, her French accent showing.

Don't call me my lady. *Don't supplicate to me.*

"I put your things away," Marie said.

"Oh." Annalise didn't remember having her belongings packed and sent over. Of course, it must have happened. How distracted she had been.

Marie pointed to the various features in the chamber, including the neighboring sitting and dressing rooms. Then she gestured to an interior door. "And that leads to your husband's chambers."

Annalise stared at the door. Several days ago, they had spoken at a masquerade, and she hadn't known his name. Now, they would intimately know each other. There was so much she didn't know about him. The little important details that made up a person. She just had his broad strokes. It was all too quick.

"I am so happy you are here." Marie arranged bottles on a vanity. "It's been gloomy since Lady Exmore died… Oh, but you are Lady Exmore now."

No, I'm not, Annalise wanted to say. *I'm Annalise Van Der Keer.* Instead, she only smiled and wrapped her arms about herself.

Marie helped Annalise out of her wedding gown. "Do you have a special nightgown for tonight?" she asked with a knowing smile. She seemed happier about Annalise's wedding night than Annalise.

"No, just… just the ones I usually wear."

Marie gave her a mysterious smile, making Annalise feel stupid for not thinking of a pretty nightgown for her husband.

After Annalise had donned her plain nightclothes, Marie brushed out her hair until it spilled in shiny waves around her shoulders. "Here, then." She dabbed floral perfume on Annalise's neck and then left with the wedding gown folded over her arm.

Annalise was alone. The rain pinged on the windows. It

hadn't let up all day.

What did she do now?

She eyed the door. Did she visit his chamber? Did he visit hers? Who knocked first?

She felt like a five-year-old who wanted to go back home to her mother and father.

She walked to where her leather portfolios rested on a large desk. She opened the top one, which contained her letters to Patrick, and drew out the last one she had written. She turned the stationery over and hastily wrote:

Dear Patrick, I've made a horrible mistake. What have I done? What have I done? It was supposed to be you. I was supposed to marry you…

She heard a gentle tap and glanced down at the letter. Oh God, she had written to Patrick on her wedding night? What was wrong with her? She felt oddly like she was already breaking the vows she had made only hours before. She didn't have time to burn the letter, so she shoved it back into the portfolio.

"Yes," she said.

The door slowly opened, and Exmore entered hesitantly, wearing a silk dressing gown of jewel blue and crimson. She had never seen him without a starched shirt, tailored coat, and cravat. In the firelight, his skin appeared bronze. His tousled hair shone as it fell onto his forehead and almost down to his shoulders. She could make out the planes of his chest peeking out from the V opening of his robe and the curves of his muscled calves beneath the hem. He cradled a wrapped package in his arms.

Despite his casual attire, he bowed stiffly.

"Are you well?" He nervously eyed her.

Why try to pretend? She wasn't any good at acting. "I'm overwhelmed, scared, not sure I can be a marchioness, and I'm wondering if I made a mistake, but you… you look very handsome." She gestured to him. "Well, you're always handsome. But you are especially handsome tonight."

Her words had the opposite effect than she'd thought they would. Surely, stating that she felt she had made a mistake would trouble him, but his shoulders relaxed with a long exhalation.

"I'm feeling overwhelmed myself. I saw how you struggled today, and I should have been—I should have been a better husband to you."

"I understand," she interjected. "I can imagine this was an emotional day for you."

"I admit I thought I may have been too hasty, but now that I have you away from everyone and all to myself…" He studied her face. Her skin heated under his perusal. "Oh, you are beautiful."

She became conscious of her dull nightgown, her hair flowing loose. She hadn't been *dishabille* with anyone outside her family. But he was her family now. "I don't have pretty nightclothes," she stammered. "I didn't expect to be married in a matter of hours after the proposal."

"I was gazing into your eyes when I called you beautiful. I hadn't even noticed your gown." Then he made a dramatic show of looking at it. "Good God, it's hideous!"

"It's not hideous!" she cried, laughing. "It's white, boring, and functionary, and not at all romantic."

"It's wonderful to hear you laugh again." That tender smile she had missed all day finally returned. Its warmth soaked into her bones. She would have thought that being in a bedchamber alone for the first time with her husband would have elicited a case of nerves. Instead, this was the closest she had come to relaxing all day.

"I brought you a gift." He held up the package. It was the shape of a book. "I think you can guess what it is."

Their hands met as she took the package. Even the brief touch comforted her. But she instinctively drew away, as would be polite, and then remembered that he was her husband now. She could touch him without Society's censure. So she snuggled against him, letting his heat and scent soothe her.

"Ahh, Annalise," he whispered, wrapping his arms around her.

She carefully folded back the paper to reveal a book of botanical illustrations. "It's lovely," she whispered, carefully flipping through the pages. "Just lovely."

"Did you take notice of the author?"

She turned the book to the cover. "Mrs. Herbert Brockley," she marveled. "A woman botanist."

"I thought you might be inspired. Perhaps you should consider publishing a book of your illustrations and thoughts."

She looked at him comically. "I'm not the scientist. My father was. I merely draw flowers and animals as it pleases me." She rubbed the book's title that was embossed in the leather and strolled to the lamp by her bed for better light. She sat on the edge of the mattress and opened the book again. "My father always talked about creating a book, but he never did. I still have all his notes. I brought them with me."

He sat beside her. "You should make a book of your work and his in his memory."

"Do you really think I could?"

"Without a doubt."

There was no mockery in his expression, as was always present in her uncle's face, only honest sincerity. He truly thought she was talented. Without thinking, she leaned in and kissed his cheek. "Thank you for your faith in me."

He studied her, turning her self-conscious.

He reached up and tucked her hair behind her ear and then let his fingers drift down her long locks and alongside her breast. She shivered, not with dread or nervousness, but with expectation.

"I only want you to be comfortable when we are together," he said quietly. "Our courtship was too brief. I can wait as long as you need."

Her face heated as she realized he meant their marital

intimacy. This was the part where they consummated their marriage, when all their spoken vows translated to their bodies. In her mind flashed an image of their bodies intertwined. Oddly, it didn't cause her any nervousness. Only want.

"Can I kiss you?" she asked. "Or must I wait?"

He smiled and answered with his lips. The kiss started as sweet as yesterday's did, but a tension gripped her body. She couldn't get close enough to him. After a terrifying day, she needed his magic. But he drew away, and cold air met her skin.

"You are so lovely." His voice was hoarse and thick.

"Don't leave me alone tonight," she implored. "Can you stay here, even if we don't…" She had spent all her nights alone, feeling the darkness seeming to press upon her and worries accumulating in her mind.

"I will stay any night you wish."

"I wish for all of them. You said I didn't have to be alone again."

He kissed her, his body turning hard, making her aware of the muscles of his arms and chest, the slight roughness of his shaved chin, and the tinge of sweat that mingled with his cologne. Her breasts began to ache, wanting more of what he was giving her. Still, she could feel him hesitate, meting out his love. She needed to give him a sign that he shouldn't worry about her. She let her hand slide up his chest. When her fingers reached the opening of his robe, his warm, naked skin sent a wild jolt coursing through her body, as did the realization that he wore nothing underneath. She paused, feeling very much in deep waters.

"It's all right," he whispered encouragingly in her ear. The heat of his breath tingled her lobe. "You can touch me. It gives me pleasure. Don't be nervous."

She tentatively let her fingers drift inside his robe, discovering the contours of his chest and belly. She enjoyed the hums of pleasure he gave as she caressed him. Yet, when she reached the patch of curls beneath his stomach, her knuckles accidentally brushed against his swollen sex. It jutted, stone-like and thick. She was arrested, unsure what to do. She could hear his uneven breath rushing by her ear.

"Annalise," he murmured.

He took her hand, keeping his fingers safely over hers as he guided her along his sex. As she explored, his lips sought hers, opening her mouth. His tongue swirled against hers as he taught her how to touch him. His pleasure flowed through her as if they were immersed in the same current. When he opened his eyes, a burning glow in their depths appeared almost predatory, yet his touch was gentle as his lips trailed down her neck and onto her shoulder. His fingers stroked her just under the line of her nightgown, telling her that he wanted more if she would allow him.

Her nipples hardened, and a wet throb burned between her legs. She reached for the tie string of her gown. He drew back, keeping his gaze fixed on her face as she undid the knot. She drew down the sleeves until her breasts were bared before him. She felt no shyness as he took her in. She wanted to share herself with him. She wanted to be known.

"Dear Lord," he whispered. He kissed her lips as he swept his arm beneath her, resting her upon the mattress. Then his mouth glided lower and lower as he drew away her gown, revealing her entire body to him.

"You're beautiful, so beautiful," he said and let his warm tongue lap the tip of her nipple.

She released a strangled cry. Every small scrap she had picked up along the way about the intimate relations between a husband and wife was very wrong. She always imagined in her daydreams that the bride would be more passive, finding less delight in the act than the husband. Yet, as his tongue fondled her breast, she felt as though she were breaking apart with want. She writhed, pushing against him, driving herself deeper into his mouth. The pleasure was most intense between her legs, where her sex throbbed, wet and swollen.

He appeared to know how she ached for him. He let his hand drift slowly lower and lower, until his fingers rested outside her sex. There, he lingered. Did he know he was torturing her? Why wasn't he touching her, or doing something to relieve the desire that burned so strong that it hurt? She bit down on her lips, and her thighs started undulating against the mattress. She couldn't control them. Her mind might not know how to make love, but her body clearly did. It had carried around the unspoken secret all these years.

His warm breath tickled her breast. "Wife, you are killing me," he said in a hoarse whisper, and his finger finally slid lower, coming to light on the mound between her legs. A powerful sensation radiated from where he touched, sending waves across her body. And he kept moving his finger, not letting the pleasure dissipate, but allowing it to build as she whimpered. She had never known such exquisite joy could exist. She kissed his lips, his cheeks, and whispered his name, letting her tongue relish its sounds. Her body began to quake from pleasure. All other thoughts ceased except that he had to be in her body. He had to satisfy that maddening want deep inside her. The course was irreversible now.

She reached out to him, crying, "I must know you."

"We can wait." His voice was ragged.

Wait? That's all she had done for years. Wait for death, wait in silence, wait alone with unrequited love. "No, no, I can't! Please! Let me give something to you. Let me give you pleasure too."

He bowed his head, taking a deep breath as though steeling himself. Then he came to rest atop her, his robe open, shielding their bodies. She felt safe beneath him, sheltered by him as the cold rain splattered the windows. He kissed her softly, assuring her that she was lovely and brilliant as his sex pressed against her. A spasm of pain ran through her, and she released a high, humming cry as his body entered her body.

"Dear God," he cried.

She became still. She held on to his arms, feeling his body tremble. The pain receded, leaving her to marvel at the sensation of him, his power, his energy, his being inside her. She hadn't expected his presence to feel profound. Almost sacred. She touched his cheek. He turned his face to kiss her palm. Her gold wedding band gleamed in the light. The wedding vows she had uttered with fear and trepidation in the empty, cold chapel now found peace in her heart. She was a wife now. His true wife. She wouldn't be alone again.

Tears burned in her eyes.

Her dear husband misunderstood and panicked. "We can stop!"

"No, please, don't. I—I didn't know it would be so lovely. I didn't know."

The fear on his face melted away, replaced by a tender smile. His lips brushed her forehead. "And may it always be for us—lovely."

He began to move, back and forth, gently. Her body met his, complementing his motion. The intense desire returned, drawing her under its powerful current until her quaking cry mingled with his, and he withdrew, spilling wet heat onto her belly.

Later, as her spent body rested against his, she felt as though she were floating on warm golden light, even as the rain poured outside. He held her tight to his chest, and she lulled in the reassuring rhythm of his breath and thrum of his heart. She had never felt so safe and fully herself. Did he feel the same? She smiled as she remembered the pleasure on his features as he loved her. She sat up on her elbows and studied his face, taking in all its facets. She had a lifetime now to learn every little thing about him.

He stroked her damp hair, drawing a strand from her face and locking it behind her ear. A boyish smile lazed on his lips.

"I guess we waited a half an hour or so," she observed. "Is that what you meant when you said we could wait?"

"No." He tapped her nose. "I was trying to be the good, patient husband, and you spoiled all my best intentions. But in truth, I wanted to make love to you the moment I walked into this chamber and saw you with your lovely hair long and shining. I could see the outlines of your breasts in the gown that you said was boring. I found the sight quite tantalizing."

"I shall wear it for you whenever you like," she said. "And I found your robe quite fetching. In fact, *all* of you is quite fetching. I can unabashedly say that now since we are married."

His eyes turned earnest. "Are you happy you said yes?" he whispered.

She found she couldn't answer. The tears threatened again. She could only nod and kiss his lips.

CHAPTER TWELVE

Exmore needed to tell Annalise about Patrick's return. They had promised to be honest with each other, and yet, he harbored this little deceit. For the life of him, he couldn't comprehend the spell Patrick had over her. She possessed a nimble, curious mind and spirited personality. Although Patrick was intelligent enough, he didn't share Annalise's passion for learning. His mind was an uncluttered, unquestioning place dictated by the rules of Society. Her love for Patrick made no sense.

Exmore harbored the idea that if he took good enough care of Annalise, he could make her forget Patrick. This notion was irrational to his thinking mind, because he had given every last drop of his love to Cassandra, but it had never altered her heart. Annalise's situation was different. Patrick didn't love her. The love was all on her side, and it wasn't a secret. Exmore had walked into this marriage with his eyes wide open to the situation.

Nonetheless, in his heart, he could feel the cold winds

blowing Patrick's sails back to England. What would happen when she saw him? He dreaded to learn. It was one thing to *know* she loved another man. It would be quite another to see that love shining in her eyes. So he remained silent, protecting his beautiful marriage to his dear friend for as long as he could.

Theirs was an easy union. There was an abundance to Annalise—she listened, she talked, she laughed, she embraced without reservation. His all-consuming love for Cassandra had drained his energies. He had always been concerned about what she was thinking, always trying to make her happy—something he now realized he could never have done. What Cassandra had taken, Annalise gave back tenfold.

He cherished how when he walked into a room to find her, a spontaneous smile curved her lips at his sight. When he sat beside her, she automatically reached out to touch him or kiss his cheek. She desired to know the trivial details of his life. She asked about his work in Parliament, the management of estates, even boring business details. At breakfast, they would often read the morning journals and discuss the same articles. He found he didn't want to attend clubs anymore, because staying at home and conversing with his wife was far more enjoyable. And he liked being there to help her along in her new life.

The idea of overseeing the domestic details of multiple estates intimidated Annalise, even though she had managed her parents' home for several years. Exmore did his best to allay her fears, always ready with an encouraging compliment or needed support. Because she was new to the household, she couldn't readily see, as Exmore could, how the staff had fallen under her spell. She took sincere interest in the lives of their staff, inquiring about the health and family of even the lowest scullery maid. She, with the help of her loyal Mrs. Bailey, sought out little ways to improve the stations of their servants, including designating more living quarters, rationing more tea and candles, and having newer garments sewn.

Each day with Annalise carried that tingling excitement

akin to children planning their day's adventure. One or two times a week, Exmore and Annalise visited Kew Gardens or attended lectures together, where she would sit forward in her seat, mesmerized. He chuckled to himself that his wife was more entranced by comets or the chemical elements than how to fashion her bonnet. Later, they might wander to their favorite tea shop, where they stayed too long, lost in conversation, while secretly holding hands beneath the table. On days when they remained at home, one or all of Annalise's cousins might call with her Aunt Sally. Although Annalise wouldn't admit it, Exmore could see she was quietly exerting her own sway over her cousins, drawing them away from her uncle's influence and expanding their education. Exmore, to his surprise, found he didn't mind their boisterous presence. He enjoyed having a family about. An effervescent happiness filled his London house, which had been dormant with gloom for too long.

In the evenings, he and Annalise ventured to the parties, where they remained at each other's side as they met other couples. But as the hours wore on, Annalise would give him a dusky, sensual look, and he would immediately call for the carriage to take them home. There, they would make love into the early hours. Then he would drift off to sleep with the comforting warmth of her body against his. In the morning, they would make love again.

One of the many things that endeared him to his new wife was her unabashed lusty nature. Often, an innocent little kiss in his parlor led to a frolic on his desk. He was making love more frequently than he ever had in his life. It was only a matter of time before Annalise began increasing. He couldn't dispel the remaining fear from Cassandra's sad pregnancy. It remained lodged inside him, even as he tried to reassure himself with what the physicians had told him. Cassandra's condition had been a rare one, further compounded by an acute chill.

However, one early morning several weeks after their marriage, Exmore tried to push down the anxious thoughts of

Annalise's pending pregnancy and Patrick's return as the fresh light fell softly on Annalise's sleeping face. For the first time in a long, long while, he was happy.

He brushed Annalise's creamy shoulder with his lips, taking in her sweet, earthy scent—the flower and the soil. She smiled in her light sleep. He studied her a moment more, marveling at the serenity that enveloped her, and then rose and donned his robe, which had draped the vanity chair. He glanced about his wife's chamber, taking in the objects and things that were hers—the Indian shawl he gave her, her perfume bottle, the simple ruby necklace that had been her mother's. He had kissed her neck as he had unclasped it when they returned from the theater the previous evening, and then he had slowly proceeded to remove the remainder of her clothes. He smiled at the remembrance of their lovemaking.

He walked quietly by the walls, studying her father's images hanging there. He would never tell her that he thought she possessed far more talent, both artistically and scientifically, than her father. He stopped at her writing desk where the leather portfolios of her work rested. He opened the top one, so he could view her drawings and descriptions. He enjoyed studying them alone when he could slowly take in all the different elements she labored over. Otherwise, she would anxiously flit about him, finding fault in her stunning work.

He realized he had the wrong portfolio when he drew out a correspondence. He was carefully putting it back when the name *Patrick* leaped off the page. He hesitated and glanced at the bed. His wife made a soft humming sound as she shifted in her sleep.

No, he shouldn't read her correspondence. He started to replace the page, but then yanked it out again.

Dear Patrick, I've made a horrible mistake. What have I done? What have I done? It was supposed to be you. I was supposed to marry you…

What?

He reread and reread the words, as if the more he read them, he could, somehow, make them unreal. His heart raced as he pulled out more and more letters. He couldn't stop himself. *Dear Patrick… Dear Patrick…* There must have been thousands of letters. A sickening sensation knotted in his gut.

"Dearest," she murmured from her bed. She patted about, looking for him, and then rose up, rubbing her eyes. She was naked, her breasts exposed. "There you are," she said and smiled. "Come back to bed."

He gripped the pages, black rage consuming him. "What is this?"

Her lips parted as she took in the letters in his hand. "Oh no," she whispered. "It's—it's not what it seems."

"I'm glad to hear it." Sarcasm permeated his voice. "Because on the day of our marriage, you wrote that you were supposed to marry Patrick." He swallowed, his throat contracting in pain. "How could… how could you do this when—when you knew…"

"I didn't mean… I didn't… I…" She glanced down, her shoulders dropping, resigned. "I'm sorry," she whispered. "I'm so very sorry."

Her apology hardly satisfied him. More and more anger poured into him, as if it gushed from some hidden reserve inside him. "You wrote all these letters to Patrick. The man who thanked me for disentangling him from 'an ambitious, witless, unmanageable piece of fluff.'"

Her head jerked up. Her eyes were wet. "He—he said that?" Her voice cracked.

He approached her, the letters still gripped in his hand. "He doesn't love you, Annalise. Don't you understand?" He repeated his words again, pronouncing each syllable as if he could hammer them into her mind. "He doesn't love you!" He shook his head in disbelief. "How many letters are here? How many did you write him?" He flung the pages he held at the bed. They scattered on the sheets where they had made love only hours before. "Did he ever send you one letter? Just one?"

Tears streamed down her cheeks. "No," she choked.

He paced, running his hands down his face. The past seemed to have crashed into the present. Everything was coming back again, recombining into new, grotesque forms.

She pulled up the covers, hiding her body as if ashamed.

"What... what is wrong with you?" he whispered.

"I was lonely. I... couldn't talk to—to anyone."

He knew this to be true when she was alone in the country with her parents, but it didn't mitigate his anger. She had written to Patrick on their wedding day! "Well, you're in luck, my dearest," he spat. "You can give him all these letters when he arrives in London. You can tell him how you were supposed to marry him and not me."

"He's coming to London?"

The hope in her voice broke him. His ire transmuted to something icy, black, and deep.

"Yes, he should arrive any day."

"H-how long have you known this?"

"Since I saw you at the print shop."

"Why didn't you tell me?"

The look on her face—the love was still there—felt like a hard punch to his gut.

"Why?" he demanded. "What difference would it make? Would you not have married me?"

She drew in, lowering her head.

"Do you still love him, Annalise?"

She bit the edge of her lip. Tears dripped off her chin onto her chest.

"Do you? We're also supposed to be honest with each other. Do you love him?"

"I—I suppose. I—"

"Suppose? You suppose?" he shouted. "I love you." The words came out before he realized he had said them. He had never admitted to himself that he loved Annalise. He hadn't allowed himself, because he had fallen too quick to trust himself—because he hadn't wanted to be vulnerable again. Yet, the words tumbled out, raw and bleeding. He studied her, waiting, hoping she wouldn't break his heart. Hoping some miracle would salvage the moment. *Please, Annalise.*

"But—but we are friends," she stammered.

He grabbed another handful of letters from her portfolio and tossed them at the fire grate.

"No!" She rushed from the bed and snatched up the pages, crushing them to her naked chest.

He stared at her, thinking he might cry himself, as she huddled protectively over the letters. How was this happening again?

"Why did you do this to me?"

He tore from the room.

* * *

Annalise had gone too far. She had said words she couldn't take back. A hundred *I'm sorry*s wouldn't suffice. She revisited the morning scene over and over, but she couldn't correct it. What had happened would calcify into a painful memory.

He loved her. Her own husband loved her. Why did she feel miserable? She would do about anything to have those wild, obsessive feelings for Exmore that she had for Patrick. And even in this lowest of moments, she couldn't keep down the flutter of excitement in her wretched, cruel heart knowing Patrick was coming.

She decided she would be as affectionate, as lovely as possible to her husband, trying to make up for the truth she couldn't hide. But a quiet voice tugged at her conscience, reminding her that he had known. He had known all along about her feelings for Patrick. He had known she didn't love him, and he had advocated a marriage of friendship. And then he changed the rules and threw everything in her face.

Nonetheless, the morning after his discovery of the letters, she sought him out, wanting to beg for his forgiveness. He was nowhere to be found. For hours, she waited, her frantic mind immediately jumping to the worst conclusions: He had gone to a hell and was drinking and gambling. What if a woman approached him? She couldn't bear the thought of him with another. Yet, he was a marquess, and many married peers openly kept mistresses. She tried to tell herself that she was being unrealistic, yet these anxious thoughts continued to whirl in her mind as she went about her day, answering correspondences, meeting with the housekeeper about domestic matters, and greeting morning callers. She and Exmore had begun making friends with other married couples. It took so much strength to smile and laugh along with friends as if nothing was wrong. She sat across from the couples, watching their affectionate little glances at each other and felt like an impostor.

She should have gone to Holland and spared Exmore this pain. She had only tried to do what she thought was best. Exmore had told her that she made him happy, but she had to think he wasn't very happy now.

Exmore finally reappeared in the early evening. He came to her parlor, where she was speaking with the butler about a monthly order from the wine merchant. With the servant present, she couldn't leap from the table and embrace her husband as she wanted. The anger that had animated his face earlier was gone, replaced with coldness. He announced he planned to work in his library until Parliament began and walked out.

Once the butler left, she hurried to Exmore's library. She tapped on the door and entered when he said, "Yes." He glanced up.

She squeezed her hands together. "I'm so, so—"

"I have to know the details of this bill by Parliament," he said. "I'm speaking."

"Oh." She swallowed and changed tactics. "Then do you mind if I sit on the sofa and read a few letters? I only want to be near you." She often stretched out against him and read her correspondences with the beat of his heart in her ear.

"No, no, go ahead," he said without looking up.

She nervously sank onto the cushion, keeping her back

straight. She didn't know what was worse—not having him around, or having him close, yet feeling separated by an invisible wall built of icy hostility. Two hours passed in this ugly silence. She would have preferred if he had verbally sparred with her or even glowered, rather than this cold nothingness.

Finally, he rose. "I must go. Enjoy your evening." He strolled out. Not a kiss, not an embrace, not even a glance at her.

Now her own ire spiked. She wanted to chase after him and say, *You can't even hold a conversation with me about what happened?*

Three hours later, a footman delivered a note from Exmore.

I apologize, but I will be unavailable to attend the theater this evening. I think your cousin Phoebe would enjoy taking my place.

Thank heavens for the excitable Phoebe. Her effervescent enthusiasm for the play and the leading man helped Annalise survive the play. She sat next to Annalise and whispered, "Oh my goodness, he's handsome and charming. I'm wildly tingling all over."

Annalise didn't find him handsome at all. Her husband was handsome and charming. This actor, with his makeup and posturing, couldn't hold a candle to Exmore. And the depressing production about star-crossed lovers who met terrible ends did little to help matters.

Exmore wasn't home when she returned after midnight. Annalise lay in bed but couldn't sleep. Tears streamed down her face. Hadn't he said that she wouldn't have to be alone anymore? Hadn't he said their marriage of friendship would be full of laughter?

She wasn't laughing.

In the early hours, she heard movement in her husband's chambers. Where had he been? She dried her face on her sheets, rose, and tapped on his door.

"Yes." His voice was hoarse.

She slowly entered. Her husband rested in his bed, his head propped against the headboard, an open journal in his hands. A candle burned on the side table. He smelled of brandy and cigar smoke. She wanted to ask where he had been. At the same time, she wasn't sure she wanted to know.

"D-did you have a good evening?" she asked.

He set his journal beside him on the mattress. "Tolerable. And you?" He glanced up at her. This was the first time in the entire day that he had actually looked at her. She thought she might burst out in tears again.

"Phoebe had a fabulous time at the play."

"It doesn't take much to amuse her."

"I wish I could be so easily entertained."

"It's a special gift," he quipped.

For a passing moment, they had lapsed into their old rhythm of conversation, but then that moment faded away, and the raw silence returned.

"M-may I stay?" she asked.

He pushed the journal off the bed.

As she crawled under the covers, he snuffed the candle. She curled beside him and rested her head on his shoulder. She rubbed his chest with her hand, trying to release his tense muscles and get any tender response from him. She drifted her hand lower and pressed her thighs against his.

His hand locked onto her wrist. "Annalise, I need some time," he said.

He turned onto his side, putting his back to her.

* * *

Each day of the following week felt like a fresh performance of the same play, only with different characters playing the minor roles. Annalise tried to reach out to Exmore, bringing his favorite books, speaking of subjects that once drew laughs, but the harder she tried, the more he retreated from her into a cold politeness.

Two weeks since her marriage seemingly fell apart, the gray morning found her staring at the blank page on her writing desk. No amount of tea could lift her doldrums. Her pen hovered over the page, her mind bursting with words to say, but she didn't know who to tell them to. She couldn't write to Patrick anymore. And her husband was actively avoiding her.

She hadn't felt so despairing since the deaths of her parents. She had written to Patrick of her sadness then. Now, she had no one to talk to. She had gone beyond rationalizing what had happened that morning when Exmore discovered the letters. She wanted only to see the warm light in her husband's eyes again, as when he used to gaze at her in that beautiful time before he found the letters.

The sound of a carriage pulling up outside the home yanked her from her thoughts. Oh no, not more callers. She didn't think she was capable of making polite conversation without breaking down. She rose and crossed to the window, edging back the curtain. Her husband stepped down from the carriage. Her hurting heart rose at his sight. She turned and hurried down the stairs. The footmen were taking away his hat and gloves by the time she reached the bottom step.

"My dearest," he said, bowing. She saw something in his eyes—sadness, love, yearning? It happened too fast to tell before that cold reserve was back.

She didn't care if he pushed her away. She rushed to him and threw her arms around him.

"Ah, a happy greeting," he quipped in her ear. "You must have heard that Patrick is back and coming to call today."

* * *

Exmore felt his wife's body stiffen when it had been so soft and open. She drew away from him and wrapped her arms about herself.

He didn't know why he had said what he said. Some vengeful devil resided in him that, despite his best intentions, pushed Annalise away. He had rambled through the days, moving from club, to coffee house, to tea shop, to bookstore, to Parliament, to gaming hell, and all the while, she had consumed his thoughts. At hells, women had approached him, but their smiles, conversation, and touch had all grated. No one could replace Annalise.

Yet, whenever he was near Annalise, an ugly rage seized ahold of him that kept her at a distance. He knew what he had done wasn't fair. Theirs was not a love match. He had known she still loved Patrick when he asked her to marry him, yet there had been something so visceral about the written words, *It should have been you.* Why did she have to write that sentiment?

His rational mind didn't want to hurt Annalise, but his heart punished her for not loving him, and for Cassandra not loving him as well.

He had been musing over these thoughts earlier that morning when crossing Piccadilly. He had looked up and spied Patrick and his father approaching from the opposite direction. Before Exmore could pretend not to have seen them, Wallis nodded his head, acknowledging Exmore.

"Patrick, welcome back." Exmore had greeted the men through tight lips when their paths met. Exmore remembered Patrick as a self-absorbed youth, that stage of young manhood when Patrick had possessed a very limited view of the world, and that narrow perspective had revolved entirely around himself. It had been an exuberant confidence born of ignorance. Exmore had looked into Patrick's bright, unclouded eyes to see little had changed about the brash young man. The only visible difference was that Patrick was even more handsome, his face leaner and more tan, his frame larger and more muscular.

A mere bow hadn't been good enough for Patrick. He had drawn Exmore into a hard, back-slapping embrace. "It's great to be home," Patrick had said. "Good to see you. My father tells me you married Miss Van Der Keer. *My* Miss Van Der Keer." He had laughed, clearly having no hard feelings. "Something must have changed your mind after that harsh lecture you rang over me about her. Maybe you had your eye on her all along, eh?" More laughter.

Exmore hadn't reminded Patrick that he had been married

to another woman at the time of Patrick's departure to India.

"Let us all go to the club and talk as proper gentlemen," Wallis suggested. Wallis had exhibited a meekness around Exmore since the wedding.

Exmore excused himself, claiming he was on his way to meet with his man of business. Exmore remained coldly polite to Wallis out of familial duty, but he would never forgive the man for insulting Annalise.

"Then I shall call later today," Patrick had said brightly, as if his visit would be the pinnacle of Exmore's day and not the nadir.

Now, Exmore didn't know how to feel. He wanted Annalise to witness how little Patrick cared for her. Yet, he didn't want her to hurt even more. So much hung in the balance. The perilous game he had dared to play was ending. He wouldn't emerge the winner.

Annalise had been right. Friendship wasn't enough for a marriage. He couldn't make Annalise love him, just as he hadn't been able to make Cassandra love him. He had been a fool, and now he would see the consequences of his idiocy play out before his eyes. His heart ached like it had during those weeks after Cassandra's death. What had he done?

* * *

Patrick arrived two hours later. Exmore met him in the drawing room.

Annalise didn't come down, and Exmore began to think that she wasn't coming. His relief was short-lived when he saw the door quietly open, and Annalise slipped into the room. She wore the same clothes as she had earlier. The sunlight glowed through the strands of hair falling from her lace cap.

Patrick, who had been thinking aloud about the kind of horse team he wanted to put together, trailed off mid-sentence. His lips parted. "Annalise," he whispered.

Her eyes widened. Patrick stared at her, seeming to lose track of the moment. Then he shook his head as if awaking. He rose to his feet. "You look…" He gestured to his face.

"Lovely. Quite lovely."

For a long moment, neither Patrick nor Annalise spoke, but gazed at each other. Raw emotion saturated the air. Exmore's heart felt like it was contracting. Why did he feel he was intruding on a tender lovers' moment? And one of the lovers was his wife. He desired to stalk from the room, get on his horse, and leave behind London and the disaster his life had become.

"Please," Annalise said to Patrick and gestured to a chair. She glanced at Exmore. He looked away. He wouldn't let her see his pain.

"I'm sorry for my appearance." Patrick nervously patted his richly embroidered waistcoat. "India's finest tailors," he scoffed.

Annalise slowly sat, her hands gripping the armrest. "Did you enjoy your time in India?" Her voice had turned breathy and soft.

"Every hour away from London was torment. Appalling climate and equally appalling inhabitants. I set forth making my way there and ignored the rest."

"I'm sorry," she said. "I've read such delightful accounts of the customs and people. I thought that I should very much like to go."

"Surely you can find more comfortable corners of the world than a mosquito- and dung-infested cesspool," he quipped.

"But the art and traditions—"

Patrick waved his hand. "Ornate rubbish. All of it." He rubbed his lips and chin while studying her again. "I can't decide what about you has changed so radically. You are different. What have you been doing these years?"

Exmore waited for her to say that she had married. She made no mention of it, but said, "My parents died. I don't know if you heard in India."

Patrick visibly stiffened. "I'm sorry." He paused, digesting the news. "I'm sorry. I remember how you were always telling me delightful stories about them. How you used to laugh about your father coming in from the fields with insects crawling all over him. And how your mother would sing louder than the other ladies in the church."

"Yes," Annalise whispered.

Exmore swallowed his bitterness. He didn't know these stories.

"I wish I had known them," Patrick said solemnly.

Another painfully laden silence infused the room. Exmore could hear the unspoken question that couldn't be asked: What if Patrick had never left? Where would they all be now?

Patrick turned to Exmore. "So, when did you know she was the lady for you?" Beneath the amicable tone was a challenge.

Exmore wasn't going to divulge anything about his feelings for his wife. He made a vague reference to the masquerade party. Patrick returned his pointed, bright gaze to Annalise. "Do you enjoy being a marchioness? You didn't seem the sort when I knew you. Too casual and always laughing."

"I—I'm still adjusting," she stammered. "It's very difficult some days."

"Ah, but you must adore having parties," Patrick continued. "Remember how we met at

Lady Denning's musical evening? You challenged me to sing Bach, and I embarrassed myself, but did it to win your admiration." He hesitated, considering his words, an introspection Exmore hadn't seen in him before. "I… when I was in India, I would think about those days, you know. They seemed… sweeter. I missed them."

Annalise regarded him for a moment, and then her eyes drifted to the window. Exmore couldn't read her expression. Patrick had all but announced he had longed for her. She must be thinking about what would have happened if she hadn't married Exmore. She would have been free to marry the man she had loved all along.

Exmore reached for the decanter on the table beside him.

Patrick continued digging about in his nostalgic memories. Annalise remained fixed on the window. Exmore sipped from his glass and followed Annalise's gaze. A dull brown finch was perched on the sill. As soon as Exmore saw it, the bird flew away.

"I—I have a headache," Annalise said suddenly, interrupting Patrick's continuing reverie.

Patrick bolted from his chair and rushed to her as if Exmore wasn't there. "I'm sorry. Let us send a servant for your present relief." He touched her shoulder, and Annalise released a high, quiet hum.

Exmore rolled the burning brandy on his tongue and stifled the urge to strike Patrick.

Annalise's eyes trailed down to where Patrick's hand rested upon her. "No, thank you. I—I need to rest." She crossed to the door and then stopped, turning back. "Welcome back to London, Mr. Hume. I hope you are happier here than in India." She studied him a second more, then her eyes lit on Exmore. He busied himself pouring another brandy. She walked out of the room.

For a moment, neither man spoke. Exmore drank from his brandy, wishing he could hasten the glow of inebriation. He didn't offer Patrick a glass.

"How extraordinary," Patrick began, wagging his finger in the air. "I think you once said that she wasn't fit to be a gentleman's wife. Her nature was too wild and unyielding. When I defended her, you said she required more grace than she possessed to be my wife. Whatever changed your opinion of her?" He tried to make his words sound innocent. Exmore wasn't tricked. He heard the accusation in them.

"Don't remind me of what I said then," Exmore growled.

"But I listened to you. I followed your advice. I sailed across the world because you told me to."

Exmore shot to his feet. "You put up no resistance. You didn't fight for her at all. You walked away from her, breaking her heart. She deserved better."

Patrick opened his mouth and then shut it. After a pause, he said, "I broke her heart?" He seemed awed by this knowledge, his ego swelling at the realization that he possessed such power. "Well, I suppose you've mended it, haven't you?" He chuckled, a low, menacing sound—a laugh he must have acquired in India. "Just don't forget whom she loved first, my cousin. I could have had her."

Exmore made no words of farewell to Patrick. He simply set down his glass and strode out. It was the best option to keep Patrick's handsome face intact.

Exmore glanced up at the empty space that had once been occupied by Cassandra's portrait as he walked up the stairs to Annalise's chamber. Their marriage had ended in irreversible death. His and Annalise's marriage would continue in name and nothing else. They couldn't live in this tangled mess they were caught in, especially when the man she truly loved loitered about London.

He had made a mistake persuading Annalise to marry him. This sham of a marriage was his fault. Now he had to do his best to undo the damage he had inflicted, and then he would disappear into a gaming hell.

If she wanted Patrick, then he would give him to her. Exmore wouldn't say a word against her if they were discreet about their affair. But Exmore wouldn't wait around to witness the love she could never give to Exmore lavished on Patrick. Exmore wasn't strong enough to feel that kind of pain. For a few beautiful weeks, Exmore had thought he could rise above the ashes of his life after Cassandra. He had believed he could build something new and strong, but he had based his hope on a shaky foundation.

Annalise had been right that night so many years ago when she had vehemently cried that she would love Patrick forever. She had been right that friends shouldn't marry. What had he done to her? To himself?

He tapped on her door. "Annalise," he whispered.

She opened the door. Her eyes were red-rimmed, her cheeks damp. Scattered across the floor were the letters to Patrick. They were strewn haphazardly, as if she had thrown them.

"Please, please," she said and gestured him inside.

He drew in a steeling breath and began the proposal he didn't want to make, a pragmatic solution to this sad union. He had only to get out the words, and then he could disappear into a numbing bottle of brandy for the next months. "Perhaps we can live separate lives—"

"Is it too late to say I love you?" she cried.

"What?" Had he heard her correctly? No. He was afraid to believe. His heart had been damaged by hope before.

"Is it too late to say I love you?" She pressed her hand to her mouth, sobs shaking her shoulders.

"Oh, Annalise," he whispered. He tenderly drew the tear-wetted strands of hair away from her cheeks.

"I don't know the man who called today. I surely don't love him. I don't even know him. All this time…" She closed her eyes. "What have I done? I've caused so much trouble out of my foolishness. I've missed you so terribly."

"Hush," he tried to soothe her. "Don't let it trouble you." Her misery ached in his own chest.

"I saw him next to you, and in my heart there was nothing for him. Nothing. Empty. All my love was for you. He was a stranger. But I wrote all those letters to him. Every day. I wasted so much time. And I drove you away. I hurt you. And yet, I can't… I can't…" She searched his face, looking for an explanation.

"You can't what, my love?"

"I can't burn the letters!" she cried. "You are right. Something is very wrong with me."

"May I see them?" He knelt beside her and began to read.

My mother is in pain. She writhes. The medicines no longer help. I'm not ready to let her go. Is it selfish to still need your mama when you are grown?

He replaced that one with another.

My father taught me a game. I had to name all the birds that come to perch on our hedges. Now I know their names and calls. I see the beautiful coloring of bluebirds, the velvet red heads of the woodpeckers, and clever bead eyes of the crows. Once you stop and truly look, there is more and more to see.

Then he read:

The physician says my father has a few months to live. He bears the news with more dignity than I can muster. I'm so terrified of death, yet he says it's as natural as the migration of birds and rebirth of flowers. I do not see cycles, only ends. Too many ends.

He studied the letters, all in her handwriting, in joy, grief, and wonder. Her life's days laid out before him.

She sank beside him. "I'm so very sorry. Nothing I can say will make up for what I've done."

"Hush." He drew her into his arms and rubbed his cheek against her silken hair. To think he had tried to toss the letters in the grate, almost unwittingly destroying her written history. "May I have them? I want to read them and know all your stories, your life. I will cherish your letters."

She drew back, her brow lowered in confusion. "But they were written to another man."

"No," he whispered. "These weren't to Patrick. You have such a lovely heart, you needed to love someone. Someone who would listen to you when you had no one to talk to. A friend. I think… I think you made Patrick over into the man that you needed, and you loved that version, a dream version who gave you solace and strength."

Her lips trembled. "I was so scared then."

"I know," he said quietly. "I wish I could have been there for you."

"Me too. You bind me to this world. I've been so miserable." She rested her head on his chest. "I had loved Patrick so obsessively—you saw me then. I thought I couldn't love you because I don't feel that way. I was such a fool."

"No, don't say that." He caressed her back with his hand. He was touching her again. All turbulence in his heart calmed with her in his arms again.

"I wish I had known. I don't love you with that wild fever that I did Patrick... well, in the short time that I truly loved him. I know now that I love you differently. I love you quietly, deeply, in a place that reaches deeper than the heart. My father said you know more in the silence, and yet, once again, I missed it. I was looking for something loud, not perceiving the quiet love surrounding me."

"I'm sorry I have been so cold. I thought about you all the hours. I missed you, and yet—"

She put her finger on his lips and then let it slip to his heart. "Shhh, I understand. You needed a wife who loved you as you deserve to be loved. And I do. I truly love you. I will love you forever. There will be no one else for me."

He remembered her shouting similar sentiments to him years ago, frantic in her sorrow for another man. Now, the words of love fell from her lips, a stillness within them. They were as real and unbending as gravity and the cycle of tides.

"I love you," he whispered. "Tell me your stories and thoughts. I shall never push you away again."

She raised her lips to his. He drifted on their softness. A bitter journey had come to an end in a kiss, and a new, happier journey began. In that kind moment, he didn't feel any fear for the future. Days of laughter, children, pictures, flowers, books, tea, and conversation stretched out before them.

When she finally pulled back from their kiss, her eyes were shining with that mischievous light he adored.

"I don't think our marriage of friendship is going very well," she observed.

"I'm afraid there's nothing to be done about it. We will have to be a true love match."

She laughed, the kind of relieved laugh that came after a trauma had passed. The radiance lit her face again. All the sadness had scattered away.

CHAPTER THIRTEEN

My Dearest Husband:

While I do love England, I wish my country would spare my beloved his parliamentary duties this season. Alas, one more week until you return from London, and three weeks, according to the midwife, until our child is born. I know you worry about me, but please don't. The midwife assures me that our unborn and I are progressing very well, even though I feel as if I'm as large and lumbering as one of our milk cows.

Little Bella checks every few hours during the day to see if her new sibling has arrived. She is delighted when she places her hand on my stomach and feels the baby kick. "I think it's trying to get out, Mama," she said this morning. She has already named her sibling Philomena. When I suggested that she may have a little brother, she replied that Philomena would do for him as well. Yesterday, we drew coccinellids together on my bed, and I have included her darling picture for your pleasure. It's a family portrait. The coccinellid on the left is you. "You know he's Papa because he has more spots," she told me. I shall let you interpret that as you may. She explained that I have another wiggly coccinellid inside me, and that is why my ladybird takes up the entire right side of the page. See how Bella has drawn herself between us, holding our little insect hands. "I love Mama and Papa more than anyone else in the world," she assures me and warms my heart. I sometimes think my heart can't hold any more love—that I have gorged on love and now I'm full—and yet, my heart swells anew with the idea of holding our new one.

Thank you for recounting your delightful dinner with Phoebe and her husband. I always thought that a dashing young gentleman with a passion for the theater would sweep away her heart. It's rather ironic that she would fall passionately in love with a staid barrister. Alas, what he lacks in drama, he makes up for in kindness, adoration, and taking such good care of her. Her letters are filled with droll domestic stories, and still the ever-glorious Phoebe, she keeps me abreast of the latest London plays. Her accounts are far more amusing than the newspapers' versions.

I'm grateful that Aunt Sally and her other daughters have come to us. She is recovering quite rapidly from her husband's death and has been a great help to me in my confinement. She goes into the village and performs the charitable works that I would normally do. Already, she has made numerous friends. All ladies must consult her before buying fabric or having a gown made. I daresay, when you return, you will find that we are becoming the most fashionable village in all of England!

My love, I fear I must take you to task. You did not warn me that our new curate was excessively handsome and single. Before anything could be done about the alarming matter, Shelley's heart fell victim. Now, the poor man is beyond consolation because he feels he cannot properly provide for her. As I blame you for this sad state, so you must rectify it. I think a wedding in the late summer should tidy up the situation nicely.

Last Friday, I received a letter from Mr. Visser congratulating me on my book's publication. I had tears in my eyes as I read his fine praise of my work and my father's. He asks me when I shall publish a second volume. I am wildly flattered, yet I fear that I *haven't the time, but still my head whirs with ideas. My father left so many papers, and the fields and moors here teem with beauty. My father would have loved it here. Sometimes, I imagine him and Mother walking arm-in-arm along the paths.*

I love you, my dearest husband. I pray for your safe return to us. A part of me is missing when you are gone. I glance at your dining room chair thinking you will be there, or I start to search for you when I read an interesting article, and then I remember that you are gone. The nights are the cruelest. Away from me, you are even more present in my mind. It is simply not enough to console myself with memories of your tender embraces. I have stored up weeks and weeks of kisses and tender embraces for you when you come home. I'm so impatient that I fear that I will bestow them on you all at once when you arrive. Until that sweet moment, I keep you in my heart.

Your loving wife.

The End

Dear Gentle Reader,

It's been a true joy and blessing to work with Emily and Grace again. They are wonderfully supportive, creative, and intelligent ladies. Sometimes our writing process makes me feel like I'm ten again, asking my friends to play, except now we play with words instead of dolls and dollhouses.

I hope that you enjoyed Annalise and Exmore's love story. If you would like to read more of my work, please visit my website at susannaives.com to find excerpts from my other stories or sign up for my infrequent newsletter. Sign up here: http://eepurl.com/bO51hv.

Happy reading,

Susanna Ives

The Governess and the Norse God

Grace Burrowes

To those who feel out of place at the ball,
even when wearing a mask and carrying a hammer

CHAPTER ONE

"You'll make all the other Vikings jealous, Papa, for you look splendidly savage."

Darien St. Ives, Marquess of Tyne, looked—and felt—a proper fool strutting about the nursery in trews, crossed garters, linen tunic, and fur cape.

"My choices were a highwayman, of which there will be dozens, a Titan, which would necessitate indecent attire, or this."

"My papa is the best Viking ever," Sylvie declared with the limitless loyalty of a seven-year-old. "Your longboat would be the longest, and the monasteries you sacked would be reduced to... to... mere reticules."

It's not that kind of sacking. Miss Fletcher, the girls' governess, had instructed Tyne on the inappropriateness of correcting Sylvie's word choices when the child was trying to be gracious. He knelt and scooped up his daughter, the only plunder worth capturing in the nursery.

"You think I cut a dash?"

Sylvie squeezed him about the neck. "The ladies will swoon

at the sight of you. When you brandish your long sword, your enemies will tremble with mortal dread."

The ladies would swoon with boredom. Tyne's weapon of choice was a sharpened pencil most days, his shield an abacus. Solitude was his preferred fortress and the mathematical error his sworn foe. For a settled widower, the vast reaches of the marquessate's estate ledger books were adventure enough.

"Papa, you forgot to shave."

This worried the girl. She was easily worried, having lost her mother at the age of four and not having found Miss Fletcher until six months ago. The intervening two and a half years had been a succession of failures in the governess department, for which Tyne blamed himself.

As heir to a marquessate, he'd had governors and tutors from the age of three. The lot of them had been priggish, sedentary, and forever spouting rules.

Miss Fletcher was about as sedentary as a lightning bolt, though she spouted rules—at her employer.

You shall tuck Sylvie in on the nights that you are home.

You shall kiss both girls on the forehead before departing on the evenings you go out.

You shall recall their birthdays, and you shall most especially note the anniversary of their mother's death with a family outing to some location their mother enjoyed.

You shall resume socializing, so your daughters know that life moves on and they need not surrender to grief forever.

You shall bestow on your daughters the occasional bouquet of flowers, for how are the young ladies to know what to expect of a gentleman if their own papa doesn't comport himself as one?

For a small woman, Miss Fletcher had an endless store of commands and warnings. By the time she'd arrived, Tyne had been grateful for anybody who brought a sense of competence and order to his children's lives, and her approach had borne fruit.

Sylvie hadn't had a nightmare for months. Amanda was playing the pianoforte again.

"I did not shave," Tyne informed his daughter, "because Vikings were a rough lot. I'm trying to be authentic to my role."

Sylvie's solemn gaze said she was considering whether this excuse would wash. "You need a name, Papa. Vikings had grand names."

Oh, right. Sven Forkbeard. Harold Battleax. Ivan Bignose. All quite barbaric. "If I had an eye patch, I could be Tyne One-Eye."

"Not Tyne," she said, wiggling out of his grasp. "Then everybody would know who you are."

Lately, Tyne himself had felt a sense of his identity fading. He was the marquess, of course. He voted his seat in Parliament, he dined at his clubs, he made the occasional speech in the Lords regarding economic matters. At Yuletide, planting, and harvest, he opened the ancestral hall to the neighbors and tenants.

The year was a succession of predictable moves, like an old-fashioned court dance: Holidays in the country, remove to Town. Opening of Parliament, beginning of Lent. Polite invitations during the Season to make up the numbers, waltzes with wallflowers.

A restful lot, the wallflowers. He liked them and envied them their anonymity.

Then came grouse season, which he usually spent at the family seat, pretending to tramp about with a fowling piece on his shoulder, while searching for a place out of the wet to read for a few hours.

Harvest, the opening Hunt Ball. The holidays in the country... All the while, his daughters grew taller and more articulate. His estates prospered, and he... he missed Josephine, though he hadn't known his marchioness all that well.

"You should be Thor," Sylvie decided. "You need a hammer."

"How shall I waltz while carrying a hammer at Lord Boxhaven's masquerade?"

"You set the hammer down, Papa, just as you'd set down a

cup of punch. Or you could hang it from your belt."

An untoward image came to mind of Thor's hammer swinging from Tyne's belt and smacking a dancing partner in an unmentionable location. This was what came of wearing crossed garters and a fur cape.

"To bed with you, darling Sylvie," he said, picking her up again and carrying her into her bedroom. "Miss Fletcher will not tolerate even a Norse god keeping you up past your bedtime."

The nursery maid rose from the rocking chair next to the hearth and ducked a curtsey.

"Doesn't Papa look dashing, Helms?"

"Very dashing, Miss Sylvie." The woman was likely twice Tyne's age and silently laughing at him. Perhaps he did need a hammer. "Sweet dreams, Sylvie," he said, kissing her forehead. "If I see any unicorns, I'll capture one for you."

"I want a blue one," Sylvie said, scooting beneath her covers. "With a sparkling purple horn."

How could this fanciful child be his offspring? "Blue with a purple horn, of course."

"*Sparkling* purple, Papa."

"Your wish," he said, making her the sort of court bow that always earned him a smile. "Now say your prayers and go to sleep, or Miss Fletcher will hurl thunderbolts at us."

He escaped the nursery to the music of Sylvie's giggles. He had bid good night to Amanda before donning this outlandish costume. She'd grown too big to cuddle or carry about. She was acquiring the knack of a rational argument, which too few people practiced on a marquess.

Soon, she'd put up her hair.

Soon after that, Tyne's hair would sport some gray at the temples. Life was passing him by, which ought not to be possible when he was wealthy, titled, in great good health, and content in every particular.

Thirty-three was hardly ancient.

Perhaps he'd stop by the livery and find himself a

convincingly stout mallet to carry about the ballroom. Anything to put off attending the masquerade for even an additional five minutes.

* * *

"He's gone," Lady Amanda said, watching the coach pull away from the front drive two stories below.

She was thirteen years old, too young to have her own sitting room, but Lucy Fletcher had found the marquess to be a creature of habit rather than convention. When he gave an order—such as "Move my older daughter into her own bedroom."—he was in the *habit* of being obeyed. The largest bedroom on the nursery floor other than Lucy's had a sitting room; *ergo,* into that bedroom, Lady Amanda had been moved.

"But where is Papa off to?" Amanda murmured, letting the curtain at the window drop.

Lucy had no idea what events graced Lord Tyne's social schedule for the evening, but Amanda was at the age where adults fascinated her in a way they didn't interest younger children. To little Lady Sylvie, the marquess was simply Papa. He had sweets in his pocket or a scold to deliver. His other adult obligations were mysterious, vaguely annoying details to Sylvie.

Amanda, by contrast, was intrigued with her father's adult responsibilities.

What *was* a marquess, historically speaking?

What did the House of Lords *do* all evening that Papa had to be there so late?

Why did that simper-y Mrs. Holymere wiggle her fingers like that at Papa in the park?

Lucy knew exactly why the pretty widow wiggled her fingers—and her hips—at the marquess. He was too good-looking, too titled, too wealthy, and—worst of all—too decent not to gain the notice of some wiggly widow in the very near future.

So Lucy would do for the girls what she could while she was governess here, little though that might be.

"We can hope your father is enjoying a social outing," Lucy said. *For a change.* If Lord Tyne were one-tenth as attuned to polite society as he was to the politics of the realm, he'd have four engagements each night.

"How will I be invited to tea dances if Papa has no social connections?" Amanda asked, flouncing onto the sofa. "I won't have any callers, I won't be granted vouchers to Almack's."

"You'd best prepare yourself for holy orders," Lucy said. "Start memorizing the New Testament, because you will need the comfort of all four Evangelists in your endless old age."

Amanda's chin came up in a gesture reminiscent of her father. "I'll go to tea dances when I'm fourteen. I'm thirteen now."

Lucy took the place beside her, because this great eagerness to grow up, to be treated as a young lady, was normal. For a marquess's daughter to be normal, rather than hopelessly spoiled or regularly hysterical, was rare in Lucy's experience.

"You are thirteen years and three months," Lucy said. "Give your Papa some time to find his bearings. He is not a man prone to precipitous action. Your aunts have many connections."

Amanda made a face, such as Sylvie made when somebody forgot to sprinkle cinnamon and sugar on her porridge.

"The aunties have babies. I'm never having babies. Aunt Eleanor says children ruin a woman's figure."

Amanda had only the merest beginnings of a figure, thank heavens. "Your aunt is approaching her fourth confinement. She is entitled to be testy. Will you read tonight?"

"You can't teach me more card games?"

Of course Amanda would ask that tonight. "I'm fatigued, Amanda. Perhaps another time. If the weather's fine tomorrow and your lessons go well, we can picnic in the park."

"With Syl-vie," Amanda said, martyrdom oozing from all three syllables. "I am the elder by six years, but I never go anywhere without her. I can't wait to put up my hair."

"Find a book, write to a cousin, experiment at your vanity with your combs and hair ribbons." Lucy half-hugged Amanda and rose. "I'll see you tomorrow."

"Good night, Miss Fletcher." Amanda remained on the tufted sofa, a precocious child left all alone for yet another evening.

Lucy knew how that felt. "Would you care to join your father some morning for an early outing in the park?"

Amanda had grown two inches over the winter, which meant she'd become too tall for her pony. His lordship had grumbled when Lucy had pointed out that the hems of Lady Amanda's habit nearly dragged on the ground, but he'd also come home the next day leading a dainty gray mare named Snowdrop.

"An early outing?" Amanda twiddled the gold tassel of a purple velvet pillow. "How early?"

"Dawn, when the mist is rising from the Serpentine, and the day is full of possibilities. All the fashionable gentlemen and not a few ladies ride at dawn."

Amanda set aside the pillow and crossed to her vanity. "Sylvie will never get up that early."

To be included in a family outing, she would. "She'd need a nap if she managed to waken at dawn."

Amanda pulled the black ribbon from her right braid. "She hates taking naps."

"While I love a refreshing respite in the middle of the afternoon. Those being in short supply, I'll bid you good night."

Before Amanda could ask for help arranging her hair, choosing a book, or deciding on a poem to memorize, Lucy slipped out the door. The hour was early by fashionable standards, but for a governess who had to change into a costume and find her way to a masquerade ball, time was of the essence.

* * *

The masquerade was becoming noisy, the inevitable result of polite society donning masks and then partaking of the mayhem passing for mine host's lemon punch. In the ballroom itself, Boxhaven's mama and grandmama would prevent outright debauchery, but in the garden shadows and unused parlors, mischief would abound.

Under the minstrels' gallery, a centurion leered down the bodice of a shepherdess in the manner of centurions from time immemorial. A portly satyr danced by with his arms about Good Queen Bess. The lady's skirts would likely keep her horned partner from living down to the potential of his costume on the very dance floor.

Tyne silently promised himself escape in fifteen minutes.

"Good evening, sir," drawled a voice to Tyne's right. "What a fine figure of a Norseman you make."

Ye gods. Lady Artemnesia Chalfont was nicknamed Lady Amnesia, so predictable was her habit of leaving a reticule, glove, or fan behind at a social call. She'd retrieve the item at the time of her choosing, and she always selected a moment when the bachelor sons of the household were on hand to play Find the Glove at my lady's direction.

"My thanks for your compliment," Tyne said, bowing. "I gather Roman legend inspired your own ensemble." She was Diana, aptly enough. She'd hunted Tyne for the past two Seasons, though she didn't appear to recognize him now. "I believe I saw a centurion patrolling beneath the minstrels' gallery."

The dance floor was full of the usual assortment of highwaymen, Rob Roys, a Louis Quinze with his Madame de Pompadour, and Greek goddesses. Couldn't have a masquerade without a few dozen bow-wielding ladies waltzing about in their dressing gowns.

Tyne was the only Thor so far. Thank heavens he'd bothered with a half-mask, or Lady Artemnesia would have started plaguing him the moment he'd arrived.

"Come now," Lady Artemnesia said, smacking his arm with a closed fan. "Should I trouble myself with a mere centurion when I can instead pass the time with a *god*?"

The centurion put his hand on the shepherdess's shoulder,

and she sidled out from under his grasp. Because he didn't remove his paw from her person, the strap of her gown was momentarily pushed off her shoulder and drooped down her arm. She reassembled her bodice, her mouth compressed in a line.

"Perhaps the centurion is free to dance," Tyne said, holding up the sledgehammer he'd rested headfirst against his boot. "I'm rather encumbered by my accoutrements."

"What a mighty hammer that is."

Seven more minutes, and Tyne would have outlasted his personal endurance record at a masquerade.

"Blasted thing is heavy," he said. "Puts a crimp in even a god's waltzing."

What sort of shepherdess carried a spear rather than a crook? And what *was* that upon her head? The young lady besieged by a Roman army of one had positioned her spear in her right hand, the same side upon which Maximus Gloriosus stood. His hand was back on her shoulder, his thumb brushing over her bare flesh in a most familiar manner.

"You will excuse me," Tyne said. "I believe I've spotted my partner for the next set."

"But you said you weren't dancing."

Tyne bowed and propped his sledgehammer on his shoulder. "I'm not."

He sauntered along the edge of the ballroom, earning some stares. The sledgehammer was a lovely touch, quite authentic. Perhaps he'd start a fashion for carrying sledgehammers rather than sword-canes on Bond Street.

"Excuse me," Tyne said, bowing to the spear-wielding shepherdess with the bizarre millinery. "I believe my dance is coming up."

Gloriosus glowered at him. "The Valkyrie isn't dancing. She told me so herself. I'm sitting out with her."

Behind her half-mask, the lady's blue eyes flashed perdition to presuming soldiers. "I said I was not free to dance *with you*, sir. I suggest you find somebody who is."

Gloriosus was the Honorable Captain Dinwiddie Dunstable, an earl's younger son who had apparently suffered a few blows to the head in the course of his military career. He was as stupid as he was indolent, and he stood much too close to the lady's spear for his continued good health.

Tyne offered his arm. "Madam Valkyrie."

She shoved her spear at Gloriosus. "You may have this, to fend off all the women doubtless waiting to importune you for a turn on the dance floor."

She was a compact little creature, her hair pinned back under some winged copper contraption that might have been concocted of spare kitchenware. Her mask obscured her eyes and half of her nose, and her complexion was English-lady pale.

"We needn't dance," Tyne said, leading her in the direction of the gallery. "I've grown fond of striding about with a sledgehammer on my shoulder. If I set my hammer aside in this company, somebody's likely to steal it, and then I'd lose my magical powers."

"A guest at this gathering would steal a sledgehammer?"

"A guest, a footman, a maid. Some of the extra staff hired for a social gathering can be less than exemplary. It's a fine tool and the property of a god, after all. No telling what imps or fairies might yearn to wrest it from me."

She peered up at him, as if visual inspection might reveal how much of the punch Tyne had imbibed. "It's a hammer, sir. A handle and a weight, for smacking things."

"Like most well-made tools, this hammer has probably been handed down from father to son to nephew. One replaces the head, the other replaces the handle, and yet, it's the heirloom hammer, carrying a craftsman's share of pride from one generation to the next. I call that magic, and I'm a god, so you mustn't gainsay me. A pouting god is an unpredictable creature."

He found them a cushioned bench beneath a burned-out sconce. The guests strolling the garden were doubtless enjoying more of nature's delights than Tyne would consider decent, while the gallery was both quieter and cooler than the ballroom. A fine place to spend the three or four minutes remaining of his penance with…

How embarrassing. He could not place the Valkyrie's voice, though she sounded familiar. Educated, of course, and not particularly regional.

"We could dance if you insist," he said. "I'll secret my hammer behind an arras."

"Thank you, no. My personal Praetorian Guard might think himself welcome to renew his attentions. Is that all people do at these affairs? Leer and flirt and swill punch?"

"I'm told this is called socializing among the English."

She stretched her feet out before her. "I'm English, rather than who I appear to be. You must forgive my lack of familiarity with masked balls."

She wore sturdy half-boots instead of dancing slippers. The Valkyrie were known to be unsentimental ladies, though half-boots were astonishingly practical.

"Isn't that rather the point of a masquerade?" Tyne asked. "To be somebody else for a short time, to impersonate a more daring, dashing creature than one is in truth?"

"I'm impersonating a friend," she said. "Somebody I went to school with. She asked me to attend, wearing this costume, so she might for once stay home and rest. I am not deceived, though. She wanted me to have an adventurous evening. I'm ready to fly back to Valhalla, if this is society's idea of an enjoyable evening."

The Valkyrie were also honest, apparently.

"I have a suggestion," Tyne said, rising. "Like the conscientious, plundering Viking that I am, why don't I make a pass through the buffet? The least you're owed is some sustenance before you give up on your adventure."

"I'll guard your hammer," she replied. "I love fruit and cheese above all combinations."

Tyne rested the long handle of his hammer against the side

of the bench. Because the sconce was unlit, he couldn't see his companion in detail, but he could *hear* that she was smiling.

So was he. "I'm to be on watch for a blue unicorn with a purple sparkly horn. No other breed will do. Guard my hammer well, Madam Valkyrie."

He strode off, wondering if the single cup of punch he'd sampled had addled his wits. He was about to set a new record for his appearance at one of Boxhaven's masquerade balls. Sylvie would be proud of him, and Amanda would think him quite silly.

Though, as to that, he hadn't even confessed to Amanda where he'd be spending his evening. And poor Madam Valkyrie. The notion that anybody could meet with adventure at a venue as tedious as a masquerade ball was absurd. Tyne could locate strawberries, though, and oranges, and stewed apples.

But what on earth could he find to *discuss* with the lady while they consumed their victuals?

* * *

"Fruit and cheese," Thor said, passing Lucy a plate. "Also some ham, for I imagine all that flying you Valkyries do from battlefield to battlefield is hungry work."

He settled beside her on the bench, the furniture creaking under his weight. He was blond and Viking-sized, and the cape swirling about his shoulders and hint of golden beard on his cheeks gave him a dashing air.

Lucy took the plate, which was heaped high with food. "I can't possibly eat all of this."

"That's the idea," he replied, bumping her with his shoulder. "You eat as much as you like, and I'll deal with the rest. English plates are too small for a man of my northern appetites."

"Melon," Lucy said, picking up a silver fork. "I lose my wits in the presence of fresh melon."

"Your adventurous spirit has been rewarded. What else would make this evening enjoyable?"

"Peace and quiet, though this cheese is scrumptious." Blue

veins, pungent flavor, creamy texture. The perfect complement to the melon.

Thor used his fingers to pop a rolled-up slice of ham into his mouth. "You sound weary, Madam Valkyrie."

His earlier comment, about flying from battlefield to battlefield, was more apt than he knew. Lucy's specialty was children who'd lost a parent. Even the aristocracy boasted a sad abundance of the half-orphaned. Wealthy parents might not take much notice of their offspring, but the children noticed when a parent died.

The agencies that placed governesses knew Lucy dealt well with such families, and thus she'd landed in Lord Tyne's household.

"I don't typically keep such late hours," she said, spearing a strawberry. "I'll pay for this tomorrow."

"Try sitting in Parliament. Why the wheels of government can only turn after dark has ever confounded me. I've a theory that most men have a quiet dread of the ballrooms and dinner parties, and Parliament schedules its debates and committee meetings the better to spare its members the social venues."

Lord Tyne seemed to thrive on his parliamentary obligations, though he also struck Lucy as a man in want of sleep most of the time.

"What would you rather be doing?" she asked. Perhaps Thor was an MP, though at this gathering, a titled lord was more likely.

He considered another rolled-up slice of ham. "I'm watching for stray unicorns. The work is hardly exciting, but you meet all the best people."

Was he *flirting?* "And you get to carry a very fine hammer about all evening."

"A consummation devoutly to be wished."

They ate the fruit and cheese—Lucy took a single slice of ham—in companionable quiet. "Take the last strawberry," and "Should have found you a spoon for the apples," the extent of the conversation. Marianne wouldn't understand how this qualified as an adventure for Lucy—sharing a plate with a strange god—but Lucy was enjoying herself, mostly.

"Do you read much Shakespeare?" she asked.

Thor set the empty plate on the floor to the side of the bench. "I'm a literate Englishman, so I'm supposed to say yes. The truth is, I haven't had time to read for pleasure in years. Now, I'm called upon to read to my children occasionally, and they seem to like that. If I have a choice between brushing up on *Romeo and Juliet*, or spending an hour in the nursery, I've lately chosen the nursery."

He was married. This revelation should not have disappointed Lucy—she'd be back in her own bed in little more than an hour—but his marital status reminded her that this was a masquerade. He wasn't Thor, she wasn't in search of an adventure, or a *unicorn*.

"*Romeo and Juliet* isn't exactly light reading," Lucy said. "You're better off enjoying the company of your own children rather than reading about somebody else's doomed offspring." She'd never liked the tragedies, particularly tragedies that left the stage littered with dead adolescents. "Your children will thank you one day for reading to them."

He relaxed back against the wall, stretching long legs before him. "Have you children, that you can offer me such an assurance?"

"I had a papa. He read to us."

"I'm sorry for your loss." Those quiet words, spoken not by a bantering deity, but by a very human man who was himself a father, nudged Lucy's mood in a sad direction.

"Papa was a god," she said. "Jovial, wise, bigger than life, kinder than kind. He knew what to say, he knew when to say nothing. I miss him."

Which was why she grasped the world of a grieving child.

"I miss my wife," Thor said. "Trite words, and we had a trite marriage. We'd known each other since childhood, had always expected to marry one another. We suited wonderfully, and yet, we barely knew each other. There's nothing trite about grief, particularly when bewilderment and guilt get into the mix." He laid his hammer across his lap. "My apologies for burdening you with such conversation. Loneliness makes fools of us."

Why couldn't Lord Tyne be this insightful? He was a good man, an honorable man, but sometimes, Lucy wanted to shake him. Perhaps his lordship needed some enchanted creature to kiss him, to waken him from his parliamentary bills and estate ledgers.

The wiggly widows would allow Tyne to stay lost in his politics and accounting, and that would not be a happy ending for Lucy's employer.

"What would help?" Lucy asked. "What would ease your grief and rekindle your joie de vivre?"

He lifted his hammer and considered the battered weight that made it an effective tool. "Joie de vivre is in short supply at Valhalla. As you doubtless know, we go in more for gory sagas, epic wrestling matches, and kidnapping maidens who don't belong to us."

He had a very nice smile, though Lucy wished he wasn't wearing a half-mask. She'd like to see his eyes more clearly. His voice was that of any well-educated Englishman, much like Lord Tyne's voice, but Thor's conversation included humor and honest emotion.

"The wrestling matches sound interesting," Lucy said as a satyr galloped past with a giggling nymph in tow.

The gamboling couple apparently didn't notice Lucy and Thor sitting in the shadows, for the nymph allowed herself to be caught, then pressed against the wall for a protracted kiss. The sight should have been ridiculous—the satyr's horns sat askew on his head, the nymph's golden wig was similarly disarranged—but the sheer glee of the undertaking made Lucy cross.

The nymph wiggled free, gave the satyr a smack on the bum, then darted off down the gallery.

"Ye gods and little fishes," Thor said, rising and shouldering his hammer. "I do believe it's time I kidnapped a maiden."

He took Lucy by the hand and led her off into the shadows.

CHAPTER TWO

What consenting adults got up to was no business of Tyne's, but he'd be damned if he'd be made to watch an orgy.

"I apologize for that… that… scene," he said, ducking out of the gallery and into the corridor that would take them to the front of the house. "I've overstayed my tolerance for the evening's entertainments. I will find your escort and take my leave of you."

He didn't want to. The lady was easy to talk to and sensible. Miss Fletcher, who answered to the same proportions as Madam Valkyrie, though with fewer curves, was also sensible. So why did Tyne feel as if he had to mentally prepare for every interaction with his children's governess?

"Are we in a hurry, sir?"

"A tearing hurry. Outside the purview of the chaperones in the ballroom, first the wigs fall off, and then clothing starts flying in all directions. I should have known better, but one loses track of time. Why otherwise rational human beings, who will nod to one another cordially in the churchyard, must comport themselves like—"

The Valkyrie planted her booted feet and brought Tyne to a halt. "You are not responsible for their folly, and I'm hardly an innocent maiden to be shocked by kisses and flirtation."

Tyne peered at her, but the damned masks made interpreting an expression futile. "I was shocked. Some kisses are meant to be private."

"I was affronted, but mostly I was amused." She linked her arm with Tyne's. "If we're to find my escort, he's the only monk in the crowd."

The monk was Jeremy Benton, Lord Luddington, heir to an earldom. The Valkyrie moved in good company, though Luddington was a flirting fool.

"I expect Brother Monk will be among the last to leave. Shall I escort you home?" The offer was out in all its well-meant, bold impropriety before Tyne could call it back. Down the corridor, glass shattered and a roar went up from the crowd in the cardroom.

"I'll need my cloak," Madam Valkyrie said. "I can't parade across London looking like this."

"Not without your spear, you can't," Tyne said. "Take my cloak. What it lacks in fashion, it makes up for in warmth."

He draped the fur cape about the Valkyrie's shoulders and fastened the frogs. The cloak reached nearly to the floor on her, which would afford her both warmth and modesty.

A laughing footman ran past—full tilt—with two shepherdesses in pursuit.

"Time to leave," Tyne said, offering his arm. "I believe that was Lord Malmsey impersonating a footman."

"Interesting strategy. I should at least tell Brother Monk that I've found another escort."

Tyne tripped the next escapee from the ballroom—a man dressed as a jockey—by the simple expedient of tangling the man's boots in the handle of the sledgehammer.

"Find the monk and tell him the Valkyrie is being escorted home by a trustworthy friend."

"I say, is that—?"

Tyne hefted his sledgehammer across his shoulders, like a pugilist stretching with an oaken staff. "Find him now, please."

The jockey saluted with his riding crop. "Will do, guv."

Tyne took the lady's hand, lest some marauding pirate carry her off, and led her through the front door. The night air was brisk, the drive lined with waiting coaches and lounging linkboys.

"We'll wait half an hour for my coachman to get through this tangle," Tyne said. "Do you live far from here?"

Her hand was warm in his—apparently, Valkyries were no more inclined to wear gloves than Norse gods were. The familiarity of clasped hands inspired in Tyne a mixture of awkwardness and pleasure. He hadn't held hands with a lady since he and Josephine had courted. He had forgotten the comfortable friendliness of joining hands. He stood beneath the wavering torches, telling himself to turn loose of his companion and trying to summon his coach forward with a wish.

He wasn't a leering centurion or a frisky monk, and yet, dropping the lady's hand would seem more gauche than pretending he was at ease with the presumption.

"I live not far from here," Madam Valkyrie said. "We could walk the distance by the time your coach arrives."

"Fine notion. Lead on, if you please."

"You're sure it's no bother?"

How he wished she'd take off that dratted mask, but then he'd have to remove his own mask and reveal himself to be not a god, but rather, a shy marquess toting a sledgehammer through Mayfair.

"No bother at all, though I need a name for you. In my mind, you're Madam Valkyrie, which conjures images of strapping shield-maidens and longboats with bedsheets flapping from their rigging."

"You have a vivid imagination, Thor."

"If I am Thor, perhaps you could be Freya?"

"A goddess. That will serve."

They reached the foot of the drive, and Freya turned left, in the direction of Tyne's neighborhood. This was coincidence, of course, not good luck, fate, or divine providence. Certainly not a sign from on high, or Valhalla, or anywhere else of any import. Nonetheless, in the lowly region of Tyne's breeding organs, notice had been taken that he was in proximity to a female of marriageable age and interesting temperament.

"What made you decide to be a Valkyrie tonight?"

"I didn't. I'm impersonating a friend, and she chose to be a Valkyrie. Why are you Thor?"

"The costume was simple. The cloak you're wearing was sent to me by a cousin in Saint Petersburg. Crossed garters are a matter of some purloined harness, and the sledgehammer is borrowed. Add an old shirt and some worn chamois breeches and riding boots, and you have a god."

Also a surprisingly comfortable ensemble. No cravat half-choking a fellow, no sleeve buttons at his wrists, no waistcoat that must lie just so under his exquisitely tailored evening coat. Perhaps wardrobe alone explained why the Vikings were such a cheerful lot.

"This thing on my head," Freya said. "I feel as if I'm wearing a copper pot on my hair. It's beastly uncomfortable."

That Tyne should enjoy rare liberty from the tyranny of his tailor while Freya suffered seemed unfair.

"Let's have it off, shall we? Whatever stewpot gave up its life to become your helm won't be missed if it should end up in yonder bushes."

"Please," she said, dropping Tyne's hand. "The dratted thing pinches behind my ears." She tried to lift the helmet off, but some bolt or other caught in the collar of her cloak.

"Let me," Tyne said, moving behind her. He explored along the edge of the cape's collar with his fingers—gently and thoroughly—finding warm skin and soft tresses in addition to fur snagged on a joint in the metal. He ripped the fur and lifted the helmet. Calling upon long-dormant cricket skills, he tossed the helmet up and used his trusty sledgehammer to bat it off into the darkened square beside the walkway.

The helmet landed with a *clonk* many yards away.

"Better," Freya said. "My thanks."

She'd wrapped a scarf about her hair, like a turban, so Tyne was deprived of even hair color as a hint to her identity. She made no move to take his hand, but rather, twined her arm through his in proper escort fashion.

Well, drat. What was a god to do? Tyne had not the first clue how to comport himself with a goddess, but a gentleman made pleasant conversation with a lady.

"You mentioned that your papa read to you. Have you any favorite tales?"

"I loved the myths and legends, the stories with fantastical beasts and clever maidens. Improving sermons put me to sleep, and fables, with their thinly disguised moralizing, bored me."

"A woman of particular tastes." Miss Fletcher was such a female. Tyne had the odd thought that she'd be pleased with him for this night's version of socializing. "Do you still love the fantastical stories?"

She was silent until they reached a corner. "No, I do not. The heroic feats and strange lands are fine entertainment, but one grows up. The amazing accomplishments become dealing with disappointment, finding meaningful employment, and learning the uncharted terrain of adult responsibility."

She sounded so sad, so resolute.

"I had a tutor once," Tyne said, "who claimed that no great problem was ever solved without creativity and courage. The fables and legends can help us be courageous and creative. Perhaps you should resume their study."

He'd like to give her a book of fables or a compendium of the world's mythologies.

Or a kiss. Perhaps he should whack himself on the noggin with his borrowed sledgehammer.

"An interesting notion," she said. "What of you? Do you love to reread certain books? Know classical tales you can recite almost by heart?"

"Wordsworth's poetry is still wafting about in the dungeons of my memory, and I was quite fond—"

Freya stumbled on an uneven brick and pitched against Tyne. "I beg your pardon."

"Steady on," Tyne said, slipping an arm about her waist. She had a lovely figure, and he didn't turn loose of her until she had clearly regained her balance. "How much farther? I can summon a hackney if you're growing fatigued."

"I'm managing." She sounded as if she was uncertain where she'd left her abode. They were only two streets up from Tyne's town house, a delightful coincidence, in his estimation.

He resumed walking, his pace slower. "Will you think me unbearably forward if I ask whether a particular swain has caught your fancy?"

Now, he was grateful for his mask, though he wished he could read Freya's expression. This late in the evening, the neighborhood was only half conscientious about keeping terrace lamps lit.

"My affections are not engaged," Freya said. "I admire… a man, but he's much taken up with affairs of state, and my esteem is that of a distant acquaintance only. I suspect I would like him, given a chance to know him better, though I don't see that chance befalling me."

Her affections were not engaged. That was good. As for the rest of it…

"I'm sure he's a decent sort," Tyne said, "but he sounds as if he'd bore you silly before the conclusion of the first set. Best look elsewhere for a man worth your attention."

She turned at the corner, onto a street where not even half the porch lamps were lit. Tyne didn't know his neighbors well, and he certainly wasn't acquainted with the families on this street—not yet.

"How can you form an opinion of a man whom I myself don't know that well?"

"Because he's an idiot," Tyne said. "A goddess admires him from afar, and he takes no notice. Trust me on this, for I am a god, and the workings of the mortal male are well known to me." He was a fool, but a fool who was enjoying his evening for the first time in… years?

"Do you fancy a particular lady?"

They'd reached a portion of the street where not a single household had bothered to light a lamp. This was providential, because some admissions were more easily made under cover of darkness.

"I notice my share of women," he said. "And those ladies are lovely, and sweet, and could easily become dear, but because I never had to learn the art of romantic persuasion, I know not how to make my interest apparent. I know not, in fact, if my interest qualifies as genuine liking, loneliness, or the base urge that motivates a great deal of male foolishness."

Or something of all three.

"You won't learn the answer to that conundrum if you simply watch the ladies waltz by on the arms of other men," Freya replied. "You can't expect them to divine your thoughts by magic."

Miss Fletcher would have offered that sort of observation, and she would have been right. Again.

"Is this where you live?" Tyne asked, for she'd brought them to a halt before a house from which not a single light shone.

"My friend bides here."

Tyne took a moment to count how many houses lay between the closest door and the corner.

"You advise me to make my feelings known," he said. "In the manner of a plundering Norseman, I'll do just that. I'd like to kiss you, if you'd be comfortable allowing me such a liberty on a deserted street at a quiet hour. I've enjoyed your company very much, Freya, and—"

She mounted the steps that led to the covered porch, where the darkness was dense indeed. Tyne followed, and she passed him what could only be her mask.

"Your plundering needs work, sir. Allow me to demonstrate." She plucked off his mask and tossed it aside, then braced herself with a grip on Tyne's shoulder, cupped his cheek with her free hand, and kissed him.

* * *

So this was adventure, to stroll down a darkened street with a strange gentleman, discussing highly personal subjects and wishing the night could go on forever.

In the company of her tall escort, Lucy felt daring, bold, and oddly safe. With Thor, she wasn't simply a governess owed the courtesies shown to a member of a marquess's staff, she was a female to be protected against all perils.

The greatest peril had become her own curiosity.

Not the long-dormant curiosity of the eager girl. Lucy had weathered that risk with a dashing infantry captain named Giles Throckmorton III. She'd hoped for passion of mythic proportions and reaped only rumpled clothing, awkwardness, and some anxious days. Three weeks later she'd received a nigh-illegible letter from Giles releasing her from any obligation arising from "that dear, brief friendship."

For months, she'd pined and paced and considered writing back to him, protesting that she would wait, she could be patient, and they'd had more than friendship. Except… they hadn't *even* had a friendship. They'd had a foolish, awkward moment. She had burned his letter years ago, when she'd learned that Giles had married a Portuguese lady and was growing grapes and raising children with her on the banks of the Douro.

The curiosity that gripped Lucy now was more dangerous for being more mature. Thor raised philosophical questions: How much of Lucy's yearning for male companionship was simply loneliness? She attributed loneliness to the Marquess of Tyne, but perhaps it belonged to her as well.

Did his lordship even sense that he'd caught her interest, and what if he had? Was he politely ignoring her, for Tyne was unrelentingly polite? Was Lucy willing to embark on that trite convention of bad judgment, an affair with her employer?

This conversation with Thor would stay with her long after

she'd bid him good night, and later—under bright sunshine—she'd consider the conundrums he'd raised. Now, she'd send him on his way with a kiss.

He was tall enough that Lucy had to go up on her toes to kiss him. He accommodated her by bending his head and taking her in his arms. The handle of his hammer hit the porch rug with a soft thump, and Lucy got a whiff of bay rum before she learned the true meaning of the verb *to plunder*.

Thor's strength was evident in the security of his embrace. He knew how to hold a woman, how to bring her body against his in a manner that offered shelter as well as intimacy. He was no green recruit to the ranks of manhood, but rather, a seasoned campaigner who could conquer by negotiation.

Lucy pressed her lips to his and half missed her target, getting the corner of his mouth, which kicked up in a smile. He corrected her aim by settling his lips over hers—*I'm here, you see?*—a greeting and then a tease with his tongue.

He tasted of cinnamon, from the stewed apples, and patience which was all him. Lucy gradually understood that she was being invited to explore as he did, his fingers tracing over her features and his tongue acquainting her with his mouth.

She had fallen for the army captain's clumsy charms, even knowing her soldier was more enthusiastic than skilled.

Thor was skilled enough to hide his enthusiasm, to build Lucy's interest instead. By the time she rested her forehead against his chest, she was hot and disoriented, and in no doubt that she was desired by a god.

Who is he? His shirt was of the finest linen. His scent up close included the sweet smoke of beeswax candles. He came from means, he was well educated, and unlike Lucy, he had the leisure to regularly mingle with the fancy and the frivolous.

His hand wandered her back, while Lucy tried to gather her wits and mostly failed.

"We must part," he said, "for the hour grows late, and lingering in London's night shadows is never well advised. May

I see you again?"

He wasn't asking to pay a call on her, and that was just as well, for his lordship's housekeeper had been quite clear that Lucy was not to encourage the notice of any followers.

"That might not be wise." Though it would be adventurous and—with him—passionate.

Thor turned loose of her and picked up his hammer. "Wasn't it you who said I must make my sentiments known, madam? You who encouraged me to speak of my feelings lest opportunity be lost forever? I'm honestly a dull fellow. I'll not be snatching you away to my mountain hall or plying you with mead until you're lost to all sense. I'd thought another quiet stroll might appeal, or an ice at Gunter's."

Lord Tyne took his daughters to Gunter's, one of few venues in London where the genders were free to mix socially. If Tyne should get wind that Lucy was meeting with a gentleman, he'd be curious, at least.

"The Lovers' Walk," she said. "Vauxhall, a fortnight hence at eleven of the clock. I'll wear your cape."

"A fortnight?" Clearly, he'd hoped to see Lucy sooner, and that gratified more than it should.

"If either of us should fail to appear, we'll know that a single encounter will have to suffice. One of those charming young ladies might return your interest, and I might engage the notice of my busy, distant gentleman."

Though, how likely was that, when Lucy had bided under his lordship's nose for months, and he'd done little more than hand her out of carriages and ask her to pass the teapot?

A linkboy trotted past, the lamplight giving an instant's illumination to an aquiline profile and hair curling with the evening damp.

"We are to be prudent deities," Thor said. "That ought to be a contradiction in terms."

She liked him. Liked his lively mind, his subtle humor, his skillful kisses. If nothing else, this evening had proved that she could like a man and that there was more to passion than she'd known with her randy captain.

"I will be a prudent, impatient goddess for the next two weeks," she said. "On that thought, I shall bid you good night."

Lucy had chosen this house because a pair of widowed sisters lived here. They would neither hear a conversation on their porch, nor spare the expense of candles kept lit through the night. They would assuredly keep their front door locked, however, and thus sending Thor on his way was imperative.

He leaned down to kiss Lucy's cheek. "Eleven of the clock, Vauxhall. Two weeks. Until then, I'll see you in my dreams."

He strode off into the darkness, pausing only to scoop up his mask. She watched him go, waited another ten minutes, then found her mask and hurried down the walkway toward home.

* * *

"Do my eyes deceive, or has the Marquess of Tyne made a social call?" Lord Luddington asked, ambling to the sideboard. "Hair of the dog or tea?" He lifted the glass stopper from a decanter and let it clink back into place.

"Neither," Tyne replied, "though of course you should dose yourself with whatever medicinal will ease your present ailment. I trust you kept late hours last night, as usual?"

Luddington had been the sole monk at the previous evening's bacchanal. Sole, but hardly solitary.

He pushed sandy-blond hair from his eyes and poured himself a tot of brandy. "The ladies at the masquerade were much in want of company, and my charitable nature had to oblige them. I didn't see you there, but then, how can the blandishments of a masked ball compare with parliamentary bills regarding turnpike watermen?"

"Without those watermen—"

Luddington held up a hand. "Please, Tyne, no politics. I truly did overexert myself last night. The ladies were all agog about some chap who'd decked himself out as Thor. You never heard so much twittering and cooing about the size of a man's hammer before, and nothing would do but they must compare… well, the night was *long*, so to speak."

Tyne had already returned the sledgehammer to the stable. "Thor, you say? Not very original."

"What would you know about originality? He had the hammer, the fur cape, the trews, the whole bit. Strode about the ballroom with his shirt half unbuttoned and sent the ladies into quite a stir. I reckon he went back to Valhalla with some toothsome shepherdess, for nobody knows who he was."

"A good-sized fellow?"

Luddington peered at Tyne over the rim of his glass. "A bit taller than you, more broad-shouldered. More the strapping specimen, less the scholarly politician."

Insult warred with amusement, though Tyne had time for neither. Miss Fletcher had requested an interview with him before supper, and Tyne dared not be late.

"You doubtless escorted a lady to the festivities. What did she make of the Norseman?"

Tyne posed the question while peering out the window to the garden behind the house. Daffodils were making an effort, and the tulips weren't far behind. He waited, his back turned to his host, and hoped for a name.

"The plaguey female ran off. Some tipsy jockey told me she'd departed the premises with a woodsman or a barbarian of some sort, and my sister will tear a strip off my backside, for I didn't see any woodsmen. Saw plenty of pillaging and sacking as the evening wore on, not that I'm complaining."

"Your sister dislikes woodsmen?"

Luddington downed half his drink, then refilled his glass. "You don't know Marianne. She entrusted some friend of hers to me, an acquaintance from finishing school, and then I lost her. Marianne frowns on brothers who lose her friends. *I* frown on me for losing her friend."

"Then Marianne ought not to send her friends to masquerades, where the entire point of the evening is to lose one's identity. You don't know the name of the female whom you lost?"

Tyne had little acquaintance with Marianne Benton, though she'd made her come out a good ten years ago. If she was Freya's contemporary, then Freya was a mature woman, a point that weighed in favor of keeping Tyne's next appointment with her.

"I wasn't supposed to know who she was," Luddington said. "I prefer not to be burdened with a lady's secrets—or a shepherdess's—for even Boxhaven's masquerades are not monuments to strict propriety. Next time he holds one, you should go, Tyne. Do you good to get out and socialize with a friendly nymph or two."

Luddington gave him a bored look that suggested Tyne's secret was being kept—for now.

"I'll bear your suggestion in mind, though a hammer strikes me as a particularly inane fashion accessory when a gentleman's usual purpose is to stand up with the wallflowers. Good day, Luddington, and next year, consider escorting a Valkyrie instead of a shepherdess. I'll leave you to your hair of the dog and show myself out."

Luddington gestured elegantly with his glass, spilling not a drop. "A pleasure, Tyne. As always."

Tyne made his way home, his steps taking him past the house where he'd kissed his goddess the night before. He'd been up early out of habit and taken a morning stroll through the back alleys of the neighborhood, pausing to inquire at the mews regarding the sixth house from the corner.

A pair of devout older widows dwelled there—both stable boys had agreed. The ladies kept a pony cart for trips to Hounslow, where one of them had a son who was a schoolteacher. No young lady had ever bided with them, and the son was unmarried.

Freya, in other words, had lied. Tyne did not care for dishonesty, but a lady was entitled to her privacy when a masked man asked for kisses in the dark. He hadn't exactly been forthcoming himself.

Her demeanor had suggested she'd have little patience with

a dull marquess who could spend fifteen minutes debating which waistcoat to wear for a speech fewer than a dozen men would hear.

He set aside thoughts of Freya, for another forthright female awaited Tyne in the family parlor, one whom he was equally unlikely to impress with his speeches, ledgers, and politics.

"Miss Fletcher, good day."

She set aside her book and rose. "Your lordship." The light in her eye suggested a battle was about to be joined, and Tyne barely refrained from smiling in anticipation.

CHAPTER THREE

The scent of England was always Giles Throckmorton's first impression of home: briny and brisk regardless of the weather, with an undertone of ancient geology, as if the stony hills ringing Portsmouth lent an aged, unchanging bedrock to even the smell of the place.

The languages he heard along the docks and in the coaching inn's common were mostly English, with smatterings of French, other Continental tongues, and the occasional American accent. The variety would have been still greater in Portugal, for that nation had made seafaring even more a part of its soul than England had.

"Good to be home again?" Giles's brother, John, asked, stepping down from a smart traveling coach in the inn yard.

"Always good to be home, but it's beastly cold here."

John clapped him on the back. "This is a fine spring day, nearly hot, but every time you come home, you complain of the cold. Portugal has made you soft."

Portugal had made Giles desperate.

He returned to England yearly, mostly to get away from his

children, also to gain a respite from the alternating work and worry of the vineyard. He'd learned enough of the winemaker's trade to realize wealth was accumulated over decades, if not generations. Worries accumulated overnight.

"How are matters in Portugal?" John asked as Giles's trunks were loaded onto the back of the coach.

John was being tactful, but then, John was a diplomat, always haring off to some treaty negotiation or conference.

"Matters in Portugal are difficult. The twins grow in mischievous tendencies as well as height, and the younger two follow the example of their elders. Without Catalina to mind the domestic concerns, I'm hard put to give the vineyards the attention they're due."

"You were married to the lady for years. Of course you still miss her."

Giles missed Catalina's ability to charm her father and brothers into assisting with the vineyard. He missed her management of the nursery and the household, however mercurial that management had been. He'd loved and admired his wife, and loved and admired the notion of building a vineyard empire with her.

But more than a year after her passing, there was also much—*much*—Giles did not miss about her. The guilt of that admission was tempered by the notion that if the boot had been on the other foot, Catalina would likely have felt the same about him.

"Do you like your wife, John?"

John pretended to study how the groom secured a trunk to the boot. "I like Agnes exceedingly, more with each passing year. We are friends first and spouses as a result of that friendship. Agnes understands me, and I very much value her counsel and affection."

Catalina's counsel had often been delivered at high volume and to the accompaniment of shattered porcelain. Her affections had become rare after the birth at long last of a daughter. Had Catalina not perished of a lung fever, the marriage would doubtless have found firmer footing as the children matured.

Giles had assured himself of that happy prognostication often in the early days of widowerhood. For the past few months, he'd taken to assuring himself that an English wife, one inured to the tribulations of the nursery and happy to improve her station even at the cost of journeying to a foreign land, would solve many of his troubles.

"Agnes will be so pleased to see you," John said as a fresh team was put to. "We very nearly dropped in on you after our last jaunt to Gibraltar."

"I would have been delighted to receive you." A lie, that. Without Catalina to nip at the house servants' heels, the staff did the bare minimum in terms of cleaning and maintenance. The harvest last year had been disappointing, and competition in the port market was fierce.

Giles was determined to take an English bride back to the chaos he'd left behind in Portugal, and his efforts in that regard would start with Miss Lucy Fletcher. The lady had cause to recall him fondly—very fondly, in fact. He'd paint a romantic picture of his fiefdom in Portugal, play a few bars of the grieving widower's lament, and take Miss Fletcher away from the drudgery of her life as a governess in the household of some stodgy old marquess.

Giles was even handsomer than he'd been as a youth. Lucy was doubtless plainer than ever, and sweeping her off her feet would be the work of a few weeks' courtship.

* * *

Miss Fletcher had insisted that she and Tyne dispense with the bow-and-curtsey ritual. Tyne had wanted to object—a gentleman extended courtesy to everyone, not only to the people he sought to impress—but she'd pointed out that he did not bow to the housekeeper and would feel ridiculous doing so.

"You asked for a moment of my time," Tyne said. "I trust Sylvie and Amanda are well?"

This was all Tyne knew to do with her—discuss the girls, be polite, keep his questions to himself. Freya's comments came back to him, though: How was a woman to know Tyne esteemed her if he never gave voice to his sentiments?

Miss Fletcher was nothing if not tidy, though today her hair was arranged more softly about her face. Her dress was a high-waisted blue velvet several years out of fashion, and the color flattered her eyes. If he said as much, she'd likely box his ears with her book.

"Lady Sylvie and Lady Amanda are in good health, my lord. Both, however, could stand to improve their equestrian skills."

Tyne had ridden like a demon almost before he'd been breeched. He missed that—riding hell-bent at dawn, his brothers thundering along beside him. Josephine hadn't had much use for horses, or the stink, horsehair, and mud that inevitably resulted from time in their company.

"Did you or did not you," Tyne said, "recently scold me into buying Amanda a mare to replace the equine sloth she was previously riding? If she can ride a pony, she can ride anything."

"With the pony, she was on a lead line most of the time. A lady should be in command of her own mount."

Miss Fletcher wore a lovely scent, not one Tyne had noticed previously. Minty with a hint of flowers.

"What were you reading?"

She edged to the left two steps, putting herself between Tyne and the discarded book. "I was merely browsing, awaiting your arrival."

He reached around her. *Myths, Fables, and Ancient Legends of the North* by Roderick DeCoursy.

"Are you in want of adventure, Miss Fletcher? Looking for an exciting tale or two?"

She took the book from him. "And if I am? Do you suppose because I am a governess that I don't enjoy a light dose of excitement from time to time? We can't all be devoted to ledgers and parliamentary committee meetings."

She was in fine form today, very much on her mettle. "Regardless of my boring proclivities, I will not subject my daughter to unnecessary risks. You are working up to a demand that I take the girls riding in the park."

Ah, he'd surprised her. She didn't retort until she'd turned to the shelves. "Most children on this square are taken for regular outings in the park on horseback. My *request* would have been reasonable."

She was trying to reshelve her myths and fables, but the library had been arranged for Tyne's convenience, and she was petite, relative to him. He came up behind her, took the book from her, and slipped it onto the shelf above her head.

She turned, and abruptly, Tyne was improperly close to his daughters' governess. She regarded him steadily, neither affronted nor welcoming.

"What is that scent?" Tyne asked, leaning down for a whiff of her hair. "It's delightful."

She apparently found the toes of his boots fascinating. "Did you just pay me a compliment, my lord?"

He had the odd thought that she'd fit him much as Freya had were he to take her in his arms—which he was not about to do. He did, however, treat himself to another sniff of her fragrance.

"I did, and now that I know the heavens do not part, nor the end times arrive as a result, I might venture to pay you another. I'd take the girls riding, except I have no notion how well Amanda's mare would deal with such an outing."

He stepped back, though he wished he knew which myth or fable Miss Fletcher had been reading.

"Surely you bought a quiet mare for your daughter?"

"Shall we sit? I've been running all over Town today, and last night went later than planned."

Miss Fletcher had fixed notions about what constituted excessive familiarity between employer and governess. She joined the family for informal meals, always arriving and leaving with the girls. She attended services with them. If Tyne took the young ladies to call on family, Miss Fletcher did not go along.

And yet, the girls were blossoming in her care. Tyne had no doubt she would give her life for them, and surely her ferocious loyalty excused Tyne's vague fancies regarding a woman in his employ. He tugged the bell-pull and prepared to embark on a small adventure of his own.

"You're ringing for tea?" she asked.

"Am I to starve for the sake of your etiquette, Miss Fletcher? Supper is hours away, and I'm peckish. Perhaps you could stand some sustenance yourself."

She looked tired to him, as if an afternoon spent curled up with that blasted book wouldn't have gone amiss. She perched on the edge of the sofa, like a sparrow lighting on an unfamiliar windowsill. Had some loss or heartache made her so careful with social boundaries? The idea explained much, including a love of fairy tales masked by a brisk lack of sentimentality.

"A cup of tea while we discuss an outing for the girls would be permissible," she said.

"Two cups," Tyne replied. "They're quite small. If Englishmen were sensible, they'd drink their ale from tea cups and their tea from tankards. We'd all get more done that way, and the streets would be safer."

"Back to Lady Amanda's mare, if you don't mind, sir."

Tyne did mind, but he was nothing if not persistent. Freya had been right—fate would not hand him a marchioness and the girls a step-mama. He hoped his Valkyrie kept their appointment in two weeks, mostly so he could thank her for inspiring his determination where Miss Fletcher was concerned.

"You refer to my daughter's lovely mare," Tyne said, "whom the auctioneer assured me could canter from one moonbeam to the next, never putting a hoof wrong. I'm not of a size to ride the mare myself, else I'd take her out the first few times. If she should shy at the sight of water or prove unruly in traffic,

Amanda will take a fall, and matters will deteriorate apace."

"Can't the grooms take her out?"

"My grooms disdain to ride aside, and Snowball is a lady's mount."

"Snowdrop, my lord."

"Mudbank, for all I care. I propose that you take out the mare, Miss Fletcher. I will ride with you, so the horse can accustom herself to the company of my gelding. If all goes smoothly after several trial rides, Amanda can join me for a hack."

A fine plan, so of course Miss Fletcher was scowling. She didn't pinch up like a vexed schoolteacher, but her brow developed one charming furrow, and her lips—she had a pretty mouth—firmed.

"My habit is hardly fashionable, my lord."

"But you do have one, and you have neglected your adventuring sorely. Ride out with me, Miss Fletcher, and call it an adventure."

A tap on the door saved Tyne from elaborating on that bouncer. No lady had considered any time in his company adventurous, with the possible exception of Freya. The first footman wheeled in the tea trolley, and Tyne waved him off.

"Miss Fletcher, would you be so good as to pour out?"

Her scowl faded as the dawn chased away the night, to be replaced by a soft, amused smile. "Never let it be said I allowed you to starve, my lord. Have a seat. You prefer your tea with neither milk nor sugar, if I recall."

That she'd noticed this detail pleased him, thus proving that he was addled. "You are correct, while you prefer yours with both."

Her smile became a grin, and she fixed Tyne's tea exactly as he preferred it.

* * *

Lucy was lucky to get on a horse once a month, if Marianne wanted to hack out on Lucy's half day. The outings invariably left her sore and frustrated.

Sore, because she didn't ride often enough to condition her muscles to the exertion.

Frustrated, because as a girl growing up in Hampshire, she'd ridden almost every day when the weather had been fine. The weather this morning was very fine indeed, though brisk enough that the horses would be lively.

The prospect of starting her day with a gallop in the park had her in a happy mood, despite her out-of-date riding habit, despite the early hour.

"Up you go," Lord Tyne said when Lucy had been ready to lead the mare over to the ladies' mounting block.

His lordship looked fixed on the task of assisting Lucy into the saddle, and she was in too good spirits to argue with him. His grasp around the ankle of her boot was secure, and when he hoisted her into the saddle, she got an impression of considerable—and surprising—strength.

She took up the reins as his lordship arranged her skirts over her boots, a courtesy her brothers had never shown her.

"Thank you," Lucy said. "If you could—"

He was already taking the girth up one hole. "The stirrup is the correct length?"

"Yes, my lord."

He walked around to face the mare. "Behave, madam, else it shall go badly for you."

So stern! For an instant, Lucy thought his warning was for her. Then the marquess stroked his gloved hand gently over the mare's neck, giving the horse's ear an affectionate scratch.

"Miss Fletcher tolerates no disrespect," he went on, "and any high spirits must be expressed within the confines of ladylike good cheer."

Ah—he was teasing. He was teasing *Lucy*, for one could not tease a horse.

"Walk on, Snowdrop," she said. "An entire park awaits our pleasure. If his lordship thinks to interfere with our enjoyment, it will go badly for him."

His lordship swung into the saddle without benefit of a

mounting block and walked his gelding alongside the mare.

"We'll start slowly," he said as the horses clip-clopped down the alley, "because you ladies have not kept company before. Attila, stop flirting."

The gelding, a substantial black with a flowing mane, whisked his tail.

"He's a good lad," Tyne said. "Up to my weight, calm in the face of London's many terrors, but he's shamelessly spoiled for treats. About the mare, he cares not at all. For the slice of apple in your pocket, he'll be your personal servant."

"I brought carrots."

"Carrots might earn you an offer of eternal devotion. Where did you learn to ride?"

As they navigated the deserted streets of Mayfair at dawn, Lucy saw a new side to her employer. He was an attentive escort, pleasant company even, asking her one polite question after another and listening to her answers.

Actually listening, to the story of how she came to be able to write with either hand.

"I was determined not to fall behind my brothers in my schoolwork, and yet, my wrist was broken, not sprained. I had to learn to write with my left hand or suffer the torments known only to younger sisters with very bright older siblings."

"You were allowed to climb trees?" his lordship asked as the horses walked through the gates to the park.

"If one is to invite one's dolls to tea in the treehouse, one had best be a good climber. Shall we let the horses stretch their legs? Snowdrop has been a pattern card of equine deportment."

Attila, on the other hand, was prancing, apparently ready for a gallop.

"Let's trot to the first bend in the Serpentine and then find room for a more athletic pace."

Tyne was being careful with her, giving her and the mare a chance to become cordial. Attila was having none of it and all but cantered in place as Lucy cued Snowdrop into a ladylike trot. A few other riders were up and about, but today was

Thursday. Most everybody of note had likely been at Almack's late the previous evening. They would miss this glorious morning in this gorgeous park.

Attila had taken to adding the occasional buck to his progress, which his lordship rode with the same equanimity he showed toward parliamentary frustrations, feuding footmen, and cross little girls. Truly, not much disconcerted Lord Tyne, a quality Lucy hadn't much appreciated in recent months.

"This way," Lucy called, turning Snowdrop onto a straight stretch of bridle path. "Tallyho!" She urged the mare into a canter, and joy welled, for the horse covered the ground in a beautiful, smooth gait.

Tyne let Attila stretch into a canter as well, and the gelding soon overtook the mare, though Snowdrop refused to be baited. She kept to the same relaxed, elegant pace, and every care and woe Lucy had brought with her into the saddle was soon cast away.

When the horses came down to the walk, Lucy was winded, while Tyne had plenty of breath to scold his horse.

"You, sir, are a naughty boy. You wanted to show off for the ladies, though how you expect to gain anybody's respect by bucking and heaving yourself about in such an undignified manner beggars all comprehension. You should be ashamed of yourself, and"—the gelding began to prance—"anticipate the cut direct from Miss Snowdrift if you ever attempt to stand up with her again."

Tyne's chiding tone was offset by an easy pat to Attila's shoulder.

"Do you always talk to your horse, my lord?"

"Is there a proper English equestrian who doesn't?"

"No," Lucy replied, "and the conversation is invariably witty and charming."

"Do you imply that I could be witty and charming, Miss Fletcher?"

Despite his bantering tone, Lucy suspected the question held some hint of genuine curiosity. "I dare to imply that very possibility, my lord." He was also an athlete, with natural ease in the saddle, strength, skill, and fitness Lucy would not have suspected based on the time he spent penning correspondence or drafting bills.

Another feature of his riding was tact. He reminded his horse to behave; he chided; he did not bully.

"I speak honestly when I say that you ride well, Miss Fletcher. We must get you into the saddle more often, because you clearly enjoy yourself there."

A governess did not expect such consideration. "I love to ride—really ride, not merely mince along on some doddering nag wearing a saddle. I sometimes forget that."

"Why is it," Tyne said, "the voice of duty can drown out all other worthy considerations? We must make an agreement, Miss Fletcher, to remind one another that an occasional gallop in the park, an afternoon with a good book, a picnic even, are all that makes the duty bearable sometimes."

The gelding snorted, the mare swished her tail. As the horses walked along beneath greening maples on a beautiful morning, Lucy realized once again that her employer was lonely and that part of his devotion to duty—like hers—was a means of coping with the loneliness.

"I will honor that pact," Lucy said, "though picnicking with two high-spirited children isn't exactly my idea of a treasured joy."

"Who said anything about dragging that pair along? I meant picnicking in the company of a congenial adult of the opposite sex. Perhaps even—one delights to contemplate the notion—reading to her on a blanket spread upon the soft spring grass, or sharing a glass of wine with her while she cools her bare feet in the summer shallows of an obliging brook."

Oh, how lucky that lady would be. Tyne had a beautiful reading voice, and his grip on a wineglass had the power to rivet Lucy's attention. She had discovered months ago the pleasure of sketching his lordship's hands, trying to capture their grace and masculine competence with pencil and paper.

As he tormented her with further descriptions of his summer idyll, Lucy's imagination went further: What would his hands feel like *on her*?

"You are quiet, Miss Fletcher. Has the company grown tedious? Shall we have another gallop? And I do mean a gallop. You and Snow-moppet are fast friends now, and I know you want to see what she can do."

"One more run," Lucy said, "and then we must return to the house, for the children will be rising."

Lord Tyne aimed Attila back up the path they'd cantered over earlier. "The children have highly paid, highly competent nursery maids to attend them, a staff of four in the kitchen to feed them, and various other domestics to ensure there's no falling out of windows, climbing of trees, or other wild behavior. After you."

He gestured with his riding crop. Attila pretended to spook, and Snowdrop lifted easily from walk to canter and from thence to a tidy gallop.

Some of Lucy's joy in the outing had fled, because she was soon to reunite with her duties. She'd change out of her habit and into the drab attire of the governess, correct the children's manners at the breakfast table, and turn her attention to… irregular French verbs.

The mare seemed to share Lucy's diminished glee, for her gallop was less than exuberant by the time the path joined one of the park's larger thoroughfares. Lucy slowed Snowdrop in anticipation of that turn and realized the mare wasn't simply tiring, she was… off stride.

"Miss Fletcher!" Lord Tyne called from three lengths back. "Something is amiss with your mount. She's favoring the right front, blast the luck."

He was out of the saddle in a smooth leap before Attila had come to a halt. The gelding stood obediently as Lord Tyne lifted Snowdrop's right front hoof.

"She's picked up a dratted stone. Why the bridle paths are strewn with gravel, I shall never know." He produced a folding knife, flipped it open, and applied the tip to the offending stone. "Some lord or other ought to introduce a bill forbidding the use of gravel on bridle paths. The poor beast could have been seriously injured. Walk her a few paces, if you please."

He set down the mare's hoof and tucked the knife away.

Lucy directed Snowdrop across the grass rather than along the gravel path. "She's not right," she said. "She's not lame, but she's not right."

Attila snatched a mouthful of grass, but otherwise stood like a sentry where Tyne had dismounted.

Tyne regarded the mare, his hands on his hips. "If this outing has caused Snow Princess to become lame, Amanda will ring a peal over my head that makes the bells of St. Paul's sound like a polite summons to the family parlor."

"I can walk," Lucy said. Though hiking through the streets of Mayfair with her riding skirts over her arm was hardly an appealing prospect.

"Nonsense," Lord Tyne replied. "You shall take Attila, and I will walk."

They'd left their groom loitering with the other grooms at the gates of the park. "I could take the groom's horse."

"James brought out an unruly ruffian by the name of Merlin for this outing. He'd run off with you for the sheer pleasure of giving me a fright. Damned beast should go to the knacker, but James is fond of him."

Tyne approached the mare and held up his arms. "Down you go, Miss Fletcher."

Lucy unhooked her knee from the horn, gathered up her skirts, and eased from the saddle, straight into Lord Tyne's arms.

* * *

Tyne had been ready to curse aloud, to damn all lame horses, all pebbles, and all parliamentary bills for good measure, until Miss Fletcher slid into his embrace.

He'd been striving mightily to achieve a tone of harmless banter and failing at every turn. Miss Fletcher had made the requisite charming responses, but she didn't simper or flirt, she didn't offer any bold conversational gambits of her own. The sum of the morning's accomplishments had been to prove that she was a natural equestrian, and he was a failure as a flirt.

Fancy that.

Then Miss Fletcher slipped from the saddle on a soft slide of velvet and lace, and the fresh morning air became tinged with the fragrance of mint and possibility. She was warm from her exertions, and her arms rested on Tyne's biceps, while his hands remained about her waist.

"Your skirt," Tyne said, reaching behind her, "is caught on the billets. I'll have you free in no time."

The lady could not move, because she was pinned to the horse's side by her habit. The moment was theoretically dangerous and exactly the sort of mishap that inspired gentlemanly assistance with a lady's dismount in the first place.

Tyne eased the fold of velvet from between the lengths of leather, though his task required that he all but crush Miss Fletcher against the horse.

She didn't appear to mind. In fact, she might have leaned into him, and she certainly kept her hands on his arms. For a moment, she was embracing him while he fussed with yards of damned riding habit and tried not to let a particularly eager part of his anatomy become obviously inspired by her closeness.

Which was no use. He had to step back, lest public improprieties ensue.

"I can walk," Miss Fletcher said.

I very nearly cannot. "That won't be necessary. If you'd hold the mare's reins, I'll switch the saddles, and we'll be on our way shortly."

That exercise took enough of Tyne's concentration that he regained a measure of composure. Then, however, came the challenge of hoisting the lady onto Attila's back. Because the gelding was considerably taller than the mare, a simple hand around Miss Fletcher's ankle would not suffice.

"Step into my hands, and I'll boost you up," Tyne said. "Attila, you will stand like a perfect little scholar reciting his sums, unless you want to make the knacker's acquaintance before sundown."

Attila stood. Miss Fletcher gathered her skirts over her arm and lifted a dainty boot into Tyne's cupped hands. She scrambled aboard Tyne's horse and took up the reins, leaving Tyne to do further battle with the sea of velvet.

He tightened the girth a hole, took up the mare's reins, and sent Attila a warning glower. "You will walk, with all pretensions to dignity, horse. Set one hoof wrong with Miss Fletcher aboard, and you will never lay eyes on a carrot or apple again, not if you live to be thirty and win the Derby in three successive years."

"He's trembling with fear," Miss Fletcher said, patting the wretched beast. "A quaking mass of equine nerves, my lord. If you'll show the way, we shall summon all of our courage, put our complete trust in your leadership, and brave all the terrors awaiting us. Is that not what an adventure requires?"

Tyne's spirits lifted at the sight of her smile—for she was smiling at him, not at the stinking creature trying to impersonate a harmless lamb.

"As long as you're having an adventure, Miss Fletcher, my joy in the day is complete."

"As is mine."

That was ladylike banter, by God. In an entirely acceptable, though unmistakable, manner, she was bantering with her employer and possibly even flirting. Tyne tried not to smile the whole distance back to the house, and Attila came along, as docile as a perfect little scholar.

* * *

Because the mare was recovering from her stone bruise, Lucy was excused from riding out again with his lordship. In little more than a week, she'd face the choice of whether to keep her assignation with Thor, or let her single encounter with him fade into fond, if frustrating, memory. She had the odd notion that if she discussed her choice with the marquess, he'd offer her considered, disinterested advice, much as a true friend would.

But did she want to limit the marquess to the role of friend? He'd been *charming* on their dawn ride, attentive, considerate… very nearly swainly. He'd shared a longing to read to some lucky woman on a picnic blanket, to admire her bare feet…

"I find you once again among the fairy tales," Lord Tyne said, striding into the library on Saturday afternoon. "Where are the children?"

He was looking all too handsome, blond hair slightly disarranged, suggesting he'd been at his ledgers. His blue eyes were impatient and held a hint of mischief.

"Sylvie has taken it into her head that Amanda and I are too old to join the nursery tea parties, and Amanda has decided that sketching embroidery patterns does not require my assistance or the distraction of a younger sibling. That they are amusing themselves, and separately, is a good sign, my lord."

Tyne gestured to the other reading chair positioned before the hearth, and Lucy nodded her assent. He was so mannerly, so—

He plucked her book from her hand. "I knew it. Mr. DeCoursy has carried you off again. He will simply have to wait his turn today, for I'm intent on carrying you off as well."

Lord Tyne was mannerly *most of the time*. "I'm not exactly a sylph, your lordship, and I object to being hauled about."

"No, you do not, else you'd never have lasted a single waltz at the tea dances you were doubtless forced to attend. From my observation, too many fellows do little more than haul their partners about. Why the waltz hasn't been outlawed for the preservation of the ladies' toes is a mystery for the ages."

He wore no coat, which was unusual for him, and a trial for Lucy. She knew now how strong those arms were, how muscular his chest. She had become fascinated with his wrists—sketched them for an hour last night—and they were on view because he'd turned back his cuffs.

"Perhaps some obliging fellow of a parliamentary bent might draft a bill outlawing the waltz," Lucy said. "Do you happen to know an MP who might oblige?"

Tyne rose and shelved the book. "Why would I associate with such a prosy old dodderer when I can instead kidnap fair maidens and take them to Gunter's?"

Maidens, plural. "You'd like to take the girls out for an ice?"

"Not without you," he said, extending a hand to her. "If I take them by myself, I'm outnumbered. Any papa knows that's bad strategy. I also lack your ability to settle their squabbles with a calm word."

Lucy took his hand and rose, though she was capable of standing unassisted. She simply wanted to touch him and wanted him to touch her. The short time she'd spent in Thor's company had awakened some mischievous inclination in her, or made her loneliness—and her employer—harder to ignore.

"The girls squabble to get your attention," she said. "If they were boys, they'd resort to fisticuffs for the same reason."

"Some boys scrap for the pure joy of it. My younger brothers were always at each other, until Papa threatened to send one to Eton, one to Harrow, and one to Rugby."

His younger brothers had likely been trying to get *his* attention. "Did you scrap for the pure joy of it?" She'd pictured Lord Tyne as a quiet, dignified boy—or she had until they'd ridden out together.

"I was the oldest, and thus the largest. I had to let them come at me in twos or all at once to make the fight fair. You will think me quite the barbarian, but I did enjoy horseplay as a youth."

She smoothed her hand over his cravat, which was a half inch off center. "You scrap with the boys in the House of Lords now, don't you?"

His smile was downright piratical. "You've found me out. Let's mount a raid on Gunter's, shall we? A spot of pillaging lifts the spirits of any self-respecting barbarian."

Lucy took his arm, which was ridiculous, but so was fisticuffs for the joy of thrashing one's siblings, so was categorizing a barberry ice as plunder, and so was entertaining fanciful notions regarding one's employer.

"Perhaps we ought to take a blanket to spread beneath the maples," she said. "Raiding on such a lovely day might tire out your foot soldiers."

"Excellent notion," his lordship replied, pausing at the foot of the main stairs. "You will doubtless do a better job of ordering the infantry from their barracks. I'll meet you here in ten minutes."

He strode away with his characteristic energy, and Lucy watched his departure with uncharacteristic longing. Berkeley Square boasted no babbling brook into which she might dangle her bare feet, and his lordship simply wanted assistance with the children—not some sighing damsel for him to read poetry to.

What Lucy wanted was becoming increasingly unclear, though barberry ices were her favorite treat, and that was insight enough for the day.

CHAPTER FOUR

Tyne's habit had been to avoid imposing on Miss Fletcher's time unnecessarily. If he was taking the children to call on family, their governess could better use that hour to steal a nap, visit friends, or drop in on the lending library.

He'd apparently erred, for the children were much better behaved when Miss Fletcher was on hand to quell insurrections before they became outright revolts. The first attempted insurrection had come from Sylvie, who had wanted to bring along a platoon of dolls.

"You may bring one," Miss Fletcher had said. "Provided you and your doll of choice are back downstairs in the next five minutes."

The next sign of rebellion came from Amanda, who refused to sit next to a doll. Miss Fletcher solved that dilemma by placing herself beside Sylvie and Lady Higginbottom, the privileged doll of the day.

Amanda took her place beside Tyne on the backward-facing seat, which occasioned an outthrust tongue from Sylvie. Miss Fletcher pretended to be absorbed in retying her bonnet ribbons rather than remark Sylvie's rudeness or Amanda's return fire.

"You spend your entire day with these rag-mannered tatterdemalions, Miss Fletcher?" Tyne asked. "I marvel at your fortitude. What flavor of ice do tatterdemalions prefer?"

"What's a tatter… tatter the dandelion?" Sylvie asked.

"An unkempt, roguish vagabond," Miss Fletcher said.

"I want to be a tatter… a roguish vagabond when I grow up," Sylvie said. "Lady Higginbottom and I will be the scourges of the high toby too."

"Then you and your doll will be taken up by the sheriff," Amanda retorted, "and bound over for the assizes. If I'm lucky, you'll be sent to the Antipodes to serve out your days in hard labor."

"What manner of sister," Tyne observed, "would rather send her only sibling halfway around the world than join her in an adventure? I do wonder if such a sister should even share an ice with her family."

"Sorry, Syl," Amanda muttered.

"We wouldn't hold up *your* coach," Sylvie replied. "We'd brandy our pistols and protect you."

"Brandish," Amanda said, gesturing with her parasol. "Brandy is that nasty potion Papa keeps on the sideboard in his study. Brandy makes your throat burn and your nose run."

Miss Fletcher cast Tyne an admonitory glance: *Your adolescent daughter has sampled the brandy. You will not roar and carry on about it in front of Lady Sylvie or me.* Her gaze held sympathy and humor, and Tyne was reassured. He had sampled his papa's brandy at a much younger age than Amanda was now, and it had made his throat burn and his nose run too.

Another good sign, in other words, that Amanda was exhibiting normal youthful curiosity.

"We're here!" Sylvie shouted, bouncing on the seat. "Lady Higginbottom wants a lemon ice. I shall have maple."

"Elderflower," Amanda said as the coach came to a halt.

"Miss Fletcher? You might as well give me your order now."

"Barberry," she said. "Which treat would you like, my lord?"

The treat he longed for was a kiss from Miss Fletcher, which was all wrong. They were in a coach with two children and a doll, she'd done nothing other than smile at him, manage the children, and share a few moments bordering on the parental. In her plain straw bonnet, she was hardly alluring, and yet…

She was *his* Miss Fletcher, and he'd held her in his arms, and now his imagination was like a horse newly escaped from captivity.

"I'll want a nice, refreshing serving of patience," Tyne said, climbing from the coach. The children spilled forth, while Miss Fletcher made a more dignified exit. She perched on the step, her hand in Tyne's.

"Girls, you will mind your father, or there will be extra sums for all of next week."

"I like sums," Sylvie said. "So does Lady Higginbottom."

"Capital cities, then," Miss Fletcher said, making a graceful descent. "We are in a public venue, and our deportment reflects on the dignity of your papa's house. Best behavior, or his lordship won't be inspired to invite us out again."

Was she warning him to be on his best behavior?

Miss Fletcher shot him a wink and dropped his hand. "They'll try hard for about five minutes, but cakes and ices have never been known to settle children down."

Nor did winks settle down grown men. Tyne placed the order and took Sylvie's hand as they crossed the street to the grassy, shaded square, a groom carrying their treats. Miss Fletcher chose the spot under the maples for their blanket, and Tyne allowed himself one moment to wish that the children might have been gamboling away the afternoon with some obliging cousins out in Kent, while Tyne…

Gamboled away the afternoon with Miss Fletcher in a secluded meadow far, far from the Mayfair gossips. In little more than a week, he had to choose whether to keep his assignation with Freya, and the lonely, bored part of him that could be intrigued with a single kiss was inclined to do that.

The part of him that had daughters to raise, parliamentary bills to put forth, and a lovely governess underfoot wasn't inclined to pursue a fairy tale when the genuine article was already sharing his household.

The ices were consumed, and the children resumed bickering until Miss Fletcher suggested they entertain themselves with the ball she'd thought to bring along.

"Amanda will soon be too dignified to kick a ball about in the park," Miss Fletcher said. "She should enjoy playing with her sister while she still can."

"When the family removes to Tyne Hall this summer, we'll get up some cricket games with the cousins," Tyne said. "My sisters all play, and the best pitcher of the lot is my brother Detrick's oldest girl."

Another pair of girls joined in the game of kickball—Lord Amery's oldest and some cohort of hers with a deadly accurate left foot. Much yelling and argument about rules ensued, as it should when children played out of doors.

"When you remove to Tyne Hall, I ought to seek another post," Miss Fletcher said. "The girls are moving on from their mother's death, and you should find them a governess whom they won't associate as closely with their grief."

What the hell? Tyne had been lounging about on the blanket, propped on one elbow.

He sat up. "Your logic eludes me. The time of grief was more than two years ago, when their mother went to her eternal reward. Your tenure with the girls has been a period of improving spirits, better sleep, and a happier papa. Why should I now tear the children away from somebody who has brought them such boons?"

Miss Fletcher's gaze remained on the girls, who were trying to kick the ball straight at a dignified old maple, and—with the exception of the left-footed terror—mostly failing to hit their target.

"Are you a happier papa?" Miss Fletcher asked. "If you

are happy enough to consider courting another marchior that's reason enough for me to seek a different post. I overstepped with your children, because I knew they without a mother's love. Your new wife will fill that role, and the children's loyalties would be torn if I stayed on."

"Good God, now you have me married to some woman I've never even courted. Have you been reading too many fairy tales, Miss Fletcher?"

"Perhaps—or not enough of them. Promise me you'll think on this, my lord. I can assist with the choice of a successor governess, if that's not getting above my station. There's no hurry, but you should give the notion some consideration."

Tyne considered *the notion* for two entire seconds and found it dreadful. "You have it all wrong, Miss Fletcher. One doesn't pike off as soon as the bonds of affection have been secured. I know not what experience put that ridiculous idea in your head, but you will only hurt the children if you leave us now. Amanda is facing the hardest years of a young lady's life, Sylvie will need a steady anchor as her sister makes her bow, and I won't have my daughters cast aside because your courage has failed you."

She untied her bonnet ribbons and would have retied them, except Tyne plucked her millinery from her grasp. Whatever losses had inspired her into a life in service were doubtless to blame for this harebrained plan to leave. She honored somebody's memory by remaining within earshot of grief, much as Tyne kept Josephine's portrait in the formal parlor.

"If we're to have a proper argument, madam, at least do me the courtesy of looking me in the eye while you threaten desertion."

"You need heirs," Miss Fletcher retorted, snatching the bonnet back. "Male heirs of your body. You're a marquess, need I remind you."

"If you think I can forget for one instant that I bear the responsibility for an old and respected title, you have been doing too many sums. Need I remind *you* that I have seven

hews thriving in my brothers' nurseries, which are heirs
gh to secure any succession?"

ough sons would be lovely. Noisy, boisterous, little
ws who rode like hellions, tracked mud into the house,
and drove their parents barmy.

"Where's Sylvie?" Miss Fletcher asked, scrambling to her
feet. "I don't see Sylvie."

"She's deserted us," Tyne said, rising. "Gone off without
giving notice."

"Badger me some other time, my lord. I don't see her
anywhere." A thread of panic laced Miss Fletcher's voice. "I'm
her governess and I've lost her in the middle of London. This
is awful."

The panic was contagious, for Tyne had never before
misplaced a daughter. "She can't have gone far," he said,
invoking a calm he did not feel. "We'll find her. Steady on,
Miss Fletcher. Let's talk to the other girls."

But neither Amanda nor her friends had seen Sylvie slip
away, and though the square was small and plenty of people sat
on benches or in coaches by the roadside, Sylvie was nowhere
to be found.

* * *

How could Lord Tyne be calm, how could he think at all,
when Sylvie was missing?

He was utterly composed. He dispatched the two grooms
to work their way around the square, bench by bench, asking
after Sylvie. Amanda and her friends did likewise with the
children, while Lucy's heart hammered against her ribs and
guilt hammered her conscience.

"She could have been snatched away," Lucy said, gaze upon
the busy streets surrounding the square. "She could be lost,
she might have been knocked witless by a passing carriage, and
she's so little, nobody would even—"

"Miss Fletcher," Lord Tyne said, putting a hand on each of
Lucy's shoulders. "This is not your fault, and we must look at
the situation logically. Sylvie is a sensible child. She has had

your example to guide her for quite some time, and she knows better than to dart into traffic. She will not take foolish risks, will not talk to unsavory people, and will not leave this area without us."

He took Lucy by the hand and led her back in the direction of the coach.

"Where are we going? We can't leave, not with—"

"We have searched the square, and unless Sylvie has learned to levitate straight up into the boughs, she's not here. We must check the coach and the coaches of acquaintances who happen to be enjoying the square. Thanks to you, Sylvie has many little friends, and she might even now be cadging another ice with one of them."

That... that made sense. Lucy's panic subsided the least bit. "I still feel responsible. She's a little girl, and I am her governess."

"While I am merely her father? You are being ridiculous. This outing was my suggestion, Sylvie is my daughter, and she will be fine, assuming she survives the scolding we'll give her."

His tone was cool, his grip on Lucy's hand steadying. His lordship inquired at three different coaches, and still no Sylvie, not even a sighting of a child who might be Sylvie.

"We need to look in one last place," his lordship said, escorting Lucy back across the street to Gunter's. "I should have started here, because I have every confidence that we'll find the prodigal and her accomplice slurping maple ices and looking entirely—"

"There you are!" Lucy said, dashing among the tables and wrapping Sylvie in a hug. "We looked everywhere for you, and I was so worried. Sylvie, you must *never* again give us such a fright."

Sylvie yet held her spoon—she was indeed enjoying another maple ice—while Mrs. Holymere looked on with tolerant amusement from the seat at Sylvie's elbow.

"I had to get Lady Higginbottom," Sylvie said when Lucy could stand to turn loose of her. "I forgot her, and I'm not supposed to be forgetful. Mrs. Holymere helped me cross the road and said we should wait for Papa to come fetch me." The girl looked uncertainly from her father to Lucy and then set aside her spoon to pick up her doll. "Am I in trouble?"

Mrs. Holymere beamed at the marquess. "Of course not, my dear. Looking after you for a few moments was my pleasure, and you really must not let this delicious ice go to waste. My lord, won't you join us? Lady Amanda is somewhere about too, isn't she? Perhaps the governess can take the child back to the square while we enjoy some adult conversation."

The governess. Mrs. Holymere turned her smile on Lucy, clearly expecting *the governess* to take Sylvie by the hand and disappear for so long as it pleased Mrs. Holymere to publicly flirt with the marquess.

Sylvie took Lucy's hand, and Lucy had picked up the half-eaten ice when Lord Tyne offered Mrs. Holymere a bow.

"While I thank you for aiding Lady Sylvie, I am not free at this moment to tarry. Good day." He plucked Sylvie up onto his hip, passed Lucy the spoon Sylvie had been using, and strode in the direction of the door.

Lucy offered the barest curtsey and marched after him.

The ride back to the house was taken up with Amanda chattering about Rose and Winnie, her kickball opponents, and Sylvie debating the merits of maple ices over those flavored with lemon. Happy, normal babbling about an enjoyable outing on a fine spring day.

When the coach pulled up in the mews, the girls scampered into the house. Lucy climbed out last, accepting Lord Tyne's hand to assist her to the ground.

"You are still upset," he said, keeping hold of her hand as the coach pulled away to the carriage house.

"I am furious."

"With Sylvie?"

Lucy shook her head, willing herself to remain civil, to keep to her place.

"With me?" Lord Tyne asked.

"You were wonderful. You kept your head, you didn't panic, you applied common sense and persistence, while I wanted to run up and down the walkways shouting Sylvie's name."

"That would have been my next step as well, having exhausted all other possibilities. If you're not wroth with me or Sylvie, then who has earned your ire?"

Standing this close to Lord Tyne was distracting, but not distracting enough. All over again, Lucy saw Mrs. Holymere's smirk, heard her dismissing *the governess*, the better to be seen sharing an ice with the marquess.

Lucy stalked the half-dozen paces across the alley and into the garden, Lord Tyne following. "I am furious, my lord, though I know I shouldn't be. I am furious at Mrs. Holymere for dragging an innocent child into her machinations, for pretending to be Sylvie's friend, for entirely disregarding the difficult position she put a little girl in. Was Sylvie to suffer a birching for the betterment of Mrs. Holymere's designs on you? Do you know how far back that would set the poor girl?

"Sylvie was trying to fetch her doll," Lucy went on, "which I have admonished her to remember to do over and over, and that woman, that manipulative, sly, flirting menace to the peace of the nursery, had the audacity—"

Lucy was pacing a circle around the smallest fountain in the garden and came smack up against his lordship.

"I'm sorry," she said. "I ought not to criticize my betters."

"Mrs. Holymere is not your better. If I had any doubt of that before today, I'm convinced of it now. You must calm yourself, Miss Fletcher. Sylvie is safe. She was at no time in danger, and a few reminders about keeping us apprised of her whereabouts are all the repercussions she should face."

"I am not calm," Lucy said. "This is why I should leave. I love those girls, and that is unpro— unprofessional of me." Her breath hitched, and she tried to turn away, but there was the marble sculpture of a laughing boy, his half-tipped urn eternally spilling into the pool at his feet.

Lord Tyne passed her his handkerchief, put his arms around

her, and drew her close. "You aren't going anywhere, not at the moment. Now, have a good cry—however one defines such an oxymoron—and then we must talk."

Lucy indulged her tears, because the comfort Lord Tyne offered was irresistible. To be held, to be cosseted, to be allowed for once to share an emotional burden… The relief was as exhausting as her worry over Sylvie had been. She never cried—almost never—but to think of Sylvie in harm's way, lost, alone, at the mercy of an unkind fate…. That was worth a few tears.

"My nose is probably red, and my cheeks are splotchy. Allow me some time to repair my toilette, and I'll be happy to—"

"Miss Fletcher… Lucy, if I may be so bold. I hope you know I would never trifle with the help?"

She took a seat on the nearest bench, because his lordship's reassurance was anything but cheering.

"Of course I know that, sir. You are all that is kind, and I'm simply overset."

He came down beside her. "With good reason. Sylvie gave us a fright, or rather that Holymere woman did. I knew her husband, so I attempt to be courteous to her, but my courtesies are at an end."

"You'll cut her?" Lucy liked that idea exceedingly.

"I will be merely civil, which is all the rebuke allowed to me as a gentleman. You are quite fond of the girls."

Hadn't Lucy said as much? "Which is why I should find another post now, my lord. I will grow more attached, and that cannot end well for anybody." The words hurt, but that pain was familiar, unlike the growing attachment Lucy felt for his lordship.

"And yet," he said, "I cannot abide the notion of you leaving us."

A sad silence went by. The garden was coming into its fragrant, colorful summer glory, but like the flowers blooming in such abundance, Lucy's time in Lord Tyne's household would soon be over. She nearly started weeping all over again, which made no sense.

A trip to Gunter's was not an adventure. A man who kept his head when a small child went missing was not a dashing flirt.

Lord Tyne was so much more than that. "We can speak further of this later, my lord. I am, as you say, not at my best."

He assisted Lucy to rise and stood staring down at her. Lucy could almost hear him rearranging mental chess pieces, hear him choosing the phrasing by which he might offer her a higher salary to remain in his employ. She did not want a higher salary—had no need of it, in fact.

"When we speak later," he said, "please consider that while I would never trifle with a woman in my employ, and your privacy is inviolable, and I am not keen on being trifled with myself, if you should ever be inclined to show me the sort of regard that—"

"Excuse me, my lord, Miss Fletcher." The first footman stood several yards up the garden walk. "I apologize for intruding, but the gentleman has been waiting for some time."

"What gentleman?" Lord Tyne asked.

Regardless of the gentleman's name, Lucy wished him to perdition. Whatever his lordship had planned to say mattered more to her than some gentleman pacing in the parlor.

"He's an acquaintance of Miss Fletcher's," the footman said. "Says he's an old friend, a Captain Giles Throckmorton, and he'd be very pleased if Miss Fletcher could spare him a few minutes of her time."

* * *

"Miss Fletcher was wild with worry for you, Syl." Amanda had been worried too.

"Mrs. Holymere said I was to come with her, and I needed to fetch Lady Higginbottom." Sylvie situated her ladyship back among the other dolls on the nursery shelf. "I think Papa was angry with me."

Amanda flopped into the rocking chair where, when she'd

been smaller than Sylvie, she'd climbed into her papa's lap and fallen asleep while he'd read to her. The memory made her sad now, which was silly.

"If Papa was angry with anybody, he was angry with Mrs. Holymere."

Sylvie took the other rocking chair, her feet not reaching the floor. "John Coachman calls her Mrs. Holy Terror. She smiles too much. I told her I'd already had an ice, and I'd helped Lady Hig finish hers too, but Mrs. Holymere insisted I stay with her to have another."

Mrs. Holymere's agenda had become clear to Amanda when the woman had called upon Papa several weeks ago, pretending to need his advice about how to manage her domestics. Amanda had every confidence Mrs. Holymere was a dab hand at managing her servants, her friends, and half the bachelors in Mayfair.

The housekeeper had said as much, and Cook and Mr. Drummond, the butler, had agreed with her.

"Mrs. Holymere wants to marry Papa," Amanda said. "Wants to add him to the staff she manages."

Sylvie set her chair rocking. "Papa is a lord. Nobody manages him but Good King George."

"Miss Fletcher manages him. She made him take us to Gunter's for ices, and now he has the knack of it on his own. She's the reason he sometimes brings us flowers, Syl, and before she came, you weren't even taking breakfast downstairs."

Sylvie's chair slowed. "I like breakfast downstairs. I like Miss Fletcher. So does Lady Hig, and Miss Twitlinger, and Her Grace of Dumpwhistle, and the Honorable Mr. Woddynod. Mr. Hamchop doesn't like anybody."

Amanda liked having Sylvie at the breakfast table. With a younger sister underfoot to get jam on the table napkins, mash up words, and speak too loudly, Amanda felt more at ease.

"Breakfast was awful before Miss Fletcher came. Papa hid behind the newspaper and forgot I was there."

"How could anybody forget you, Manda?"

The question was genuinely perplexed, and guilt rose again to upset Amanda's belly. "I forgot you, Syl. I was so busy trying to kick the ball at that tree, I didn't realize when you'd wandered off. I'm your older sister. I should have kept an eye on you."

Sylvie hopped out of her chair and went to the toy chest. "I waited until it was your turn to kick before I went to fetch Lady Hig. I didn't want anybody to know I'd forgotten her again."

"Do you ever get tired of playing with dolls, Syl?"

"Yes, but there's nobody else to play with, unless Miss Fletcher has me invite Rose or Jessica or Clementina or Daisy or Maude or Lizzie or—"

"Who does Miss Fletcher ever play with, Syl?"

"Grown-ups don't play. I can't find my tops."

Grown-ups did play. They played fancy dress-up and called it a masquerade. They played all manner of card games, and Papa had once said Parliament was a glorified cricket tournament.

"Mrs. Holymere wants to play with Papa."

Sylvie left off plundering the toy chest. "You said she wants to marry him. She told me that I have been too long without a mama, and Papa needs to do his duty by the session."

"The succession, the title. She meant we need brothers, though we have seven male cousins on the uncles' side. Mrs. Holymere wants to marry Papa so he can have sons with her."

"Will brothers play with me?"

Amanda crossed the room to fetch a pair of spinning tops from the mantel. "From what I understand, brothers are a little bit of a friend and mostly a bother. Miss Fletcher writes to her brothers often." Papa did not seem to bother the aunties, though he called upon them more often than they called upon him.

"Miss Fletcher has the most beautiful handwriting," Sylvie said. "I want to learn to write as she does, without getting ink all over my blotter."

Amanda had developed beautiful handwriting under Miss Fletcher's tutelage. She was also tackling her third Beethoven sonata and, according to Miss Fletcher, was already equal to any of Herr Mozart's challenges.

"Papa can do his duty by the succession without involving Mrs. Holymere," Amanda said.

"You found my tops!" Sylvie took the one painted with blue and white rings. "Let's have a race!"

They'd been playing this game forever, setting both tops spinning until one toppled, and the one still whirling was the winner. Amanda rolled back half the carpet, Sylvie plopped to the floor, and Amanda tried to do as Miss Fletcher had done on the blanket in Berkeley Square—fold gracefully to her knees, then shift to one hip, legs tucked aside.

That was harder than it looked, like most attempts to emulate Miss Fletcher.

"How is Papa to find me some brothers without marrying another lady?" Sylvie scrambled to her feet and fetched Lady Hig and Her Grace of Dumpwhistle—they had made their come outs together, after all.

"Papa could marry Miss Fletcher."

Sylvie whipped the string off her top and set it spinning on the smooth oak floor. "Miss Fletcher isn't rich or fancy."

"Papa's not fancy, and he likes Miss Fletcher a lot. They smile at each other when they think we're not looking."

Sylvie watched her top, still going at a great rate, more of a blue blur than a highly polished wooden toy.

"We have had a lot of governesses," Sylvie said. "Miss Fletcher laughs and hugs me, and she doesn't say I'm too old for my dolls."

"She makes Papa listen and makes him talk to us."

"He wishes us good night now. I like that, but how do we make sure they marry?"

"We tell Papa, and he proposes to Miss Fletcher, and they marry."

The top wobbled, then fell to its side, all momentum gone.

"I don't think it's that simple, Manda. Wind your string, and we'll have our race."

"We'll talk to Papa and maybe to Miss Fletcher. We'll give them the benefit of our informed guidance."

Informed guidance, according to Miss Fletcher, was to be esteemed as highly as a pot of chocolate and fresh shortbread, but not quite as highly as heavenly intercession.

"I'll tell Papa that Lady Hig didn't like Mrs. Holymere *at all*. Start on the count of three."

Amanda counted with Sylvie, in the age-old nursery tradition, and then they let their tops fly.

Even though Sylvie was only a little girl, her complicity with Amanda's plan was a comfort. They would talk to Papa and to Miss Fletcher. Exactly how they'd go about that task without being able to consult either source of wisdom first was a puzzle.

Amanda enjoyed puzzles. She loved her papa and Miss Fletcher, thus she would find a way to give them the benefit of her guidance—and Sylvie's and even Lady Higginbottom's, if that was what she had to do to bring Papa and Miss Fletcher together.

CHAPTER FIVE

Giles Throckmorton had been handsome as a youth, and the years had only improved his looks. A young soldier had matured into a man with some character to his features, a subtle dash to his attire, and gravity in his gaze.

Lucy noted those developments impersonally, for Mr. Throckmorton's arrival had interrupted some sort of declaration from Lord Tyne—a declaration or a disclaimer. Lucy hadn't been sure if his lordship had been about to confess a *tendresse* for her or to warn her not to develop one for him.

A bit late for the warning. Any other employer would have blamed the governess when a child went missing. Lord Tyne had solved the problem, taken responsibility for it, and reassured Lucy most kindly afterward.

"Mr. Throckmorton." Lucy curtseyed. "Your call is unexpected."

He bowed. "You are ever tactful. I think what you mean is, my calling upon you is a great presumption. I had to come nonetheless."

"Lord Tyne will not turn me off for receiving an

acquaintance from long ago," Lucy said. "Shall we be seated?"

Giles took the only wing chair—he'd been shown to the formal sitting room—and he looked quite at home there. The Portuguese sun had burnished his blond hair to gold, and the effect of the elements on his complexion was to make the blue of his eyes more vivid.

He wasn't as tall as Lord Tyne, not as muscular either.

"You look the same," Giles said, studying Lucy as if she were a portrait. "As pretty as ever."

He was up to something. Lucy had brothers, and those brothers had wives, and those wives kept her informed of every scrap of gossip from home. Giles regularly came back to England, and not once had he brought his children or his wife, not once had he called upon or asked about Lucy.

"Mr. Throckmorton, please don't take this as rudeness on my part, but your opinion of my appearance is of no interest to me. I am happily employed in a very respectable house, and I hope to remain in that blessed state for some time."

He smiled, and heavens, that smile had matured in Portugal as well. Giles had always had more charm than was fair, and he'd learned to add a dash of regret to his gaze, a soupçon of self-mockery that blended humility with amusement.

"You won't believe me, Lucy, but more than your affection, more than your lovely appearance, more than your humor, I've missed your common sense, and you are right: My opinion of your good looks is of no moment. I merely remark the obvious. How have you been keeping?"

A friend could ask that.

"I do very well, thank you. My work matters to me and allows me to use my gifts for the benefit of others." Flinging the reality of Lucy's situation at Giles's feet felt good. She hadn't married, hadn't taken any other lovers, but she'd made a good life for herself. "I trust your family thrives?"

"John is a natural-born diplomat. He sends you his regards, as do my sisters. They've kept me apprised of your situation, though I gather they haven't done the same for you in my case."

His sisters had never so much as sent Lucy a note after she'd removed to London.

"I did not feel I had the right to inquire after you." Lucy hadn't, in fact, spared Giles more than a passing thought since she'd come to Lord Tyne's household. "You wrote me the once, years and years ago, and I took your letter for a polite admonition not to spin fancies where you are concerned."

He rose and studied the portrait of the late marchioness that hung over the sideboard. "My children are all in good health, but perhaps you had not heard that I was widowed more than a year ago."

That explained the sadness in his gaze, the gravity where a high-spirited young man had been. "I am sorry for your loss, and I know your children must miss their mama terribly."

The thought of those children tugged at Lucy's heartstrings, and she even felt some genuine compassion for Giles. He'd been a young man going off to war, and Lucy's choices where he was concerned were her own responsibility.

"The children and I are a little lost." He sent Lucy an unreadable look. "Sometimes more than a little. I can be honest with you, Lucy. My marriage was not a bed of rose petals, and I know my wife had her frustrations where I was concerned, but we muddled along, and we loved our children."

"Of course you did. Tell me their names."

He resumed his place in the wing chair and spoke with fond exasperation about four small children clearly bereft of their mother's love. Somewhere in the discussion of the children, Lucy recalled that Giles had been her first love, if a very young woman's foolish fancies could be called love. He was a good man, and according him that honor allowed Lucy more compassion for her younger self too.

Giles was a father, older, wiser, and undoubtedly sadder. Lucy had been desperately upset over his only letter, but eventually, she'd seen that he'd done her a kindness. The war had gone on for years, and too many soldiers had never come home.

Waiting for him could have been so much futility ending in bereavement.

"Twins are always a challenge," she said. "I've noticed that if I make the effort to refer to them as individuals, using their names rather than simply calling them 'the twins,' or 'you two,' I have fewer problems. I've also noticed that always dressing them alike, in the manner of matched footmen on display, isn't wise."

Giles sat back as if startled. "I had never thought… I had never considered… But then, in the army, when the drill sergeants are dressing down the recruits, the sergeants refer to the lads in collective insults—'you lot,' 'you disgraces.' When they praise a man, they always single him out by name."

"It's a detail," Lucy said. "Probably of no significance at all."

"I doubt that, and yet, none of the nurses, tutors, and governesses I've employed ever once put forth these insights."

An odd moment went by, during which Lucy had the sense she was being reassessed, and that old affection—or whatever Giles had brought to this reunion—was being supplemented by new respect. The clock chimed the hour, and he stood.

"Might I call on you again, Lucy? We haven't nearly begun to catch up. I have much to tell you about Portugal and about the business of making port. The land is beautiful in a way I can't describe, not as tame as dear England, and the people are wonderful."

"I am torn," Lucy said, rising. "While I am glad to know you prosper, and I wish you every joy, I do not want to create any mistaken impressions. I love my life here, Giles, and I love Lord Tyne's children. I am prospering too, in my way, and the terms of my employment do not contemplate that I will be socializing with many gentleman callers."

"I do believe I have just been given a preemptory spanking," he said. "I understand your situation, Lucy, but even a governess is entitled to meet an old friend on her half day."

Where was the harm in that suggestion? He'd go back to Portugal, and Lucy would be able to close the door on a youthful indiscretion that she'd never quite come to terms with.

"I can meet you for an ice at Gunter's on Tuesday at two of the clock. If I'm not there, assume my duties intervened, as they sometimes do."

Or she might have changed her mind, as she seldom did.

"I'll look forward to it," Giles said, bowing over her hand. When Lucy would have withdrawn her fingers from his grasp, he smoothed a caress to her knuckles, then kissed the back of her hand. No other gentleman had ever taken such a liberty—nobody except Giles, who apparently hadn't lost all of his youthful audacity.

Lucy snatched her hand back, ready to deliver a sound scold, but Giles strode to the door.

"Until Tuesday, Lucy. I'll be counting the hours."

* * *

Tyne met Miss Fletcher's guest at the door, for Captain Throckmorton by rights ought to have called upon Tyne, then asked after Lucy. He ought, in fact, to have brought a mutual acquaintance to make introductions between host and caller too. That he hadn't observed those courtesies made the whole question of chaperoning the call awkward. The housekeeper was out for the afternoon, and the senior maid enjoyed her half day on Saturday.

Tyne took an interest in these details of the household schedule because Miss Fletcher had informed him months ago that he must. No lady of the house was on hand to maintain domestic order. The staff had to know somebody was in charge or slacking—a transgression sufficient to threaten the peace of the realm—might ensue.

"Captain Throckmorton, good day."

Throckmorton was a good-looking devil and several years younger than Tyne, damn the luck.

The captain bowed. "Do I have the pleasure of encountering Lord Tyne?"

"You do." A purely masculine pause ensued. Tyne took

control of the figurative snorting and pawing by handing Throckmorton his hat. "Any friend of Miss Fletcher's will always be welcome under my roof, provided that friend comes in good faith. We *cherish* Miss Fletcher, and her happiness matters here."

Throckmorton apparently had little experience with parliamentary flag signals. What sounded like a pleasantry could be a threat, which Miss Fletcher's caller would understand the instant he misstepped.

"Lucy is an old and very dear friend," Throckmorton replied. "I've been remiss to let the connection lapse in recent years, but my regard for her is of long standing. I rejoice to know that her situation here is so comfortable."

Tyne all but shoved Throckmorton's walking stick against his chest. "She is *Miss Fletcher* to you."

"I beg your pardon. You are right, sir. Miss Fletcher."

Never had Tyne wanted so badly to smash his fist into another man's jaw, but Miss Fletcher would scold him about fisticuffs in the foyer, setting a bad example, and jeopardizing the decorum of a peer's household. She might even assign him a list of sums. The altercation would be worth the set-down, if she'd scold Throckmorton as well; but, alas, Tyne was the host. Miss Fletcher had firm ideas of how hosts should behave.

Hosts should show a polite interest in every guest. "Will you be in England long, Mr. Throckmorton?" Tyne had consulted with Drummond, who as butler had gleaned that Throckmorton was visiting from his vineyards in Portugal and had known Miss Fletcher before deploying to Spain as a captain in Wellington's army.

Drummond was overdue for an increase in wages.

"I haven't decided how long I'll stay," Throckmorton said. "I'd forgotten how lovely the land of my birth is, and now that my children are once again in need of a mother, I'll likely be spending more time here."

Meaning Throckmorton was in need of a wife. "My condolences. All I can tell you is that the pain of losing a spouse fades, but the ache never entirely leaves you."

Throckmorton's expression of genteel sorrow faltered, suggesting he'd alluded to his widower status out of something other than paternal devotion to the children he'd abandoned hundreds of miles away.

He pulled on his gloves. "My thanks for that sage observation. Army life gives a man some perspective where death and loss are concerned, but your view is also appreciated."

How bloody gracious of him. "My years in Lower Canada afforded me the same perspective. The winter alone cost us many good soldiers." Tyne had served for only two years and mostly in peacetime. Papa had decreed that a man destined to help run an empire ought to see something besides sheep pastures and ballrooms before he sat in the Lords.

In the military, Tyne had become proficient in all manner of card games, perfected his aim with a rifle, and learned to tolerate cold the like of which no self-important grape farmer would ever encounter.

"I'll wish you good day," Throckmorton said, bowing. "Until next we meet, my lord."

"Until that happy occasion," Tyne said, signaling Drummond to open the door. "Should I not have the pleasure of encountering you again, safe and swift journey home when you rejoin your children."

Tyne summoned the same smile he used on junior MPs spouting radical notions. *Out you go, lad, and mind your manners around Miss Fletcher.*

Throckmorton had no choice but to accept his dismissal, and Drummond closed the door.

"Is Miss Fletcher to be at home to Mr. Throckmorton in future, sir?" Drummond asked.

If Tyne said yes, he was admitting into his home a potential competitor for Miss Fletcher's services as a governess. A nursery full of bereaved little souls in Portugal would call to her, as they should to anybody with half a heart.

Throckmorton was also a competitor for her affections.

His posturing, his attempt to circumvent propriety, his use of informal address… Tyne had every sympathy for a grieving widower, and no patience at all for a manipulative bounder.

And yet, if Tyne said no, that Miss Fletcher was not at home if Mr. Throckmorton called again, then Tyne was disrespecting the lady's independence. After all she'd done for Tyne and his children, she was owed, and she surely had earned, his respect.

"You must ask Miss Fletcher," Tyne said, "and inquire of her as well whether our housekeeper ought to join any future calls that Mr. Throckmorton pays on my household."

More than that, Tyne could not in good conscience do— not until he'd completed the awkward conversation with Miss Fletcher that Mr. Throckmorton's arrival had so inconveniently interrupted.

* * *

We cherish Miss Fletcher, and her happiness matters here. Lord Tyne had spoken at sufficient volume that Lucy had heard him in the formal parlor. Giles's half of the conversation had been harder to discern, which was just as well. Eavesdroppers never heard any good of themselves.

Though, to be *cherished…* His lordship did not posture for the sake of impressing anybody, least of all a casual caller.

"I have seen Mr. Throckmorton out," the marquess said, wandering into the formal parlor. "If you'd like a chaperone for any future calls, please let the housekeeper know."

"Thank you."

He took the piano bench. "What are you thanking me for, Miss Fletcher?"

Being yourself. "Being protective. Giles is an old, old friend, but I hadn't seen him for years. People can change over time."

His lordship spun around and opened the cover over the keys. "You call him Giles."

What mood is this? "I knew him when I was a girl, and before he left for Spain, we had something of a flirtation."

"Are you being delicate?"

"Yes." And euphemistic. *A mutual pawing* would have been

a more accurate description. The thought made Lucy smile, which, where Giles was concerned, was a relief. What a pair of young nodcocks they'd been.

"You recall him fondly, in other words." His lordship began the slow movement from Beethoven's Piano Sonata No. 8 in C minor, often called *Pathétique*. The first theme was lyrical and lovely, and he played it at the flowing, calm tempo the composer had intended.

"Mr. Throckmorton would like me to recall him fondly." Lucy had come to this realization somewhere amid Giles's recitations regarding his children. Why was he making this effort now?

The marquess played on, and Lucy wished she might simply enjoy the music. Amanda got her musical talent from her papa apparently, and Sylvie showed signs of the same gift. Giles's visit had further disrupted an already unsettling day, though, and Lucy had questions for the marquess.

"How many children does he have?" his lordship asked.

"Mr. Throckmorton? Four, including twins."

"Twins."

Twins, spoken in that tone, with that expression, suggested somebody had committed a dire offense.

"Will you leave us to help him raise his twins, Miss Fletcher?"

The notion that Giles had been looking for a governess— an English governess experienced at dealing with grieving children—had only begun to form in Lucy's mind. If so, he'd have been better off approaching her in writing with an offer of a post instead of pretending to call on an old friend.

Much less presuming to kiss her hand, for pity's sake. "I haven't been offered that opportunity."

His lordship brought the music to a sweet, stately close rather than carry on to the more tempestuous, contrasting theme.

"I am confident that you will be offered that opportunity. If it's in your best interests to pursue such a post, then you should."

That was what a true friend ought to say, and what nobody ever had said to Lucy. "I thought you sought to keep my services, not toss me onto the first boat bound for Lisbon."

His lordship closed the cover over the keys. "You will be tempted, by the children in his nursery who are doubtless struggling for want of their mama's love, by the notion that an old friend deserves your loyalty at a trying time, and—we have always been honest with each other, have we not, Miss Fletcher?—by the excuse to leave a situation here which has come to mean much to you."

He rose, and Lucy thought he was finished expounding on her motivations, which he'd identified more clearly than she could have herself.

"What is wrong with being useful?" she asked.

Lord Tyne drew her to her feet and again kept hold of her hand. Unlike Giles, he wasn't flirting. Lucy wasn't sure exactly what his lordship was about. He didn't seem angry, exactly, but then again, when Sylvie had gone missing, he hadn't shown any sign of anxiety either.

"Being useful is a worthy goal," he said. "Compassion and service should figure prominently in any meaningful life, but what of joy? What of pleasure, dreams, hopes, and wishes? Children grow up, Miss Fletcher, and devoting yourself to their well-being while ignoring your own is a scheme that will leave you old and lonely. Fond memories are some compensation for decades of your life, but you deserve more than that."

Thor would have admonished her thus, and at that moment, Lord Tyne put Lucy in mind of her Norse god.

"What were you about to say to me in the garden, my lord?"

"In the—? Ah, that. I'm not sure those sentiments are relevant now. Perhaps after Captain Throckmorton has returned to the wonders of Portugal, I might recall what point I was trying to make."

I will kill Giles. "Whatever you have to say is of interest to me, sir. Your happiness matters to me too."

His brows rose. "A cheering revelation. I'll see you at dinner, Miss Fletcher."

He leaned down to brush a kiss to her cheek and strode out, closing the door softly behind him.

CHAPTER SIX

Lucy heard not a word of Vicar's sermon, so preoccupied was she trying to sort out emotions, options, and innuendos.

Lord Tyne had kissed her cheek, which for him amounted to a bold declaration, but of what? Good wishes on a venture in Portugal? Support for Lucy's ability to choose a course? His attachment to her as a member of the household?

Something *more?*

She should ask him, she *meant* to ask him, except that he'd again become the remote, reticent man whom she'd met when she'd first joined his household. The children must have sensed his mood, for they didn't exchange a single whisper during the service.

After church, his lordship took the children for Sunday dinner at Lady Eleanor's house, leaving Lucy to begin and then tear up three different letters to her oldest brother's wife. What was Giles about? What had shifted in his lordship's regard for his children's governess?

And what was Lucy to do about Tuesday night's assignation with Thor?

About her Tuesday afternoon meeting with Giles?

The life of an adventuress is complicated. Freya would have known that. Lucy was making a fourth attempt at correspondence when she heard the jingle and clatter of the coach in the mews. Curiosity had her setting aside her pen and capping the ink, because the children hadn't been gone long enough to enjoy a Sunday meal with family.

"Manda is sick," Sylvie announced before Lucy had untied the child's bonnet ribbons. "Papa said I might get sick too, but when I asked him if he could get sick, he didn't answer me." Sylvie gave her father a half-hopeful, half-peevish look.

"Your father has a very strong constitution," Lucy said. "Illness befalls us all, but his lordship appears to enjoy great good health. Amanda, what's amiss?"

"Her throat hurts," his lordship replied. "She's congested, she aches. Every symptom of the blasted flu, in other words."

Illness terrified this household, and for good reason. The marchioness had been well one day and at death's door a fortnight later. The best physicians, the most fervent prayers, had been useless against the sickness that had befallen her.

Lucy put her hand against Amanda's forehead. "No sign of fever. Your eyes lack the characteristic shine of one battling influenza." She aimed a glower at the marquess. "Amanda has very likely caught a spring cold or taken some blooming flower into dislike. Come upstairs, and we'll cosset you with willow bark tea, lemon drops, and card games."

"I've sent for the physician," the marquess said, joining Lucy and her charges on the stair.

"I don't want to see a doctor," Amanda retorted. "I have a cold. You heard Miss Fletcher, Papa."

"A cold or a hay fever," Lucy said. "Neither one should inconvenience you for more than a few days. Sylvie, you will write a story to amuse your sister during her convalescence. Your lordship will inform the physician that his services are not needed, and I will see the patient settled in her bed."

Lucy put an arm around Amanda's shoulders—the girl was

growing so tall—and spared his lordship a quelling glance.

Steady on, sir. We've dealt with this before.

Sylvie had come down with chicken pox a month after Lucy joined the household, and Amanda had had colds in both spring and fall. Illnesses happened, and with good care and luck, most children recovered. The blow to a parent's confidence likely did permanent injury.

Lord Tyne paused at the top of the steps. "I don't see the harm in having Dr. Garner drop around—"

"Today is the Sabbath," Lucy said. "Leave the poor man one day of peace. Amanda has a sniffle, possibly a cold. She has no serious injury, no signs of infection, no fever. She will be well in no time."

Lucy continued with Amanda into the girl's bedroom, leaving Tyne and Sylvie holding hands at the end of the corridor. The picture they made, father and daughter, equally worried, equally brave, made Lucy's heart ache, but what they needed was her calm and good sense.

So, calm and sensible she would be.

"Are you truly ill, Amanda?" Lucy asked when the door was closed. The first time Amanda's courses had befallen her, she'd been practicing duets at the home of a cousin. Because Lucy had instructed the girl regarding contingencies, Amanda had known to plead a megrim and always have cloths in her reticule. She'd been returned posthaste to Lucy's care.

Lord Tyne had paced outside his daughter's bedroom for nearly an hour before Lucy had been able to explain the situation to him. His reaction had been relief rather than embarrassment. He'd observed that the late marchioness had been known to use the poppy on occasion to ease the same indisposition.

That conversation had given Lucy the first hint that his lordship not only worried for his children, he also loved them—desperately.

"I'm sick," Amanda said. "A cold, as you say. My head aches, my throat itches, and I sneezed three times in a row."

"Is that what had your papa summoning the physician?"

"Yes, but how can one not sneeze?"

"Into bed with you. Prepare to be spoiled and pampered out of your sneezes. We'll get you a pile of old handkerchiefs, because they are the softest, and some peppermint tea to help clear your head."

Amanda yawned. "Do I have to take the willow bark tea too?"

"That will ease your headache and any soreness of your limbs," Lucy said, starting on the hooks at the back of Amanda's dress. "Change into your nightgown, and I'll be back to redo your braids more loosely."

"Papa is worried." Amanda sounded more forlorn than anxious. "Will you stay with me? He'll fret, and then Sylvie will have nightmares, and it will all be my fault, because I sneezed."

Lucy hugged the girl. "Nobody can help sneezing, and of course I will stay with you." She kept the embrace brief, because Amanda had also inherited a certain dignity from her father.

Amanda hugged her back. "You won't leave us, will you?"

Oh, dear. Lucy stepped away. "I beg your pardon?"

"That man who called on you yesterday, the friend from your girlhood. Mr. Drummond told Cook that your caller is a widower living in an exotic land, and he might be trying to entice you away from us. I shouldn't like that, and Sylvie—"

"Will have nightmares," Lucy said. "All children have nightmares, Amanda, but nobody has offered me a post in a far-off land, so we needn't discuss this."

"Good."

Lucy fetched the book of Norse fairy tales and read to Amanda until the child dozed off. The evening was spent in the same manner, with a break to marvel over Sylvie's tale of Her Grace of Dumpwhistle's public altercation with Mr. Hamchop-who-doesn't-like-anybody. Several times, Lucy heard Amanda's bedroom door opening and closing. She didn't have to look up to know Lord Tyne was peeking in on his daughter—and fretting.

Lucy fell asleep in the chair beside Amanda's bed, the book of fairy tales in her lap. When Monday morning came, Lucy was in her own bed, with only a vague notion of how she'd arrived there.

She'd been carried in a pair of strong arms, laid gently on the mattress. Her slippers had been eased off, then she'd been covered with not one but two quilts. The fairy tales were on her bedside table, and her slippers were by the side of the bed.

She recalled a soft kiss to her forehead, and she recalled—with embarrassing clarity—returning that kiss with a desperately heartfelt embrace that she'd never wanted to end.

* * *

"For God's sake, are you a horse or an overexcited puppy?"

Attila kicked out behind, hopped left, and propped on his back legs. Because Tyne had been up too late Sunday night worrying over Amanda, Attila hadn't left his stall since Friday. By Tuesday morning, the gelding was an unruly ball of unspent energy.

"Then let's run," Tyne said, aiming his horse at an empty stretch of bridle path. The park was more than three hundred acres all told, but none of the paths afforded the miles and miles of open country that Tyne and his mount needed to truly gallop off the fidgets.

This was all Miss Fletcher's fault. Tyne had thought to press a good-night kiss to her forehead, and mayhem had ensued. The happiest, most unexpected, inconvenient... She had lifted herself into his embrace and held him for a long, aching moment in the night shadows.

And then, her kiss, ye gods her kiss. As if he'd been slumbering in some fairytale castle of old, her kiss had wakened desire and determination in equal measure. Freya's parting gesture had been intriguing; Lucy Fletcher's sleepy passion was riveting. She'd held nothing back, had clung to him as if her dearest secret longings could be fulfilled only by him. Tyne had hung over her recumbent form, returning her passion and longing to do more… Except that lady had clearly been exhausted, and very likely she'd been kissing a phantasm from a dream.

I want to be the lover of her dreams and the man at her side when she wakens.

The emotions that had coursed through him as he'd shared that fervent embrace with her had been wonderful—joy, hope, desire, affection—and terrible—uncertainty, loss, despair. And while Tyne abhorred drama, that embrace had answered one question for him: He was very much alive, very much still human, and that was a good, if painful, gift.

In the morning, Miss Fletcher made no mention of what had passed between them the previous night. She hadn't so much as hesitated at the door of the breakfast parlor.

Perhaps she had no recollection of that heated embrace, but Tyne was haunted by it.

"That will do for now," he said, bringing Attila down to the walk. The horse's sides were heaving, but one short burst of speed wouldn't be enough for him, just as one heartfelt embrace wasn't enough for Tyne.

"But was she clinging to me, to some conjured shadow from her imagination, or to Throckmorton, may God rot him straight to the bottom of the river Douro?"

Tyne's mind was made up on one point: Two weeks ago, he'd kissed a stranger on a darkened front porch. The encounter had been sweet and unexpected. That passing delight could not in any way compare to the depth of his regard for Miss Fletcher. She had seen him and his children through many difficulties, from illness, to grief, to adolescent awkwardness.

"She's loyal, loving, resourceful, and she won't let me slack as a papa. I suspect she wouldn't let me slack as a husband either." *Or as a lover.*

Attila snorted.

"You're a gelding. Your opinion on the matter is uninformed."

Tyne set the horse to cantering back up the path and spent another half hour humoring his mount's high spirits. By the time the horse was clip-clopping up the alley to the mews, the creature was sweaty and docile, not a buck or a hop left in him.

"My attachment to Miss Fletcher is beyond doubt," Tyne concluded as the stable came into view. "But have I engaged her affections?"

Attila sighed, a big, horsey, side-heaving exhalation.

"You are telling me I'm making this too complicated, and as usual, you are right, my friend. I must risk losing the woman my children adore—the woman I adore—and plainly state my intentions. She'll either laugh and decamp to Portugal, or she'll become my marchioness."

For there could be no un-saying a declaration of intentions, no battling those words back into a sealed box, never to be recalled. No un-leaping over the precipice once honest emotions had been disclosed.

"Tomorrow," Tyne said, patting Attila's sweaty shoulder. "I'm expected at Eleanor's for dinner this evening, and choosing the proper words requires some thought. Freya might wait for me briefly tonight, but I suspect she's already come to her senses as well. A future isn't built on a single kiss, no matter how lovely or adventurous that kiss might be."

Tyne's logic was sound, his mind made up. Now all he needed were the right words and endless courage. He could forgive himself for forming an unreciprocated attachment, but his daughters would never pardon him for driving Miss Fletcher away to dratted Portugal.

* * *

Amanda's cold had done as colds did and given her a passing inconvenience. By noon Tuesday, she was back to bickering with Sylvie, and Lucy was more than ready to pitch the pair of them into the garden fountain.

"I am going out this afternoon," she said, coming upon her charges by the garden fountain. "I suggest you ladies spend the hours between now and supper in neutral corners."

"What are neutered corners?" Sylvie asked.

"Neutral," Amanda said, punching the air. "Like when pugilists rest between rounds of a fight."

"What are pew… puganists?"

"Pugilists," Lucy said. "Combatants, bare-knuckle fighters. You and Amanda are cross with each other today, and I cannot bide here to referee your verbal sparring. I'll be back well before supper."

"Where are you going?" Sylvie asked.

"Don't be rude, Syl."

"I'm not being rude. I'm being curious. Miss Fletcher says a curious mind is a gift from God."

Miss Fletcher is sometimes an idiot. "Sylvie, I have a few errands to see to, and that's what half days are for. If you truly wanted to impress me, the two of you might consider working on your duet."

Older and younger sister wore identical expressions of distaste.

"I'm off," Lucy said. "Behave, please."

"Yes, Miss Fletcher." They spoke in unison, and Lucy hurried through the garden gate. She turned to drape the latch string over the top and saw two girls, holding hands, regarding her departure with forlorn gazes.

A movement in an upstairs window caught her eye. Lord Tyne had pulled back the curtains in his study and stood at the window watching the tableau in the garden. Lucy waved to him—he'd been excruciatingly proper since Sunday night— and he nodded in response.

Lucy took that nod as acknowledgment that she and the marquess had unfinished business. He was having dinner with his sister's family tonight—thank heavens—and Lucy had matters to tidy up with Giles and with a certain Norse god. Then, by heaven, she and Lord Tyne would finish the discussion they'd begun in the garden on Saturday.

And—if she was brave and he was willing—they'd resume the kiss that had haunted her dreams since Monday morning.

As she made her way to Berkeley Square, Lucy gave up wondering what his lordship had been about to say and embarked on the fraught exercise of determining what *she* wanted to say. Instead, a list grew of admissions she was reluctant to make:

I have become that pathetic cliché, the governess in love with her employer.

I am still young enough to give him sons, truly I am. I hope.

One can be lonely in a house full of people.

I desire Lord Tyne. I want a future as his wife and as step-mother to Sylvie and Amanda.

All too soon, she was in front of Gunter's and approaching Giles, who lounged on a shaded bench across the street. He rose and tipped his hat as Lucy came up the walkway.

"My dear, lovely to see you."

She was not his dear. "Good day, Giles. Shall we order our ices?"

He offered his arm. "I suppose the proprieties require it."

Lucy's predilection for barberry-flavored treats required it. "What is your favorite flavor?"

"The offerings here are all so much cold sweetness," Giles said, patting her fingers. "Gunter's is an excuse to profit from a clientele that seeks to mingle with members of the opposite sex. Lemon will do for me."

Giles could be blunt. Lucy had forgotten that. He wasn't entirely wrong, but neither was he correct. "I bring the children here often, and I dearly hope amatory matters have not yet caught their fancy."

"So you're a nursemaid as well as a governess?"

Good gracious, he'd left his manners in Portugal. "Lord Tyne accompanied us on our last outing. Is he also a nursemaid?"

"He's something of a bore, if you ask me. Does he interrogate every person who calls upon you?"

"He did not interrogate you. Perhaps you'd best place our orders, Giles."

Except Giles hadn't asked her what flavor she wanted. He

came back from the counter with two lemon ices and carried both across the street, then settled himself beside Lucy on a bench.

The moment put Lucy in mind of their youthful encounters. Giles had strutted about, making pronouncements that were supposed to paint him as a worldly, sophisticated man-about-town, while Lucy had wondered if her company meant anything to him. Then he'd turn up flirtatious just as she was about to leave him to his self-importance, and she'd—

"I have missed you, Lucy Fletcher." He drew his spoon from his mouth slowly, his lashes lowered.

Lucy used her spoon to swirl the letter T into the top of her ice. "Thank you. I have also thought of you over the years. Is there something in particular you want to discuss with me, Giles?"

A few people loitered around the square or strolled beneath the maples, but the conversation would not be overheard. Lucy wanted this appointment concluded, and she wanted her late-evening appointment with Thor over with as well…

If she even kept it. She was under no obligation to appear. What would be the point? She did still have his cloak—a beautiful article of clothing—and should return it to him. She didn't anticipate another kiss from a stranger with any joy, though, and she ought not to be haring about after dark on her own.

"You thought of me from time to time?" Giles replied. "I will content myself with that admission, because I know you were raised in a proper household. I also know that you've strayed, Lucy."

Lucy set aside her ice, which was too sour by half. "I *beg* your pardon?"

"Come now," Giles said, holding a spoonful of ice before Lucy's mouth, as if she required feeding like an infant. "We have a past, you and I. An intimate past. Surely that means something to a woman who in all these years has never married."

Lucy gently pushed his wrist aside. "It means we were very foolish, very long ago, also very lucky that our foolishness didn't have unfortunate repercussions. Giles, are you thinking to offer me a post as governess to your children?"

The lemon ice slipped from his spoon onto his thigh. "*What?* As *governess?*"

"Of course, as governess. I am a governess and a very good one. I'm particularly skilled with children who've lost a parent, and yours fit that sad description."

He tossed the remains of his ice to the grass beside the bench. "Lucy, you cannot think that I'd travel the ocean, call on you personally, and regale you with the details of my situation simply to offer you employment?"

"Of course not. You travel back to England to see your family, not to see me, but why else would you bother to call on me after sending me exactly one letter since the day you left for Spain?"

He regarded her with a pained expression, as if she'd made a weak jest. "I am attempting to embark on a proper courtship of you, Lucy. I know you regard yourself as in possession of experience no blushing bride ought to have, but of all men, I am the last to judge you for that. You'll like Portugal, and I know you love children, else you'd never have consigned yourself to a career caring for them."

Lucy had the sense she'd been thrust into some other woman's life, a poor creature expected to flatter and fawn over any male buffoon who made calf's eyes at her.

"Giles, at the regimental ball, you encouraged me to drink from your glass of punch, and you kept that glass refilled. I had never before, and have never since, been tipsy. I hold myself entirely responsible for my actions, but you are very fortunate that my brothers didn't get wind of your behavior. I can assure you, no gentleman has since doubted my good name."

He stared at the empty walkway. "Has any other gentleman paid you his addresses?"

This conversation had all the earmarks of one of Sylvie's

grand dramas involving Her Grace of Dumpwhistle and Lady Higginbottom.

"I have attracted the respectful attention of the occasional gentleman. More than that is no concern of yours. I consider you a friend from my girlhood, Giles, one who became a passing fancy on his way to war. I am unwilling to leave my present post to join you in Portugal on any terms."

Lucy refused to give him the comfort of the you-do-me-great-honor speech, because he hadn't done her any honor whatsoever. The nerve of him, showing up after years of silence, and all but proposing…

Giles used a handkerchief to dab at the damp spot on his breeches. "I will try to change your mind, Lucy. You must allow me that. I've been hasty, leaping to conclusions, making assumptions. We were fast friends when we were young, passionate lovers for too brief a time. I have four motherless children, including twins, and you love children."

As if twins were some sort of parental prize? As if he'd been the one to carry those twins or bring them forth into the world? "Giles, you must put this notion aside. I am content with my present post."

"But you are very nearly *in service*," he retorted, balling up his handkerchief after he'd succeeded only in spreading the stain. "Don't you long to have a household of your own? Children of your own? You once assured me you yearned to see foreign lands, sail the sea, and sample exotic cultures. You told me you longed to follow the drum because you were so infernally bored with England. Don't you long for those things still?"

Well, no. Once upon a time, what Giles offered would have been all Lucy had ever dreamed of. Once upon a time was for fairy tales.

"Giles, I have sufficient funds of my own. My parents saw to that, and my brothers have managed that money very competently. If I want to travel, I needn't marry to do so."

"You have *money*? And still you spend your days wiping the

noses of other people's brats?"

Lucy got to her feet lest she start laughing at his version of a governess's responsibilities. "I love children. Surely that concept isn't unheard of?"

"No," he said, rising. "Not at all unheard of. I see I have been precipitous and that your situation is not what I thought it to be. I refuse to give up, though, Lucy. What you need, what you deserve, is the proper wooing you should have had years ago. If I should call on you again, you will receive me, won't you? For the sake of old friendship?"

She ought not. She ought to send him packing with a flea in his presumptuous ear, but widowers could be a desperate lot, and their dignity should never be avoidably slighted.

"Lord Tyne told you himself that I'm welcome to see old friends, but you mustn't entertain false hopes, Giles."

"No false hopes," he said, bowing. "But perhaps a few new hopes."

Lucy left the square with a new hope of her own: that Giles would sail back to Portugal with some other blushing bride at his side, and make that journey soon. His four children doubtless missed him desperately, though in recent years, Lucy had stopped missing him at all.

* * *

"We want to talk to you," Sylvie said.

Her expression was solemn, making her look much like her mother. Josephine had had an inherent gravity that Tyne hoped would not entirely overtake her daughters, not so soon.

"Do I mistake the matter," he asked, "or are we not in conversation already? Whose turn is it to select my cravat pin?"

"You are grown up," Sylvie said, advancing three more steps into Tyne's bedroom, all but dragging Amanda by the hand. "You can choose your own cravat pin, like I choose what dress to wear every day."

Miss Fletcher's handiwork at its subtle finest. Give the young ladies choices, she'd said, and they'll learn to exercise independent judgment.

"I haven't much sense of fashion," Tyne replied, "but you're correct. I am capable of making an adequate selection."

"The sapphire." Amanda dropped Sylvie's hand. "It brings out the blue in your eyes."

Tyne would have chosen something more subdued. "The sapphire it is, a gift from your dear mama, like the two of you."

"Mama would want you to be happy," Sylvie announced with such conviction that Tyne suspected it was a rehearsed conclusion, or one supplied by Amanda.

"I am happy." That approached telling his daughters a falsehood, though one kindly meant. Tyne was grateful for his life, he was abundantly blessed by good fortune, he was hopeful… But happiness had eluded him for a long time.

"Happy like when Mama was alive," Amanda said. "We think you should marry Miss Fletcher."

Pain stung Tyne's chest as he stabbed himself with his sapphire pin. "Blasted, dashed, deuced,"—Sylvie's eyes grew round—"perishing, dratted, infernal,"—Amanda was grinning—"accursed, wretched, *damn*."

"Papa said a bad word." Sylvie was ecstatic.

"He was overset," Amanda crowed, quietly. Tyne's daughters were ladies.

He assessed himself in the mirror. No blood, which was fortunate for his valet's nerves. "I am *not* in the least overset. I am ambushed by a pair of…"

They'd gone serious at his severe tone, watching him with the same wariness he used to feel toward his own children, before Lucy Fletcher had joined the household and made a family of them.

He knelt and opened his arms. "I've been waylaid by a pair of insightful young ladies who take my welfare very much to heart."

Sylvie barreled at him full tilt, while Amanda graciously permitted herself to be hugged. Tyne reveled in their embrace, and to hell with wrinkled linen, being late for dinner, and admitting his aspirations to his children.

When he turned loose of his daughters, Sylvie went skipping around the room. "You have to woo Miss Fletcher, Papa. Bring her flowers and steal kisses."

"And give her chocolates," Amanda added with an earnest nod. "She liked the French chocolates."

At Amanda's urging, Tyne had given Miss Fletcher chocolates at Christmas, months ago. "Excellent suggestion. What else?"

"You should read to her," Sylvie said, tripping on the carpet fringe, then skipping in the opposite direction. "She always reads to me, and she loooooves books."

"Do you think she'd enjoy my rendition of Norse fables?"

"I think she'd enjoy your version of anything," Amanda said. "You're handsome, kind, and intelligent. Do you know how to kiss, Papa? The uncles might have some ideas how to go about it."

"Your mother took care of that aspect of my education." Bless her for all eternity.

"Then," Sylvie said, climbing the steps and bouncing onto Tyne's bed, "when you've brought Miss Fletcher chocolates, and read to her, and vowed your every lasting devotion, you ask her to marry you!"

Amanda sent her papa a grown-up smile: *everlasting.*

"Such a campaign will take time," he said. "You must not say anything to Miss Fletcher or to the staff. This will be a family undertaking. Are we clear?"

"Because," Sylvie said, leaping from the bed, "it's *personal.*"

Tyne set the sapphire cravat pin back in his jewelry box. "Exactly. Very personal, and there's no guarantee I'll be successful."

"But you won't muck it up, will you, Papa?"

He chose another cravat pin, this one more subdued, also unlike any he'd seen in London ballrooms or house parties in the shires.

"If my objective is to ensure Miss Fletcher's happiness, then success is assured. My regard for her is such that I truly do want her happiness above all things, though my hope is that marriage to me will fulfill that aim."

"What's that?" Sylvie said, peering at his cravat pin.

"My lucky cravat pin," Tyne said. "This stone is very rare, coming from only one area of Derbyshire. It's called Blue John and found nowhere else in the world." The color was halfway between lavender and periwinkle, the stone a cross between marble and quartz, subtle rather than sparkly, and unique.

"Why is it lucky?" Sylvie asked, crowding in beside him at the vanity.

"Because Miss Fletcher gave it to me for Christmas." A highly personal gift, from the lady's home shire. She'd blushed when he'd thanked her, another precious rarity. He rose and beheld himself in the cheval mirror. "Will I do?"

"You're merely dining at Aunt Eleanor's," Sylvie said. "You don't have to be fancy for that."

"You look splendid, Papa."

Tyne did not feel splendid, but he felt *alive*. Ready to take on challenges and woo at least one lovely damsel, if she was willing to be wooed. If she wasn't, he'd make a gentlemanly effort to change her mind. Mr. Captain-Come-Lately from Portugal would have to find some other English rose to plant in his Portuguese vineyard.

Or some such rot.

"I'm away to dinner," he said, kissing each daughter on the forehead. "Don't give Miss Fletcher any trouble, and remember: not a word of my marital aspirations. I must conduct this campaign as I see fit, with no helpful interference from the infantry."

"Come, Sylvie," Amanda said, marching to the door. "We must talk."

That sounded ominous, though Sylvie skipped from the room happily enough. Tyne did not skip from the room, but headed down the steps five minutes later, prepared to endure a long evening making up the numbers at his sister's dinner party.

He was plagued by the vision of his Valkyrie waiting alone on the path for a suitor who never arrived, though the image of himself being left in the chilly darkness wasn't any more appealing. Perhaps he'd go to Vauxhall—that was the gentlemanly thing to do—and perhaps he'd leave fairy-tale kisses in the shadows where they belonged.

CHAPTER SEVEN

Giles had been assigned to intelligence work in the army, though army intelligence had often struck him as a contradiction in terms. His tasks were usually no more dangerous than sitting outside a rural inn and counting the number of wheeled conveyances going past in an afternoon, watching to see which farmer was riding too fine a horse for the condition of his acres, or listening at tavern keyholes and interviewing soiled doves.

He'd learned how to follow someone without being obvious, though, and thus he was inconspicuous as he followed Lucy Fletcher from her garden gate late Tuesday evening.

The only explanation for her dismissal of his proposal was that she had another fish on the line, another gentleman panting after her. Why shouldn't she? She was pretty enough—considering her age—she liked children, and she was trapped in the household of a priggish lord. Even a vicar's cottage, where she could be mistress of her own humble world, would appeal by comparison. She'd be a fool to give up such a prospect if the gentleman had nearly come up to scratch.

She'd been so confident in her rejection that Giles concluded his rival must also figure in the lady's immediate schedule.

Clearly, Giles had been correct, for Lucy wore a long, elegant cloak with the hood pulled up. A sleek town coach stopped in the mews for her—no crests showing—and she quickly ascended.

Naughty, naughty lady. But then, Giles knew she had an adventurous streak. He kept up easily with the coach—nobody went galloping through London at night—and hopped onto the boot of a passing carriage to follow the lady across the river.

To Vauxhall. Where else did lovers meet on cool and cozy nights?

Lucy was intent on a specific destination, for she directed her steps straight to the Lovers' Walk, no safe place for a lady. She was, of course, on her way to an assignation. Otherwise, she'd never have gone even a short distance beyond the bright illumination elsewhere in the gardens.

She stopped under a stately oak, one casting deep shadows. The occasional couple, trio, or quartet strolled past, but they seemed to notice neither Lucy nor Giles loitering farther down the walk.

Giles's plan dropped into his head all of a piece, as his best inspirations often did: Lucy was intent on meeting a lover here in the dark, and Giles would oblige her. When she realized that all caps truly were gray in the dark, and one swain could make her as happy as another, he'd have advanced his cause considerably, if not won the day.

* * *

Lucy had long ago deduced that the Lovers' Walk was not as dangerous a venue as most chaperones wanted their young charges to believe.

In the first place, torches were placed at intervals, albeit wide, shadowy intervals. In the second, the path was frequented by those intent on discretion. Nobody was peering too closely at anybody else, by mutual, tacit agreement. In the third, the path was far from deserted. While not thronged by foot traffic, a lady crying out in distress would be heard and assistance forthcoming.

Of course, that lady's reputation might emerge from the incident irreparably scarred, but her physical safety was at little risk.

Lucy's confidence was further bolstered by the cloak she wore, a loan from Thor and marvelously warm. She'd drawn the hood up before leaving Marianne's coach and had put Mr. DeCoursy's Norse tales in her reticule in case she needed to defend herself from untoward advances.

Not that Thor would make any of those. He was a gentleman, of that Lucy had no doubt.

She was also convinced, however, that he was not *her* gentleman. He was a lovely memory, a very fine kisser, and a man deserving of every happiness, but—

Footsteps along the walkway on the far side of Lucy's oak gave her pause. A man's tread, though soft, even stealthy.

"My dear?" He spoke barely above a whisper. "Is that you?"

If Lucy peered around the tree, she'd give her location away, and yet, she could not be certain that was Thor's voice.

"Madam, I beg you, don't keep me in suspense. This is the appointed time and place, and I'm here, as agreed."

Lucy stepped out from behind the oak. "Punctuality is likely one of your many fine attributes."

She'd recalled Thor as somewhat taller, but perhaps her recollection wasn't accurate. In the darkness, all she could tell for certain was that a man in a top hat and greatcoat stood a few feet away.

"You came," he said, stepping closer.

Without his hammer, he seemed less a god and more a man embarking on a clandestine flirtation.

"As did you, though you must know that my purpose for keeping this appointment was simply to acknow—"

He took her in his arms somewhat roughly. "I've missed you so."

What? and *This is not Thor* occupied Lucy's mind

simultaneously. The scent of this man was wrong, the shape of him wrong.

Giles? "Turn loose of me," Lucy hissed. "Get your paws off me this instant."

"I've thought of nothing but you," he replied. "Of what we both long for."

Good God. The cloak hampered Lucy from using her knee, so she tried to stomp on her assailant's foot, but he was nimble, and she was being bent back off her balance.

One moment Giles—this had to be Giles—was planting wet kisses on her chin, the next he expelled a solid, "Ooof!" against her cheek.

"Get away from her," said a cold voice. "Get your filthy presuming hands off of her, or next time, I'll use this sledgehammer to do something more than poke you in the ribs."

Thor had arrived. Lucy knew that voice, that shape, and even in the shadows, she could see he'd brought his signature fashion accessory.

Giles stood panting beside the tree. "Who the hell are you?"

"I'm a Norse legend, and you are the disgrace who's about to bolt hotfoot up this path, unless you want to be the fool I put period to at dawn."

"Go," Lucy snapped. "I never want to see you again, and don't think your identity is unknown to me. Thank every guardian angel you possess that you survived this encounter and stay far, far away from me in future."

Giles hesitated one instant, while Thor shouldered his sledgehammer, then Giles did indeed take off at a dead run up the path.

His footsteps faded, though Lucy's heart was still pounding. "Your arrival was timely, sir. Thank you."

"I considered bringing my usual walking stick, but realized you'd have no way of identifying me if I looked like every other strolling swain. Try being inconspicuous while toting a sledgehammer. It's impossible."

He sounded testy, and human, but still formidable. She could not see his features clearly, but she recognized the manner in which he carried his signature accessory.

"I almost didn't come," Lucy said.

"I almost didn't come either. Shall we find a quiet bench?"

Well, that was a relief. Also somewhat lowering. Lucy made sure her hood shaded her face and took Thor's arm. He was considerate, matching his steps to hers, and giving her time to organize her thoughts. They found a bench in the shadows on a side path, and Lucy spared a moment for regret.

Thor was impressive and doubtless a lovely man, but Lucy's heart was spoken for, even if the gentleman did not return her interest in the same way. She had respect in Lord Tyne's house, she had love after a fashion, and friendship.

"Is this an instance when courtesy requires the gentleman to go first?" Thor asked.

"You almost decided not to come," Lucy said, "but changed your mind, for which I am most grateful."

"Gratitude. A fine place to start. When you came upon me at the masquerade…"

"You came upon me, sir. Rescued me from a centurion with wandering hands."

"My name is Darien," he said. "I see no harm in sharing that with you, for I am very much in your debt."

Darien wasn't the most common English name—Lord Tyne was a Darien—but neither was it a name Lucy heard every day.

"As I am in your debt, Darien."

"If you'd like me to call that scoundrel out, I'm pleased to oblige. You said you know who he is."

"He's former military. Meaning no disrespect, but he might know his way around a firearm."

"I'm former military and a dead shot, but no matter. I'm also a widower. You knew that much about me."

Lord Tyne had served for a few years in Lower Canada. Why Lucy should recall that tidbit, she did not know, though people in love tended to hoard details about their beloved.

And she was in love, surprisingly so, though not with Thor.

"I know you lost your wife several years ago, but if you think to court me, Darien, then I fear I cannot encourage you."

He was quiet for a moment, another quality Lucy liked about him. He didn't chatter, didn't need to hear his own voice. Truly, he'd make some woman a lovely spouse.

"Perhaps your affections are elsewhere engaged, as mine are. Two weeks ago, I was content to pine after a worthy young lady and ignore my own longings. You told me that I did the woman a disservice by not declaring myself, and I agree with you. When we conclude our appointment, I will focus my energies on winning her affection, but my resolve in this regard…"

Lucy waited, though he sounded very much like Lord Tyne, in his rhetoric, in his willingness to put aside his own desires to look after the needs of others, in the very timbre of his voice.

He even wore the same scent as Lord Tyne.

Oh.

Dear.

Oh, damn and drat. Of all the painful ironies… Of all the infernal injustices. Of all the heartbreaks.

"You woke me up," he said, giving Lucy's hand a gentle squeeze. "I was bumbling about, watching my children grow older, making brilliant, dull speeches in the Lords, and going slowly mad. Right beneath my nose is a woman whom I esteem greatly, one as ferocious as a goddess on behalf of those she loves, one who can laugh at herself and at life, one I honestly adore."

Lucy managed to speak around the lump in her throat, for that young lady was very, very fortunate. She could not think who the lucky lady was, for Lord Tyne was discreet, and his social calendar his own.

"I'm sure you'll make her quite happy."

"I'm not half so confident of my success as you are."

Hope leaped, the hope that this paragon he'd determined

to court might not appreciate the gem life was handing her.

"Then the lady must be a dunderhead, sir. If she fails to appreciate you, she must be the greatest featherbrain ever to float down from on high, for I'm sure—I'm certain—that your esteem would be the most precious treasure that young lady could ever claim."

Another silence stretched, likely relieved on his part, tortured on Lucy's.

"Well, then," he said. "Do I conclude that your circumstances are similar to my own? Have you determined to pursue the distant gentleman who has caught your appreciative eye?"

Must he sound so brisk, so cheerful? "You conclude correctly. I harbor little hope that he'll ever hold me in the same regard I do him, but we respect and care for one another within the limits of our situation. I am content with that."

Or I will learn to be. A tear trickled hotly against Lucy's cheek. She didn't dare raise her hand to brush it away.

"Then we can part friends and wish each other well," his lordship said, "if you so choose, but I'd like to share with you one other aspect of my evening, before I escort you to your coach."

Lucy nodded, all she could manage in the way of communication.

"My children accosted me as I prepared to go out for an evening at a relative's house. They are delightful girls and blessed with the courage of their convictions. They counseled me regarding my future, in no uncertain terms, and then went giggling and conspiring on their way. I thought to be about my appointed rounds, when the children stopped me again at the foot of the stairs."

What could the girls have been about?

"They faced a moral dilemma," Tyne said. "Somebody about whom they care enormously had apparently made free with a possession given to me years ago. They'd seen it laid out on the lady's bed as they'd come to my apartment to assist me with my toilette. The girls didn't know whether to tattle, confront the thief, or hope a misunderstanding was afoot. I told them a misunderstanding was afoot."

His voice had become painfully gentle. "I know you, Lucy Fletcher, and I know you would never, ever steal a fur-lined velvet cloak from your employer."

Lucy Fletcher.

Mortification surged over Lucy, heating her neck and face. "I didn't want to go to that damned masquerade, I vow this. I only went to appease a friend, and I rue… I don't rue the decision, but I never want you to think—"

"Lucy, I know you," he said, drawing her to her feet. "I know you are ferocious in defense of those you love. I know your integrity is bottomless. I know you have more kindness in your smallest finger than most people have in both hands. I know that if I can merely convince you to stay on as governess, then my heart and my household will be the richer for your generosity, but I also know that you kiss splendidly, and I am determined to court you."

* * *

"Court me?"

Tyne took Lucy in his arms, though that overture required courage on his part. In the night shadows, he couldn't tell consternation from disbelief from horror, and a man in love was capable of tremendous blunders.

"Yes, court you. I told myself as I made my way here that I could be the distant gentleman who'd caught your fancy—or it might be some other lucky soul. If I am not that man, I want to be him, Lucy. I want your kisses, your scolds, your future. I want to read fairy tales to you and live them with you, complete with the messy parts—the lost and sick children, the gossiping domestics, the ever-multiplying nieces and nephews. I've made enough grand speeches to last a lifetime, but this is the only speech that matters. May I court you?"

She put her arms around him as if weary. "You seek to court me, and you think I'm fierce."

Her crown fit perfectly beneath his chin. "You have

dragged me grumbling and fussing into being a proper father to my children. You have ensured I am not a stranger to my own siblings. You listen to the upper servants when they would drive me barking mad with their petty complaints, though they aren't petty, of course. You have rescued me from becoming that worst affliction known to society, a speechifying politician. I'd be aiming for a Cabinet post…"

She bundled closer, and Tyne forgot all about Cabinets and posts, though the image of a bed popped into his head. His bed, with himself and Lucy beneath the covers.

"You are awful," she said. "Why didn't you simply reveal yourself after you'd run Giles off with your sledgehammer?"

"I thought that was Throckmorton. If he's that easily routed, no wonder his children rule his roost."

Lucy tipped her head up so the cloak fell back. Tyne could not make out her expression, but she remained in his embrace, from which familiarity, he took a certain degree of—

She kissed him, gently—an invitation to trust.

"I did not reveal myself," he said, "because you might have chosen to content yourself with some other man. In that event, I would have encouraged you to wake the poor nodcock up with the sort of direct speech you serve to me regularly. You might have been mortified to think you'd kissed your employer by mistake—not once but twice—and I didn't want the sweetest, loveliest kisses I've ever… oh hell."

He kissed her back and found the lady was smiling. Then she got a fistful of Tyne's hair, and then *he* was smiling, and then he had her up against the nearest oak tree—or she had him—and all manner of public indecencies nearly occurred, except Lucy's feet got tangled up with the handle of the sledgehammer. She grabbed Tyne for balance, and they both ended up laughing so hard they nearly went top over teapot into the hedge.

While Lucy tried to compose herself, Tyne located his hat and the offending sledgehammer, then offered her his arm and escorted her back to the coach.

Where she promptly went off into whoops again, pausing only long enough to agree to marry him.

EPILOGUE

"I do believe that the lack of a blue unicorn with a sparkly purple horn will forever live in Sylvie's heart as the only imperfection in our wedding ceremony." To the casual ear, Tyne doubtless sounded his usual self: calm, self-possessed, articulate. The typical English lord offering his opinion on the weather.

Lucy's was not the casual ear, and her new husband was smiling like a Viking with a longship full of plunder.

The coach rattled away from the wedding breakfast, Sylvie and Amanda tossing rose petals at the boot, the crowd of family waving and cheering in the midday sun. Lucy's brothers had brought their families to Town for the event, as had Tyne's many siblings, and talk of a house party had already started.

Tyne took Lucy's hand and kissed her gloved knuckles, then began undoing the pearl buttons that ran from her wrist to her elbow.

"The wedding was perfect," she said, "because you were my groom. I still say we ought to have wed by special license."

Tyne had refused her request, insisting on every propriety—

while anybody was looking. Behind closed doors, he'd subjected Lucy to diabolically skilled kisses, whispered promises, and caresses of shocking intimacy. On every occasion, though, he'd stopped short of anticipating the vows.

He paused with her glove half unbuttoned. "Our siblings would not have had time to assemble had the ceremony been performed on short notice, and you deserved to meet my family before you became part of it. They're a loud, opinionated, rumgumptious lot of—"

"Of wonderful people. Much like my own family." She switched arms, so he could start on her other glove. "You did not want our firstborn to arrive too soon."

He held her palm against his cheek, and through the thin kid of her glove, Lucy felt the heat of his skin.

"How can I focus on these thousands of buttons, how can I attend to anything, when you tempt me with talk of progeny?"

"Get used to it, my lord. You are married now, and you have tempted me without mercy for the last month." She patted his thigh—*not* his knee—and he drew down the window shade. A week before the wedding, Lady Eleanor had whisked Lucy and the girls to her ladyship's household, which had been wise but irksome.

The girls had needed some time to sort out Lucy's transition from governess to step-mother. A new governess had to be interviewed—Tyne had ceded that decision to Lucy—and fittings without number had to be endured.

"I nearly stole into your bed more times than I could count," Tyne said. "With my valet sleeping in the dressing closet, I did not want to start talk below stairs."

"Did you ask Eleanor to open her home to me?" Tyne would do that, would be that discreet and considerate—also that dunderheaded.

"No, I did not, though my valet will be sleeping elsewhere henceforth." He had both of Lucy's gloves half undone, loose enough that he could draw them off. "That veil business next."

"All you need do is remove some of the hairpins," Lucy

said, "but be careful. I hope our daughters might wear that veil someday."

He paused, leaning his forehead against Lucy's shoulder. "*Our* daughters. Have I told you that I love you? Have I told you that *our* daughters love you? The damned pantry mouser had better love you, or I'll banish him to the stables."

This demonstrativeness was either a benefit of marrying a widower, or simply Tyne's way of being conscientious. He *told* Lucy he loved her, *told* her he loved to look at her, to touch her. He was surprisingly affectionate, taking her into his lap, sitting beside her of an evening in the parlor, holding her hand when they walked into church services on Sunday mornings.

His fingers searched gently through her hair for pins, though he found rather too many, and before Lucy could tell him to stop, not only her veil, but the chignon fashioned at the nape of her neck had come undone. He drew the veil away and piled it atop the gloves on the opposite bench.

"You'll arrive to Boxhaven's estate looking ravished. I like that idea."

"If I'm to look ravished," Lucy said, "hadn't you ought to look ravished as well?"

"Valid point." He took Lucy in his arms, and for the few miles they had to travel before breaking their journey, she did her best to kiss, caress, and tease him into a nearly ravished state. When they alighted from the coach in the estate's forecourt, Tyne's cravat sported two entire wrinkles, his hair was a trifle mussed, and he was missing one glove.

Nonetheless, he was every inch the polite guest when he addressed the housekeeper.

"Her ladyship and I will take dinner in the library after we change out of our wedding attire. We will ring for assistance if we require it."

The housekeeper beamed at them, Lucy beamed back. Tyne had prevailed on the Marquess of Boxhaven for use of one of his rural properties to break their journey. The marquess, the same fellow who'd hosted the masquerade ball, had cordially obliged.

"I'm not used to being a ladyship," she said, taking Tyne's arm as they ascended a curving staircase. "I'm not used to being a mama, not used to being a wife."

Tyne knew where he was going, for he'd visited Boxhaven at this property in years past. "We will learn together, my dear. I have been a husband before, but I haven't been *your* husband. Nobody would call me a quick study, though I'm diligent and motivated to excel in my new role. I'm also motivated to get all that damned frippery off of you."

"Language, my lord."

He bowed her through a doorway to an elegant parlor that adjoined a sizable bedroom. A bed of enormous proportions sat under green velvet hangings, and trays holding tea and sandwiches were on the sideboard.

"Right now," Tyne said, "I am entirely yours, and not a lord at all. Would you think me very forward if I suggested we put that bed to use in the near future?"

How polite. How aggravatingly self-disciplined. "I'd think you completely backward if you so much as reached for a sandwich, when all I want is to reach for you."

Tyne came to her, wrapped his arms around her, and all the kissing and teasing in the coach was so much dithering compared to the passion he unleashed on Lucy. His embrace was possessive rather than polite—as was hers. His kisses were plundering, his patience with her clothing nonexistent. He growled—Darien, Lord Tyne—growled—and buttons hit the carpet. Fabric tore, and Lucy tossed his beautiful morning coat in the general direction of a chair.

"We must—" He tried to step back, but Lucy was having none of that. "We must repair to neutral corners."

Like pugilists. "You must undo my buttons." Lucy swept her hair off of her nape and gave him her back.

"I have grown to loathe buttons." Nonetheless, his fingers were swift and competent, and he was equally proficient with her stays. He insisted on removing her shoes, kneeling before her, but Lucy insisted on undressing him too.

She took her time with his sleeve buttons, his cravat, his watch, all the trappings of the lord that covered up the reality of the man: fit, muscular, and endlessly desirable. When she had him down to his breeches, he tugged on her braid to draw her near.

"If you touch me even once more, I will have you on your back on the rug, Lady Tyne."

She pressed her hand over his heart, loving the slow tattoo beneath her palm. "Do you promise?"

Ah, that smile. The Viking smile that assured her, yes, he promised. He promised to love her thoroughly and often, to make all the waiting worth the wonder to follow.

"I have married a goddess," he said, scooping her into his arms and striding into the bedroom. "May I be worthy of that honor."

Oh, to be plundered by a god who knew how to wield his hammer. Tyne gently set Lucy on the bed, stepped out of his breeches, and settled over her without once taking his gaze from her.

She wiggled beneath him, wrapping her legs around him. "My shift?"

"Is the only thing holding my dignity together," Tyne replied, kissing down the side of Lucy's face, from her temple, to her cheek, to her neck. "Though that won't last long. I'll make it up to you, Lucy. For the next three decades, I'll make it up to you if you'll excuse my haste on our wedding day."

She did not excuse his haste. She abetted it, with slow caresses and long kisses, with wandering hands and well-aimed shifts of her hips. When Tyne had eased inside of her, and Lucy was nearly weeping with frustrated desire, he stilled.

"I have dreamed…" he whispered. "I have longed for this moment with you."

"For all the moments," Lucy replied. "To hold you as physically close as I hold your love in my heart." He'd been right to have the banns cried, right to give her weeks to anticipate this joy, but she'd have to tell him that later, for he'd begun to move.

His loving was relentlessly controlled, his tempo escalating by maddeningly deliberate degrees, no matter how Lucy urged him on. She surrendered to his superior command of strategy—for now—and nigh unbearable pleasure was her reward. When she was drifting down from torrents of marital bliss, Tyne let go of his ferocious self-restraint, and the pleasure cascaded through her again.

They were both panting when he eventually stilled over her. The covers had been kicked halfway off the bed, and Lucy's shift was hanging from one corner of the cheval mirror.

Ye gods, ye Norse, Greek, and Roman gods and goddesses.

"I like that," Tyne said as Lucy's hand smoothed over his backside. "I think you left claw marks there."

How smug he sounded. "Don't gloat." Lucy pinched him in the same location, and he laughed. "What a wonderful sound," she said. "My lover's laughter."

He eased from her and crouched on all fours, passing her a handkerchief from the night table. When had he thought to put that there?

"You'll need sustenance now," he said, climbing from the bed and strutting into the sitting room. "I'll need sustenance. I am her ladyship's devoted lover."

He was also—yet another surprise—unselfconscious about his nakedness. What a delightful quality in a husband and lover.

The smile he wore as he brought Lucy the tray from the other room was frequently in evidence in the ensuing weeks, months, and years, the smile of a happy, much-loved Viking. He wore an even more tender smile when—forty weeks to the day after the wedding—she presented him with little Thor.

And little Freya.

And all the rest of the Tyne pantheon who came after the twins. The first time Sylvie was permitted to hold her baby siblings, she declared them even better than a blue unicorn, in which opinion, even her sister (who had begun to put up her hair) concurred.

THE END

Greetings, Dear Reader!

I hope you enjoyed Tyne and Lucy's tale of moonlit kisses and plans gone awry. There's just something about a guy with a sledgehammer, isn't there? In my next novella collection, *No Dukes Allowed* (May 2018), our hero isn't packing big tools, and neither does he have a title. How architect Alexander Morecambe thinks he's going to win the hand of Eugenia, Dowager Duchess of Tinsdale, I do not know. (Excerpt below—might contain a few hints.)

If you're in the mood for a full length romance, my fourth Windham Bride, *A Rogue of Her Own*, just came out in March. Charlotte Windham has met her match in Lucas Sherbourne—but has she met the love of her life? If you haven't read this one, the **ordering links are here**: graceburrowes. com/bookshelf/a-rogue-of-her-own/#order

I'm also working on another True Gentlemen, **My Own True Duchess**, which will come out in June. This is the story of Jonathan Tresham, a charm-deficient ducal heir, who gets tangled up with Theodosia Haviland, a widow with little tolerance for self-important aristocrats. She needs a goodly sum of money, though, and Jonathan needs to outwit the matchmakers, before they choose the wrong duchess for him. Necessity is the mother of happily ever afters? Excerpt below.

If you'd like to keep up to date with all of my new releases, sales, and special projects, you can sign up for **my newsletter, here: graceburrowes.com/contact/**. If you're interested only in new releases, deals, and discounts, then following me on Bookbub is a good way to get the information you want without the cat pictures (though my kitties are ALL adorable).

Happy reading!
Grace Burrowes

FROM ARCHITECT OF MY
DREAMS
BY GRACE BURROWES
IN NO DUKES ALLOWED

Adam Morecambe has good reasons for keeping his distance for titled society, and yet, when it comes to Eugenia, Dowager Duchess of Tindale, distance is the last thing on Adam's mind. He's an architect, and even though he knows better, when it comes to Genie, he's building a castle in the air…. So why is she lowering the drawbridge, just for him…?

A sharp rap on the parlor door startled Adam from dreams of carved wooden flowers and freckled geese. His boots dropped to the floor, nearly clobbering an indignant marmalade cat.

"Where did you come from?"

The cat squinted, and the knock sounded again, more firmly.

"Come in."

The Duchess of Tindale presented herself, looking as feminine and pleasing as she had in Adam's dreams, but wearing a good deal more clothing. He rose from behind the desk, holding his unfinished sketch in a manner that hid the evidence of his wayward imagination.

"Mr. Morecambe." She popped a brisk curtsey. "I'm looking in on you, as a hostess ought to. Do you have all you need to make your sketches?"

"I apparently needed a nap," he said. "That is a diabolically comfortable chair." He shrugged into his coat as casually as he could, though Her Grace had been married. A man in dishabille would hardly shock her.

"I have remarked the same on the occasion of tending to my ledgers," she said. "The combination of accounting and that chair induces sleep even first thing in the morning. I've sent off a note to Petworth House."

Petworth was the finest collection of interior woodcarving in all of England, possibly in all the world.

"I beg your pardon?"

"I hope Friday suits your schedule. Godmama's gardener vows the weather will hold fair for the rest of the week. We can make a picnic of the outing."

She was inviting him on a tour of Petworth. Also a picnic. *With her.*

On the occasion of Adam's first encounter with the duchess, he'd swept her into his arms to spare her a soaking. The contact had startled him. He'd not held a woman closely for ages, hadn't wanted to. His every spare moment and thought went to building his business, and he liked it that way. Her Grace had tolerated the embrace for exactly two instants before she'd righted herself and shaken her skirts, but they had been lovely instants.

She was sturdy, lively, and friendly. None of which explained why Adam wanted to kiss her.

"I trust Lord and Lady Egremont will not be in residence?" he asked.

"Off to Paris. We'll have the place to ourselves."

To themselves and an army of servants. "Friday, you say?" Adam mentally rearranged lunch with friends as well as four other appointments to see properties for sale.

"Have you a conveyance? We can take my traveling carriage or the landau if the weather's fine."

"I'll drive," Adam said, lest he find himself plodding through the countryside, when the time could be better spent marveling at the wonders of Petworth. "Shall we leave around eight in the morning?"

"Earlier," she replied, tidying his sketches and handing

them to him. "We have the long hours of daylight, we might as well use them. Leave the picnic basket to me, and plan on a lovely day."

"The crack of dawn then," he said, bowing over her hand as best he could with his sketches tucked under his arm. "I'll look forward to it."

The prospect of a day bouncing along the lanes of Sussex had her beaming at him, and her pleasure turned an unremarkable countenance luminous. Her eyes lit with such benevolence, that Adam held onto her hand longer than strictly proper. She had a subtle beauty, not the boring, cameo-perfect appearance of her friend, but a personal loveliness that would make the hours until Friday morning long.

And busy. She saw Adam to the front door, where no servant sat in attendance collecting gossip and spying on the walkway.

"Do you know," Adam said, "I do believe you are my favorite duchess in the entire world."

"How many duchesses do you know, Mr. Morecambe?"

"Two." Not strictly true. As a youth, he'd once been introduced to the Duchess of Seymouth, who'd regarded him as so much dung clinging to her slipper.

"You are my favorite architect."

"How many do you know?"

She went up on her toes and brushed a kiss to his cheek. "One, and I am looking forward to getting to know him better."

Adam tapped his hat onto his head, accepted his walking stick from her, and left the house without even taking the time to examine the fine Palladian window above the lintel.

* * *

Order your copy of **No Dukes Allowed!**

MY OWN TRUE DUCHESS

Mr. Jonathan Tresham, heir to a dukedom, has sought the privacy of an unused parlor to negotiate with Mrs. Theodosia Haviland for certain personal services. The negotiations are off to a bumpy start...

"I don't want a perishing duchess!"

Mr. Tresham had raised his voice, though he was insisting rather than shouting. Theodosia was pleased with his reaction nonetheless. He'd managed the situation with Bea, managed Diana's obstinance in the park, and managed any number of presuming debutantes. Theo was cheered to think Mr. Tresham had found a situation he could not confidently handle on his own.

"What *do* you want? You are to become a duke, God willing. Dukes are married to duchesses."

"Might we sit? I'll spend the rest of the evening enduring bosoms pressed to my person while I prance around the ballroom with a simpering, sighing, young woman in my arms. My feet ache at the very prospect."

Theo began to enjoy herself. "Poor dear. You must have nightmares about all those bosoms."

He smiled, a rueful quirk of the lips that transformed his features from severe to... charming? *Surely not.*

Theo took a seat and patted the cushion beside her. "Speak plainly, Mr. Tresham. The bosoms await."

He took the place beside her. "Plain speaking has ever been my preference. I left England after finishing at Cambridge, and went abroad to make my fortune. In that endeavor, I was successful, but the whole time I ought to have been taking a place among polite society, making the right associations, being a dutiful heir, I was instead making money on the Continent."

Without any partners, he'd said. "Why Cambridge? You would have met more young men from the right families at Oxford."

Theo really ought to scoot a good foot to the side. She'd taken a place in the middle of the sofa, and Mr. Tresham was thus wedged between her and the armrest. There was room, if they sat improperly close.

He was warm, however, and he wasn't shy about discussing money. Theo stayed right where she was.

"Cambridge offers a better education in the practical sciences and mathematics. I am something of an amateur mathematician, which skill is helpful when managing a fortune." He gazed at the fire, his expression once again the remote, handsome scion of a noble house.

Theo had the daft urge to tickle him, to make that charming smile reappear. He'd doubtless offer her a stiff bow and never acknowledge her again if she took liberties with his person.

"You offered me plain speaking, Mr. Tresham, yet you dissemble. No ducal heir needs more than a passing grasp of mathematics."

He opened a snuff box on the low table before them. Taking snuff was a dirty habit, one Theo had forbid Archie to indulge in at home.

"Would you care for a mint?" Mr. Tresham held the snuff box out to her.

Theo took two. "Tell me about Cambridge."

He popped a mint into his mouth and set down the snuffbox. "My father went to Oxford. He earned top marks in wenching, inebriation, stupid wagers, and scandal. I chose not to put myself in a situation where his reputation would precede me."

Most young men viewed those pursuits as the primary reasons to go up to university. "I gather he was something of a prodigy in the subjects listed?"

"Top wrangler. So I became a top wrangler at Cambridge."

Ah, well then. "And you've taken no partners in your business endeavors. Can't your aunt assist you in this bride hunt, Mr. Tresham?"

"Quimbey's wife doesn't know me, and she's too busy being a bride herself. She and Quimbey are…" He fiddled with the snuffbox again, opening and closing the lid. "Besotted, I suppose. At their ages."

Mr. Tresham did not approve of besottedness at any age, and Theo had to agree with him. Nothing but trouble came from entrusting a heart into the keeping of another.

"They are off on a wedding journey of indefinite duration," Mr. Tresham went on. "They are reminding me that soon, Quimbey will not be on hand in any sense. He's an old man by any standards, and I have put off marriage long enough."

Theo patted his arm. "They are also leaving you a clear field to make your own choices, which seems to be a priority with you."

He crossed his legs, a posture far more common on the Continent. "Possibly. They also asked me to move into the ducal townhouse during their absence, supposedly to keep an eye on the staff and the damned dogs. Pardon my language."

"And you capitulated because of the dogs."

He crunched his mint into oblivion. "A pair of great, drooling, shedding, barking, pests. Caesar and Comus. You've met Comus, Caesar is larger and more dignified."

"You want me to help you find a bride?"

"Precisely. I haven't womenfolk I can turn to for first-hand information, haven't friends from school who will warn me off the bad investments. In this search, I need a knowledgeable consultant, and I am willing to pay for the needed expertise."

A consultant, but not a partner, of course. "Why should I do this? Why exert myself on behalf of a man I don't know well. I could end up with another woman's eternal misery on my conscience."

Another smile, this one downright devilish. "Would you

rather have *my* eternal misery on your conscience?"

Well, no. Mr. Tresham was little more than a stranger, but he'd been kind to Diana, he was dutiful toward his elderly relations, and he'd make a woman of delicate sensibilities wretched.

"How would my matchmaking to be compensated?"

"Your role has two aspects: Matchmaker and chaperone. I will accept only those invitations where I know you have also been invited. You will simply do as you did with Dora Louise's ambush in the library—guard my back. You will also keep me informed regarding the army of aspiring duchesses unleashed on my person every time I enter a ballroom."

Theo got up to pace rather than remain next to him. "And my compensation?" Five years ago, she would have aided Mr. Tresham out of simple decency. Archie's death meant she instead had to ask about money—vulgar, necessary money—and pretend the question was casual.

"I could hire any number of men to serve as discreet bodyguards," Mr. Tresham said. "You will be more effective for being unexpected, and for knowing my pursuers. I'm not buying merely your eyes and ears, though, Mrs. Haviland. Please be very clear that I am also buying your loyalty."

"My loyalty comes very dear." In some ways, loyalty was a more intimate gift than the erotic privileges a courtesan granted to her customers.

Mr. Tresham rose. Manners required that of him, because Theo was on her feet, but must he be so tall and self-possessed standing in the shadows? Must he be so blasted, *everlasting* attractive?

"Name your price, Mrs. Haviland."

* * *

Order your copy of **My Own True Duchess**

CPSIA information can be obtained
at www.ICGtesting.com
Printed in the USA
LVOW12s1716180418
573963LV00003B/566/P